MY FIFTY FRETTING YEARS. Copyright 1980 by Ivor Mairants. All rights reserved. Printed in the United Kingdom. No part of this book may be used or reproduced in any manner whatsoever without written permission except in the case of brief quotations embodied in critical articles and reviews. For information write Ashley Mark Publishing Co. c/o Summerfield, Saltmeadows Road, Gateshead, Tyne and Wear NE8 3AJ, England.

FIRST EDITION SEPTEMBER 1980

Typeset and printed in Great Britain by
Campbell Graphics Ltd., Newcastle upon Tyne NE1 2AR

ISBN 0 9506224 3 5 PAPERBACK

'MY FIFTY FRETTING YEARS'

A Personal History of
The Twentieth Century Guitar Explosion

by

IVOR MAIRANTS

ASHLEY MARK PUBLISHING CO.
©1980 IVOR MAIRANTS

To my wife
who for fifty years
has backed me up and
played second fiddle to a guitar.

'MY FIFTY FRETTING YEARS'
Contents

Introduction 7
Foreword by Eric Sykes 9

Part One – Autobiography

1. From East to West 13
2. Roy Fox's Band 33
3. Freelancing 40
4. War 47
5. Geraldo 55
6. Central School of Dance Music 70
7. Consultant 75
8. Mission to Moscow 79
9. Ivor Mairants Musicentre 101

Part Two – The Steel Strung Guitar

10. The United States 110
11. Maccaferri and the Other European Makers . 121
12. Lifting of Dollar Restrictions 127
13. The Great Guitar Pioneers 139
14. The Post War Electric Guitarists 173
15. The Wes Montgomery Era – Before and After 197
16. The Nylon Strung Guitar in Popular Music and Jazz 217
17. Arrangers and the Guitar 224

Part Three – The Classical Guitar

Introduction 250
18. Andrés Segovia 253
19. The Ladies 258
20. My Friends The Recitalists 279
21. Mainly Spain 305
22. The Flamenco Guitar Tutor 319
23. From Gut to Nylon 331
24. The Ramirez Dynasty 337
25. The Craft in Spain 349
26. A World of Classical Guitars 363

Coda 381
Perfect Cadence 385
Appendix 387
List of illustrations 390

'MY FIFTY FRETTING YEARS'

INTRODUCTION

During the half-century between 1930 and 1980 the guitar rose from obscurity to unprecedented popularity.

My own first faltering entry into the field of music started about the same time with the banjo, which I played before progressing to the instrument which became my musical tool, my inspiration, my constant companion and, of course, my means of livelihood.

Every struggling guitarist will understand that the title I have selected is not just a meaningless pun but relates to the difficulties confronting most players in their desire to master this most satisfying of all fretted instruments. Segovia says 'it is like an orchestra seen through a pair of reversed binoculars; small and of lyrical intimacy'.

An apt title for the complete story about the origins of this ancient stringed instrument would be *Five Thousand* Fretting Years but I am content to confine my story to the 50 years which I have experienced.

Although few players have the ability to make the guitar sound like a 'miniature orchestra' the fascination lies not only in the musical completeness both in solo performance and accompaniment, but also in its ability to portray a variety of musical styles.

The first guitar playing I ever heard was performed on a steel-strung instrument whose specific function was to play dance music and jazz, but later, when I heard Segovia literally make his words come true by creating 'an orchestra seen through a pair of reversed binoculars' on a classical guitar with gut strings, I realised that there was another guitar world.

Flamenco music is another area in which the function of the guitar cannot be substituted with authenticity by any other instrument – not even by an orchestra.

But I doubt if the popularity of the guitar would have reached its present level without the advent of amplification. When the pick-up was attached to the steel strung guitar and the sound was transmitted through a loudspeaker, it was on the road to equality with the other orchestral instruments, even to its use in the symphony orchestra. However, these electrifying events were very far removed from my own beginnings.

Acknowledgement

I would like to pay tribute to my wife Lily, Cyril and Valerie Howard and Maurice Summerfield for their help and encouragement in completing this book.

Ivor Mairants
London 1980

Photographs

All photographs are from the author's personal collection with the exception of the photos of Teddy Bunn p.163 which is courtesy of Pete Tanner and that of Carmen Mastren p.161, courtesy of Bill Spilka.

'MY FIFTY FRETTING YEARS'

FOREWORD

I'm glad that Ivor Mairants has written another book on the guitar, because it was mainly due to his earlier efforts that I became interested in Flamenco, Jazz and indeed all aspects of this fascinating instrument. Without any prior knowledge of music I found his earlier books readable and readily understandable.

Whether you are a casual strummer or an ardent student of the guitar, a book by Ivor Mairants seems to me to be an essential, and for all the help he has given me in the past, I wish him well with this new publication.

ERIC SYKES
London 1980

'MY FIFTY FRETTING YEARS'

PART I

AUTOBIOGRAPHY

With my parents, Solomon and Sarah Thema Mairants

Part One

Chapter One

FROM EAST TO WEST

I was born in 1908 in a small Polish town not far from Plock on the River Vistula, and was the only child of very religious parents. My father was a Talmudic scholar and remained so all his 52 years, meditating with God while my mother did her best to run a small shop, selling haberdashery in Poland and later, tobacco and confectionery in London, usually resulting in poverty or somewhere near to it.

In 1913 my father performed a very heroic deed and braved the journey to London where he thought he would receive a little help from his rich uncles who were well established in the cloth business; but when my mother and I arrived in 1914 about a month before the first World War (August 1914) it was evident that no such help had been given. God knows how my father made a living (in the then predominantly Jewish East End) apart from being sustained by his deep religious beliefs. (He was known as 'Reb. Shelomo' by the congregation.)

But earning a living or not, I have never ceased to thank him inwardly for bringing me to my adopted country with its tolerance and opportunities for a life of freedom of thought and culture, where I soon learned to speak English in the East End elementary school, close to our one room abode.

When I reached teenage, I had a desire to receive a better education by entering a secondary school, but not being eligible for a free scholarship place because of my foreign birth (and I doubt if I was clever enough to win a scholarship), I cajoled my parents to pay for my schooling at Raine's Foundation School in Arbour Square about a mile from where we lived. It was there, at the age of 12, that I first consciously heard the sound of music from the school orchestra (which, by the way, included Sid Phillips on clarinet). No doubt part of the curriculum included music but my first really positive connection came through my crystal set.

When I was 14 or 15 I became keenly interested in wireless, making my own crystal sets, and it was through the earphones that I heard the Savoy Orpheans broadcasting from the Savoy Hotel. But the orchestra did not impress me as much as the solo tenor banjo played by Pete Mandell in his own composition *Take your Pick* which became a standard for both plectrum banjo and tenor banjo.

When, at the age of 15, I was forced to leave school due to lack of money for school fees, my father sold me down the river as a salesman in the woollen warehouse of his cousins S.N.G. & A. Mackover in the Whitechapel Road, and there I earned 12/6d a week, from which I was allowed 2/6d all to myself.

Somehow the banjo must still have prompted an interest in the back of my mind because, after saving £3.00, I bought a banjo I saw displayed in the window of Ebblewhite's music shop in Aldgate and began to practice assiduously – even at lunch times.

I was offered a gig three months later and had the satisfaction of playing with other musicians (piano and drums) and receiving 7/6d in addition. What a wonderful way of making a living!

I discovered a magazine called *BMG* devoted to the interests of the banjo, mandolin and guitar, and decided to ask its editor, Emile Grimshaw (a prominent figure in banjo playing and composing) for tuition. My connection with Emile Grimshaw really opened the door to my entering the music profession. Although I had only 12 lessons from him, his interest in my career went far beyond that of a teacher.

Back at the woollen warehouse, S.N.G. & A. Mackover took a hand in my fate by engaging a new secretary/book-keeper. She was a smasher aged $15\frac{1}{2}$ and just out of school. It was love at first sight for me and more or less for her; what more could a fellow want! We went to see Paul Whiteman's Band with Mike Pingatore (the hunchbacked banjoist) playing figure eights with his right hand and producing a sound like a peal of bells.

Ted Lewis and Vincent Lopez were other bands of the day we enjoyed and from whom I caught some inspiration.

By 1927 I had joined my third dance band. The first was The Valencians, a seven-piece, the second the Florentine, a six-piece where I first met Harry Gold (the saxophonist and leader of The Pieces of Eight who is my oldest friend in the profession) and the third, Fred Anderson's Cabaret Band. The Cabaret Band was a busy, semi-professional six-piece band comprising pianist/leader, trumpet, alto, sousaphone, drums and myself, gigging around Stratford, Ilford and East Ham and winning many contests.

My girl friend, Lily Schneider, usually accompanied me to the public dances, doing what all faithful girl friends do, *i.e.* help carry instruments for the boy friend. Being a very good ballroom dancer, she was in constant demand as a dancing partner and I was able to keep an eagle eye on her to see that she came to no harm.

My tenure with the Cabaret Band lasted from April 1927 to July 1928 and was instructive, remunerative and enjoyable, but at the end of 1927 Emile Grimshaw recommended me for an audition with Al Starita, who then led a band in the plush restaurant of the Piccadilly Hotel: the banjoist/guitarist Len Fillis was leaving to join Fred Elizalde at the Savoy Hotel and he needed a replacement. Emile Grimshaw (whose son Emile Jnr. was also a famous fretted instrument player) was 'in the know' and thought I might secure this plum job.

Here I must digress a little. Just before this event I had heard a record of Boyd Senter (an American ragtime clarinettist) accompanied by a most wonderful sounding guitar also taking a very rhythmic extemporised single string solo. The name of the guitarist was Eddie Lang, and I could not rest until I had myself acquired a guitar. Naturally, I asked Emile Grimshaw for advice and it so happened that Emile Jnr. had designed a flat top, steel-strung, double cutaway guitar of generous dimensions and sound, which I bought and began to finger. What I did not know about this guitar and did not realise until about three years later was that the fingerboard was too wide for plectrum playing and that the string tension was too taut, owing to the strings being too distant from the fingerboard. Whether the neck had begun to warp or whether the neck was fitted at too obtuse an angle to the body I do not recall, but by the time I found out, my left hand developed muscles it never had before, almost to the point of paralysing it. But eventually my strong left hand helped me to produce a full, loud sound, proving that nothing is ever *all* bad.

The taut, high string-action fault, due to a warped neck, high bridge saddle or some other maladjustment, is still prevalent among some guitars and innocent newcomers still fall into this trap, both in steel-strung and nylon-strung guitars.

Back to my Starita audition, where I presented myself at his sumptuous Jermyn Street (off Piccadilly) flat. Al Starita was friendly and asked me to play from tenor banjo orchestral parts (consisting of musically notated chords without chord symbols) and I did this without difficulty, although when I was asked about my ability on the guitar I ventured the naive opinion that it was conducive to natural and sharp keys and not to flat keys, not realising that most music written for dance bands is in flat keys to suit the E♭ and B♭ saxophones and the B♭ trumpets. However, the gentlemanly Mr. Starita invited me to play one session on the job. So the following night I presented myself, suitably attired, with tenor banjo in a room of carpeted elegance where the band played with a soft rhythmic pulse which matched the Piccadilly Hotel atmosphere. Seeing me, Al Starita acknowledged my presence and Len Fillis (then England's No. 1 and only guitarist) vacated his chair and I took his place and began to play.

'Have you a mute?' asked Mr. Starita. I could not believe my ears; I had never heard of a banjo mute so I shook my head and continued to play. I must have been showing off my fancy rhythms when Sidney Bright (for it was Geraldo's twin brother at the piano) bent towards me and earnestly hissed 'Play four in a bar'. But I couldn't have taken his advice because I failed to be appointed as Len Fillis's successor. So it was back to the Cabaret Band after this brief moment amongst the elite.

I later wrote to Len Fillis requesting some guitar tuition but he replied in the negative and as I knew no one else who played the guitar, I learned from records and guitar music using my own intuition to guide me. Fortunately, I discovered the Segovia arrangements of Bach, the music of Tarrega, and compositions by Turina which were written for Segovia and fingered by him. Many years later I was particularly pleased with this passage from his autobiography of the years 1893–1920 (page 14, published in 1976 by Marion Boyers).

'I would like to point out to those guitarists who might be reading this that the fingering of my few diatonic scales and other exercises dates from this period (about 1910 when I was 17) and though unpublished they are being used by masters and students today. I have never had to change or modify them since; my experience, acquired through many years of practice, still relies on those early studies of mine. Having intuition and a will to work in the service of skill, one can find unsuspected means of shortening the rough road of apprenticeship.' No one could have put it better.

In spite of my failure to pass my audition for Al Starita, Emile Grimshaw had not lost faith in me and once again recommended me, this time to play solo guitar behind the screen at the New Gallery Cinema in Regent Street W1, to bring to life a scene from the silent film *Ramona* (1928) starring Dolores del Rio and Warner Baxter. There were three performances every day for a two week run and very often Lily Schneider sat next to me watching the film from behind while the pit orchestra (whose music was fitted by Louis Levy, the film conductor) and Florence de Jong, the organist, sat silent.

I had not given up my day job, which now earned me £2 per week, and was still a member of the Cabaret Band earning about £9 or £10 per week, but it was not long before I gave up both and turned professional.

Once again my guardian angel Emile Grimshaw recommended me, this time to Percival Mackey whose banjoist Emile Grimshaw, Jnr was about to join Jack Hylton. Percival Mackey's Band was rated third best after Jack Hylton's and Jack Payne's Bands.

I was not quite 20 (and looked younger) when I presented myself for approval. Percival Mackey was due to open a fortnight's engagement at the Alhambra, Leicester Square (on the site of the present Odeon cinema). It was a super stage-band show, and I was required to play guitar and banjo, sing, and take part in a musical extravaganza built round a tune called *47 Ginger-Headed Sailors* in which I acted as the pirate who abducted the girl (Monti Ryan); I grew a moustache to hide my youthful features.

I said goodbye to S.N.G. & A. Mackover and to Fred Anderson's Cabaret Band, and in August 1928 opened at the Alhambra for a fortnight, playing, singing and acting for the princely sum of £14 per week, having renounced my 'steady job' security (?) forever in favour of one of the most precarious professions known to man, *i.e.* doing what you enjoy and getting paid for it.

Besides playing at the Alhambra we also recorded for the Dominion Record Co., my first experience of a recording studio, with Dan Ingman (features editor of the *Melody Maker* and later producer of the Horlicks Hour on Radio Luxembourg) on drums. Then my touring days began with a week at the Birmingham Hippodrome followed by a month at the fabulous Wintergarten Theatre in Berlin.

Berlin 1928

I was quite oblivious of the fact that there was a political power struggle going on in Germany which would culminate in Hitler coming to power; I only saw Berlin as the fun city of the world. Prostitution was official and protected and female virginity among teenagers was rare. Nude sunbathing was a popular pastime beside the lake at Wansee outside Berlin, and international artistes filled the music halls such as the Wintergarten and the Admiral's Palast.

We really had a ball doing one 20 minute performance per night, leaving time to visit the other shows at the Admiral's Palast, to see the first talkie with Al Jolson as the Jazz Singer and to watch the girls go by.

My room mate and companion was Issy Bonn (then the singer Benny Levin) and we had a few adventures. We once strayed into the El Dorado (a palatial transvestite establishment) where the barman, opening his shirt front, greeted me with 'I'm Daisy, feel me'! In my innocence, I was nonplussed. The clientele, whether sitting at tables or dancing, were all dressed in the height of female fashion, their faces superbly made up to look like gorgeous females. As the only two male males there, we must have looked very odd and out of place.

Generations before computer dating, the table telephones of the five-floor Haus Vaterland were used to do the job. Every floor represented a restaurant of a different country and one was free to contact the occupant of any table. There were 'wein stube' in abundance and one could shop at the (now burnt out) department store of Hermann Tietz, a magnificent, monumental building near the Tiergarten.

We were lucky to have found digs off the Kürfürstendam (the Bond Street of Berlin) and coupled with the sinecure of one short show a night and the intoxicating cosmopolitan atmosphere backstage – at the newly built Wintergarten – we had a marvellous time. The smell of the grease-paint and the roar of the crowd is really a most potent drug.

The month passed only too quickly and after a not very successful tour of the south of England including Plymouth and Devonport, the band was disbanded.

From riches to rags in one short episode! Well, one could always wander down to Archer Street.

Archer Street is a short street behind Shaftesbury Avenue in the West End where musicians meet. It is like an open air club with all amenities: the pub, the cafe, the barber shop and the characters. Whereas Damon Runyon had Harry the Horse, Archer Street had Jack the Yank (a drummer who did one boat trip to the States and returned with a permanent Yankee accent).

Sometimes the police made a blitz and cleared the street, claiming that we caused an obstruction, but as the police made their exit at one end, the musicians made their re-entrance at the other end.

I did not find any work in Archer Street on my couple of excursions, and, in fact, hardly knew anybody, the penalty I paid for starting at the top and not coming up through the ranks, but once again Emile Grimshaw came to my rescue.

This time he asked me to join the banjo quartet he was forming to go into C. B. Cochran's 1929 revue *Wake up and Dream* with music by Cole Porter, who personally attended some of the rehearsals to rewrite some of it.

This was a new world to me, and after a fortnight at the Palace Theatre, Manchester, we opened in a blaze of publicity at the London Pavilion, Piccadilly, where I received a basic £12 per week.

Well, there were certainly some innovations in that show. Leslie Hutchinson (Hutch), rising on a platform singing and playing his piano, Elsie Carlisle (who died in 1977), then the leading torch singer, standing alone, spotlighted in a diaphonous gown, singing *What is this Thing Called Love?*, Jessie Matthews in her first leading role singing and high-kicking opposite Sonnie Hale, and Dame Anna Neagle, then known as Margery Robertson, a humble chorus girl. The show lasted 10 months and all we did was to play two choruses of *Wake up and Dream* on stage, blacked up and dressed in the period costume of San Francisco before the earthquake and fire. But it was worth blacking up for! With extra sessions the money was good and the work easy.

The banjo quartet also made many records for HMV and Decca and fulfilled other engagements, but my one regret was that I never took lessons from a fabulous flamenco player named Rodriguez who accompanied Tina Meller, a flamenco dancer whom Cochran had imported from Spain.

Near the end of the run, Lily Schneider and I decided to get engaged, hoping to get married in 1931, but the road to 1931 proved to be a little bumpy. While I was sitting pretty in 1929, comfortably tucked away in the make-believe world of the stage, the dance band world outside had been changing and the banjo had almost disappeared in favour of the guitar. With few exceptions like Ambrose at the Mayfair Hotel, where Joe Branelly was still playing the banjo, bands employed either a guitar or neither. Of course, there was always the Savoy, the residency of Dave Thomas who was succeeded by his son Bert on guitar when his father died in 1930.

Still, I had been practising the guitar in my spare time, and had also added the Hawaiian guitar to my collection of fretted instruments, an accomplishment which often helped me to secure work in the next few years.

My next job was far less glamourous than the one at the London

Pavilion and physically about a hundred times more work. It consisted of a solid slog of five hours, six nights a week, on the guitar with a 15 minute break, playing in a five-piece band at the Roadhouse Club in Leicester Square led by pianist Harry Gordon. But it did one thing for me during six months residence; it strengthened my fingers almost to the point of overstraining the muscles, so that by comparison, all my future guitars were easy to play because of their lower string action. In addition, I had memorised the chords of many popular tunes.

Once again I became involved with the theatre but this time in the pit orchestra at the London Hippodrome in the Clayton and Waller production of *Sons O' Guns*, a musical about the 1914/18 war (with the action in France) starring Bobby Howes and Binnie Hale. I probably got the job because of my ability to play the Hawaiian steel guitar.

The orchestration called for a solo guitar chorus in a number called *Why?* (Why is there a Rainbow in the Sky?) sung by Bobby Howes, to be played on the Hawaiian steel guitar as a romantic interlude, while he was indulging in some stage business between vocal refrains. There were no electric guitars in 1931 and a plectrum guitar would have been inaudible hence the more sustaining Hawaiian guitar.

The musicians in the orchestra were quite a different category of human beings from those I had previously encountered in the profession. Those in the top West End bands were aloof and proud of their instrumental capabilities; in Mackey's band they were more down to earth but keen on music and fun. Those in the pit were older, more hard bitten and cynical (some having had more glamorous jobs like Charlie Pemmell, former lead trumpet with Jack Hylton, who died in 1979), and were in it strictly for the money. During a long tacet it was either cards or picking horses, an attitude which mystified an eager young musician like me, but also broadened my experience and did me no harm.

One experience I had so far missed was playing with jazz musicians of any brilliance, but my gramophone and radio set were my teachers. Apart from Eddie Lang, who had recorded *Bullfrog Moan* and *A Handful of Riffs* with Lonnie Johnson, I listened to Louis Armstrong and transcribed his solos for guitar and memorised them. Some of my favourites were *West End Blues, Beale Street Blues, Bessie Couldn't Help It* and *Basin Street Blues*. Nineteen-thirty was rich in available jazz records including the Rhythm Boys, the Boswell Sisters, the Mills Brothers, all with guitar in the backing groups, Jimmy Lunceford's Band, Red Nicholls, Frankie Trumbauer, Bix Beiderbeck and Jack Teagarden. Then, of course, there was Duke Ellington whom I heard not only on records but directly from the Cotton Club, New York, on my home assembled shortwave set. I had continued building radios ever since my early crystal sets and now had a six valve shortwave set which brought in the US stations after midnight till about 3 or 4 a.m.

Listening to Ellington from the Cotton Club sounded quite different from the cut and dried performances on record. No wonder we lagged behind the Americans in the jazz field. How could British musicians receive the inspiration transmitted first-hand to their American counterparts? However, we were imbued with this spirit for a couple of hours during 1933 when the orchestra played a concert at the Trocadero, Elephant and Castle with Freddie Guy on guitar and the other legendary figures we had come to know through records; Johnny Hodges, Freddy (Posy) Jenkins, 'Bubber' Miley, Barney Bigard, Arthur Whetsel (who played jazz fiddle), Sonny Greer, Juan Tizol (composer of *Caravan*), Joe 'Tricky Sam' Nanton, Cootie Williams and Rex Stewart. None of these guys ever lost their magic.

I was very familiar with these arrangements, having transcribed *Rockin' in Rhythm* from the record and later presented it to Joe Loss soon after he opened at the Astoria Ballroom in September 1930. He did not always have a guitar in the band, although later Jimmy Messini did sing and play guitar for him, when, in 1932, Joe went into the Kit Kat as relief band to Roy Fox. Hence, I often played for Joe in broadcasts and recordings.

By the time *Sons O' Guns* closed near the end of 1930, I had become a little better known to musicians which brought me to the notice of Marius B. Winter who plied a good society trade and had other valuable connections. He was always cheerful and friendly; the popular conception of a real English gentleman, completing the image by driving a Swallow (predecessor to the Jaguar) sports car. His equally charming sister Irene acted as his secretary. He played at functions of all kinds, at mansions, large houses and hotels, with groups of varying combinations, sizes and instrumentations.

I soon discarded my tough playing Emile Grimshaw Jnr. double cutaway and bought a Martin 00–18 with a double scratchboard which was then listed in the US at 45 dollars (today, it is around 1,200 dollars) and supplemented my usefulness with steel guitar solos played on my National steel guitar. Listening to the records of the Boswell Sisters gave me the idea of writing for a vocal trio and before long I called on my old friend Harry Gold, who was then working with a trumpet player named Les Lambert.

We rehearsed a few numbers with myself singing melody (it was the easiest part), Harry top harmony and Les bottom harmony, and the result was a vocal trio. I brought the trio to the notice of Marius, who was delighted to be able to add a vocal trio who were also able to more than hold their own on alto and trumpet. Thus began a long working and social friendship and the birth of Roy Fox's Cubs who became England's foremost vocal trio.

In the spring of 1931, Marius arranged for a five-piece group to entertain at Selfridges Roof Garden tea rooms which proved to be a cosy two hours' weekday stint, and while gigs were not too plentiful I joined Geoff Gelder's band at Quaglino's Restaurant, St. James Street, which was also very pleasant, adding to my savings in preparation for my wedding on 18 October that year.

So here I was, in my 23rd year, with an assured income (so I thought) of well over £20 a week.

'All of a suddenly' as Max Bacon used to say, I woke up one morning in June feeling extremely ill (I do not want to bore the reader but I must confess that for a number of years I had suffered severe pains in my lower abdomen to which doctors had paid little heed). I tottered over to the London Hospital (which was a few minutes walk from where we lived) and after two major operations and the removal of the offending parts, my life was saved and after a long convalescence I returned to freedom in time to honour my most important engagement to date; my wedding on 18 October 1931. As they say in show business 'the show must go on' and it certainly did with Marius and the boys giving their services as a wedding present not to mention a silver dish. And so I began married life, happy to be alive, but broke.

While I was out of commission many changes had been taking place both to the personnel and the style of dance music, but I think the one which caused a major change round of musicians and was to affect the future of the thirties was the Roy Fox Band which opened at the Monseigneur Restaurant in Jermyn Street in May 1931 and seriously rivalled Ambrose's popularity, almost overnight.

In another way, Ray Noble, whose recording band included members of both Fox's and Ambrose's bands, also had a good effect on the standard of sophistication. Ray Noble used Al Bowlly for vocals but in Roy Fox's band Al doubled on guitar. Ray Noble's regular guitarist was Bert Thomas who was now using a Gibson L–7 arch top with an oval sound hole, although in 1932 he also used a Maccaferri for a while.

Entertainment habits and restaurant sites also changed. As more people owned motor cars (not I, I hasten to say), it led to the building of bypass roads and places of entertainment, food, drink, dancing, swimming and tennis. One such roadhouse was The Spider's Web off the Watford By-Pass. The arrangements for installing the band were in the hands of Edgar Jackson, a one-time editor of the *Melody Maker* turned gramophone critic and agent, and upon the recommendation of drummer Maurice Burman (a friend of Edgar's who had seen the trio perform) we three were engaged.

To complete the five-piece band a pianist named Jack Nathan was brought in from the semi-pro world and so The Spider's Web Band was formed. The three friends had now become five friends and were to remain so until death did us part (in the case of Maurice Burman and Les Lambert who both died prematurely).

Although the five-piece only stayed there for a few months, it was really the prelude to our joining Roy Fox because, left to our own devices at the Spider's Web we made ripples which reached the West End and leading musicians used to come and enjoy our 'hot' performances.

Summer came, another band went into the Spider's Web, and Maurice Burman went to the Dreamland Ballroom, Margate, with Stanley Black on piano and Albert Harris on accordion. Harry, Les, Jack and I found a nice berth with Jack Padbury at the Princes Restaurant in Piccadilly. Jack Padbury led the band, playing saxophone and clarinet, and besides the 'Four Musketeers' there were Johnny Cantor, violin and Kenny Knapper on drums.

The Princes job was excellent, everybody was happy and I had again changed my guitar to a Martin C–1 model, carved arched top 'f' holes which had much more punch than the 00–18.

Many celebrities used to come in, and one evening when a very expansive wide-smiling Louis Armstrong (who was then appearing at the Palladium) made a visit, I played him his chorus from his record *Bessie Couldn't Help It* and he happily scratched his name on the pickguard of my guitar. A stone's throw from the Princes Restaurant the famous Roy Fox's Band was providing music at the expensive Monseigneur Restaurant but apparently all was not well in the Fox camp resulting in the abdication of his leadership. Lew Stone, the band's pianist/arranger who had conducted during Fox's previous absence through illness, took over officially in 1932 retaining the existing personnel with the exception of Sid Buckman the lead trumpet. When Roy had been engaged to play at another West End spot and required a new band, Maurice Bruman recommended his old friends and one night they both appeared at the Princes Restaurant to 'look us over'. The result must have been favourable for the next day Roy made us an offer we could not refuse. Jack Padbury was in tears but I, for one, was able to soften the blow by recommending Albert Harris who had changed from playing accordion to guitar.

After extensive rehearsals the new Roy Fox Band opened at the Cafe Anglais in Leicester Square on 26 October 1932. Albert McCarthy wrote in his book 'The Dance Band Era':– 'Fox's second band ... was built around a nucleus of five musicians who played at a club called The Spider's Web and once more, it was an immediate success'. (p 89.)

The Valencians, 1926.

The Florentine Band, 1927.

Fred Anderson's Cabaret Band, 1928.

Percival Mackey's Band, 1928.

Emile Grimshaw Banjo Quartet.
(Left to right) Stan Hollings,
Emile Grimshaw, Ivor Mairants,
Monty Grimshaw.

Clifford Essex

Eddie Lang with the Mound City Blowers.

Vega Banjo Catalogue, 1928.

Marius B. Winter Orchestra.

Louis Levy Orchestra 1937 – 'Lord Babs' – film.

Roy Fox Orchestra.

Roy Fox Band 1932 – about to embark for Brussels.

Advert for 'Spring Fever' a guitar solo.

'MY FIFTY FRETTING YEARS'

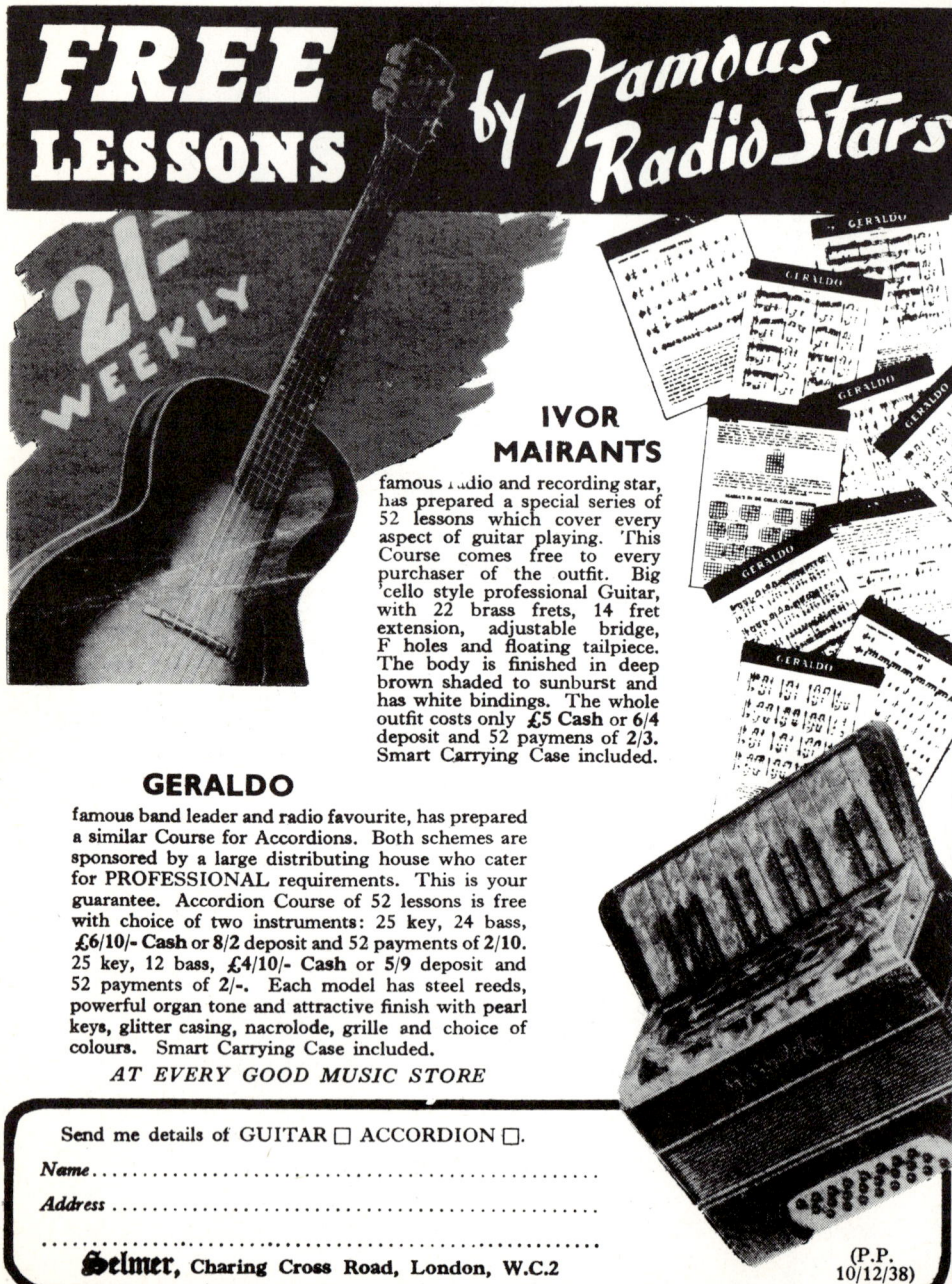

FREE LESSONS by Famous Radio Stars

2/- WEEKLY

IVOR MAIRANTS

famous radio and recording star, has prepared a special series of 52 lessons which cover every aspect of guitar playing. This Course comes free to every purchaser of the outfit. Big 'cello style professional Guitar, with 22 brass frets, 14 fret extension, adjustable bridge, F holes and floating tailpiece. The body is finished in deep brown shaded to sunburst and has white bindings. The whole outfit costs only £5 Cash or 6/4 deposit and 52 paymens of 2/3. Smart Carrying Case included.

GERALDO

famous band leader and radio favourite, has prepared a similar Course for Accordions. Both schemes are sponsored by a large distributing house who cater for PROFESSIONAL requirements. This is your guarantee. Accordion Course of 52 lessons is free with choice of two instruments: 25 key, 24 bass, £6/10/- Cash or 8/2 deposit and 52 payments of 2/10. 25 key, 12 bass, £4/10/- Cash or 5/9 deposit and 52 payments of 2/-. Each model has steel reeds, powerful organ tone and attractive finish with pearl keys, glitter casing, nacrolode, grille and choice of colours. Smart Carrying Case included.

AT EVERY GOOD MUSIC STORE

Send me details of GUITAR ☐ ACCORDION ☐.

Name..

Address...

Selmer, Charing Cross Road, London, W.C.2

(P.P.) 10/12/38

Advert for postal guitar lessons 1938.

Chapter Two

ROY FOX'S BAND

I was now a member of a 'name' band which meant that we were regularly heard by the general public through the means of radio and recordings and by the comparative few who had the means and the inclination to sup and dine at the Café Anglais.

Each musician in the 12-piece band was an excellent sight-reader. Sid Buckman, who shared lead trumpet with Les Lambert, was also a very pleasant vocalist and played the 'whispering' trumpet attributed to Roy Fox as the Whispering Trumpeter.

Les Lambert played the jazz solos and sang in the vocal trio (named The Cubs) with Harry Gold and myself. Harry switched from alto to tenor sax and remained a tenor player throughout his career. Rex Owen played lead alto and doubled on clarinet, soprano sax and flute. Hughie Tripp played second alto and 'hot fountain pen' (a single reed wooden whistle) and the second tenor sometimes played baritone sax but had no solo attributes. Eric Tann on trombone had an important function playing sweet solo passages and completing the brass trio. George Gibbs, a well known figure on double bass also doubled on sousaphone when the occasion demanded. Jack Nathan served as the resident arranger and general musical factotum and Maurice Burman, always a rhythmic up-to-date drummer, added showmanship and fresh ideas in music which he would illustrate either on the piano or on the cornet, which he always played in E♭.

There had, of course, to be a 'crooner' and the man selected was then very well known as a recording artiste. His name was Jack Plant and he sang everything in a higher key than everybody else in the business and with perfect diction, but he was no Bing Crosby or Frank Sinatra where phrasing was concerned.

The Fox band had the advantage of the best arrangers in the business, some freelance like Ben Frankel and Van Phillips, or staff arrangers like Stan Bowsher who worked for Peter Maurice; all arrangements were paid for by the publishing company whose sales were assisted by regular broadcasts from the Café Anglais.

After a period of rehearsals the band settled in on a specially built platform and played immaculately, apart from the broadcasts when we let ourselves go where required.

I did the arrangements for The Cubs, and now and again wrote for the band as well, using a few rules and my ear. After the band's first late night broadcast the critics hailed us as one of the top three, the others being Ambrose and Lew Stone.

All the bands in the West End establishments finished at 2 a.m., when many of the musicians would congregate at the Foyer Restaurant of the Coventry Street Corner House which stayed open all night.

We were now accepted as members of the magic circle which included storyteller Max Bacon (drummer with Ambrose), Max Jaffa (violinist with Jack Harris at Ciros, a superb raconteur), Joe Crossman (first alto with Lew Stone) then the supreme saxophonist of Great Britain, George Melachrino (multi-instrumentalist) then at the Savoy, Jack Miranda and many other famous musicians like Teddy Brown (xylophone) and Sam Browne (vocalist with Ambrose).

Apart from the fact that membership of this privileged group was one of the perks of working in a top band, it rounded off our education in double entendre and sophisticated gossip. Those never to be repeated early morning sessions provided more laughs than any dozen comedy script writers.

One night at the Café Anglais, a guest waltzing round the postage stamp dance floor asked Roy if he would like to take the band to Brussels to play for the King of the Belgians, and Roy thought it was a 'leg-pull'. But it turned out to be genuine and we all flew over in a tiny aeroplane (our first flight) to play a Command Performance for King Albert of the Belgians at the L'Agora Theatre in Brussels. When I plunged my life savings of £3 into buying a banjo such an event was beyond my imagination!

Roy was always even-tempered, very pleasant and, although somewhat aloof from the musicians, nevertheless engendered an even atmosphere between us.

Things at the Café went smoothly, aided by a friendly atmosphere among the boys but after three months we discovered that we were to move to the Kit Kat Restaurant situated under the Capitol Cinema in the Haymarket where we opened on 16 January 1933. The Kit Kat was much larger than the Café Anglais and the clientele less sophisticated but, for Roy, it was a step into the more popular field of entertainment leading to stage performances on the Gaumont British circuit as well as the Kit Kat. This was a period when cinemas were supplementing films with variety shows, following the American pattern.

At the Kit Kat the playing was split up between two bands for which Joe Loss was brought in from the Astoria. It has been said that the people came to the Kit Kat to enjoy listening to Roy Fox's Band and dancing to Joe Loss's Band, but it was Joe who outdistanced the whole pack. Apart from Sidney Lipton who still quietly officiates at the Grosvenor House and supplies bands for many functions, Joe Loss is the only remaining bandleader of the 30's to retain an unassailable position with the British public, culminating in the award of the OBE in the Queen's Birthday Honours list of June 1978.

After rehearsing an entertaining stage show, we embarked on a full scale variety and cinema tour, reaching as far into the outer suburbs as time and travel would allow. Sometimes we would fit in a recording session in the morning and a broadcast at night, but it was all grist to the mill of a full entertaining life with extra money for extra work, although paying extra money was not one of Roy's strong points.

When summer came and the Kit Kat closed for a month, we toured Holland and Belgium for a fortnight then proceeded for a fortnight's residence at the Casino in Deauville, France, known as a millionaire's playground where our soft music was merely a background to the quiet conversation of the wealthy in the regally appointed restaurant of the Casino.

It was also more or less a playground for us because of the short working periods, and my wife, who was then pregnant, joined me to benefit from an ideal summer in this superbly French seaside resort.

It is said that there is nothing like travel to broaden one's outlook and it is not just the travel but what one discovers in the process. Well, here in Deauville, we discovered a small group comprising guitar, flute, piano, bass and percussion, also playing at the Casino and at its nightclub the 'Brummel' performing Latin American music equal to any Carlos Jobim/Stan Getz combination. Had they existed today, they would have acquired an international reputation.

The leader's name was Don Barreto, a Cuban, resident in France, who played a four string National guitar with a metal body (the same as my own steel guitar), and he composed the most fascinating rhumbas and other Cuban music, his guitar solos being interlaced with jazz fills-in from the flute. They were without doubt years ahead of their time. One of our favourites was *Mi Amor Esta en el Vallée* and this piece inspired Maurice Burman to write a rhumba called *La Majestica* to which I added an interlude. We broadcast it regularly using a similar combination of instruments, later recording it for Decca. Eventually I arranged it as a guitar solo which was published by the Peter Maurice music company.

Alas, the summer idyll soon ended and we were back on the old slog with not a dull moment. One of my most anxious and exciting moments happened when my daughter Valerie was born, waking the household with a healthy cry at five in the morning of 19 December 1933, after refusing to take the leap for a couple of days.

Beyond our immediate work schedule we knew little of what the future had in store for the band. Although we were fairly well paid and living comfortably, I, personally, had no idea of the importance played by the band's broadcasts, records and public performances in helping Roy's personal fortunes, but suffice it to say that he had acquired a mansion in Stormont Road, Hampstead, opposite the Heath, *and* a Rolls-Royce car.

We were the last to hear of our vacating the Kit Kat, to open at the Café de Paris on 5 March 1934.

In a way this was a step up the social ladder insofar as the Café de Paris was frequented by the Duke and Duchess of Kent and high society. On the other hand, the size of the band was cut down to match the smaller area, and we again reverted to a society type of dance music apart from our broadcasts and when we accompanied the cabaret.

The cabaret was really the prime attraction and often included artistes of international fame. The artistry of Sophie Tucker at close hand was phenomenal and so natural was her performance that one would never have believed that each sob, aside and movement was rehearsed to perfection with the aid of her pianist, Ted Shapiro.

About 20 years later, while in London for a London Palladium season, she presented me with my certificate as the No. 1 guitarist in the *Melody Maker* Popularity Poll, May 1952.

Nöel Coward, the master of sophistication, absolutely mesmerised the audience. Dougie Byng, with his outrageous innuendos, had everyone rolling in the 'chaises longues'. In contrast, Ben Blue's comedy was good clean fun acting as ringmaster to a performing flea while his assistant stood by holding a large block of ice in his arms until they almost froze off.

Soon we heard rumours that we were to leave the Café, not to move to another West End club but to go on tour. The rumour was true and we left the Café de Paris on 10 May for a tour of the variety halls of Great Britain and Ireland, combining live shows and dances with broadcasts and records.

Naturally, feelings in the band were mixed and I certainly did not relish going out of town for any period, but a bee does not leave the honeypot so easily, especially if there is no alternative jam in sight, so off we went.

From then on it was Roy Fox the touring band in and out of London or Glasgow or Dublin or Aberdeen until August 1937.

From September on when my daughter Valerie was nine and a-half months old it was the touring family Mairants. The first time round it's a lot of fun, playing around by day and in the theatre at night. Top of the bill, hosts of admirers, getting to know all the acts on the bill and learning life backstage in the music hall.

We saw acts grow from small to second top billing. Ted Ray, Jimmy James, Ted and Barbara Andrews (Julie Andrews parents), Norman Evans ('Over the Garden Wall'), Lucan and McShane, Murray and Mooney, Donald Peers ('By a Babbling Brook') – you name them – we topped the same bill.

Guitar style was slowly changing. Eddie Lang had died on 26 March 1933 after a tonsillectomy and Dick McDonough had become the most outstanding guitarist to be heard in England especially for his guitar duets *Chicken a la Swing* and *Stage Fright* with Carl Kress. These compositions had an important influence in changing guitar style from the hard picking, high string action of Eddie Lang to a lower string action and a smoother picking producing a light swing. Another important influence was the sophisticated chordal harmonies of George Van Eps. A few of us used to rehearse in the theatre in the mornings and Maurice Burman suggested that I write a guitar solo based on a few bars of melody which he played to me on the piano; I thought about it and produced *Spring Fever* which we used in our broadcasts.

Evidently this was heard by Alex Kraut, artists and recording manager of Decca, and next time the band was at the Chelsea studios, he asked if I would like to record it. I thought it a good idea and contacted Albert Harris who was then broadcasting a solo composition called *Dedication* (to Eddie Lang) in a BBC programme entitled *Soft Lights and Sweet Music*. Albert readily agreed to play second guitar to my solo and for me to play second guitar to his and so the date was set up for the session. For some unknown reason this took place in a huge warehouse in Upper Thames Street which the Decca Record Company were then using for large orchestras. We both used Epiphone guitars, Albert playing an Emperor and I a de-luxe model.

The record was issued on the expensive Brunswick label and was considered a milestone by those who cared. The musical magazines and periodicals of July 1935 were very kind and said we had made guitar history.

Encouraged by our breakthrough, we wrote and recorded two more guitar pieces. Albert did *Kaleidoscope* and I followed my *Spring Fever* with *Summer Madness* which was recently broadcast on BBC radio in a request programme (much to my surprise). After all, 40 years and all that!

Considering how little the guitar meant to the public in those far-off days, Albert and I were certainly fortunate in receiving the backing of the Decca Record Co. Albert was at this time the leading and most sought-after guitarist in London and I was still firmly rooted with the touring way of life; but returning home from Liverpool one early Sunday morning during 1936, severe adhesions gripped me in my old operations and I was taken off to Middlesex Hospital where I stayed six weeks hovering between 'to operate or not to operate'. There was no operation but a grave warning to take it easy for six months.

I returned to work after a couple of weeks of convalescence having written another solo, this time *Autumn Harvest* which I later recorded backed by Albert's *Yankee Doodle Plays a Fugue*. I feel it is a pity that it was before the days of vinyl and long playing records.

Although when I returned to the Fox fold at the Holborn Empire we faced an enthusiastic audience, it seemed that business was not up to expectations (is it ever?) and as always the chopper was about to fall on the musicians' salaries.

Cuts were suggested which I decided The Cubs would resist. We, in fact, survived the cuts but noting the ever-increasing number of diamond bracelets on Mrs. Dorothy Fox's elegant arms in comparison to the lowering of the musicians' pay, I could not reconcile the difference.

It was obvious in other ways that the writing was on the wall for 'Roy Fox's Band' and in August 1937 I left after I had given a month's notice, Harry Gold leaving at the same time. Harry Thorne took my place and the band continued for another year before Roy departed for Australia.

Even at this time the guitar was still not considered a very important instrument, certainly very expendable as far as bands were concerned.

Chapter Three

FREE-LANCING

When I joined Roy Fox in October 1932, I was a 24 year old married man (or should I say 'boy') who, in spite of serious major abdominal surgery regarded life as fun with music. When I left in August 1937 I had been somewhat steeled by my experiences. Now, as a family man with a mortgage to repay and no savings, a slightly more serious view of life was required.

The glamour had been a little intoxicating; so had playing in the best West End restaurants, variety halls, Royal Command Performance, broadcasting and recording. I had enjoyed writing and recording my own compositions but the sum total of savings was nil. Two lessons could be learned from my experience. Although every young man should tour and learn about people and places, it is difficult to travel and to retain any money for the future. Next, touring may mean prominence with the interested public but back in London the people who provided employment did not know me; so I just had to wait.

For six months I just about scraped together enough to keep going but I had plenty of time to practise while waiting to be called. I had gone to see a Segovia recital during 1937 and the effect of this performance was both thrilling and shattering. I had never before heard such guitar tone, phrasing or expression and realised that my own poor sounds were like a cat scraping across a tin roof, but in a few months I recovered some of my confidence and, at least, had a goal to aim for.

In the meantime, I gave a few guitar lessons, did some broadcasting and even TV, but it was all very spasmodic.

A free-lance musician's workload is always spasmodic, although there are a few exceptions where one has more work than it is possible to handle. But the demands made upon one's versatility as an instrumentalist know no bounds. One rises to one's highest capabilities and thrills at the results when in the company of great artistes. Is it a wonder that people are attracted by its glamour?

We musicians are ourselves affected by the quality of the music we play and those with whom we play it, receiving inspiration from great performers. I have found this equally true whether accompanying Ezio Pinza in *Don Giovanni* under the baton of Sir Thomas Beecham or accompanying Rosemary Clooney in *Come-on-a-my-House*; whether playing the *Tango* by Stravinsky under Bruno Maderna or busking an accompaniment to an unknown piece sung by Sammy Davis, Jnr. I can still recall the wonderful sound of the great Dennis Brain (killed in a motor accident) when he broadcast with us in a small jazz combo which also included Art Pepper the brilliant jazz American saxophonist.

My free-lance experiences after leaving Fox were, in fact, equal to a post-graduate course in musical adaptation.

As to how I made a living during 1937/8, I can give the picture by consulting my diary. An entry for Sunday, 3 January 1938, states: H. M. Weedon (Bert Weedon) of 1 Ashford Road, East Ham, E6, £4 for term of six lessons.
For writing an article in the *Melody Maker* £2.
6 February 1938. One solo performance for BBC Empire broadcast at 2.45 a.m. $6\frac{1}{2}$ guineas.
A film session at Denham Studios for Muir Matheson £7.10.0.
A film session at Sound City Studios, Shepperton £5.8.4. while a TV session from Alexandra Palace earned me 5 guineas. Fees, as you can see, fluctuated according to the employer and the engagement.
Week commencing 1 February, broadcast from St. George's Hall (since burnt down) £3.10.0.
Half-session at Pinewood film studios £2.10.0.
Broadcast from London Casino for Bert Firman £4.
Total for the week of 21 February, £10.

But there was a slight improvement the following week.

The work included film sessions for Ben Frankel, Louis Levy and Muir Matheson, a recording for Bert Firman, a morning film session at Gainsborough Studios, Islington, then a dash to Denham Studios for the afternoon, total for the day £5.16.8., then an Empire Broadcast in the late or early hours. All in all for the week £25.15.8. Jolly good.

But the following week was jolly bad – a gig at the Albert Hall £4.17.6. and payment for the *Melody Maker* article £2.2.0. total £6.19.6. The week of 14 March I was saved from extinction by Jerry Hoey who engaged me for a teatime broadcast from the Piccadilly Hotel for which he paid £3 and that was it for the week.

In the midst of this period of keeping the wolf from the door, there were, of course, some highlights. Once, at the Abbey Road studios on a session conducted by Walter Goehr, the solo artiste turned out to be the great Gigli recording two Neopolitan songs, *La Marechiara* and *La Danza*. We rehearsed and in a guitar and voice passage Gigli wanted to move the tempo, pause and return to the original tempo. So Mr. Goehr asked the two of us to rehearse it together and there I sat with my guitar while Gigli, standing in front of me, sang in his own inimitable way while I followed as if glued to him. What a thrill! When we were ready to record, he stood waiting for the red light and no red light appeared. All of a sudden, without warning, Gigli sang *It's a Long Wait to Tipperary!* and everybody folded up with glee.

I could continue with many more musical tales but will confine myself to one terrifying experience of that period. After all, everybody has had a most nerve-shattering experience in their career or they haven't lived.

One day, to my surprise, the manager of the London Philharmonic Orchestra, then resident at the Royal Opera House, Covent Garden, asked me to play the mandolin for three performances of *Don Giovanni* at the Royal Opera House under the baton of Sir Thomas Beecham with Ezio Pinza and Richard Tauber taking the two leading roles.

I had never played mandolin but was loth to refuse such an interesting engagement so I accepted and borrowed a mandolin from Andy Wokowsky who *could* play the mandolin and duly presented myself for the first rehearsal in the foyer of the Opera House.

I had prepared myself by practising this tiny instrument and in my ignorance thought the mandolin sound would be well covered by the huge orchestra. When Sir Thomas called 'Act 2 Scene 2 *Serenade*' I sat down on the chair provided in front of the orchestra and awaited the fall of the baton. Down came the stick and I was off –

la-da-da-da-di-da, tum-tum-tum, etc.
1 and 2 and 3 and 1   2   3

but instead of my melody notes being drowned by the orchestra, they rang in solitary isolation accompanied only by a boom, ching, ching, from the bass and 'cellos.

Having played the eight bars introduction, I thought Don Giovanni would appear to sing the *Serenade* but not at the first rehearsal. So I had no option but to plough through to the end with a repeat.

When I had finished, Sir Thomas smiled and said 'Very nice' while, to my great surprise and mystification there came acclaim from the string players tapping their bows on the backs of their viols. I later discovered the reason for the approbation.

On previous occasions the mandolinist had broken down somewhere along the line triggering off some choice remarks by the Maestro but this time, a hole in one.

On the day of the opening, everything was arranged for my comfort. Microphone in correct position, ensuring a good balance and a small accompanying orchestra suitably arranged behind me. This took place offstage beside the wings so that the assistant conductor could watch Sir Thomas and convey the beat to me.

The opening night came and the moment had almost arrived. I had my finger ready on the fingerboard to come in on the beat and the blood was pumping so loudly in my temples that I could not hear a thing. Furthermore, I had not bargained for the fact that there was a recitative before my entrance and I had to follow a certain chord from the harpsichord. At this moment I neither knew when it would come nor could I hear it; it was absolutely terrifying, but somehow I did start at the right time and once having started, the going was secure. One rises to a sense of occasion and although completely gripped by tension, experience, determination and technique blow you along.

On 3 June the name Ambrose appears in the diary. I did a broadcast with George Elrick (the disc jockey and theatrical agent) then a drummer and bandleader, in the morning and another with Ambrose in the afternoon, which brings me to the next part of my story.

Ambrose's Band

Now we come to Bert Ambrose, the most legendary and talked-about British bandleader of the Thirties. The darling of society, the golfing partner of Edward, Prince of Wales, the big gambler, spender and lover. That is not to say that his band was other than the best in the land and when his secretary Joan 'phoned to ask me to do a broadcast, I was more than pleased.

I attended the rehearsal for this 3 June Friday night broadcast from the Café de Paris and when we finished, Ammy (as he was known by the profession) asked me to join him for a cup of coffee.

Much to my surprise, he asked me to become a regular member of his band. Although I had not been in a regular berth for about a year, I declined the invitation. When he demanded to know the reason for my refusal, I confronted him with stories I had heard about the way he behaved to his musicians. A heated argument ensued, Ammy denying that he did anything of the sort. The proof was, he said, the high salaries and the high standard of musicianship in the band. Well,

I could see it was no use prolonging the shouting match and I was really very keen to join the best band in the land as it then undoubtedly was.

The following Monday, 6 June 1938, I joined Ambrose at the Café de Paris. It was exhilarating playing with that rhythm section comprising Bert Read (piano and arranger, to be followed by Bert Barnes), Max Bacon drums and Tiny Winters bass, which swung with a light lilt. The brass, with Tommy McQuater, Max Goldberg, George Chisholm and Eric Breeze, even now speaks for itself, and the saxophones led by American jazz virtuoso Danny Polo with Billy Amstell (the English Bud Freeman) on tenor, Joe Jeanette on second alto and Sid Phillips on baritone (and arranging) completed the ensemble. There were also two fiddles, one of whom conducted for the cabaret and the other was there to fill up the harmony, but they were a sort of separate entity. Ammy led the band with an impeccable sense of tempo and in this respect I learned a lot from him and would always follow his tempo fluctuations.

Every band engenders its own atmosphere and this was my third experience with a regularly employed combination of musicians.

The members of Percival Mackey's band accepted me as a pleasant young novice; in Roy Fox's band we were equals starting together with young men's thirst for fun and adventure, taking our work in our stride, but in Ambrose's band it was different. Everyone, as Ammy would say, was a 'Prime Minister' and he wasn't far out. Each player was to a certain extent the 'best', jealous of his reputation as an instrumentalist and often touchy about criticism, to the extent of not speaking to one another. Sometimes Ammy and one or two of his star musicians were at daggers drawn. The one thing that held the band together was the quality of the players, who, having obtained satisfactory pay for the job, played their best, sometimes reaching great standards of ensemble and individual musicianship. It was a hard school and set the high standard I was happy to maintain. After the strict discipline of Ambrose (and in films, Louis Levy), I was never frightened by any martinet of the stick.

After the initial argument, Ammy and I got on very well. He and I both came from the East End of London, had a not too dissimilar background and understood the same type of humour known as dry, sardonic, satirical or sour. Whatever it was, we always got along very well. In spite of the master-servant or employer-employee relationship, we were on the same wavelength. I had a soft spot for him and he was very comfortable with me around. When, on the day after my son Stuart's birth on 3 July 1938, I announced it in the bandroom, Ammy, with a mischievous glint in his eyes, said 'Well, what do you want, applause?'.

Although he was below medium height, he was of strong stature and well built. His aquiline features were emphasised by a ridge down each cheek which the profession knew as 'f' holes and he was known to be a tough egg with a rough tongue. Whenever he felt like complaining about his bunch of 'Prime Ministers', it would always be in an aside to me, speaking with his bow hand beside his mouth: 'Listen to those foghorns' (saxophones). 'It sounds like a ship coming in!' or 'Listen to that drummer, all he's interested in is eating sweets and playing drum breaks, not keeping tempo!'.

If any drummer kept tempo and played with a lift, it was Max Bacon. Another time but to another drummer, 'Listen to him chopping! Tell him to play sideways!' which was Ammy's way of saying 'Play a smooth rhythm'.

He really loved jazz, and whenever Danny Polo, George Chisholm or Tommy McQuater excelled themselves, he was elated. One could write a book about 'Ammyisms'. How can you resist appreciating a man who describes an arrangement as sounding 'like brown paper' or 'a piece of string'?

There was also a very soft sentimental part to his character as illustrated by the way he treated the two violinists in the band. The management instructed Ammy to dispense with the two violinists and they were given a fortnight's notice. The fiddlers, however, decided to ignore their dismissal and stayed on until the end of the band's engagement and Ammy did not have the heart to stop their wages.

We really got on very well and I was very upset in later years to see the great man sliding down the road to obscurity.

When I heard of his lonely demise in a Leeds hospital I recalled with sadness the contrasting scene at his grand apartment off Park Lane, which he also used as his office.

He had asked me to see him about a future engagement and Joan (his secretary) admitted me and returned to her office while I waited for the great man to appear. Eventually he slouched in, wrapped in a heavy woollen check dressing gown, looking like death warmed up. He might have had a losing streak the night before, who knows? When he opened with 'Look at me, I could have been a millionaire had I not been a gambler!'.

I was saved from replying by the telephone ringing and the reappearance of Joan saying that Sir Edmund Crain was on the 'phone from Birmingham and wanted the band to play for his daughter's 21st birthday party. 'Tell him I can't do it', 'But Mr. Ambrose' pleaded Joan 'The date is open'. Still Ammy refused but Joan prevailed upon him and impatiently he gruffly gave his answer 'Tell him it'll cost him £600'. Joan was shocked at the excessive figure, but Ammy answered that Sir Edmund could take it or leave it. He took it and we eventually fulfilled the engagement.

When the Café job finished, we went on a tour to Holland and Belgium, then began a British tour opening at the London Palladium and including Cork and Dublin. Ammy had great plans for the band in 1939 but the commencement of the war put a stop to that.

Chapter Four

WAR

'The day war broke out' I was on holiday in Lancing (on the South coast) where I had rented a bungalow for my wife and two children, Valerie and Stuart, as well as a maid, and was commuting to London for broadcasts and sessions with Lew Stone, Van Phillips, Ambrose, Bert Firman and anybody else who required my guitar services. But after the announcement on 3 September 1939, all music stopped and nobody knew what the future would bring. I knew of no musician who had had that kind of experience and for all I knew that was the end of music.

Anyway, when our lease on the bungalow ended we returned home to await developments.

Less than a month after the declaration of war, the Café de Paris re-opened (it was the first West End restaurant to open after the war), and Billy Bisset and his band (who had been resident there) returned at a cut rate. When the Musicians Union organiser came to investigate, he learned that the musicians were being paid £5 per week although the agreed union minimum had been £10 weekly (before the war). It seems that the management considered this a princely sum in view of the fact that 'there was a war on' and no other West End venue employed musicians, but the Musicians Union thought otherwise and soon agreement was reached to pay the £10 minimum.

The management then decided to install a band with a bigger reputation and asked Bert Firman (who had been at the London Casino) to form a band. And that is where I came in; indeed, lucky to land a job even at £10 per week and I was not the only one to accept that rate. George Melachrino, a star performer lately with the Savoy Orpheans, came in on saxophone, violin and vocals, Freddy Gardner, featured soloist of the Six Swingers and Ray Noble Band, played first alto, Harry Parry, a jazz clarinettist and leader of his own group, played second alto and clarinet, Cecil Norman, a very much in demand sessioneer, played piano and Wally Morris, who had always been in great demand on the most lucrative commercial sessions, played double bass. Altogether the band consisted of trumpet, four saxes and four rhythm with Bert Firman leading on violin and the whole lot for just over £100 per week.

Less than a month later, business was better than ever and Ken (Snake hips) Johnson and his West Indian Band was engaged as an added attraction. But this caused a dispute between Bert Firman and the management whereupon Bert handed the leadership of the band over to George Melachrino and resigned.

Meanwhile, Bert Ambrose had been re-engaged by the Mayfair Hotel and asked me to rejoin him and, regretfully (because George Melachrino and I had become very friendly) I returned to my previous employer who with his usual astuteness had again assembled a wonderful band of 'Prime Ministers'. Stanley Black piano, Jock Cummings (later, Maurice Burman) drums, Tommy McQuater, Max Goldberg trumpets, George Chisholm, Les Carew trombones, Joe Crossman, Joe Jeannette, Billy Amstell, Andy McDevitt and Harry Smith reeds, Jack Cooper and Evelyn Dall vocals. Later, in 1940, Anne Shelton auditioned and got the job. Believe it or not she was only 13 at the time. But we were in for a bumpy ride.

In June, the British Expeditionary Force evacuated France and after Dunkerque came the Blitz. There were many near misses in those wild night rides of 5 miles from Berkeley Square to my home in Cricklewood. Once the roof of my car was blown off and another time the garage near my house was flattened. But that was not everything.

By the end of September Ammy had had enough. He gave notice to terminate at the Mayfair, left me in charge of the band, part of which left *en bloc* to join the Air Force and form The Squadronaires, and took off for Torquay. One would think, therefore, that London was emptying but my book shows a different picture. In spite of late and disturbed nights, I was freelancing with Lew Stone, Peter Yorke, George Scott Wood, Troise, Mantovani, Percival Mackey, Felix Mendelssohn, Carrol Levis, Louis Levy, Billy Thorburn and Bert Firman. The film studios at Ealing and Elstree were in full swing and so were the recording and broadcasting studios.

Lew Stone
It was now October and the Battle of Britain was raging nightly in the air. I had passed my army medical and while awaiting my call-up I was freelancing when Lew Stone asked me to join him at the Dorchester Hotel in Park Lane.

It was a pleasant little band, with my friend Lew officiating at the piano and satisfying the musical requests from the diners and winers in the restaurant. I must add that there was an added attraction. Since we had had some extremely near misses at home from the incessant night bombing, we had sent the children to Devon and my wife was therefore on her own when I went out to play at night, and when Lew offered me the added inducement of the use of the comfortably bunked air raid shelter under the Dorchester which my wife would share, what could be better?

But this state of affairs did not last very long. On 17 October, ten days after I had settled in, the old twisted bowel trouble struck again while I was on the bandstand, and I was removed to Middlesex Hospital for more major surgery on my ninth wedding anniversary.

A few days after I had been sliced up and trussed up, a landmine fell across the street just missing our ward and I was removed to a Military Hospital where the patients kept a daily tally of the air battle as announced on the radio and where our intellectual care was under the supervision of young Mary Churchill (now Lady Soames) who, as our librarian, walked around the ward with a trolley of books.

When I was discharged from the hospital two months later, I was still unfit for the nightlife of the Dorchester Hotel and after one appearance I bade the job (and the air raid shelter) farewell.

(Left to right) Mario Maccaferri, Chappie D'Amato and Jack Hylton – Paris 1930.

Ivor Mairants with his C.I. Martin guitar, 1932.

10,000 dancers on the floor at the Wintergarden Ballroom, Blackpool.

Ambrose

Ivor Mairants with Premier Vox electric guitar 1936.

Geraldo's Orchestra embarking for Germany, 1946.

Geraldo's Orchestra, Samson and Hercules Ballroom, Coventry, 1947.

Ivor Mairants and Albert Harris, Decca Studios, Upper Thames Street, London, 1935.

Ivor Mairants with Vega acoustic/electric guitar, 1945.

This time a Zenith guitar with Eric Robinson at BBC Television Studios.

Chapter Five

GERALDO

One cynical expression in the profession is 'When one door closes another slams in your face!' but it was quite the opposite on this occasion.

Geraldo, who had been resident at the Savoy Hotel with his Gaucho Tango Band, had, a few months earlier, become Director of BBC Dance Music and unbeknown to me had kept the guitar chair open for me. When he heard that I was out of hospital and available for work, he offered me the job which consisted of doing a minimum of nine broadcasts per week.

'The Duke of Bond Street' as he later became known in the profession (because of his immaculate dress and formal public image) proposed a salary of £12 per week (the Musicians Union minimum) which I refused and this tall, handsome but rather graceless conductor added £2 to his original offer. Eventually I accepted, as a temporary measure, providing he allowed me the freedom to campaign for a higher Musicians Union minimum. He readily accepted my conditions and I am pleased to relate that we were able to raise the low pay that the BBC had become accustomed to paying musicians.

I performed my first Geraldo broadcast on 22 December 1940 at the Maida Vale studios. It was the first of thousands of broadcasts, gramophone recordings, TV shows, concerts and dances to be performed in the following eleven and a half years.

We took part in many important events from playing the troops off before embarking on the eve of D-Day on 5 June 1944, and later that year entertaining them in France, Belgium and Holland, to Royal Command Performances at Windsor Castle, Buckingham Palace and the London Palladium.

My guitar was featured in every performance of the dance band, no doubt adding to the emergence of the instrument and helping me to be voted top guitarist in the *Melody Maker* Polls for about six or seven years.

Until I joined the orchestra, my acquaintance with Geraldo had been very limited. I knew he played the piano and had been at the

55

Savoy Hotel with his Gaucho Tango Orchestra but little beyond that. Unlike all the other bandleaders I had worked for, he never gave a bar in for nothing (*i.e.* beat one, two, three, four) perhaps in deference to his classical training. However, during a rehearsal in my second or third broadcast, he brought his baton down for *In the Mood* at a much faster tempo than I was used to, and I did not respond.

Seeing that I had made no attempt to play, Gerry stopped the band and, mystified, said 'What's the matter?'. I answered that I had been surprised by the fast tempo. 'Well, what should the tempo be?' he asked. I was beginning to feel distinctly uncomfortable wondering whether he was being sarcastic or seriously requiring information, but decided to take him seriously with a 'Do you really want to know?'. 'Yes I do' he replied, so there was nothing for it but to play a few bars on my own at the acknowledged Glenn Miller tempo.

Without further ado, he directed the band into the new tempo! I had never experienced any similar situation where a conductor had demonstrated his vulnerability but was not too proud to take honest advice.

When I realised that he often watched for my reaction to a new arrangement, I had to guard against overt expression, but once I really put my foot in it.

A few months later, Maurice Burman (my best friend) joined the band on drums and wrote a new piece called *Soft Shoe Shuffle*, a lilting melody aptly described by the title, which was arranged for the band by Phil Cardew, an excellent musician and arranger for whom I had often played. Phil came along, put out the parts and we played it through; a simple orchestration which allowed the band to swing lightly, featuring Harry Hayes on alto-sax in the second chorus then ending quietly and simply.

Without giving the matter a second thought I turned round to Maurice and under my breath said to him 'Does he call that an arragement?'. This ill-considered remark nearly stifled *Soft Shoe Shuffle* at birth and Maurice held it against me for some time. Fortunately, talent wins in the end and it became one of our regularly broadcast numbers. It was also recorded on Parlophone and later reissued on a Geraldo LP.

Ben Frankel and one or two other arrangers wrote some scores for the various combinations, large and small, but it was George Evans who did most of the scores, often including some attractive passages for the electric guitar or acoustic guitar backgrounds. At the same time chords were becoming fuller, richer and more chromatic and required to be identified by the guitarist and there were many discussions between us before deciding the symbol that would identify the chord quickly and correctly. For example, G7 aug.5th (sus B♭) was much more of an eyeful to read than G7 + 5 + 9, *ie* (G.B.D♯.F.A.♯).

It was still a few years before chord symbols were regularised and it is still necessary to use your ear in order to play the best inversion.

But not only were the chords changing, the personnel was changing, due to call up's for the Armed Services.

The Rhythm Section eventually included Jack Collier (tonally and technically a great master of the string bass), Maurice Burman, Sidney (Gerry's twin brother) on piano and myself, and did not change for five or six years until Maurice became ill.

The saxophone section often changed and sometimes, when a last minute call of army duty prevented Harry Hayes and George Evans from attending a broadcast, we were left with only one alto and tenor, the alto players varying at this period and the tenor played by Aubrey Frank until he joined the RAF.

Gerry battled on without turning a hair as if there were nothing amiss. When Jimmy Coombes returned to the Guards, Ted Heath joined on trombone as a team mate in the brass section to Joe Ferrie, Alfie Noakes and other trumpet players.

In spite of our nine broadcasts per week, I was still freelancing with Lew Stone and others, and then came the time when I rejoined Ambrose on 5 May 1941 to add another nine broadcasts each week for six weeks. This may sound unreal but for those weeks I played with both Gerry and Ammy, either dashing from studio to studio or, if the same studio was being used for both bands, just staying where I was while the personnel changed around me.

Nat Temple, who played alto and clarinet for Geraldo until he joined the Grenadier Guards, was also a member of the Ambrose Orchestra at this time. I would often be late for rehearsal because one broadcast finished later than the other rehearsal commenced, but I was always in my place when the red light signalled that we were on the air. The schedules were often pretty tight, as shown by the entries in my diary:

		Rehearsal	Transmission	*Studio*
Same day	Geraldo:	5.00 p.m.	7.20 – 8.00 p.m.	Criterion, Piccadilly Circus
	Ambrose:	7.00 p.m.	9.00 – 9.20 p.m.	Paris Cinema, Haymarket

Same day	Ambrose:	10.00 a.m.	11.30 – 12 noon	Paris
	Geraldo:	Open House		
		4.00 p.m.	7.00 – 7.40 p.m.	Paris

Same day	Ambrose:	Rehearsal		
		12.30 p.m.	1.30 – 2.00 p.m.	Criterion
	Ambrose:	5.00 p.m.	6.30 – 7.00 p.m.	Criterion
	Geraldo:	6.00 p.m.	7.15 – 8.00 p.m.	Paris

The last pair of broadcasts required a fast getaway, a sprint round to Regent Street, down two flights of stairs, get set and play the opening theme when the red light went on, with no panic. The music was, of course, all in order. The above is just a sample of the daily round and I was still attending Middlesex Hospital for deep X-ray therapy.

Early in 1941 I received my call-up for the Royal Ordnance Corps, but since I was still attending hospital my doctor did not think me fit to 'storm the defences of Tobruk' and after another medical I was downgraded.

Meanwhile, ever since the Café de Paris incident, when the Musicians Union had been able at least to maintain the pre-war minimum rate of pay, I had become more and more interested in Musicians Union work. Eventually I became the Musicians Union Steward of Geraldo's Orchestra and in 1942 was elected to the London District Committee as well as serving a term as Vice-President a year later. It was then that I was sent as a delegate to the TUC (held that year in Blackpool) which really gave me the opportunity of meeting trade unionists in industry.

Musicians are always regarded as a bit of a novelty, and perhaps for that reason I was introduced to Ernest Bevin who was then Minister of Labour, and found him to be a very jovial individual. Shaking my hand which was buried in his big fist, he radiated a good-humoured personality. I could never believe that this was the same

Bevin who took an implacable stand against entry into Palestine by the displaced Jewish refugees during his term of office as Foreign Minister in the 1945 Labour Government.

Back at the musical front, our large output of broadcasts was devouring new arrangements in large quantities, so there was plenty of scope for introducing new ideas.

My first idea revolved around a Russian tune, no doubt inspired by the Soviet Union entering the war on 21 June 1941 and I called it *Russian Salad*, further prompted by my enforced near-vegetarian diet.

I have always liked to work in small groups so I arranged *Russian Salad* for clarinet (Nat Temple), alto-sax (Harry Hayes), flute (Geoffrey Gilbert), electric guitar and rhythm. The group became known as the 'Geraldo Swing Septet' and due to our many broadcasts it became popular with listeners as far away as the Sahara Desert. I followed with *Seafood Squabble* and recorded both tunes for Parlophone, the former *(Russian Salad)* now reissued on the same Geraldo LP as *Soft Shoe Shuffle*.

But since the Septet had become part of the show, more numbers were required and the next two were *Spring Prelude* and *Overhead Drive*. Bosworth & Co. published them all and Mr. Bosworth himself kindly proposed me as a member of the Performing Rights Society (PRS).

Although few recordings reached Great Britain commercially from the United States, one did arrive which was of great interest to me. It was called *Picking for Patsy* written and played by Alan Reuss on Parlophone 1942 Super Rhythm Style series No. 54–R2856, and I liked its light bouncy melody so much that I transcribed it and added it to my regular broadcasting repertoire for an unamplified guitar.

A pity the Atlantic Ocean divided us; guitarists on this side could have gained so much. Another guitarist none of us ever met was Charlie Christian, *the* greatest jazz guitarist of the 40s, whose influence far outweighed Lang's in his short span of life. The guitar world was shocked to hear that their idol had suddenly died at the age of 23 on 2 March 1943, less than three years after he had come to prominence with Benny Goodman.

I had, of course, listened to most of his recorded work and had transcribed many of his solos so it was like losing a close friend and teacher, and I paid homage to him by writing a dedication which I called *In Charlie's Footsteps*. It was, no doubt, inspired by his *Solo Flight* in the style of a miniature jazz concerto. Wally Stott orchestrated it for the band and it became quite a favourite especially of Jack Collier, our bass player. He, too, was always well featured especially when Trigger Alpert, the fantastic bass player with Glenn Miller, presented him with a solo called *Trigger's Fantasy*. One thing led to another in the form of a duet between us called *Spotlight for Two* composed by both Trigger Alpert and Barry Galbraith who was then playing for pianist/arranger Claude Thornhill.

During 1944, when Glenn Miller's Band was stationed in England, I became very friendly with Carmen Mastren, his guitarist, and when he showed me the score of a guitar solo with orchestral accompaniment I lapped it up eagerly. Before long, I recorded both *Two Moods* by Carmen Mastren and *In Charlie's Footsteps* for Parlophone accompanied by Geraldo's Orchestra. I was certainly fortunate in receiving help and inspiration from musicians and their music and this was by no means confined to guitarists.

After the fall of France, Stephane Grappelly made his home in London and formed a delightful group for broadcasting, comprising George Shearing on piano, Coleridge Good bass, Ray Ellington drums and vocals and myself on guitar. My first airing with them was performed on 24 December 1944, and the inspiration that was generated in those broadcasts was tremendous. The orchestrations were quite skeletal, liberally sprinkled with jazz solos and I can honestly say that George's tremendous playing drove me to fluency beyond my own bounds.

Stephane too, was not only a great extemporiser but a warm friendly person with many artistic talents; he came round to my house in 1956, three years after Django Reinhardt had died to ask me to join him in a re-formed Hot Club de France but I had to decline. Firstly because I could never step into a dead man's shoes and secondly, there were better Django players than me around. As Stephane had his violin with him we had a little jazz session for our own enjoyment. It did prove that Stephane was a sincere friend. His charm, his lovely smile, his natural bonhomie and his modesty have never deserted him and his playing is as excellent as ever today.

It is often surprising that although 'there was a war on' (as we were often reminded), music played quite an important part in people's lives and so did films. In fact, I was commissioned to write a Spanish guitar solo for a scene in the film *He Found a Star*, the leading roles being taken by Vic Oliver and Sarah Churchill (later husband and wife).

The fact that I did not then play 'Spanish' guitar but 'plectrum' guitar did not seem to worry anybody, least of all me, and I had the cheek to add *Spanish Dance No. 5* by Granados and *Fandanguillo* by Turina to my broadcasting repertoire. It could not have done any harm because in 1943 Francis, Day & Hunter, the publishers, were receiving requests for a guitar tutor, requests that could not be fulfilled. Francis, Day & Hunter who were the British distributors of the Eddie Lang tutor were unable to replenish their stocks because of the dollar restrictions (so I discovered much later) and so I was brought into the picture. I had a call from John Thackeray of Francis, Day & Hunter who commissioned me to write a plectrum guitar tutor of some 36 pages, but when I returned to him with only half a book and my full allotment of pages used up, he agreed to my request for 72 pages.

The Ivor Mairants Complete and Up-to-date Guitar Tutor in Theory and Practice, was first published in 1943 and after many editions the copyright was renewed in 1965 having become a standard work.

From my account it would seem that music revolved round the guitar. That was not so; the music featured on guitar was but a drop in the ocean for which I, in retrospect, seemed to be acting as a hot gospeller for fear of the drop submerging altogether.

There were few dull moments in our increasing Geraldo band schedule. On 13 November 1944, a month or so after Brussels was liberated we cast off from Newhaven in a Liberty Boat and landed across the Channel in Dieppe to spend 16 days touring France, Belgium and Holland at the request of General Montgomery.

We were the first of the bands to entertain the troops in the European Theatre of Operations and performed many concerts to about 70,000 Allied troops, playing in all kinds of places; the Marigny Theatre on the Champs Elysées in Paris, the tiny Marie Antoinette antique theatre at Versailles for SHAEF (Supreme Headquarters of the Allied Expeditionary Forces) and by contrast various packed, dimly-lit halls in Holland, particularly one in Tilberg where most of the electricity generators had been destroyed by the retreating Germans. In Brussels we were presented to General Montgomery who came to see us backstage and to say that although he had often heard us play, this was the first time he had had the pleasure of seeing us.

The Supremo of this superb variety show (which included the fabulous Josephine Baker), was Noël Coward at his most imperious, an attitude resented by Gerry. Noël was, of course, the darling of the top brass but as I pointed out to Gerry, it was the band that provided the troops' favourite entertainment, not Noël Coward.

After a number of adventures involving detours, land mines and sweet Dutch children once fed on bread made of crushed tulip bulbs, we arrived back in England, land of the flying bombs. These vaguely guided missiles often seemed to end up near my house so I sent my wife and children to Glasgow where they stayed with the parents of Ernie Shear, who was a pupil of mine. My reason for mentioning this will soon be evident.

One night in January, I was in the process of setting up my guitar and amplifier for a late-night broadcast from the BBC Paris Cinema studio in Lower Regent Street. I had plugged the lead of the Vega electric guitar into the AC/DC amplifier and holding the instrument in my left hand, I took the amplifier mains lead and looked round for a suitable power socket. My mains lead had a bayonet plug at the end and the only suitable thing I could see was a metal prompt-light stand with a matching socket into which I inserted the plug. Still holding the guitar in my left hand, I switched on the amplifier then clasped the prompt stand in order to place it in a more favourable position when **WHOOSH!** I became transfixed. There I was, standing with the guitar in my outstretched left hand and the prompt stand in my right hand as if crucified. An agonising pain shot across my chest and as the pain increased my vision began to fade. I tried to cry out for help but no sound came; I had been struck numb and dumb and my life was being painfully and silently extinguished.

The musicians were seated in their places ready for rehearsal unaware of my predicament but, fortunately for me, the producer Peter Duncan who was surveying the studio through the control room window, saw me standing alone in a stiff unnatural position and realised what was happening. He immediately pushed up every switch on his control panel and finally hit the one that controlled the prompt stand. When I regained consciousness I was lying on the floor and as I opened my eyes I saw Maurice Burman standing over me pouring water on my face. Looking up at him I remember saying 'Mind my new suit!'.

Peter Duncan, looking rather pale and shocked, said that in all probability I had about eight seconds to go before asphyxiation. Imagine my feelings when I thanked him realising that he had saved my life.

When I recovered my equilibrium the thing foremost in my mind was the broadcast which my wife would be listening to in Glasgow, expecting to hear my guitar and if not why not. So I picked up my guitar and discovered that the top three strings had disappeared and melted across my left hand leaving three long weals. First Aid put some ointment on my hand then I replaced the strings and was ready just in time for transmission.

This incident led to an enquiry by the BBC regarding proper safety regulations for electrically operated instruments and resulted in special separator transformers being installed in every studio. No longer is a guitarist allowed to plug an amplifier lead directly into a mains socket. Other lives may well have been saved as a result of my near miss!

After that midnight broadcast, Jack Collier and I went to pick up our cars parked in the side-street but mine was not there; it had been stolen. Talk about salt on the wound.

In 1945 Geraldo's band embarked on a variety tour, turning us once more into gypsies or schoolboys freed from home rule, playing the usual (and some unusual) pranks. For instance, every time Ted Heath came into his hotel bedroom he found the wardrobe lying on the bed instead of standing by the wall, not – let me assure you – due to poltergeist. Not that we had anything against Ted, he was a very good practical joker and gave as good as he got, like unscrewing the stopper from underneath Maurice Burman's wash-basin so that the water emptied straight out on to the floor.

Jokes aside, Ted had done well on royalties from *Thanks for that Lovely Week-end* written by his wife Moira and himself and, financially fortified by a maturing endowment policy, had decided to take the plunge and form his own band. He left Gerry during the tour much to Gerry's annoyance, partly, I suppose, because we had made a big feature of Ted's tune and helped it to success and partly because Gerry hated anybody to leave unless he gave them notice himself.

However, during Victory in Europe week in June 1945, while we were playing at the Empire, Newcastle, Ted upped and left for home, fame and fortune.

Between VE Day and the end of the year a number of changes had occurred in the Geraldo band line-up. My old friend Jock Bain had come in on trombone and we were joined by 'The Man with the Golden Trumpet', Eddie Calvert, to team up with Freddie Clayton and Alfie Noakes.

There was also a strong battery of vocalists – Carole Carr, Sally Douglas, Archie Lewis and a new male vocalist. Actually, Gerry christened the new male vocalist Dick James which may well have been an omen for the future publisher of the Beatles.

At the end of the year we were again invited to entertain the troops, but this time they were known as the BAOR.

Our Christmas and New Year tour in Germany was very extensive and altogether we gave about 130 performances, playing in camps, local theatres and in some fabulous fairy-tale schlosses where we feasted with Air Vice-Marshalls downwards after the show, being served by an abundance of liveried stewards.

We travelled back on the first VIP train to traverse the Rhine on a single track Bailey Bridge built by the Royal Engineers, and slowly reached Calais. In fact, we arrived in London on 2 January 1946 just one hour before we were due to go on the air.

Tight schedules were taken for granted. Flying back to London from Belfast after a tour of Ireland, one of the two propellers packed up. We made a quick turn-round to Belfast and eventually picked up another plane which flew us safely to London but only just in time to get into the Maida Vale BBC studio, set up, sit down, and open our books before the red light went on for *Tip Top Tunes*.

June 1946 heralded a new era in entertainment ... television; and on 8 June, Victory Day, Geraldo made the first TV appearance of his career. Transmissions came from Alexandra Palace and here is an eye-witness account from a *Melody Maker* reporter:

'There was an air of expectancy in Studio A. The temperature was already stifling as the brilliant lights blazed down upon the piano, painted a pale matt blue to offset undue reflection ... upon those members of the orchestra who would have to face close-ups and whose features, therefore, had been painted to resemble death masks. The vision cameras were focussed, the mobile mike hovered overhead, the leader stood with baton raised. The boys settled down, electricians stood at the ready. In one minute the red light would come on, thereafter there would be no mistakes, no retakes, no cutting. Perfect stillness. And into the soundproof studio wafted strains of a symphony orchestra. Panic! Wildly, musicians, producer, cameraman, electricians, sought the source of the interruption. It was coming from the band itself! From the back of the saxophone section! Ivor Mairants gasped. It was coming from his electric guitar amplifier well beyond his reach beneath Sid Bright's piano. Induction from a nearby low power transmitter had, apparently, transformed the amplifier into a receiver. About to rise and stifle it, the red light winked, paused, glowed, held him rooted to his chair. Down came Geraldo's baton – 'Hello again! We're on the radio again . . .' together with the Henry Wood Promenade Concert from the Albert Hall'.

Nothing could be done until the cameras were off the orchestra, when I dived under the piano and switched off the amplifier.

It did happen just once more, this time in the middle of a programme. Gerry was just about to announce the next number when a very cultured voice broke in with 'This is the BBC Home Service. Today in Parliament.' I reached over to the amplifier and switched off, allowing Gerry to collect his thoughts again and make his announcement.

Berlin next stop
For the third year in succession we were invited by General Montgomery to provide the music for our Forces in Germany and this time the main centres were to be Berlin and Hamburg where two new NAAFI centres were to be opened.

Many parts of Berlin were in a sorry mess. Wertheims, Berlin's largest department store, was just a shell, the windows of the Hermann Tietz building revealed the sky behind them. A further feature of the Berlin skyline was the dome of the burnt-out Reichstag. The Wintergarten Theatre and the nearby Friedrichstrasse Bahnhof were a shambles. The Hotel Adlon, close to Unter den Linden, had once been Berlin's top hotel and was used during the war to house the top Nazi officers, but all that remained of it was the piece of wall bearing its nameplate. The open space opposite was dominated by the new, imposing War Memorial built by the Russians, guarded by a lone Russian soldier and as I watched the changing of the guard I felt the irony of the situation.

The Oranienbourg Temple, the central synagogue of Berlin, which had been set on fire by the Nazis was also but a shell, and Kürfürstendam, the Bond Street or Knightsbridge of pre-war Berlin, was flattened. There were still a few shops open which preferred to receive payment in cigarettes (value seven marks each) than in currency and the nightclubs were again operating in the cellars of the buildings to which there were no upper floors. The once five-storey multinational restaurant Kempinsky's Haus Vaterland no longer had any upper floors. It just functioned as a street level cafe.

We could not leave Berlin without a visit to Hitler's Chancellery, a large building with long wide corridors posted (every few yards) with high rectangular pillars leading to Hitler's study. The huge chandelier had been broken and I continued the process by breaking another piece off as a souvenir.

Where there had been wood block flooring and wooden panelling, these had been removed by the Russians who were, in fact, loading the stuff on trucks at that very moment. Then we went round the back where we descended into the network of underground concrete rooms in Hitler's air raid shelter. What ghosts those cold corridors conjured up!

The NAAFI Club opening generated great excitement, the BBC announcements being delivered by our late lamented friend Franklin Engelmann (known in the BBC as 'Jingle'), who said he thought of me as sitting on a pogo-stick with a lead attached.

We were very popular in Berlin and had the pleasure of being the only British band to broadcast over the American Forces Network (AFN). In fact, so many troops were unable to gain admittance that we put on a second show to save a riot.

We were soon on the move again. We left the Russian Zone and passed the now familiar Bad Oyenhausen on the way to Hamburg where we repeated our successes.

Near the Bahnhof big business was going on in black market deals of all kinds and one of our lads bartered something for a good camera, which he smuggled home hidden in the crotch of his underpants.

In England we still had some sort of blackout and rationing so a small group, including my wife and a few friends, spent a holiday in Switzerland, world of bright lights, white sheets, food galore and sunshine, before returning to England, home and Geraldo.

Our broadcasts were soon cut down to four or five a week so I suppose Gerry had to find other work for the band and every summer we found ourselves in Blackpool as resident band at the Wintergarden from periods of six to about twelve weeks, some years more, some less, supplementing our work with broadcasts, dances and Sunday concerts. It had its moments, but being in close proximity with the same people became rather prickly at times and I was beginning to long for my freedom. There were also other kinds of friction, rates of pay not the least of them.

During one winter, a tour of the Scottish Ice Rinks was proposed which, because of the proposed cut fees, was unsatisfactory and being the steward of the band, I strongly advised against it.

In order to explain the situation, Gerry arranged a meeting at his Bond Street office and during the discussion he tried to explain how impossible it would be for him to find the money to pay us what we wanted. One Scottish newcomer to the band was very touched by Gerry's story and exclaimed, 'Well, you don't expect him to dig it out of the ground'. 'No' I quickly retorted with some sarcasm, 'but he can always sell his Rolls'. That broke the meeting up and Gerry did not speak to me for weeks. He was really upset so I eventually admitted that it had been a thoughtless remark.

We did eventually do the Scottish tour and were paid the full fees.

Besides working for Gerry, I had formed a guitar group for broadcasting which in its time included many of my professional colleagues – Billy Bell, Dave Goldberg, Roy Plummer, Jack Llewellyn, Ike Isaacs, Bert Weedon, Ernie Shear, Frank Deniz, Alan Metcalfe and even part-time guitarist Jack Duarte. I was also involved with an increasing amount of other recording and broadcasting work, one of these activities being with Winifred Atwell, the pianist. Ever since I had played on her Decca record of *Jezebel* and *Black and White Rag* (on her 'other piano') which had become a best seller, she insisted on my doing all her sessions. As well as making records together, we visited theatres to make public recordings for commercial radio and also played for the Queen in private at Lady Zia Wernher's home 'Luton Hoo' and in public for a Royal Command Performance at the London Palladium.

The Fading Fifties
Dance band fans and writers about popular music always consider the 30s as the Big Band era, but are dubious about their quality during the 40s and 50s – and Albert McCarthy in *The Dance Band Era* pp. 129 writes 'but it is worth noting here that a number of musicians were, by the mid-forties, showing signs of disenchantment with their lot'.

Brian Rust, in his book *The Dance Bands* goes even further when giving his verdict as the war ended, ' "Swing" had had its day. The top bands had not progressed much in the war years' pp. 149.

I would not have thought so, nor would the British Musicians working in the good bands, nor would the *Melody Maker* readers who voted in the annual Polls which began in 1944.

Year	Top Band	2nd Band	3rd Band	Top Guitarist
1944	Squadronaires	Geraldo	Carl Barriteau	Ivor Mairants
1945	Squadronaires	Geraldo	Skyrockets	Ivor Mairants
1946	*Swing Band* Ted Heath	Geraldo	Squadronaires	Ivor Mairants
	Sweet band Geraldo	Ted Heath	Skyrockets	
1947	*Swing Band* Ted Heath	Geraldo	Squadronaires	Dave Goldberg 2nd Ivor Mairants
	Sweet Band Geraldo	Cyril Stapleton	Ted Heath	
1950/1	*Swing Band* Ted Heath	Vic Lewis	Geraldo	Ivor Mairants
	Sweet Band Geraldo	Stapleton	Joe Loss	
1953	Ted Heath	Jack Parnell	Geraldo	Ivor Mairants
1954	Ted Heath	Johnny Dankworth	Jack Parnell	Ivor Mairants

In 1954 the *New Musical Express* Poll results were:

1954 NME	Ted Heath	Jack Parnell	Ken Mackintosh	Ivor Mairants

which points to the fact that new dance bands were being formed and that styles were not stagnant. However, it will be seen that by the end of the 40s Geraldo's band no longer had a clear lead but had to compete with Ted Heath, The Squads, The Skyrockets and Cyril Stapleton.

However, Gerry still had the best arrangers who gave the guitar as much scope as the score would allow. In any case the guitar was now considered as a voice practically on equal terms with the other instruments of the orchestra and there were a number of excellent guitarists who could cope. The most prominent were Dave Goldberg, Pete Chilver, Roy Plummer, Jack Llewellyn, Lauderic Caton, Laurie

Deniz, George Elliot, Billy Bell, Bert Weedon and later Ike Isaacs who came to London from India in 1946.

Young people now wanted to learn to play the guitar more than ever and pupils were taking up more and more of my time so that my home was becoming a teaching establishment. Although I had always liked to share my love of the guitar with keen pupils, it seemed that a home should be a family affair, so with the help of my wife I decided to establish a school to accommodate all those who were seriously interested in study.

In September 1950 I opened the Central School of Dance Music and as I became more involved with the school and with freelance work I could see the Geraldo era drawing to a close, and I finally left the band on 12 July 1952.

Chapter Six

THE CENTRAL SCHOOL OF DANCE MUSIC

The CSDM got off to a flying start with an impressive array of star teachers for whose support I was very grateful.

The opening line-up read like a poll winners' chart – Johnny Dankworth, Dougie Robinson, Keith Bird and Aubrey Frank (saxophones); Jack Brymer (clarinet) Kenny Baker and Alan Franks (trumpet); Laddy Busby and Jock Bain (trombone); Sid Bright and Malcolm Lockyer (piano); Jack Collier (double bass); Eric Delaney and Jock Cummings (drums); Bert Weedon, Ike Isaacs and myself (guitar); Enso Topano and Lorna Martin (accordion); Alan Dean (vocal); David Miller (broadcast presentation) and Wally Stott and Roland Shaw (arranging). It was an incomparable panel of teachers.

Soon it was evident that I needed an assistant principal. Wally Stott with great perspicacity suggested Eric Gilder who was then directing the Geraldo Choir and it could not have been a better choice; he fitted in perfectly and he was as happy as a sandboy.

One interesting experience taking me back to the CSDM took place quite recently when the jazz trombonist in Jack Parnell's Band and a leading saxophonist in the Radio Dance Band reminded me of the time when they had been pupils of the school. It was during a concert with Geoff Love's Orchestra that they challenged me to recognise them. Twenty years had elapsed and they had grown up so I failed to meet this challenge, but they had not forgotten the value of their excellent tuition. That was a truly rewarding experience.

In spite of the numbers of guitar teachers employed at the school – and they included Roy Plummer, Ike Isaacs and the late Dave Goldberg as well as myself – the demand was so great that pupils had to wait patiently when we over-ran or returned late from a session.

The keenness and enthusiasm was certainly rewarding although the rush from studios in and around London and attending to pupils almost sapped my energy. In addition, we formed a guitar group which broadcast regularly and a Jazz Academy Group which did concerts, dances and BBC Jazz Club broadcasts. Nothing did I enjoy more than paying the best rates for the musicians whose playing I loved. We even did a jazz week-end at Butlins Holiday Camp at Clacton. This was organised by an agent who shall be nameless and also included Johnny Dankworth and his band with Cleo Laine and other top artistes.

My group consisted of Bert Courtley, trumpet, Don Rendell, tenor sax, Max Harris piano, Major Holley, double bass and the fabulous Phil Seamen, drums, and myself. All dedicated jazz musicians – perhaps a little hard to handle, but tremendously co-operative.

Well, we had done one dance, and one day's clinics (*i.e.* class tuition) and the agent had arranged to pay me on Saturday at 5 p.m. Five p.m. came and went and so did 6 when I finally got a message to say that he would have the money at 10 a.m. the following morning – Sunday.

Sunday we were scheduled to play our final concert in the theatre at 11 a.m. and by 10.15 the hall was packed with young enthusiasts who had paid well for the jazz week-end. We were all set up on the stage ready to go and before I went to my assignment, I instructed the boys not to lift the curtain until I returned with the money and off I went. The agent did not show up so I went to the administrative building and asked to see the controller. Permission refused. I then strengthened my terminology to the two bully boys in the outer precincts and was ushered into the manager's office. The manager was sitting behind his desk and I briefly outlined the situation about the absentee or absconded agent and made the following speech. 'The theatre is packed to capacity and my band is all ready and waiting to perform. It is almost 11 o'clock and if the show does not go on there will be fury in front of the house and the audience will tear the seats up and wreck the place. You are in charge and I hold you responsible, so either you pay me now or there will be no show.' He did not reply but wrote something on a slip of paper, turned to the wall behind him and rapped on a small panel which soon opened. He passed the slip of paper in and a hand took it. The panel closed but soon opened with the wads of pound notes changing hands. The manager handed me the bundles which I had to stuff into my trouser pockets and I quickly and triumphantly made my way to the theatre with the good news and the curtain went up as scheduled.

My pockets were heavy but my heart was light and, needless to say, the performance was worth every single note I paid out.

On 6 September the *Melody Maker* reported that Jim Davidson, BBC Dance Band Chief, stated 'I am booking the Guitar Group's return. I have seen Ivor Mairants and told him the ball is now at his feet so far as building up his group for future engagements is concerned'.

No sooner said than done, and the group which had been tacit since 1950 (due to my being torn between the school, Geraldo and free-lance engagements) began a BBC series on Saturday 4 October 1952. The group consisted of three guitars, including myself, Dennis Wilson, piano, and Frank Clarke, bass.

At that time Les Paul had opened his Palladium season on 15 September, giving the London audience its first glimpse of a solid electric guitar, and the following Tuesday Les Paul and his wife Mary Ford were invited to the school to meet my professional colleagues and friends, and great excitement was engendered for guitar fans.

I realised the added variety a solid guitar would contribute to the guitar group and it wasn't long before I, too, had a Les Paul guitar, the only one in Great Britain (through the good offices of Messrs. Boosey & Hawkes).

With changes in personnel and instrumentation, the Guitar Group continued to broadcast for another couple of years eliciting favourable comments from the press:

Melody Maker **14 November 1953**
'Since Ivor Mairants has added accordion and drums to his combination and subtracted one guitar, the improvement has been considerable. There is now an air of artistry and gentle jazz about the group which it didn't possess before.'

It may be interesting to note that the accordionist was the now famous jazz pianist and composer Stan Tracey, who was also responsible for some of the avant-garde group arrangements. (Later, Ivor Beynon became the regular accordionist, playing brilliantly.)

Daily Mail **16 October 1954. Collie Knox calling!**
'Soothing and unusual is the music made by Ivor Mairants and his Guitar Group. Now, after a whale of a struggle to get on at all, they are successfully airborne. They soothe my nights of madness.'

The school was riding on the crest of a wave and there was a demand for some recreational activities, so what better than a Jazz Academy dance. Thus began the formation of the 'Jazz Academy Group' comprising Leslie 'Jiver' Hutchinson, trumpet, Tommy Whittle, tenor sax, Douggie Robinson, alto, Jock Bain, trombone,

Dennis Wilson, piano, Tony Kinsey, drums and Joe Muddell, bass, and myself. Besides the dances and concerts, we broadcast for the 'London Jazz' series of the BBC and although personnel changed depending on the availability of the players, it became a popular group.

The variety of work I was able to do after leaving Geraldo was greatly extended and a good proportion of it was taken up with Winifred Atwell's recordings, Radio Luxembourg shows, TV and stage appearances.

On 4 November 1952 in the middle of my other guitaristic activities, she was honoured with a Royal Command Performance at the Palladium at which I accompanied her together with drummer Colin Bailey (a protégé of mine and a pupil at the school who has since become a star recording man in Hollywood).

Other artistes in the performance included Benjamino Gigli, Gracie Fields, Vera Lynn and the Deep River Boys, all of whom I had previously accompanied. It was an exciting time, but running a school carried its responsibilities especially the responsibility of assessing the pupil's potentialities. Sometimes it was easy and obvious especially with somebody like Judd Proctor who came down from Nottingham every week (where he was working as guitarist at the Palais). He soaked in everything I showed him first time and when he returned for the following lesson his homework was perfect – a perfect pupil.

When I had a call from Ray Ellington asking me to recommend a pupil to replace Lauderic Caton (his original guitarist who was leaving) I had no hesitation in sending Judd Proctor, who mastered the Ellington guitar book in no time. The Ray Ellington Quartet featured a lot of guitar so it wasn't an easy job.

Mike Morton was in his teens when his father sent him to me from Oxford but he found it so difficult to absorb the barest basics of music, pitch or time that I gave up. It was only his father's pleading that made me persevere until I broke through his sound barrier eventually, and to my surprise Mike Morton became a good player, formed his own trio and became very successful, performing at the Empire, Leicester Square, in pop, rock and jazz. He now has his own recording studio, cuts his own discs and tapes which sometimes enter the charts and generally makes a lot of money.

I was once interviewing a young prospective pupil and tried to discover what style of playing he favoured. In doing so I demonstrated a few bars on my guitar. He watched wide-eyed and when I had finished he exclaimed 'Cor, if I could play like that I'd be a millionaire!' It only goes to show what really attracted him to the guitar.

When young guitarists ask me how they can break in to the profession I know it is a right and proper question but it is one which has no short answer. One has but to read the short biographies in Part 2 of this book to realise that the popular music profession is a most unpredictable one. Changing fashions and styles come and go but musicians with talent and determination – plus a little bit of luck – manage to stay the course.

Chapter Seven

CONSULTANT

The rise in the popularity of the guitar began in the early fifties and by the end of the decade had reached 'boom' proportions.

Les Paul's 1952 Palladium performance had introduced us to the solid electric guitar. Duane Eddy, who followed shortly with a variety tour favoured a slimline Guild electric/acoustic, but by the time Bill Haley and his Comets arrived, audiences had grown larger and were more enthusiastic.

This group played Rock 'n Roll at its loudest and wildest to an hysterical, screaming audience at the Dominion Theatre, Tottenham Court Road, whose excited shrieks of elation produced more volume than the banks of loudspeakers on the stage.

Britain's youngsters were greatly affected and they rushed to buy guitars and to create their own styles. New performers like Tommy Steele, Cliff Richard, Hank Marvin and the Shadows all came into the picture. Lonnie Donegan, who had long been a banjo and guitar player, recorded *Rock Island Line* which placed him in the front as the leader of the singing, playing, skiffling movement. The new social habit of coffee drinking established Coffee Bars where skiffle groups proudly showed off their three chord tricks.

Aided and abetted by trombone playing, fast singing Gordon Langhorn (Don Lang) I succumbed to the Rock 'n Roll avalanche and formed the Mairants/Langhorn Group, recording some titles for Parlophone and appearing on ATV in one of their spectaculars.

Behind the wall of Rock 'n Roll publicity, the classical guitar was quietly gaining ground, although classical recitals by Ida Presti (France's leading guitarist) and Maria Louisa Anida from South America attracted only small audiences. Segovia's annual appearances were always fully attended and his name was known to a public who otherwise knew nothing about the classical guitar.

Julian Bream, who had first broadcast at the age of 12, had now become famous enough to appear on the BBC TV show 'Six Five Special' in the midst of the 'Twist'. Even the Royal Academy of Music had added the classical guitar to the classical instruments curriculum. Spanish flamenco companies toured England and tourism in Spain began, aiding the romantic appeal of the Spanish (flamenco) guitar.

I myself began to take an interest in flamenco music and had lessons from visiting guitarists Luis Maravilla, Juan de la Mata and Angel Iglesias.

Guitars were now becoming an item of commerce and the first man to take advantage was Ben Davis of Selmers, London, who aided by his guitar playing PR man, Dick Sadleir, imported Höfner guitars from West Germany. On the classical side Rose, Morris & Co. imported Tatay guitars from Valencia in Spain. Cheap guitars also came from Czechoslovakia and an extremely cheap small guitar from the Soviet Union in exchange for *razor blades*!

I suppose they all served a need but I did not much care for any of them except the Tatay which, in spite of its shoddy appearance, had a good tone. Guitars, of course, need strings and Boosey & Hawkes approached me to sponsor a string bearing my name; after a couple of years of study, trial and error, I accepted the final sample and in May 1952 the 'Ivor Mairants' strings were launched. This led to my being appointed guitar consultant and buyer for Boosey & Hawkes, a position which I took seriously and enjoyed.

It must be remembered that because of the dollar exchange control, no dollar goods could be imported into Great Britain, hence the trade with Europe, but there was nothing to stop me designing a guitar similar to my Epiphone and in the end I decided to copy the design of the Epiphone Broadway arched top.

It was now up to *us* to select a guitar manufacturer (of which there were a few in West Germany) to make the instruments which were to be known by the trade name of Zenith.

There were a number of guitar makers in the district of Bubenreuth near Erlangen in Bavaria some of whom had come over from nearby Mark Neu Kirchen in East Germany and others from Schönbach in Czechoslovakia and opened small factories. They were Karl Höfner, Edward Hoyer, Klira and Freddy Wilfer. Freddy Wilfer was about to build a new factory for Framus guitars which made their debut in December 1953. Eventually there were three Zenith models, Nos. 17 and 19 non-cutaway and model 21 a de-luxe cutaway, with prices ranging from £19.00 to about £27.00.

As the demand rose and Wilfer could not meet the requirements, I had to make many journeys to Düsseldorf, Nüremberg, Frankfurt, Mannheim, Berlin, Leipzig and Czechoslovakia. In Leipzig I discovered a talented maker named Dieter Hense who later came out to West Germany and became one of the best luthiers in Europe and I must have met and seen the work of a hundred guitar makers including Herman Hauser Jnr., Oscar Teller, Dieter Hopf and Edgar Mönch.

The need for Spanish guitars was also growing so in 1954 I began what became an annual pilgrimage to the luthiers and guitar manufacturers of Spain, at first on behalf of Boosey & Hawkes and then on my own account. As the 1950s rolled on so did the demand for guitars increase. The sales in 1954 were twice as many as in 1953. In 1955 they were 150 per cent up on 1954, and by the end of 1956 sales had risen to five times the volume of 1955. By 1957 the National Press were screaming of a guitar boom. The weekly magazine *John Bull* printed a two page spread which included a personal interview, a picture of me testing a warehouse full of guitars and another with Winifred Atwell at the Palladium under the caption 'The Guitar Craze Hits Fortissimo'.

Both the *Daily Mirror* and the *Daily Mail* published my inside story about the shortage of supplies and the overwhelming demand for guitars. One northern retailer offered me a large sum in cash to divert guitars to him from one of my continental sources. I sent him and his Jag. back to Lancashire with an empty boot!

Yes! 1957 must indeed have been the year the guitar craze hit fortissimo not only in the United Kingdom but also in Europe.

An internationally organised Guitar Festival took place in the University town of Erlangen in Bavaria which received national TV coverage in which representative guitarists including myself were televised performing their own special styles before large audiences. The star, in my opinion, was Atilla Zoller from Hungary whom I called Europe's Tal Farlow. I also met the youthful Siegfried Behrend playing from Bach to avant-garde with equal ease on the nylon-strung guitar.

After doing some adjudicating and holding a 'clinic', I looked in at the October Beerfest (Festival of Beer) in Munich – an amazing sight of an unlimited number of Germans drinking an unlimited number of beers from steins, in long beerhalls along tables which stretched to infinity.

However, the object of my journey south was to go to Mittenwald. Mittenwald is the birthplace of the famous German violin maker Glotz, the main industry being violin making. In this picturesque mountain resort Leo Rossmeisel (once guitarist of Marek Weber's

Orchestra in Berlin in 1928) had set up a small factory making Roger guitars. They were made with solid timber and good craftsmanship and I had no hesitation in recommending them to Messrs. Boosey & Hawkes, who soon added Roger guitars to their catalogue. However, prior to my German visit I enjoyed a once-in-a-lifetime experience which needs a chapter on its own.

Chapter Eight

MISSION TO MOSCOW

Perhaps due to my many guitar activities coupled with my earlier involvement in the Musicians Union of which I am still a paid up member, I received an invitation from the 'International Preparatory Committee' of the Sixth World Festival of Youth and Students to be an adjudicator in the guitar section of the music competitions.

A letter followed signed by Galina Ulanova, David Oistrakh and Dmitri Shostokovitch inviting me to Moscow for a fortnight from 28 July to 11 August 1957, and after arranging for my wife to be included, I accepted the invitation.

We chose to fly to Helsinki where we were able to do some sightseeing and experience a sauna bath (a thing then unheard of outside Finland) before entraining for Moscow.

The train seemed to be full of international performers and competitors from outside the Soviet Union: sportsmen, musicians and dancers, all of whom detrained at Viborg where we boarded the Russian narrow gauge train. There was no dining car and our main means of sustenance was many glasses of Russian lemon tea supplied by the attendant who kept the samovar steaming for our 24 hour journey.

As the train drew in to the platform in Moscow, the station hall seemed packed solid with Russians greeting the foreigners, ready to transport them to their destinations, while we ourselves were greeted by a young Russian who presented us with a huge bunch of flowers. How he recognised us I shall never know but, speaking good English, he conducted us to a chauffeur-driven car which was to drive us through the packed streets to our hotel.

All the main thoroughfares had been closed to all but festival traffic, so that they could be packed with sightseers. Imagine an avenue 10 lanes wide with only a single lane in the middle left clear for traffic while the rest of this Sadyove Ring Road was packed with people wall to wall.

We, in our car, formed part of the inauguration drive but this unusual experience went only a small way towards preparing us for the fortnight which followed.

Eventually we pulled up at the front steps of the newly built 28 storey Ukraine Hotel. It was like pulling up at St. Paul's Cathedral except that this large square of buildings was a massive example of 'wedding cake' architecture facing the Moskva river. When we entered our room (also facing the river), it was being tidied by a woman who became so awestruck at seeing two strangers that she bowed herself backwards out of the room muttering 'Gospodin' meaning 'Your Highness'. We were certainly surprised by this 19th century behaviour and thought that she must have been fresh from the backwoods as one could not imagine a Muscovite mixing feudalism with socialism.

It now dawned on us that we were receiving VIP treatment and this was confirmed when the telephone rang and a female voice announced in excellent English, that she was our interpreter. 'Come up' I said, and soon a well-dressed, good looking, sun tanned blonde of about thirty-odd presented herself.

She told us that she had volunteered for this job during her holiday period from her regular teaching job at the College of Adult Education and was delighted to do so. Furthermore, she would be at our service for the whole fortnight, act as our interpreter-guide, and deliver us to the official social functions to which we would be invited. A car and chauffeur had been allotted to us for the period and all we had to do was ring for car number 46.

Here we were, not yet settled in our room and we felt that we had been transported into the ancient land of Ghengis Khan with the fair Lily Shilovskaya acting as the 'Slave of the Lamp', perhaps even conjuring up the Polovtsian Dancers for us among other miracles. In fact, she had brought the first official invitation for us to attend a reception that evening in honour of the opening of the Festival, to take place at the Prague Restaurant.

Although this event was the least sumptuous of the many that were to follow, it was still in the top class by any standards. Superb food, friendly people and scintillating entertainment.

The slogan for the Festival was 'Mir y Druzhba' – Peace and Friendship, and in this spirit we were introduced to delegates from Mexico, Cuba, El Salvador, Czechoslovakia, Venezuela, India and the Arab countries. The United Nations had nothing on this mixture. The entertainment, too, was just as cosmopolitan. A Hungarian gypsy band, a Russian balalaika and mandolin ensemble, an Eskimo group playing odd stringed zithers, and other groups from strange lands playing strange instruments.

Although one would have thought that the novelty of these unusual ensembles would have evoked great interest among the international audience, in the event the show stoppers turned out to be a French trio of harmonica, piano and drums playing a rock and roll arrangement of *St. Louis Blues*. There seemed to be no geographical limitation to the rock and roll craze. What a day! It was well into the night before we flopped into bed for the first time in three nights.

The following morning our Slav slave called to take us sightseeing in this great city, a mixture of East and West, the exotic and the tumbledown, new building projects next to wooden houses with leaky windows and standpipes in the street for domestic drinking water.

On our way to Red Square, walking along the river embankment, an odd sight manifested itself before our very eyes. A couple of women dressed in dungarees and kerchiefs, suddenly climbed out of a manhole in the pavement, sat down with their feet dangling down the hole, took out packets of sandwiches and ate their lunch. Quickly I whipped out my camera but Lily Shilovskaya begged me not to take such an uncomplimentary picture of life in the Soviet Union.

When we arrived in Red Square the queue for viewing Lenin's tomb stretched for quite a distance past the Lenin library right round to 'GUM', Moscow's huge department store.

Undaunted, Lily, the 'Slave of the Lamp' used her powers. She had a little chat with the policeman on duty and we transferred to the head of the queue, but not before the policeman had asked to have his picture taken with the two Lily's.

Eventually we descended a few flights of stone steps and entered a small black marble-lined chamber with a cordonned-off section at the bottom of the steps where two glass coffins lay side-by-side on a stone platform.

There they lay, Lenin neatly dressed in a dark suit, white shirt and black and red tie under the open-looking features, waxlike, with broadly spaced eyes and dark moustache.

Stalin, by contrast, looked rather Machiavellian, the narrow head and close set eyes matched by the drooping moustache. Although he was then in disgrace after Kruschev's denouncement, his body had not yet been removed from Russia's pinnacle of honour.

It felt good to emerge again into the sunshine and warmth of Red Square partly dominated by St. Basil's Cathedral with its onion and pineapple and cone-shaped domes and riotous colours in contrast to the rectangular red granite of the mausoleum.

The grounds of the Kremlin, open to the public, now presented an unusual sight. Not only because of the onion-shaped domes, particularly the golden glint of the magnificent tower of Ivan the Terrible set off against the black storm clouds, but also from the many colourful clothes worn by the African and Far Eastern visitors, all of which I captured with my camera (with the full approval of Lily).

That evening we saw our first variety show which was presented at the Red Army Theatre which must be the most spacious theatre of its kind — and that includes the pre-war Wintergarten of Berlin. One could even walk along between rows without disturbing the people sitting in the seats. However, even in this comfort, 20 magnificent acts became rather indigestible and we were glad to return to the quiet of our room.

The following day, Monday 30 July, all the musical juries were assembled on the stage of the 'Hall of Columns' (a magnificent building hung with crystal chandeliers, studded by marble columns) while all the competitors filled the body of the hall. Everybody on the platform was introduced to the competitors and to each other and formal speeches were made by the President and Secretary of the Preparatory Committee after which followed stunning performances of instrumental, vocal and terpsichorean brilliance brought from the vast land expanse known as the Soviet Union.

The instrumental ensembles included all the fretted instruments and for the first time I was able to see chord zithers used as solo and accompanying instruments by a group of girls from Kamchatka. There was entertainment to fill months of star billing.

Back to the job in hand (after all, we were there to do a job). We were five guitar jurists plus a referee-cum-rules adviser whose name was P. Ilyushin of the Moscow Pedagogical Institute.

The Russian juror was himself Laureate of the guitar and a professor at the Moscow Conservatoire, a man in his forties named Alexandre Ivanov-Kromskoy, while the others were Ugo Kalise, singer-guitarist and composer from Radio Roma, Bruno Hense, composer, arranger and teacher from West Germany, and Wim Gaffel, guitarist and double bass player in the Amsterdam Opera Orchestra. Bruno Hense was elected Chairman and myself Vice-Chairman, a rather formidable committee compared to the small number of guitar entrants of about a dozen.

There was a guitar quartet from Moscow, a duo from Leningrad as well as soloists from Czechoslovakia, Yugoslavia, Ceylon, East

Germany, Korea, Japan and Surinam, and the first heat was held in the Concert Hall of the Moscow University Club. We agreed to allow all but two of the competitors through to the finals, which took place on 4 August. These resulted in three competitors coming almost neck and neck, namely:

Milan Zelenka (Czechoslovakia). Playing *Fandanguillo* (Turina), *Fantasia* (Jose Vinas) and *Bonne Nuit* (Stephan Urban).
Ivao Suzuki (Japan). Own composition and *Gavotte* (Bach).
Roland Zimmet (GDR). *Suite in E Minor* (Bach), *Fandanguillo* (Turina), *Study in E Minor* (Villa Lobos).

My marking gave Zimmet 22, Suzuki 21 and Zelenke 20 (out of 25), but on aggregate the order was Zelenke 1st, Suzuki 2nd, Zimmet 3rd.

Herr Hense, to my great surprise, refused to accept these placings and wanted Zimmet to be placed first, but after I stormed in with a lecture on 'fairness according to British standards', Ivanov-Kromskoy (who nearly succumbed to Hense's pressure) suggested that the three top players each receive a gold medal; a decision accepted by the whole jury.

Time has proved the correctness of the judges' decision for they have all become leading guitarists in their own countries.

The presentation ceremonies took place in the Hall of Columns but I was unable to attend because I had arranged to record an interview as well as play an instrumental broadcast from Moscow Radio, although I did not have a guitar. However, I was lucky enough to find Denny Wright (the guitarist) who was also in Moscow working with Bruce Turner's Band playing concerts, the biggest of which was an open air performance in Pushkin Square for an audience of several thousands. Peggy Seeger, who sang and played the banjo, was the guest artiste.

Having found a guitar *and* amplifier, I went off to the studios. First I recorded the interview then was introduced to the quartet of Russian musicians who were to accompany me. They were excellent sight-readers and had no difficulty in reading the parts including the accompaniment to *Little Bo Bleep* which I had written for the occasion to commemorate the launching of the first Sputnik into space.

Now I had to rush off to the Prague Restaurant where Ivanov-Kromskoy had arranged a party for the adjudicators in a large private room. The room was dominated by a huge oval table heavily laden with an enormous selection of food and drink. Ivanov-Kromskoy and his wife were at one end of the table, the professor from the Pedagogic Institute and the rest of the jury with their interpreters were already seated and I was left to take my place at the other end of the table with my two lady escorts at either side of me.

Everything would have gone along perfectly with me had not the Russian Laureate made countless toasts which he addressed to me and to which I was expected to reply – and drink the toast. Not being much of a drinker and not being used to large quantities of vodka, I hoped to get by just by taking a sip for each toast. But this would not do for the merry Ivanov-Kromskoy, who insisted on drinking Russian style, *i.e.* linking arms and drinking bottoms-up for each toast. After seven toasts and seven vodkas, he insisted on our tasting their best Russian brandy and this I dutifully did, still being able to stand *and* talk. However, inadvertently touching my face, I discovered to my dismay that it felt numb, so I sat down and quietly waited for the party to break up.

At about 7.30 I rose to leave and fortunately, aided by the two Lily's on either side of me, was able to descend the main staircase and walk along the wide corridor to fall into our waiting car.

The following day, when the vodka veil had lifted from our numbed brains, we visited the woodwind competition which was chaired by my old friend and colleague, flautist Geoffrey Gilbert, who had now become world famous and was busy not only judging scores of entries but also giving two solo recitals, so that he was far too tired to take part in the late-night revels.

Our next call was to the popular music, dance band and vocal competition which had attracted entrants from all over the world.

Imagine my surprise when I was introduced to the Chairman, Leonid Utyesov, the Russian bandleader to whom (in the war years) we had sent records and with whom I had corresponded. His daughter (his one-time vocalist) was also on the committee and they both welcomed us with open arms. Naturally we were all delighted especially as there was no language barrier and we were all able to converse in Yiddish.

We discovered that Utyesov was, without doubt, the king-pin of popular music in the Soviet Union. He was a People's Artiste who regularly led his various combinations of bands and orchestras in performances for concerts, dances, records, radio and television, and provided the light and dance music for official and Government functions.

His personal fees and royalties must have been considerable and it was apparent that he was a rich man by any standards, owning a dacha in the country as well as an enormous apartment in a solidly built block of flats in Moscow.

Edith, his daughter (who had been the vocalist in his band) was now married to a leading film director whom she accompanied when he made working trips abroad, and was therefore dressed in more fashionable clothes than most women we had seen in Moscow, who did not have the advantage of shopping in Paris.

Further confirmation of Utyesov's affluence came when we were invited to the party he gave for the adjudicators in the Popular Music Section. This was held in the privacy of his own luxury apartment which consisted of many rooms. In the main room there was a table at least 18 feet long covered by a beautiful openwork one-piece linen tablecloth laden with an enormous number of dishes filled with a great variety of foods.

A grand piano seemed to be hidden in a corner of this large room, the walls of which were hung with antique plates, and in the adjoining room where we deposited our coats, the treasures which were displayed in the cabinets would have graced any national museum.

Seated at the banqueting table we were attended by four girls in maids' outfits and when I asked Leonid if they were friends or neighbours he replied that two were regular maidservants and two were borrowed from a neighbour for the occasion. Quite bewildering to one who understood the Soviet Union to be a classless society.

Among the 30 or so guests from France, Italy and other European countries, there were some members of his band, and when I saw a record player containing discs of Charlie Parker, Miles Davis and Dizzie Gillespie, I began a discussion with Utyesov and his men about jazz, a subject Utyesov had written about oddly in his letter to me of 1947.

Well, it soon became obvious that there was a wide gulf in jazz appreciation between Abramov, his lead trumpet player and himself, and an even wider gulf between Leonid and myself as to what was meant by jazz. In the end, he explained that he really understood very little about jazz but was very well versed in popular music and musical entertainment. I also learnt that jazz was forbidden but was smuggled in in a variety of ways. There was such a keen interest in the subject that most leading Soviet dance musicians made a very careful study of whatever good jazz records could be obtained, in spite of the edict by Zhdanov in the late forties proclaiming jazz 'decadent'.

This marvellous evening – we all entertained – came to an end at about 4 a.m. and when we eventually came out into the forecourt, our chauffeur was there where he had been all evening, to return us to our hotel.

Saturday, the Jewish Sabbath, turned out to be a day of different experiences. We asked to be taken to the Moscow Central Synagogue and accompanied by Lily Shilovskaya, we drove there and parked in a nearby street. Turning the corner and walking towards the Synagogue we suddenly came upon dense crowds of people jamming the streets solid right up to the entrance and when I asked for an explanation, I was told that the Synagogue was so crowded that there was no more room inside for worshippers. I also learned that the Israeli Ambassador was attending together with the Israeli delegates to the Festival whom the press had completely ignored, and this gathering must have been an act of solidarity with the Israeli contingent.

After Lily had explained to the silent demonstrators that we were foreign delegates we were permitted to push our way through the crowd and up the broad steps to the entrance of the building. Lily and my wife made their way upstairs to the circular gallery and I was ushered straight into a seat near the Ark (quite an honour).

The Synagogue was much larger than any I had been to, giving rise to a feature I had not experienced before, the service being relayed on a PA system so that the Cantor could be heard by the outsize congregation. I was honoured with an 'Aliyah', that is, being 'called up' to say a prayer on the bimah (platform) during the reading of the Sefar Torah (the Pentateuch), a similar 'mitzvah' (good deed) being given to the one-armed Israeli Ambassador.

In the intervals between prayers I had opportunities of conversing with some of the congregants who, between them observed caution in their statements. One said he had no complaints and was receiving his old age pension which sufficed; another, while hinting that all was not well, said it was better not to talk; a third admitted that things had improved since the death of Stalin.

My wife, up in the women's gallery, received an entirely different impression. All the women were unanimous in their desire to emigrate to Israel in spite of agreeing that they were well provided for in their old age, but that it did not compensate for anti-Semitism and all asked if there was anti-Semitism in England. But when they asked my wife who the other woman was and she told them that Lily was our interpreter, they became very angry. They claimed that my wife had no right to bring her along and refused to utter another word.

I paid my respects to the Rabbi and gave a donation, leaving with an uneasy feeling of tension. The question of anti-Semitism was often raised and I was often asked whether it was prevalent in England. A young Jewish reporter interviewing me for *Komsomolskaya Pravda* (the official journal of the Young Communist League), speaking perfect English, told me that it was impossible for Jewish graduates to obtain teaching posts in certain schools of adult education and that his father had lost his job as a journalist because of his creed and in order to make any kind of living, had to 'ghost write'. It all seemed in a way bizarre especially when I was told by members of a Georgian dance band that anti-Semitism wasn't as bad now as it had been under Stalin. The law, of course, states that racial discrimination is a crime in the Soviet Union but then it also provides that there shall be freedom of speech.

It would be very difficult to cram a greater and more exciting variation of activities in any fortnight than we experienced in Moscow. One early evening Lily Shilovskaya presented Russia's two leading exponents of the seven string guitar for me to hear in our room and their performance was unbelievable. The seven string guitar is tuned from the lowest note up

7	6	5	4	3	2	1
D	G	B	D	g	b	d

and I would say that the performance given by Alexie Kuznetsov and Victor Kruchinyin that evening could not be equalled. It held me spellbound with its technical brilliance and repertoire. They played Russian folk tunes of course, and arrangements of the music of the famous composers and my one regret is that I did not have a tape recorder for I doubt if any of my readers would ever have heard the like, which again proves that only masters can raise the standard of an instrument which is always associated with the major and relative minor three chord trick strums.

Two evenings were spent at the Bolshoi Theatre, one for a performance of *Romeo and Juliet* featuring Ulanova as prima ballerina dancing to the music of Prokofiev with the magnifient orchestra conducted by G. Rozhdestvensky, and the otner to see the opera *Aida* by Verdi, both viewed from the close proximity and comfort of a circle box. The huge stage made an equally perfect setting for the ballet scenes and the crowds of performers in the opera, including the Aida trumpeters playing the Grand March. They were two evenings to be savoured, never to be forgotten – and they were not the only ones.

We were invited to a reception at the British Embassy, to an Art Exhibition and special entertainment which included the world famous hand puppetmaster Obrastzov whom I had seen perform in London but had never met. We were introduced to him after the show and in the informal setting of the Embassy room, a conversation was carried on in English between Obrastzov, ourselves and the puppet painted on his hand between forefinger and thumb.

One would never have thought that the painted mouth between finger and thumb belonged to anyone but a saucy young lad, so real did he appear and sound, even in the closest proximity.

The most magnificent and unbelievable show, however, was the Kremlin Ball held on 5 August at 8.00 p.m., equivalent to but on a larger scale than a Royal Ball and Garden Party.

Our car dropped us at the Kremlin gates, where we gave our names to the official on duty who indicated that we could make our way through the gardens. As we did so, young people standing on the edge of the path presented my wife with flowers while, hidden somewhere in the bushes, gypsy orchestras played. As we proceeded we heard our names being relayed ahead of us over the Tannoy or Public Address system, until we reached the lawn in front of the palace, set with long tables stacked with food and drink to feed the multitude.

Soon after we arrived, Mr. Bulganin, the President, and Mr. Krushchev the Prime Minister (Messrs. B&K) and other members of the Government came out of the Kremlin Palace and joined us at the tables where we were standing enjoying the food and the fantastic scene. There they stood on the other side of the table opposite us, joining in the general conversation with those who understood Russian and although we understood not a word of it, it was interesting to see that they were most jovial with the Arab visitors who showered them with adulation and affection, drinking their health in pink champagne, taking dozens of flash photos.

Having stayed long enough to say that we ate at the same table as B&K, we started to walk around and to my amazement came face to face with a short stocky figure with broad shoulders, a strong head and full drooping moustache, the living image of the famous wartime hero and leader of the Cossack Cavalry, 'Marshall Budyony?' I enquiried, as if I didn't know. 'Da' he answered. I pointed to myself and tried to explain that I was an English musician and began to sing the song dedicated to him and his troops and which we had broadcast many times during the war, namely the *Steppe Song*. He soon caught on and putting his arm round my shoulder, joined in, singing the song with me. So there we were, walking along on the lawn in front of the Kremlin singing the *Steppe Song* at the top of our voices. No fortune-teller could have dreamed up such an incident, and it was an unbelievable magical moment.

Inside the Palace there was an Utyesov band playing for dancing until the interval, then we strolled along with two of the brass players whom we had already met – Abramov and Tartakovsky, both outstanding performers on their respective instruments and probably the best jazz players in Moscow.

The musicians in Moscow were very well dressed in comparison to the other Muscovites of the period and this was, no doubt, a reflection of their good taste and comparatively high pay – about £40 per week, not very different from the pay of good musicians in London.

Although they were members of Utyesov's big band they felt musically restricted and preferred to play in smaller groups where they were able to extemporise. Indeed, for part of the evening they combined with a bass player and drummer to perform on a platform in the grounds where they gave a fine jazz performance to the delight of an enthusiastic audience.

At midnight, instead of our being turned into poor Cinderellas, it was announced that a firework display was to take place from the top of the Palace and this was the most extravagant I have ever seen – and I have seen many. The comets came shooting off the top of the Kremlin in kaleidoscopes of colours, co-ordinated with the grace of their finest ballets. After this evening and spectacular display what was there to do but return home.

Now the fairytale was really over. As our interpreter put us on a train back to Finland and said goodbye to us at Moscow Station I left with conflicting and confused feelings about what I had seen and experienced. One thing was, however, certain; I did not find what I had believed to be Socialism. There had been far too many glaring examples of inequality to be seen. On the journey home the English boys and girls had many conflicting stories to tell about the limitations they had experienced when trying to visit Russian friends or how they were restricted in their travels, particularly to move outside Moscow. Even a broken camera and a confiscated roll of film. It had been an unforgettable fortnight, but I was very happy to return to our own muddled capitalist system which affords us a greater degree of personal freedom than most places I have visited.

Is the guitar popular there to-day? Yes, much more so than in 1957. The 7-string folk guitar is still widely played and there are numerous classical guitarists but few performers of jazz, which is not encouraged. However, the music of visiting American jazz musicians or rock groups is always received with wild enthusiasm by the Russian public, although carefully monitored by the authorities. If a Russian performer oversteps the mark, he *may* have to cut his long hair short and may not be allowed to do lucrative gigs.

Restrictions or not, the power of the guitar has captivated the Russian youth as much as those in other parts of the world. And a good thing too!

On set at Ealing Studios 'Saraband for Dead Lovers'.

Scene from 'The Battle of the River Plate' the singer, April Olrich.

Jean Simmons – the 'Film Actress of the Year', 1949.

With Winifred Atwell at the London Palladium.

Adelaide Hall presenting 'Melody Maker' poll awards, 1951.

'Melody Maker' Award 1950–51.

Red Square Moscow – 1957 – Ivor and Lily Mairants.

Alexandra Ivanov – Kromskoy.

Lily Mairants with Russian 'bobby'.

Original staff of Central School of Dance Music.

With the late A. P. Sharpe 1950, Editor of B.M.G. for many years.

Ivor Mairants Guitar Group (left to right) Joe Mudelle, Jack Duarte, Dennis Wilson, Ivor Mairants, Billy Bell, David Jacobs.

Ivor Mairants Trio – BBC Spotlight Programme.

Ivor Mairants Musicentre – 56 Rathbone Place, W1.

With Mantovani, Decca Studios, West Hampstead 1968.

Guitar section of 'Manuel and His Music of the Mountains' (left to right) Ivor Mairants, Alan Parker, Steve Guana, Vic Flick, Alan Sparkes (in front) Geoff Love, Sheila Bromberg, Norman Newall.

A copying machine at the Framus factory, West Germany.

George Benson, Ivor Mairants, Attila Zoller.

Cartoon by 'Sallon'.

Chapter Nine

THE IVOR MAIRANTS MUSICENTRE

In 1958 the School moved to 195 Wardour Street in very much larger premises and soon the wholesalers in the musical instrument industry prevailed upon me to add to my other activities and go into business. I eventually succumbed and The Ivor Mairants Musicentre was established and I hoped that my son Stuart, soon to finish his National Service, would take an interest in it.

The dollar restrictions were now lifted and we opened the Musicentre with an exhibition of guitars – Gibson, Guild, Harmony, Martin from the USA, Levin from Sweden, Höfner and Zenith from W. Germany, Tatay and Sanchis from Spain and a copy of Josh White's guitar, i.e. Martin 00–21 from Hense in East Germany. Incidentally, this was the first time I had encountered a 12-string guitar. It was made by the Harmony Company and called a Stella selling for £21. It was clumsy but strong.

It seemed as if guitarists were waiting for the Musicentre to open in order to become customers. Narciso Yepes came in in search of music and Charlie Byrd came to buy an Ignacio Fleta guitar for £150! Now there is a 20 year waiting list and one would be lucky to get one for 10 times that sum. Julian Bream came in to support his old friend, and Jim Sullivan, then doing some labouring job, came in to try a Gibson ES.345 which he played so brilliantly that I strongly advised him to throw his job up and become a professional musician. He did, and I let him have that Gibson on very easy terms.

Perry Botkin, a famous American guitarist who had accompanied Bing Crosby on all the recordings he made in Hollywood, paid a visit and demonstrated his guitar style and I discovered that he was responsible for the music in the hilarious TV series 'The Beverley Hillbillies'.

Nineteen fifty-nine proved to be even more busy than ever. Geraldo was regularly appearing on TV and I rejoined him. I was on Sunday Night at the London Palladium with Cyril Ornadel, and Stanley Black, Norman Luboff, Mantovani and Peter Yorke all came into my work schedule.

Ben Selvin, the once famous US Musical Director of the Denza Dance Band, whose recording of *You are my Sunshine* was the first gramophone record to sell a million copies, came to London to make records for RCA. The sessions were conducted alternately by George Melachrino and Billy Hill-Bowen, and Ben Selvin became known as Father Christmas because of the way he handed out cash.

I was still teaching, Benny Hill and Eric Sykes being among my keenest pupils, and while Eric Sykes was doing a season at the Palladium, I used to nip over from Wardour Street to give him lessons in his dressing room. His great love was Flamenco music and I acted as his 'straight man' when he did a comedy Flamenco feature on TV. Benny Hill (not to be outdone?) also used me on his TV show, when I left my place on the orchestra stand to play the part of a gypsy guitarist on camera (collecting two fees in the process!).

Then one night, while out at dinner with my wife, I was sitting at the table when everything went dark and I thought the lights had been dimmed but they had not. It was just that I had had a momentary blackout. This became a good enough sign for my wife to insist that something had to be given up and when we asked Eric Gilder if he would like to take over the Central School of Dance Music, he was delighted.

So ended a decade which had witnessed the growth of guitar popularity to the extent of having become not just a passing craze but an established recognised instrument that was here to stay and grow in world demand through the Swinging Sixties. Meanwhile, the premises in Wardour Street became very cramped, but through a stroke of good fortune, aided and abetted by a good friend, an opportunity arose in 1962 to take over the lease of shop premises at the Oxford Street end of Rathbone Place, and by the end of August, what had been a dark, fusty, dismal cloth shop had been completely rebuilt and redecorated to become what was then the West End's last word in luxury musical instrument stores.

It opened on 1 September 1962, exactly 12 years after the advent of the Central School of Dance Music, now in the capable hands of Eric Gilder, and at the official opening Geoff Love, Eric Sykes and other luminaries and members of the profession came in for a drink and a good luck wish.

The Beatles and The Shadows were then very strong and both Paul McCartney and Hank Marvin bought Ramirez flamenco guitars quite independently of one another to add an additional effect to their groups. I had added Ramirez guitars to our inventory in 1959 which,

IVOR MAIRANTS MUSICENTRE   103

under the new directorship of Jose III, had become supreme. In fact, Andres Segovia changed over to a Ramirez Concert from his Hauser in 1962.

One day four young fellows came into the shop and wanted to buy some Gibson guitars. These guitars had only been imported for a little while in 1962 and were still a novelty – an expensive luxury. They selected some electric/acoustics and a Rivoli bass which, altogether, came to about a thousand pounds and wished to take them there and then. When asked about payment, the spokesman said 'Charge it to our agent'! 'Who's your agent'? I asked, curious to know who was willing to stake these confident youngsters. 'Tito Burns' was the answer and, sure enough, when I 'phoned Tito (an old colleague) he said 'Yes, just send me the bill and let them have the goods. They are a group who will go far. They are known as The Searchers'.

Meanwhile, a new tower block of 29 stories rose up just along Oxford Street at St. Giles Circus called Centre Point, and two new musical instrument stores opened in magnificently sumptuous premises in this new complex. One was Messrs. Boosey & Hawkes and the other Burns Guitars, who had just produced the Hank Marvin model.

In spite of the extra competition the Musicentre won the Top Dealer Award from Gibson Guitars for 1963 and 1964. At the end of 1963 the *Daily Sketch* published a feature article which began 'If you want to get ahead get a guitar' and as evidence named Tommy Steele, Cliff Richard, Lonnie Donnegan and groups like The Shadows, The Beatles, The Searchers and The Tremolos.

Now that the press proclaimed the guitar as the biggest selling instrument in the world with America topping sales at some five million a year and the figure in Britain reaching towards the million mark, the how and when of guitars was almost as newsworthy as sport.

In 1966/7 guitars could be bought for as little as £10 for a Jose Mas y Mas to £236.50 for a concert Jose Ramirez. By 1970/1 Ramirez concert guitars sold for £365 and in 1976 they had again doubled in price to about £750 (currently priced at £995). In 1969 Frankfurt International Fair there were fewer gimmick guitars on display than in previous years and more folk, jumbo and 12-string guitars. About 30 manufacturers of varying importance displayed their wares and I fell in love with a splendid Gibson 'Johnny Smith' model acoustic with a floating pick-up and bought it on the spot although it was officially not for sale, having been specially made for the show.

The Guild Guitar Company headed by the late Al Dronge surprised me with a very good top concert model which Al Dronge was very proud of and persuaded me to stock.

C. F. Martin showed their beautiful D-45 and Nippon Gakki had the largest stand showing Yamaha guitars.

Billy Lawrence (now president of Lawrence Pick-ups in Nashville, Tennessee) was then adviser to Framus Guitars and demonstrated the varied tone colours of the Framus solid guitars. Hofner, Hoyer, Hopf and Teller were also busy showing a large range of guitars.

Helmut Schaller (who had earlier worked for Freddy Wilfer, president of Framus) was displaying his own manufactured goods. He, being a fine engineer, had produced amplifiers, pick-ups and guitar leads, but his ace card was in the production of geared machine heads. These were giving Grover machine heads a very good run and, in fact, overtaking them.

Today, the Japanese machine-head makers are copying these Schaller machine heads (which are world famous) and are competing with Schaller. Talk about stealing the eyebrows off your face!

It was not only the Japanese who were jumping on the guitar wagon. The advertising moguls of Madison Avenue, New York, also hitched a ride on the wagon by slanting their advertising to include guitars in the glossy magazines: from Viceroy Filter Tip being lit up for a man with a guitar or new wallpaper with a guitar handy in the living room.

Unheard-of youngsters became stars too fast for me to know one from another. One day a tall young man was playing a guitar in Musicentre's lower showroom and the fluency of his playing attracted my attention. I looked in, listened and watched. 'Good' I thought, 'talented, but if this boy studied the right way to play a classical guitar, he would be very good'. I complimented him and said he had the talent to become a really good player if he took it up seriously. He thanked me and bought the guitar, paying by cheque. The cheque for £500 was handed in to the office for the usual bank OK and when the girl at the bank heard that the signature on the cheque was Mike Oldfield she repeated it with great excitement which caused quite a stir at the bank. When I asked, in all innocence, 'Who is Mike Oldfield?' I did not realise that his LP *Tubular Bells* had been No. 1 in the LP charts for six months – and I had advised him to take it up seriously!

After that I took more interest in the Pop Charts.

IVOR MAIRANTS MUSICENTRE

In October 1969 my wife and I embarked on a five week investigative and buying trip round the world, going to New York, Washington, Chicago, San Francisco, Los Angeles and Hawaii, where I discovered Kamaka ukuleles, met a whole new culture introduced to us by Mr. Kamaka and introduced his Koa wood ukuleles to Britain.

From Hawaii we flew to Japan where we visited many guitar factories and had an exciting time in many out of the way places from Nakatzagawa in the mountains (where I discovered Takamine guitars) to Arima, a spa not too far from Kobe, where we bathed in the communal pool of running hot spring water and lived Japanese style.

Hong Kong, Kowloon and the new territories were a fascinating eye-opener at close quarters, and one of the first things to hit us on our initial stroll was the shrieking gaudy enormous neon advertising. The one that struck me most was the neon-lit piano keyboard that hung over the street suspended in the air advertising Tom Lee's Music Shops. I met Tom Lee who had arrived from China penniless some 17 years before and had built up an empire of five or more shops and the distributorship of Yamaha pianos, organs and guitars. He showed us the town, his shops, taught us to eat Peking duck and lent us his limousine and chauffeur for the rest of the time so that we could tour the environs, almost to China.

The contrast between Hong Kong and our next port of call, Bangkok, was enormous. The pace was more leisurely and the people sweet and charming. Here, life was lived on the river which teemed with small boats and was lined with houses down to the river's edge.

The Floating Market cannot be experienced anywhere else in the world, and to be caught up in a flat bottomed motor-propelled longboat in the middle of solid traffic jams among floating shops selling food, fruit and hot meals, paddled by young and old males and females, is an experience of a lifetime. Memories are surely made of this.

The guitar had really taken me to far away places and introduced me to an international society of friendly people, some of whom visit London and drop in to see us on our own home ground.

After my first-hand experience of the Japanese guitar manufacturing business I forecast in the *Music Business Weekly* (22 November 1969) that the very low priced Japanese guitars of acceptable quality would soon no longer be available and this may well give Valencian guitar makers a chance to come back into the British market. The first part of my forecast eventually came to pass but the Spanish manufacturers are still slow to take up the challenge. They prefer to make cheap guitars for the home market which includes the tourist trade, and the methods are still fairly primitive. Nevertheless, since 1978 they have been displaying guitar ranges at the annual Frankfurter Messe and breaking into the British and European markets.

And so to the seventies which brought along new challenges with fresh developments in playing, writing and in business. The guitar was now being used not just as an instrument for performance but as an aid to composition. Where a piano might have been used in previous decades the more portable guitar was taking its place.

The guitar has turned up in some odd places, not the least exceptional being in prison. The *Melody Maker* of 30 January 1971 featured the story of an ex-burglar serving a sentence in Dartmoor, who taught himself to play guitar from a tutor by Ivor Mairants, and became a song writer. Soon after his release he sang one of his songs on the BBC, met favourable reaction and had 30 of his songs recorded by the time the article was written. The Musicentre has many regular customers residing in HM Prisons and I myself have given a two hour solo entertainment to a 'captive audience' at Wandsworth prison.

In the classical field, I rediscovered Dieter Hense whom I had met about 15 years earlier in Leipzig, and who had now come over to West Germany. He made guitars for me which were as good as the best made in Spain but due to the adverse foreign exchange of the pound sterling against the Deutche Mark, his guitars sold for £375 in comparison to Ramirez 1–A for £365.

Masaru Kohno was now making a No. 20 concert guitar which we sold for £500 while the other models were No. 15 – £350, No. 10 – £250, No. 7 – £200 and No. 5 – £160. Today, the Kohno prices have gone up to £1,500 for the top model.

On the American side an interesting amalgamation took place between C. F. Martin and John D'Addario, makers of Darco and Martin strings. John D'Addario's family had been making strings for 160 years and in the late sixties I had discovered the qualities of Darco strings, paid a visit to the D'Addario family in Astoria, Long Island, and introduced Darco strings to players in Britain. They were instantly accepted and sales soared. Naturally, John D'Addario and I became very good friends and our mutual regard transcends business.

Now that C. F. Martin had bought Darco and John had become President of the Darco division of Martins, I bought the strings from the Darco division. Martin guitars were not selling very well in England in the early 70s because the fact that they were imported by a wholesaler made the price too high by the time they reached the consumer.

I had long considered that guitars of high quality should be sold directly by the manufacturer to the retailer and when I thought it prudent, had voiced my opinion. Well, the upshot was that John D'Addario, together with another Martin official, came to London to sound me out on the subject of direct franchise and before long the Musicentre was selling the whole range of Martin guitars at lower prices than had prevailed for years and in spite of the galloping inflation, we still have that privilege. But by 1975 John had left Martin's in his official capacity and for the first time since the D'Addario family had been manufacturing strings, founded the string-making firm of John D'Addario Inc. with strings under the name of D'Addario. Working with his wife Mary and sons John Jnr. and Jimmy, this proved to be one of the success stories of the seventies.

As the guitar business grew so did the string business and there was room for D'Addario, Darco, Martin, Ernie Ball, D'Angelico, De Merle, La Bella and now, the latest name in strings, Daniel Mari.

Daniel Mari, the son of the founder of La Bella strings Olinto Mari, offered me La Bella strings in 1960 and they were actually introduced to England by the Musicentre.

Danny is the complete guitar aficionado and knows all the best guitarists both jazz and classical and besides being an expert in string making, is somewhat of an intellectual, a music lover and a gourmet. At the beginning of 1978 he broke away from the family business and began manufacturing independently Daniel Mari strings and his strings are in the top bracket. He, too, has become one of my best friends who is treated like family by my wife and myself.

While talking about strings, I must also mention D'Angelico De Merle strings which I also introduced to English guitarists in the middle sixties through the good offices of Bill Gieson who, with the help of Gerry Barberine, continued to uphold the quality originated by the great John D'Angelico after he died in 1964. Bill Gieson was the owner of two wonderful D'Angelico guitars which I have had the pleasure of playing but, unfortunately, he passed away in his prime. Gerry Barberine, who was in charge of the marketing, continued to build up the name, quality and sales of De Merle and is also one of my oldest friends.

It would be extremely difficult to find three better companions than John D'Addario, Danny Mari and Gerry Barberine – may they live long and prosper. One can feel very rich with such friends.

In writing about my fifty fretting years, a few tragedies or failures might have made the story more dramatic but with some caution, a little foresight, good fortune, and much hard work and vigilance, I have been able to avoid falling flat on my face. Or as Jack Collier, our bass player, used to say 'Even if I fell into a proverbial load of "sweet violets" I would fall on my feet'.

Let's hope he's right.

'MY FIFTY FRETTING YEARS'

PART II

THE STEEL STRUNG GUITAR

Part 2

THE STEEL-STRUNG GUITAR

Chapter Ten

THE UNITED STATES

Gibson
When I first heard Eddie Lang play his Gibson L5 guitar producing sounds I had never heard before, I never expected to be invited to Kalamazoo or Nashville as a guest and be asked for my comments nor later to become a member of the Board of Directors of the Gibson Hall of Fame. Therefore, since the first guitar playing I heard was performed on a Gibson, I will relate their story first.

My first visit to Kalamazoo was in June 1973 after Gibson had undergone many changes in management since it first became The Gibson Mandolin-Guitar Manufacturing Co. in 1902.

Julius Bellson (a Gibson executive who had just completed the *Gibson Story* which is a proud record of the way guitars were made and marketed) presented me with a copy of their original 1903 catalogue, therefore I cannot resist quoting one opening paragraph and one graphic guitar description.

Distinctive Features of the Gibson Guitars
"All Gibson guitars are fitted with finest quality patent friction keys. All guitars have position marks inlaid on upper side of neck, thus enabling performer to catch position quickly. Bound edges are inlaid on outside of rim so as not to retard vibrations. All of our instruments are strung with special 'Gibson' strings.

Each guitar has an end pin to which cord or ribbon may be attached, to enable performer to assume the easiest possible position when standing.

On all Gibson guitars, grace and ease of execution is possible even above the twelfth fret as body is made low and oval where it meets the neck on first string side.

Bone nuts and inlaid bridge pins and end pins are used on Gibson instruments."

Note: The back of Gibson guitars should never be held flat against the clothing as it impedes vibration.

There is a picture of the Gibson Guitar Style '02' with a description from the catalogue:

"Always state whether steel or gut strings are to be used.

Specially selected Norwegian spruce top (sounding board) of regular straight grain, beautiful ebonised finish carefully selected, thoroughly air-seasoned maple rim, back and neck, dark mahogany finish, highly French-polished throughout; celluloid bound oval ebony fingerboard with 21 close narrow frets, pearl position marks inlaid on fingerboard and upper side of neck; ivory-celluloid bound soundhole, inlaid with 2 rings of fancy coloured woods and mother-of-pearl border; pearl and ebony cord pattern binding inlaid on upper edge of rim; East India mahogany bridge, handsomely inlaid with pearl ornaments; ivory bridge pins with pearl.

    Standard Size: List Price $132.98
    Concert Size: List Price $150.72
  Grand Concert Size: List Price $168.43

Style '03' is decribed as the 'Richest Guitar Yet Offered' priced $177.30; $195.95; $212.77."

Orville H. Gibson, the designer and inventor of Gibson mandolins and guitars, was the son of John Gibson who emigrated from England to the USA. Orville, who was born in Chatauguay, N.Y. in 1856 and died in Ogdensburg in 1918, played the mandolin, was very good at wood-carving and violin construction. In fact, he made a prize-winning violin then built a mandolin using the principles of violin construction so that instead of making a mandolin with a flat board top and a bowl-shaped back, he carved and contoured the top and back in what has become known as a flat back mandolin.

Although throughout its long history the guitar had assumed many shapes, no maker had considered using the carved top and back principles to enhance its tone.

Orville H. Gibson, having succeeded with the mandolin worked on a guitar using the same methods and eventually produced the carved top guitar some time in the 1870's.

By the time dance bands began their vogue in the first part of the twentieth century, a type of guitar had been invented which would become the standard for all dance band and jazz guitar playing. By the time Orville Gibson had died, Gibson had firmly established this type of guitar and when in 1920 Lloyd Loar, an established mandolin and stringed instrument player, a composer as well as an acoustics engineer, joined Gibson his developments of the guitar reached almost the highest level ever attained.

It is true to say that during his five years with Gibson he discovered innovations for the 'f' hole guitar which have become standard.

His greatest memorial to guitar posterity was the L-5 model with its two-footed adjustable bridge, adjustable truss rod through the neck, 'f' holes and the elevated finger-plate.

Of course, Gibson continued to make all kinds of guitars, including flat tops, electric guitars with that natural earthy sounding Charlie Christian pick-up, the Les Paul electric solid guitars, banjos and, later, bass guitars. But here I must return to 1928, place London, 4,000 miles away from Kalamazoo the home of Gibson.

I had by then realised the necessity of having a guitar but instead of following the footsteps of Eddie Lang, I took the advice of Emile Grimshaw and bought an EG Jnr. double cutaway flat top round hole guitar designed by my old teacher's son and marketed by Messrs Boosey & Hawkes the musical instrument people. Also, I was quite unaware of the role Gibson played in producing the instrument played by my hero, Eddie Lang, nor was I aware that Francis, Day & Hunter, the publishers and musical instrument dealers, marketed a special line in Gibsons made specially for FD & H and being used by at least three players, Len Fillis, Jackie Hill (in Al Starita's Band, the one I failed to join) and in Jack Payne's BBC Radio Dance Band.

It was not until 1930 that I decided it was time to change my E.G. Jnr guitar and so I did, to a Martin 0021 also from Messrs Boosey & Hawkes. I found that the 12th fret to the body was not very suitable to playing high chords and solos and changed it for a 0018 where the fingerboard joined the body at the 14th fret but, again, it did not possess the ideal penetrating tone required for dance band work.

Well, some people change cars for fun but I changed guitars from necessity and next time I was able to buy a Martin C.1, a carved top 'f' hole model which, although more suitable, did not have the required edge for big band work, but it was very nice to play. Had I been able to look into the future, I would have kept these instruments as museum exhibits, but being just a guitarist groping for better sounds, I just kept swapping.

THE UNITED STATES

Eventually, after playing my Epiphone Emperor for over 22 years, I felt the need for a slightly smaller, lighter sounding 'cello guitar and during 1960 arranged for New York guitarist Mundell Lowe to choose a Gibson L.5 for me.

It suited me for a couple of years but I still found the tone too percussive and changed to a second L.5 until I saw a Gibson Johnny Smith model. This instrument had a slightly wider fingerboard, a sweet tone and an easy action and was perfect for my work with Mantovani's Orchestra, but in 1971 temptation came my way.

Strolling round the Gibson stand at the Frankfurter Messe (music trade fair), I saw a new Johnny Smith model hanging up and idly played a chord on it – and that was it. I played it to my wife and (like Jim Lord in Hawaii Five-O) she said 'Book it!' and I booked it.

But my next Gibson experience was not so convincing.

The Gibson Mark Guitar

I am no Cassandra – no prophet of doom – but I do listen to the evidence of my own ears and if I am asked for an opinion I am bound to give an honest one.

The scene is the Gibson NAMM Exposition at the Pic Congress Hotel in Chicago, the time June 1975, and Bruce Bolan, a guitarist who is a master of all styles, is demonstrating a Gibson 'Mark' guitar in preparation for the following season's launching of this revolutionary instrument.

The 'Mark' guitar was a flat top Jumbo size guitar with an unorthodox bridge fitting widening from treble to bass, a heavy bridge saddle and a thick ridge round the soundhole.

After scientific and musical analysis of various patterns, the 'ideal' bracing was established and, in the end, the reaction of the instruments was carefully monitored by the most rigourous and sensitive computer-calibrated instruments.

As I was listening, a high official of Gibson asked me to examine the strutting and to give my opinion. He claimed that *now* Gibson had discovered the guitar with the perfect balance and volume. Well, I listened carefully and heard that the 3rd string was louder than the 4th and that the 5th string dominated the rest. When I played the instrument I found the action hard and the sound sharp and edgy, not conducive for smooth phrasing.

I also explained the reasons for these characteristics (in my opinion), and asked what had been wrong with the old J-45s and J-50s and SJNs (which had an attractive soft/sweet tone before they glued the struts in an electric high speed press pre-1970).

In short, I was not convinced and advised caution.

The design team I learned, was headed by Dr. Michael Kasha, Director of Florida State University Institute of Molecular Biophysics, and an authority on guitar construction, aided by master luthier Richard Schneider who finalised the external design.

Whether or not my advice was taken I do not know but it was another year before the 'Mark' was launched with great publicity and fanfares.

The scene now changes to the Frankfurt Musical Instrument Fair and this time I am asked to spare an hour by a director of Norlin (the Gibson parent company), in order to test the newly launched 'Mark' guitar in the company of the chief sales director, the European sales director and Bruce Bolen.

Bruce played, I played, we made observations, discussed and gave opinions. Bruce was enthusiastic, the others were trying hard to convince me that *now* everything was right, but I could not honestly agree with them although I admitted there were some improvements on the previous year.

However, Gibson was committed to the 'Mark' and every effort was made to popularise the new range.

I cannot give facts and figures for the next two years sales but eventually they were offered to the trade at a greatly reduced price and at these lower prices they were considered very good value.

By 1979 they were all sold and as far as I know there is no move afoot to relaunch another 'Mark' series.

C.F. Martin
Christian Frederick Martin, the founder of C.F. Martin, was born in Mark Neukirchen (now in East Germany) in 1796, the son of cabinet-maker John Georg Martin, who had himself discovered the art of guitar making.

C.F. Martin became a guitar maker and from 1826 he was the foreman in the factory of the noted violin and guitar maker Johann Georg Stauffer of Vienna and there C.F. produced excellent guitars. At the time there was, it seems, narrow mindedness and jealousy prevalent, especially in the local violin makers' guild and in 1833 C.F. Martin, accompanied by his wife, daughter, and son Christian

Frederick Jr. left his native Saxony for New York where he began his guitar making business at 196 Hudson Street.

Never really settling down in New York, he bought a piece of land near Nazareth, Pennsylvania in 1839 where the family became established, while the manufacturing prospered eventually resulting in a large factory being built about a mile away from the original site.

As we have seen, Orville Gibson was the innovator of the carved top guitar, but it was the C.F. Martin family which began the steel-strung flat top when C.F. Martin Jr. designed the crossbar bracing to enable the guitar to accept steel-strings without causing damage to the top or pulling the bridge off. Prior to that time they were fitted with gut strings.

In the summer of 1973 my wife and I were guests of the C.F. Martin Organisation and were able to appreciate the quiet rural atmosphere of Nazareth and of nearby Bethlehem (where we stayed).

The quiet atmosphere was also evident among the workers, and one could never have forecast the sixth month strike which took place in 1978/9 but, happily for the future of Martin guitars, work began again in March 1979 with the guitars looking and sounding as good as ever.

Near to the entrance foyer of the works, there is the Martin museum of guitars and one of the first that hit me was the guitar with the six-on-one-side machine head and external bolt neck adjuster, very similar to that of Stauffer of Vienna. Not knowing the connection, I mentioned it to C.F. Martin III (then a sprightly 79) and he told me his great-grandfather had, in fact, worked for Stauffer.

'I myself began my training by sweeping the floors of the factory' he told me, then learnt to play and fit strings to the guitar under the tuition of his father F.H. Martin (son of C.F. Martin Jnr. who was a very good teacher) and very soon C.F. III made a guitar for himself.

'Basically', he continued, 'the constructional principles are to-day the same but the guitars have become larger, the fretting has changed, there is a steel truss rod in the neck and the instruments are now lacquered. The big crossbar was my grandfather's idea and was modified from the fan bracing. We used to use ivory for the binding and purfling but since 1921 were forced to use celluloid (plastic)'.

The factory then employed about 240 craftsmen and craftswomen making guitars more or less in the traditional method. Some of the rims (sides) were still shaped by bending them round a heated pipe and the struts were glued and pressed by hand operated presses. Although there is a good deal of cutting and drilling machinery used for the rosewood, mahogany, ebony and spruce, each guitar still requires 300 different operations before it is completed. Nevertheless, nearly ninety guitars are produced each day which, although seemingly a good figure, is not in itself a sufficiently large number to be able to cover the costs, and since speeding up production might be detrimental to the final results, it was decided to diversify.

To-day, Martin make Vega banjos and guitars,[1] own the Darco string manufacturing, Levins of Sweden and a venture in Japan which manufactures 'Sigma' guitars, and, in future, will also make Levins.

Martins are unique in still being under the control of a member of the family, the president being Frank H. Martin; his successor, no doubt, will be his son Christian Frank Martin who is already working in the business and has for the last year been extolling the virtues of Martin guitars at the Musical Trade exhibitions.

It is so rare to find family businesses in this era that I must repeat the often published family dates.

> Founder C.F. Martin 1796-1863: C.F. Martin Jnr. 1825-1888:
> F.E. Martin 1866-1948: C.F. Martin III 1894-
> H.K. Martin (brother of C.F. Martin III) 1895-1927:
> Frank Herbert Martin, b.1930, President since 1970.
> Christian Frank Martin (C.F. Martin IV) b.1955 (sixth generation).

In 1972 the Ivor Mairants Musicentre was appointed a direct importer by C.F. Martin & Co. and continues to be in close touch.

[1]The Vega banjo and guitar company has since been sold.

Epiphone
I will now return to 1932 during which year I joined Roy Fox's Band and once again required a more powerful guitar than my C.F. Martin, but in spite of the fact that Eddie Lang produced a sound unequalled for tone, volume, depth and sonority on his L-5, the Gibsons available in London did not match up to that quality.

For that matter, no one else I had ever heard could match the Lang sound, but when comparing the Gibsons with the new Epiphone that I tried at Ben Davis's shop (then in Moore Street, Cambridge Circus), I opted for an Epiphone de Luxe and swapped my Martin for a guitar which, to me, at the time, had everything.

That guitar stayed with me until 1938 when I changed it for an Epiphone Emperor which I used for over 22 years, both acoustically and amplified with a De Armond pick-up.

I took the Emperor with me on a single trip on the Queen Mary across the Atlantic as a musician/able seaman and had the pleasure of meeting Orfi Stathapoulo, younger brother of Epi, founder of Epiphone Guitars. My guitar was in a pretty worn state and Orfi offered to renovate it and when it was returned to me the neck had been reset to improve string tension and it was better than new.

There were two Epiphone Emperors in existence which, had it been possible to join them, would have produced the best 'cello body guitar ever made – the volume of mine and the sweetness of Carmen Mastren's who played guitar for Glenn Miller's USAF Orchestra.

Orfi treated me as if he had known me for many years and told me how Epiphone had become the great makers that they undoubtedly were. In 1873 Orfi's father, A. Stathapoulo came to Boston from his native Greece and established himself as a violin and mandolin maker, but his eldest son Epi began to make guitars and settled in New York.

He specialised in the carved top guitars which were coming into vogue and built them on similar principles to Gibson but with slight modifications in shape and contour. In some ways the difference was comparable to the products of different violin masters where the thickness of the wood between the edge and the rise of the table produced altered reflections of sound.

The derivation of the Epiphone is, of course, obvious and the factory produced a large range of models namely, Emperor; De Luxe; Broadway; Triumph; Zenith; Blackstone; Olympic; Spartan.

After the war they also produced cutaway models and electric guitars. When my Emperor came back from the factory, it had been fitted with a special fingerplate shaped to include a pick-up, but I did not like the sound of it and changed back to my old fingerplate.

George Van Eps, without doubt the most respected guitarist in the field of dance music since the thirties, was a very good influence both playing their guitars and advising them, and we have to thank the Epiphone Company for publishing the George Van Eps tutor and solos.

Epi died in 1943 and the company continued until about 1956 when they sold their names and assets to the makers of Gibson guitars who began assembling the new style Epiphones at Kalamazoo; but new makers meant different guitars. Although a completely new range of acoustic, electric and flat tops was manufacturered by Gibson, it was considered that there was no room for two types of similar instruments made by the same factory. By now Gibsons had become a subsidiary of Norlin (a holding company specialising in musical instruments) and it was decided to launch Epiphone as a secondary line to Gibson and their manufacture was transferred to Japan.

Guild

Meanwhile, back in 1952, when it was obvious that the original Epiphone company was losing business, Al Dronge, a guitarist and businessman, decided to establish a new guitar manufacturing company and called it the Guild, taking five of the Epiphone craftsmen who used their skill, tools and templates to produce Guild guitars. Fortunately, the United States is a big country abounding with guitarists and coupled with Al Dronge's enthusiasm and business acumen, Guild slowly broke into the guitar market.

I had not heard of Guild guitars until the late 1950s when an American naval officer came to me for lessons and brought his guitar along. It was a flat top wide-bouted low action F-40 or F-50 which produced an excellent singing tone. The guitar had been obtained direct from the factory so my pupil (for whom I later became best man) knew quite a lot about the guitars.

I was so impressed that I introduced the guitar to Messrs Boosey & Hawkes and advised them to make arrangements to introduce Guild to British guitarists, which they subsequently did when they became the sole importers.

I first met Al Dronge in 1965 when I visited their factory in Hoboken, New Jersey, and found this to be a hive of industry. It was a busy time for Al who was about to re-marry, and his son Marc, chauffeured us from New York.

I asked if he could take me round to see John D'Angelico and he gave me the sad news that he had recently died (September 1st 1964). Marc then told me of the efforts his father had made to shift D'Angelico from the unhealthy location of his workshop in Kenmare Street (where he had suffered a heart attack) to warm, comfortable premises where he could continue his craft in more ideal conditions and advise on the design of Guild guitars. But D'Angelico was a loner and would not be moved.

In 1966, Guild sold out to Avnet, a public company, later moved to a new location in Westerly, Rhode Island and the company has never looked back.

In the early 1970s Boosey & Hawkes decided to give up the Guild agency for Great Britain and Al Dronge, knowing how much I liked the guitars and had, in fact, used the Award model, asked me to import them for the Musicentre. I was very happy to do so until the company's policy changed and they set up a distribution centre in England.

Al Dronge had a number of sporting hobbies and one of them, and a very practical one too, was piloting his own plane. One day in 1972, having to reach a destination in a hurry, he went up despite warnings of bad weather, crashed, and was killed.

The company accountant Leon Tell, was prevailed upon to become the President of the company (and, as they say, it couldn't happen to a nicer fellow) and Neil Lillian, Guild's sales chief, became vice-president.

The 6- and 12-string flat tops continue to keep up their high standard and I am pleased that my judgment of nearly twenty years ago did not fail me.

National Steel Guitar
and the Dobro Ampliphonic Guitar (since 1928)
My connection with the Resophonic National Steel Guitar went back to 1931. At the time I was absolutely unaware that the Dopyera brothers, John, Rudy, Ed, Louie and Robert, had been the inventors of the Dobro guitar and that due to many trials and tribulations which dogged their fortune, the guitars were now being made by the 'National' company. One thing I *was* sure about; in the days prior to amplification, it was the loudest and best sounding Hawaiian Steel guitar available. I think it cost £30 and brought me great plaudits when I played solos with Marius B. Winters' Band and later in Roy Fox's Band whose record of *Aloha Beloved* sold a million for Decca. I followed this up with *Sweet Leilani*, Denny Dennis singing the vocal.

In 1935 I discovered that a plectrum guitar version was available and bought one from Hessy's in Liverpool while we were on tour (price £36). I recently heard a Fox reissue which included *Rhythm in my Nursery Rhymes* sung by Mary Lee on which I backed the vocal and took a solo, and was pleasantly surprised by both the full sound and up-to-date style of the guitar.

Both guitars were of metal construction (apart from the neck and fingerboard of the plectrum model), were nickel-plated, and richly engraved with flower motifs back and front. They resonated on the principle of a triplate fitting with three vertical steel pins fitted to the end of each arm which rested on the apex of a small finely spun aluminium cone. When the strings were tightened to the correct pitch and picked, this activated the resonators and produced a somewhat amplified full sounding note, longer and thicker than on normal guitars.

In 1971 through the efforts of Ed and his young, large, energetic nephew Ron Lazar the 'Original Musical Instrument Co.' of Huntington Beach, Southern California, reactivated the Dobro story, the result of which produced the regular worldwide distribution of Dobro guitars

The types that I used to play would have made collector's pieces which would today be worth many hundreds of pounds but there again, who was to know?

One day, Ron tells me, his Uncle Ed[1] hopes to write a book with the title *The Trials and Tribulations of Dobro* revealing that everything is not what it seems in this wonderful world of the guitar.

The Dopyera family originally came from Czechoslovakia and it makes one wonder what the steel-string guitar would have been like if European guitar makers had not made their way to the States.

[1]Unfortunately no longer alive. (d. 1979.)

Jimmy D'Aquisto – Chicago July 1980.

Chapter Eleven

MARIO MACCAFERRI AND OTHER EUROPEAN MAKERS

I feel very privileged to have been able to meet and retain the friendship of so many important figures connected with the guitar, but the friendship which has covered the longest span of years must be with Mario Maccaferri. Of course, today the Maccaferri guitars of the thirties are collectors' items fetching many hundreds of pounds, and until a few years ago Mario had no idea that Django Reinhardt had become famous playing a Maccaferri guitar.

Mario was born in Italy in 1900 and in 1912 became apprenticed to Luigi Mozzani. Mozzani had been a guitar virtuoso in his time and was then very well-known as a guitar maker. Mario stayed with him until 1923, all the time learning everything he could from his master who taught him to play classical guitar (incidentally using a metal thumb pick) and make and repair guitars.

When Mario thought he had learned everything Luigi could teach him, he went off on his own and began to perform at concerts, and having a very inventive mind, worked on a new design which would be able to accommodate both gut and steel strings. He left Italy and lived in France, working in Paris, and doing concert tours.

Near the end of 1931 he came to London where I saw him give a concert at the Wigmore Hall and was later introduced to him by Ben Davis of Selmer. It transpired that Mario had gone to Ben with the design of the Maccaferri guitar (which he was playing) and asked if he could manufacture it. Ben was not in a position to do so but introduced Mario to Selmer of Paris with the recommendation to support their manufacture which Selmer of London would market. And that is how I came to play a Maccaferri guitar in 1932.

Mario was personally involved at Selmers in Paris from 1931 to 1933 and in those three years 300 guitars were made. In July of that year, he was filming in Paris with Simone Signoret and during a break in recording he went swimming. A good swimmer, he took a high dive and hit another swimmer, the impact breaking his right arm so putting him out of action as far as his concert career was concerned, and he eventually decided to emigrate to the United States.

Before going to the States he came to London where we met again and he asked me to buy his guitar music which included Ferraro, Mertz and Julian Arcas of Spain as well as some folios signed by Luigi Mozzani. I was glad to do so although I did not then know he needed the money. He soon became disillusioned with New York and returned to Paris where he stayed right until the Germans invaded France. Fortunately he escaped by boarding a ship which, as ill luck would have it, was sunk but, again, fortune smiled and he was picked up by a ship whose destination was New York, and he lived to tell the tale.

I did not meet Mario again until June 1975 when I went to see him, having discovered that he was a big manufacturer in the plastics business and owned the Maestro Manufacturing Co. in the Bronx.

We hardly recognised each other, not having met for forty years, but it was not long before we were like old friends and he pulled out two guitars for us to play on. Life can be rewarding in many ways and pleasures such as these are not often realised.

We have since met in London, and, apart from his other business interests (he is an inventive genius), he is endorsing the new Maccaferri guitar being made in Japan under the auspices of keen guitarist and businessman Maurice Summerfield.

Europe
The dollar restrictions in force during the 1950s prevented American goods from being imported into Great Britain, making us dependent on guitars from Germany and Czechoslovakia.

Markneukirchen, previously a violin and guitar manufacturing centre, was now in East Germany, which caused difficulties in trading; the East Germans were also short of the raw materials required for guitars such as good machine heads, while adequate supplies of wood were officially withheld from individual makers.

Czechoslovakia had a different problem; shortage of skilled craftsmen. Most of them, suspected of prior Nazi sympathies, had been expelled to West Germany and had taken their skills with them to Bubenreuth, Erlangen, Mannheim and other parts of Bavaria nearby and had begun manufacturing guitars and kindred instruments.

The first guitars of acceptable quality to be imported into England came from Karl Höfner, and were marketed by Selmer who built up a range of 'cello body guitars both acoustic and electric named Congress, Senator and the President, a cutaway model. Then Ben Davis asked me to lend my name to a de luxe creation, but compared to my

Epiphone Emperor it sounded very thin and stringy. I could not very well sell my big sound for a mess of potage by advertising Höfner so it was called the Committee. In any case, I had thrown in my skills in favour of Boosey & Hawkes who were then receiving guitars from Sandner of Mannheim. These guitars, sold under the Zenith label, were not very good, so I designed a 'cello guitar somewhat on the lines of Epiphone and went to see Freddie Wilfur of Bubenreuth who was about to build himself a model guitar factory with the help of the bank. This factory was being set up to build the Framus range of guitars but when Freddie Wilfur saw the blueprint I had prepared, he became agog with excitement in his eagerness to supply the new Zenith guitars for Boosey & Hawkes, and I supervised and checked them. Wilfur also made the Aristone guitars for Messrs Besson (a subsidiary of Boosey & Hawkes) although up to that time they had been made by Jack Abbott, one of the few good English makers of the period.

Arnold Hoyer, also of Bubenreuth, introduced many innovations in a bid to secure orders and even built me a guitar completely covered in nacrolacque which made it look like a guitar-shaped drum outfit.

Also to be found in Bubenreuth was Oscar Teller who specialised in classical guitars until I asked him to produce a copy of a Martin 0021 which was eventually approved by Josh White and was marketed as the Zenith Josh White model. And it was pretty good at about £24.

Nearer to Frankfurt, Willy Hopf had a well-organised factory making flat top and folk guitars more suitable for European consumption than for Great Britain. So, all in all, it was difficult to find makers who were able to match the sounds of their Stateside counterparts.

Czechoslovakia
When around 1954, the popularity of the guitar showed signs of growing, I suggested that as Czechoslovakia was supplying the English trade with a cheap steel guitar which sold at around £7, they might be interested in investigating the possibility of making really good ones for Boosey & Hawkes. I was therefore invited to go and institute the building of a range of guitars to supplement the Zenith models which we were now receiving in insufficient quantities from Freddy Wilfur.

Arrangements were made with Ligna (the Czech State Exporting Company) who financed the trip, and, taking my Epiphone Emperor carved top guitar, my Esteso classical guitar, and the permitted maximum of £5 currency, I flew off to Prague on March 18th, 1954.

Two English-speaking representatives of Ligna met me at the airport, deposited me at the then leading Alcron Hotel near Wenceslas Square, and mapped out my programme for the rest of the day.

First, a sightseeing tour of this ancient and beautiful city, at that time devoid of traffic and conspicuous with shops with empty windows. Then at 6 pm I met Stepan Urban, Prague's leading classical guitarist and teacher (middle-aged and since deceased) whose playing, sad to relate, was adequate but dull, matching the tone of his guitar, made for him by Czechoslovakia's leading luthier Franz Mettal.

Willie Wilson of Boosey & Hawkes had arrived from Leipzig and he joined us for dinner at the Alcron, where a fashion parade was being presented that rivalled any Western show. Considering the scarcity of goods in the shops it seemed rather incongruous and led to a heated discussion between our two guides about the pros and cons of the prevailing system of government.

Even more surprising was our next port of call, a Students' Ball held in the brilliantly-lit, chandeliered 'Smetana' Hall in the House of Representatives where the girls all wore white dresses and the young men, neatly dressed, danced to a modern dance band.

But to cap the day, there followed a visit to a gramophone studio where Karel Vlach (the Czech Ted Heath or Glenn Miller – as you wish) was in the process of conducting his band in a recording session for Suprafon.

Karel Vlach, a short dapper balding chap of about 40, gave us a great welcome. He soon invited me to take over on guitar and there was no other course open to me but to sit in, harnessed (or should I say 'lumbered') with the high-action East German effort used by his guitarist. Discussion after the session proved that, musically, it was very difficult for them to move with the times because there was no way of receiving new orchestrations, music or records from the West.

In a small way I was able to remedy this shortcoming by sending them a few dozen orchestrations through Ligna.

The other main topic of the day was the lack of decent living accommodation, the subject of most topical jokes all aimed at Government shortcomings.

The next day began very early for me. At 7.15 am we left for Luby in a powerful-rear-engined Tatra car and after a short stop at Karlovy Vary (Karlsbad) for breakfast and to taste the waters, we arrived at our destination about noon. After trudging our way through squelching melting snow and mud, we finally reached the head office of Cremona and were welcomed by Mr. Horsky the director of musical intrument production and co-ordinator of the town's social and works departments.

Mr. Horsky was a tall, powerful and handsome man, who had been an underground fighter during the war against the Germans. His job was to see that everybody worked in harmony.

No doubt his background and strong Party affiliations had secured him this important post because he freely admitted he knew very little about guitars although he *had* been a cabinet maker before the war.

We moved over to the boardroom and there, seated round a very large table, were the heads of Department: Export, Stringed Instruments, Commercial, Production, Technical and Research. In addition there were the two leading guitar makers, Mr. Brauer, steel-strung guitars, and Franz Mettal, classical guitars, as well as Mr. Horsky, Willie Wilson and the two Ligna boys. I had never been confronted by such a galaxy. I felt that all I had to do was to rub my magic lamp and they would produce the guitars out of a hat, like rabbits, but it wasn't quite like that.

Franz Mettal was very set in his ideas and it was very difficult for us to see eye to eye on tone and construction even with the help of my Esteso guitar.

The question of altering the angle of the neck setting in the flat top steel-strung was soon settled and all the guitars subsequently delivered were much improved so that not only did Boosey & Hawkes get the benefit but also their competitors and, of course, the guitar buying beginners. Incidentally, the cost of these guitars to Boosey and Hawkes was 25/- each!

My Epiphone guitar was greatly admired; many measurements were taken and promises made to supply early sample models. Our discussions eventually ended at 7 pm. We were then invited to make a tour of the different factories where they made not only guitars but also the whole range of bowed instruments. They even had an original Strad, Guarneri and Vihaum from which they made copies.

Exhausted, I finally fell into bed well past midnight, hoping that my journey had not been in vain, but in the months that followed, stretching into nearly two years, and after many rejections of sample guitars, I began to wonder why I had bothered. However, I do not usually give up easily, and early in 1956, after visits on behalf of

Messrs Boosey & Hawkes to the Frankfurter Messe and the Leipzig Messe I returned to Prague.

This time a woman headed Ligna's musical instrument section, and it was soon evident that she understood and sympathised with my aims for producing better guitars.

Madame Beyerova (a young war widow who spoke excellent English having been brought up in India where her father had been a major in the British Army) immediately telephoned Luby and requested Mr. Brauer to come to Prague by the next train. The following morning we met again, to hear about a sorry state of affairs. We learnt, what I had suspected, that only good craftsmen can build guitars and not just good Party members. Of course Cremona must also by then have realised this, and almost all the Cremona directors had been changed.

This time my instructions were followed as well as one could expect considering the difference in outlook, distance and their lack of materials for machine heads, tailpieces and purfling.

Shipments of guitars followed and the Zenith Range was implemented by one cutaway 'cello body and one non-cutaway, but never in sufficient quantities to satisfy the demand.

Czechoslovakia also began to produce classical guitars known as Tatra which were sold both in Great Britain and the USA and although different from the Spanish or Japanese concept, they are popular to some extent with beginners and students.

For a number of years Ligna has been exhibiting at the Frankfurter Messe and the charming Madame Beyerova (since married again) has been in charge, but I think they still wear blinkers in Luby.

Chapter Twelve

1959 – THE LIFTING OF DOLLAR RESTRICTIONS

Sweden supplemented the supply of steel-strung guitars to Great Britain with their Levin carved-top and flat-top models which, although superior to the other European makes, still lacked that certain something (in spite of their good American sales under the name of Goya).

Eventually, the dollar restrictions were lifted and this opened the floodgates to the re-introduction of the famous American guitars.

Gibson and Epiphone and eventually Fender were imported by Selmer; Martin, Guild and Harmony by Boosey and Hawkes, all adding to the excitement of the coming 'Swinging Sixties' and its demand for guitars.

The opening of the Ivor Mairants Musicentre coincided with the arrival of the American instruments and we exhibited them all.

In the lower priced field the Harmony guitars were the most popular, so much so, that the 'Sovereign' Jumbo had to be rationed to their dealers by the importers Boosey and Hawkes.

The Harmony Company also produced a range of Thin Line Electrics H.75 and H.64 as well as small, hollow-bodied Les Paul types of electrics known as Rockets 1, 2 and 3. I was very upset when, in 1976, Harmony Guitars finally gave up. How did it happen?

The Harmony Company (1892-1975)

Harmony's rise and fall should be chronicled and with the aid of Jerome King (Harmony's ex-Vice-President of production and purchasing), the co-operation of Chuck Rubovits (ex-President) plus my own personal experiences, I present a brief history.

It was 1888 when Wilhelm Schultz, a hard working mechanic, emigrated to America from his native Hamburg and found a job with the Knapp Drum Co. in Chicago. Two years later Lyon and Healy bought the Knapp Drum Company and appointed Wilhelm Schultz foreman of the division manufacturing drums, tambourines and banjos. He stayed at this appointment for two years and in 1892 commenced operations in two small rooms in a loft at Washington and Market Street (present site of Chicago's Civic Opera House) assisted by four men.

The business increased quite rapidly and 12 years later Mr. Schultz moved (for the sixth time) into a three-storey, 30,000 sq.ft. plant. By 1915 the company employed a personnel of 125 reaching annual sales of 250,000 dollars.

Sears-Roebuck (the world famous mail order house) bought large stocks of the very low priced guitars for resale to their mail order customers in the US 'hinterlands' and it seemed a logical step to buy Wilhelm Schultz's company outright in 1915.

The guitars had not yet been named Harmony but borrowed the name from one of the items in the Sear's catalogue known as Harmony House Towels. The newly acquired company, manufacturing guitars, ukuleles, banjos and drums, then became the Harmony Company. Ten years later, in an effort to improve the management, Sears appointed Jay L. Kraus, from the Sears organisation, to take charge of the company and he was so successful that 15 years later (in 1940), Jay Kraus and a group of employees bought stock control of Harmony and moved it to larger premises at 1633 South Racine Avenue.

By 1961 they had outgrown these headquarters and acquired a fine new 80,000 sq.ft. building. Then there was a guitar boom and within two years sales had trebled. This necessitated taking a further 40,000 sq.ft. of space in 1964 and by the time the Company celebrated its 75th birthday (in 1967) they had acquired an additional area of 12,000 sq.ft. as a warehouse.

It was during this era that Harmony produced 391,000 units per annum.

Anyone who was connected with guitar playing or selling at the time, could not fail to be impressed by the superb sounding Harmony 'Sovereign' guitars. In fact, no dealer in the US could afford to be without a stock of Harmony guitars which, of course, included the famous 'Stella' model, the all-time unassailable low-priced guitar that stood up to all contingencies.

The team directing this success story comprised Jay L. Kraus (whom I met in London during 1954 and from whom I learnt about

LIFTING OF DOLLAR RESTRICTIONS

Harmony guitars first-hand), President and controlling stockholder, Chuck Rubovits, who had been with the company for 32 years, and Jerome King, who had been with the company some 20 years. Despite the fact that at some periods Harmony employed 450 people, because of their worldwide export business the 'Sovereigns' were always in short supply.

In Great Britain they were imported by Boosey and Hawkes, and they had to be strictly rationed to their regular dealers of which the Ivor Mairants Musicentre was a favoured customer.

Back at the factory, processing the various guitar components — tops, backs, sides, ribs, necks and fingerboards — required a multiplicity of traditional and specially engineered machines. Parts had to be sculptured by automatic and hand shapers, planes, hand saws, routers, automatic cutters and micrometer gauged saws. At every stage meticulous handcrafting had to be combined with high volume production to produce quality instruments. This process is just an example of how the artisan was still engaged in making the guitar and had not been *replaced* by modern machinery but *assisted* by it.

So what caused the slide from a million dollar cash fluidity to bankruptcy? A few things. Sadly, Jay Kraus died in 1969, and during his lifetime he had formed a trust appointing his widow and lawyer as trustees, and both Chuck Rubovits and Jerry King were beneficiaries.

In spite of the competition from the low priced Japanese imports into the US, Harmony held its own until 1971 when Chuck Rubovits resigned as President. Whereupon the trustees appointed a new President, Mandel Kaplan, a man who, until then, had been President of Sara Lee Cookies (a biscuit manufacturing company). Not long after the new President had been appointed, Jerry King also resigned (1972), which left Mandel Kaplan trying to bake an 'all butter guitar' in competition with the low priced Japanese onslaught.

Unaware of these changes I visited the Harmony stand at the 1973 NAMM Exhibition in June and saw a whole range of guitars which barely resembled the old 'Sovereign' either in appearance, sound or price. I met the new President and pointed out to him that although the appearance of the guitars had certainly been smartened up, they no longer looked like Harmony guitars and did not sound as good as the previous instruments. Furthermore, there was some small degree of inaccuracy in the intonation, the necks seemed unstable and the prices were too high.

Mandel Kaplan was very perturbed at my unfavourable comments with which the production manager and quality control chief were forced to agree and begged me to visit the Harmony plant. Early on the following morning, Mr. Kaplan conveyed me to the plant in his new Mercedes all-electric automobile, and what I saw substantiated my fears. I saw a workforce that lacked enthusiasm or interest in what they were doing and this was evident from the way in which the sides were being bent in the old gas-heated bending machines to the haphazard way in which the struts and blocks were being glued and fitted. The wastage of broken sides stacked in bins was obvious and compared to the other large and small factories I had visited, there seemed to be no direction.

I duly relayed my observations; but only expertise, enthusiasm and experienced direction could have lifted the standard of the quality and these were not available. The inevitable happened and the Harmony Company became bankrupt less than 10 years after their successful 75th anniversary. The assets, including the Harmony name, were sold, and although it is still possible to buy a Korean made Harmony guitar, the reign of the old 'Sovereign', alas, is over but its reputation lives on, as any collector will confirm.

Kay String Instruments 1890 to 1970
The Harmony Group has sometimes erroneously been credited with the manufacture of Kay guitars but this has no foundation in fact.

The Kay Company was actually founded in 1890 and was known as the Groeshel Company specialising in the manufacture of bowl type mandolins. By the early 1900s the making of banjos was developed, to be followed by guitar making, eventually changing its name to the Stromberg-Voisinet Company.

It was the Stromberg-Voisinet Company that pioneered laminated tops and backs in 1924 at the same time arching the laminations to the shape of the 'cello guitar.

This was outstanding considering that in 1954, while I was at the factory of a West German guitar manufacturer, I saw laminations being glued together by hand in a very primitive way.

It was not until 1928 that the name was changed to the Kay Musical Instrument Co. and by 1937 they were the largest manufacturers of the famous Kay double basses to which they later added violincellos, violas and violins, and electric guitars and amplifiers.

Later, in 1964, there seemed to have been a parallel development at the Harmony Company and the Kay Company, with the difference that Kay's new factory at 2201 West Arthur Avenue, Elk Grove

Village, Illinois, was rated as one of the nation's outstanding woodworking facilities. But the end was the same and they suffered the same fate as Harmony.

Because of the upsurge in interest in electric guitars, Kay produced a double cutaway thin line acoustic-electric with two and three pickups similar to the Harmony H-75 but with a difference. The neck was attached to the body by means of four screws fitted in the heel which was really (in this instance) part of the body.

Instead of the heel sloping into the back of the neck, it was not shaped at an angle but left square with sharp edges.

When I was asked to stock this range the danger of these sharp edges was obvious to me and I suggested that the design be altered and the edges rounded off, but by the time this suggestion reached the executive of Kay Guitars, not even the glossy brochures could help the sales. Furthermore, the bass guitar was replacing the Kay double bass and at some point the cash flow (from sales) could not have equalled the increasing outgoings and the name and assets of the Company were sold.

For the record, the name of the President was Sidney M. Katz, Vice-President Robert W. Keyworth and Vice-President, Manufacturing, Joseph F. Ascherl, but in spite of brains and new models, something went wrong and I am sorry to say that I forecast their failure at the end of the 60s.

Now, Kay guitars are made in Korea and the new company markets a cheap range of classicals and flat tops which are fair value for money.

Ovation Guitars

One day in the late 1960s or early 1970s when I was abroad, a man came into the Musicentre, saw my son Stuart, and said he had a completely new steel-strung guitar to offer for sale. It was the first Ovation seen in England, with a dished back made from a fibreglass material known as Lyrachord.

The American told my son that he had been round England showing this instrument but it had been received with indifference. He did not want to take it back with him to Hartford, Connecticut, where they were made, so he was presenting it to us in the hope that we would show it to our customers and inform the Kaman Corporation of the results.

When I returned to London, I was very intrigued with this innovation made through the efforts of Charles Kaman, a very keen amateur guitarist, and owner of an aerospace company and helicopter rotor blade manufacturer.

I found the sound rather thin and tinny, quite the opposite of the full Martin sound and lacking the gentle sweetness of a good Gibson but, nevertheless, I tested customers' reactions. Guitarists were very shy of accepting it, but one day somebody bought it. Some months later the customer returned complaining that it had become very hard to finger. Upon examination it was clear that the neck had warped. The fingerboard was shaved straight and refretted only to come back to us again, not by the original purchaser but by another guitarist who had purchased it from the original owner. It was evident that the fault had re-appeared, and we attempted to straighten the neck and it appeared to be satisfactory, but believe it or not, we had that guitar back five times from different owners before we were free of it.

Guitar players in England are more conservative than those in the States and it took a few years before Ovation guitars were accepted and I must admit to being one of the sceptics who is still unconvinced of their unusual tonal qualities when compared with the best in wooden-backed conventional guitars.

The Ovation guitars did not really take off until Glen Campbell endorsed and played the amplified model, but after that event, the upsurge in the popularity and sales of Ovation guitars became the greatest success story of the decade.

Perhaps the final accolade is the use John Williams has made of the Ovation Classic, an amplified nylon-strung instrument with a long scale of $26^3/_{10}''$, probably inspired by the string length of a Jose Ramirez guitar.

Charles Kaman is a big man with big ideas and it is, in a way, a compliment to me that when he required a normally constructed line of guitars for world distribution, he selected Takamine whose factory I discovered in 1969 and whose President, M. Hirade, has since then sought my advice and opinion for effecting improvements to their sound.

James D'Aquisto (New York)
We now come to the present leading master-builder of the arched top guitar, Jimmy D'Aquisto.

He joined D'Angelico in 1951/2 when he was a teenager and worked and learned from him until he died in 1964. D'Angelico was more like a father to him than an employer and teacher, taking great care to pass on his skills. Although Jimmy was involved with every phase of the guitars made by the master, he never actually completed one of them himself. Carving the tops and backs was heavy work which became too much for D'Angelico, but Jimmy was keen and must have been a talented apprentice and, heartbroken at the death of the master, he stayed and completed the guitars in hand.

Although Jimmy wished to continue making guitars bearing the D'Angelico name, there were legal entanglements which prevented this so he decided to embark independently, making a James D'Aquisto carved top and back, steel-strung guitar using all the skill he had acquired.

By 1973 I had heard about Jimmy and knew that a few American guitarists had had instruments made by him, but I had never seen one. However, during that year I attended the NAMM Show in Chicago and was standing near his booth which displayed a solitary guitar (which had been made for Jim Hall) and was being played by Billy Lawrence.

As I stood listening, Jimmy, whom I had not seen before, introduced himself and asked me to play the guitar – an offer I dared not refuse. So, after greeting Bill Lawrence (an old friend) I sat down and began to play, when a fellow with fairish hair wearing a high necked sweater said 'Hello Ivor'. I looked up but did not recognise the speaker who, seeing my quizzical expression said 'Don't hook your up strokes' and then the penny dropped. It was Les Paul whose right hand picking I had had the audacity to criticise with the remark 'Don't hook your up strokes' when he was appearing at the London Palladium in 1952. He had never forgotten my remark and took this first opportunity to throw it back at me more than twenty years later. He then took the guitar from me and proved that he was as good as ever and immediately ordered a guitar for himself.

Never having met Jimmy before, we chatted and he then paid me the compliment of asking if he could make a guitar for me to my own specifications. I was, of course, delighted and as I had been extremely comfortable with my Gibson Johnny Smith model which I had been playing for a few years, I asked him to use that size as a model explaining that I had, some years back, found my Epiphone $18\frac{1}{2}''$ lower bout somewhat large for comfort and the Gibson L.5 slightly too deep. About eighteen months later I received the guitar and have been using it ever since, serving as a perfect orchestral guitar for rhythm playing, for accompaniment and for amplified and acoustic solo passages where I would previously have used a flat top. In fact, it is a guitar for all seasons and occasions. It is even possible to 'squeeze' a crescendo out of a single held note and I can honestly say that it is the best 'f' hole guitar I have ever played. When Joe Pass tried it a couple of years ago, he agreed with me and had a replica made for himself but with a pick-up fitted in the body instead of a floating pick-up like mine.

Jimmy has diversified the style of his New Yorker models to include solid electric guitars because of the demand, but once again, each one is made to the specific requirements of the player. This kind of collaboration between luthier and player has always been a feature in the relationship between artiste and craftsman from time immemorial.

Elmer Stromberg (d. 1955)
When Stan Kenton and his Orchestra came to England to play at the US Forces bases, I became friendly with Barrie Galbraith. I had admired his playing since I heard his solo in Claude Thornhill's recording of *Anthropology*.

He played a Stromberg guitar and some time later he offered to sell it to me, and I was tempted. I compared it with both my Epiphone Emperor and Gibson L.5, but after careful consideration I decided not to buy it.

I gave it many tests, asked many opinions and was quite sure that the Emperor had a fuller tone and was less stringy than the Stromberg, but the fact that the decision was so difficult to make, proves how good it was.

There were a number of other famous guitarists who played a Stromberg and they included Irving Ashby, Mundell Lowe, Laurindo Almeida and as far back as 1930, Freddy Guy who played with Duke Ellington.

Elmer Stromberg's shop at 40 Hanover Street, Boston, USA was visited by many players who watched him carve his guitars; he is reputed to have made over 600 guitars in his lifetime.

The Gurian Story, Michael Gurian (b. January 26, 1943)
Michael Gurian was a lad from New York with more than average talent who believed in his own ability as a guitar designer, maker and tonewood expert.

He was so confident that two highly respected figures in the music trade signed up an agreement with him as partners in a specialised guitar-making outfit, but when he moved from the Carmine Street premises to Grand Street, Michael decided to part company with his two partners.

Later Michael left New York City for Hinsdale, New Hampshire and founded Gurian guitars.

Michael is not much of a talker but in my opinion a deep thinker, with a knowledge of what makes wood vibrate and how to harness the wood to sing when shaped in the form of a guitar.

With expert knowledge and skill, it still takes guts and determination to go into business and compete with the famous and well established, and Gurian Guitars, after what must have been a determined struggle, are just about to become generally accepted.

A few years ago I agreed to import Gurian guitars and was, in fact, the first and only dealer in Great Britain to do so: I did so because I was convinced that the all-wood construction, the superb finish and the sonorous sound would sell them, but it was not as easy as that.

The British guitarist is very cautious and sceptical when he is confronted by a new-style, excellent but unknown make of instrument. For a long period guitarists admitted that the guitars were fine but they did not take a chance and buy one. For three or four hundred pounds they wanted something that was well known and familiar and who had ever heard of Michael Gurian?

The guitarists who eventually bought them loved them, but even after regular advertising and promotion the Musicentre found the pioneering job rewarding in the end but unprofitable. Michael, however, was very patient and waited, in the meantime increasing his sales in the US and in France. Now, English guitarists are actually asking to see Gurian Guitars.

Great Britain

The United States does seem to have lived up to its reputation as a land of opportunity for guitar makers and until recently at least, Great Britain has still been smarting under the slur of being a nation of shopkeepers, but as far as the guitar is concerned this is rapidly changing.

England can boast a fair number of guitar makers, some who build classical and others who build steel-strung guitars. In this section I will recall the steel guitar makers who have made some impact and who are personally known to me.

In the thirties John Abbott, working for Bessons and for a time assisted by Len Williams, was the craftsman who made the 'Aristone' guitars in both 'cello and flat top styles. The guitars sounded quite good and had a limited sale. In later years, after the war, his son Jack Abbott joined him and set up a workshop in Grafton Way off

Tottenham Court Road. Then Jack worked with a team and produced the well-known Abbott-Victor large-bodied 'cello guitar (for many years favoured by Bert Weedon).

In the early 1950s Jack Abbott supplied Bessons with their 'Aristone' guitars, but after Framus began to make Zenith guitars for Boosey & Hawkes, Besson (a subsidiary of Boosey & Hawkes), under the direction of Jack Howard, transferred the manufacture of Aristone to Framus.

Jack Abbott and I almost went into the business of guitar manufacturing but fate decreed otherwise.

Another name, not quite as well-known as Jack Abbott, is Dick Knight. Dick was a cabinet-maker and carver who became very keen on making a carved top guitar in order to supplement the better Hofner guitars imported from Bubenreuth by Selmers in the early 1950s. He did, in fact, work hard at producing a very well constructed and well finished instrument in the style of the Epiphone de Luxe. A company was established by Joe Van Straten and Dick Knight, and the guitars were marketed by Selmers of Charing Cross Road for whom I tested and reviewed the Knight guitar. But, in spite of the high quality of workmanship and appearance, the project was not successful, and only a few found their way to professional players. To date, Dick has returned to his old love of repairing and making guitars.

Tony Zemaitis
Later, in the 1960s, a guitar enthusiast who began as an apprentice cabinet-maker, found himself unable to afford a decent guitar so he made one himself copying an old Tatay. His name is Tony Zemaitis. Gradually he became more and more intrigued with the craft and eventually came to see me and ask for my support and advice about a flat top steel-strung guitar he had finished.

The shape, sound and general conception showed talent and I made some specific suggestions about the balance and texture of the tonal qualities, in particular about strengthening the treble (a universal weakness of this type of guitar). Eventually I bought some for the shop but in spite of their original appearance and tone, they were at first too expensive to be able to compete with less expensive American flat tops, but this situation did not prevail. It did not take long before prices rose for American guitars and so did the quality of Zemaitis guitars, which had begun to attract leading folk players. Subsequently, he received orders from famous players for personalised instruments with attractive inlays. Silver inlays became a speciality of

Tony Zemaitis and an outsize guitar he made for Eric Clapton, known as Ivan the Terrible, is beautifully inlaid with silver motifs and the bold front proudly displays a heart-shaped soundhole.

He was also commissioned to build a 12-string guitar for George Harrison.

Tony Zematis has an output of about 25 to 30 guitars a year and his fame has even reached the general public by means of a BBC Television documentary showing him at work. 'It couldn't happen to a nicer guy'.

Fylde

Although there are now quite a number of people who make and sell steel-strung guitars, proving once again that necessity is the mother of invention and guitar-making is not a prerogative of the United States, Great Britain, to date, has only one manufacturer whose guitars have begun to compete successfully in the world market. The brand name is Flyde and this is their story.

Early in 1970 Roger Bucknall began to build steel-strung guitars copying the leading American makes like Martin, Gibson and Guild, but these instruments made little impact. He therefore decided to break away from the mainstream style and try his hand in producing an individual sounding instrument. Afraid that by staying in London his original thoughts would be too influenced, he moved away to Kirkham in Lancashire and began experimenting in earnest. Eventually, after much research, he began to include many different variables, designs and materials, and adopted the name of Flyde taken from the stretch of Lancashire coast bearing the same name.

But all was not yet perfect. I was given repeated opportunities of examining the early Fylde guitars but was not satisfied with their construction, sound and stability until March 1978. I then agreed to be their sole London selling agent and have since then been closely in touch, often discussing details of construction, sound and finish in prolonged long-distance telephone calls. By the end of 1979 Fylde guitars became an historic success story as the first British made guitar to be exported to the US and the rest of the world, competing with all comers.

The guitars produce what has become known to players as 'The English Sound', and it is a combination of long sustained and sweet sonority. The strutting is not favoured to produce a big bass and lighter treble, but equilateral. Not only is this conducive to good balance between bass and treble, but can, with a changed nut and bridge saddle, be used for left-handed players at no extra expense. The neck is reinforced with a special alloy extrusion extending the full length of the fingerboard and built into the selected seasoned wood used for the neck. Warping is, therefore, very rare and makes the usual adjustable truss rod superfluous.

There are seven basic models, all named after characters from Shakepeare's plays. These are:
> Goodfellow (6 and 12-string)
> Calaban (with a cutaway shoulder)
> Falstaff (6 and 12-string)
> Orsino (6 and 12-string)
> Oberon (6-string)
> Ariel (a small size steel-strung)
> Sir Toby (an acoustic bass guitar)

Fylde also make a mandolin known as Lucetta and a mandocello called Octavius.

Two features are the wood purfling and the wooden nut and the instruments themselves are claimed to be 'unrivalled in their technical merits' and Roger Bucknall is sufficiently confident in the quality of his guitars to be able to offer a no-time limit to correcting any faults.

I am happy to relate a success story to which the Ivor Mairants Musicentre has contributed during the last two years.

David Bourne

My first meeting with David Bourne was during 1977 when he came to the Musicentre to collect two Martin guitars for adjustment. Apparently C.F. Martin & Co. had appointed him their official repairer on all warranty guitars supplied by them. When the guitars were returned to the shop I examined them, and the string height and intonation were perfect.

David Bourne has since established a workshop in Worthing and hopes to return to London, but wherever he may settle he will surely be known as one of Britains best makers of Steel Strung guitars.

Chapter Thirteen

THE GREAT GUITAR PIONEERS

The advent of one innovation always sets another complementary one in motion and the steel-strung guitar, especially the 'cello body, took the place of the banjo as a rhythm instrument in the dance band. This was so because the guitar provided a less clanky sound than a tenor banjo. The banjo or tenor banjo, of course, projected a more lively clout so suitable to the small jazz bands but became out of place in the more sophisticated smoother swing bands of the thirties.

Therefore, the instrument owes a debt to the pioneers of the thirties who struggled to make their instrument heard as a solo voice besides its seemingly accepted role of being 'felt' as part of the rhythm section.

These pioneers were a source of inspiration for guitarists on both sides of the Atlantic and they are the guitarists who had the greatest initial influence on me and on most of my contemporaries for nearly two decades. If some proof is required it surely appears when recalling the *Melody Maker* Poll of 1937 to seek the most popular jazz musician of the day. When this poll took place I had been on tour and out of London for about three years. Albert Harris was the foremost session musician as well as being a member of Lew Stone's Band. Eddie Lang had been dead for four years and Django Reinhardt was only known in England through the *Hot Club of France* recordings, which were only obtainable through Oriole records.

There is, of course, nothing conclusive about a poll but the figures do show in this instance that some guitarists were better known than others *and* more popular.

The other outstanding American jazz guitarists who were heard in England via recordings of the leading swing bands were George Van Eps and Alan Reuss while Dick McDonough and Carl Kress had made history in 1935/6 with their guitar duets. Eddie Condon, although only a rhythm player of a *four string* guitar had, nevertheless, been involved with Chicago style jazz from as early as 1927 with Red McKenzie and the Chicagoans and later with Red Nichols, Bobby Hackett and in the 52nd Street clubs. Although, as I said, he never played a solo note, he is reputed to have known the chords of any number that he was asked to accompany. He was still leading his own band when he died in 1973.

Laurence Lucie played for Benny Carter, Lucky Millander and Fletcher Henderson and although little was heard or known of his playing, his association with three great bands gave him status. Needless to say there were dozens of other excellent guitarists in America who were unknown in England.

Here is the placing in the *Melody Maker* Poll 1937 Guitarists International Section and the voting. Incidentally, Eddie Lang polled the largest number of votes for any individual musician.

1. Eddie Lang   1737
2. Django Reinhardt   245
3. Dick McDonough   83
4. Albert Harris   54
5. Alan Reuss   45
6. George Van Eps   28
7. Eddie Condon   22
8. Laurence Lucie, Carl Kress,   both 16

In the British Section the figures were as follows:

1. Albert Harris   1287
2. Ivor Mairants   438
3. Danny Perri   36

(Danny Perri was an excellent Canadian guitarist working in London.)
4. George Elliot, Joe Young   each 27
(George Elliot recorded with the Six Swingers and other house bands at EMI. Joe Young was the English 6-string counterpart of Eddie Condon.)

6. Alan Ferguson   25
(Reputed to be a good jazz player but there was never any evidence of his having been heard in the flesh or on record.)

7. Archie Slavin   23
(A popular young guitarist who later joined Lew Stone and Ambrose.)

8. Len Fillis   22
(Len Fillis had been *the* leading player and, in fact, the only player in the later 20s, recording solos, as well as with *The Bright Sparks* on

THE GREAT GUITAR PIONEERS   141

Parlophone and, of course, a star with Fred Elizalde's Savoy Hotel Band.)

9. Joe Brannelly   21
(Banjoist and guitarist with Ambrose. Came to me for a few lessons but his forte was choosing songs for Ambrose like *When Day is Done* and *Body and Soul.*)

10. Sam Gelsley   19
(Originally a pupil of mine then playing with Jack Harris at Ciros.)

11. Jack Llewellyn   17
(A brilliant soloist and sight-reader and a disciple of Django. Played at the Grosvenor House with Sidney Lipton Band and later a prolific sessioneer and member of my guitar group for a while.)

Billy Bell, who was equal to most and better than some, was not mentioned, but well deserved to be, and it is interesting to note that both Billy Bell and George Elliot who used to work together in Pasquale Troise and his Mandoliers and Banjoliers are both still working as session guitarists forty years on.

It is sad to say that Teddy Bunn whom I consider one of the greatest jazz guitarists who ever lived did not even receive a mention in the International Section.

Here then is a closer look at the great guitar pioneers who influenced me and thousands of others in the thirties.

Eddie Lang (born Salvatore Massaro) (b. Philadelphia 25.10.02 d. 20.3.33 New York)

If I were asked which guitarist I would have liked to have met most of all I would say Eddie Lang because it was his guitar playing on the Brunswick record *Some Day Sweetheart* (with Boyd Senter, clarinet) that set my flame alight, still to burn with love for the guitar.

His tone was full and throaty, the rhythm was alive and the phrasing perfection in style. Altogether the sound projected a warmth heard only from great performing musicians or singers.[1]

The sound and individuality of his guitar playing has never been successfully equalled. In his field he was a musician well in advance of the times and there were few of his calibre. The fact that he played in

---

[1] Eddie Lang's L5 is still in existence and the owner says that the original strings are still fitted. The sixth string is .085, .020 more than the heaviest sixth I have ever seen. There is also a covered second. The heavy gauge strings would account for the heavy tone.

the Piccadilly Hotel, London in 1926 with a combination known as the Mound City Blue Blowers meant nothing to me at the time, because I had not yet taken up the guitar or heard of Eddie Lang.

The Gibson Master Guitar – Style L5

Gibson guitar similar to one used by Eddie Lang.

Mentioning this visit, Lang remembered how he enjoyed London and how charming the English musicians were to him, spending time showing him all the sights.

Imagine my chagrin when, many years later, during a conversation with Sidney Bright, the pianist (with whom I worked for ten years in Geraldo's Band), I discovered that *he, too*, was then at the Piccadilly Hotel, had met Eddie Lang and could not remember a thing about him.

From all accounts, his own written one included, Lang was a real professional, excellent at his work, in fact the best, a genial companion and like most greats, modest about his accomplishments. It was, however, said that he did not read music, a slur on his abilities which I never believed, but it was probably spread around because his ear was so keen that he did not have to see the music in order to play his part (which would only have been a chord chart). Furthermore, his upbringing belies this. His father had been a maker of guitars in Italy and when Salvatore was one and a half his father kept him out of mischief by making him a 'musical instrument'. It consisted of a cigar box with a broom handle attached and a strong thread was used for the strings.

After a few years had elapsed he began to study the violin and played in the orchestra at the school he attended – and one cannot do that without learning to read music.

Also attending the same school and playing violin was the one and only Joe Venuti who became Eddie Lang's inseparable pal, a fact very much confirmed recently by octagenarian Joe Venuti who, in an interview, said 'The reason I could work well with Eddie was because he was a great accompanist. Instead of playing a G7 when a dominant chord was called for, Eddie would approach it through a D minor or D minor seventh to G7. Instead of playing a plain G major chord he would add the major seventh and so on'. (something unheard of in those far-off days of simple harmonies).

Many pianists thought he was playing wrong chords but neither Venuti nor Lang let on.

After leaving school Lang's first real job was playing *violin* with a Charlie Kent who signed him up for four years but when the banjo came into fashion, Mr. Kent decided that he would prefer a banjoist to a violinist and for Eddie, having 'fooled around' with a guitar, the banjo presented no difficulties.

His next job was with the Scranton Sirens where he met and first played with Tommy and Jimmy Dorsey.

Eddie Lang considered his first break came when he joined the Mound City Blue Blowers who wanted him to play banjo, but as they already had one banjo player he suggested being allowed to play guitar and so improve the combination. Needless to say, it was very successful and it was with this combination that he played in London during 1926. No wonder that London was not agog with the guitar playing of Eddie Lang. It had not yet been heard of!

On returning to America, Venuti and Lang formed their own band to play at the Silver Slipper Club, Atlantic City, then moved to the Playground Cafe in New York while at the same time making a number of records under the Venuti-Lang heading, leading various large and small combinations.

Among the small combinations that Lang formed and enhanced was one with Lonnie Johnson (1880-1970) an innovator of twice Lang's age who played guitar with an easy swing bending the blues with plaintive feeling. Johnson must have had a profound effect on Lang's solo style because there are close similarities both in phrasing and feeling. Nevertheless, the difference between their playing was quite distinct. The main difference lay in the string tension. Johnson had a lower string action which enabled him to phrase smoothly and bend the blue notes without effort while the sound sustained; on the other hand Lang's phrasing was tighter and more percussive. While both expressed their music in the same plaintive manner, Lang's tone was more due to his greater intensity of vibrato which created a warmer feeling. Johnson's jazz style was sometimes influenced by ragtime, Lang's style was more sophisticated harmonically and certainly he was the master at accompaniment (*50 Years of Jazz Guitar,* CBS 8825 would confirm this opinion). These qualities gave Lang limitless opportunities for combining his jazz talents with other musicians in the whole spectrum of dance music. He and Venuti, in fact, joined the most prominent dance band of the time, Roger Wolfe Kahn, and played with him until he disbanded the outfit.

During this period Eddie Lang was a prolific recording guitarist as well as recording his own solos, among them Rachmaninov's *Prelude, Just A Little Love A Little Kiss, April Kisses, Lilac Time* and *Rainbow's End.*

The duo also played in vaudeville with Jack Benny before joining Paul Whiteman who had been after them for some time, but was unable to engage them until their three-year contract with Roger Wolfe Kahn had run out.

Then off they went to California (May 1929), where they spent ten months (with a break from August to October) filming *The King of Jazz,* which Eddie Lang enjoyed immensely.

After returning to New York they continued their connection with the film by playing in theatres which projected the *The King of Jazz.*

The instrument which Ed Lang played throughout his later career was made by Gibson although in some recordings with Red Nicholls and Chauncy Moorhouse he used what looked like a Martin 0-18 or 00-18, that is, a flat top round hole guitar. The numbers he enjoyed most were *Happy Feet* and *Bench in the Park* with Bing Crosby, containing gems of accompaniment. Lang, in spite of his obvious inspiration through Lonnie Johnson, became the innovator and leading guitarist of his time and right from the inception began a new trend in the existing dance band world, evidenced by the fact that Dick McDonough was still playing the banjo on sessions with Red Nicholls and his Five Pennies when Lang was already playing his little Martin 00-18 guitar.

Nevertheless, *The Gibson Story,* written by Julius Belson, gives little credit to Eddie Lang for the extremely important part he played in bringing the 'cello guitar to the notice of American and European dance band guitarists.

In his short lifetime, his guitar playing made more impact on listeners then any other guitarist of the period, so much so that four years after he had died he was voted the most popular dance musician in the 1937 *Melody Maker* Poll.

He died on 20 March 1933 aged 31, due to complications developing after a tonsillectomy, while he was working as regular accompanist to Bing Crosby with whom he was reputed to be earning 1,000 dollars a week.

What a dreadful calamity. One can only speculate as to the development of his playing had he lived to be an octogenarian like his lifelong pal, Joe Venuti.

Dick McDonough (1904-1938)

In the hierarchy of great innovators of plectrum guitar style, I would say that Dick McDonough carried on where Eddie Lang left off. Lang and his immediate contemporaries used a high string action which required great pressure on the strings from the left hand coupled with an attacking right hand picking, but McDonough changed that to the more lightly picked smoother style which first made its mark in the Dorsey Brothers Orchestra record of *By Heck* (Brunswick Rhythm Series No. 180).

Although the volume and tone of Lang had to be sacrificed, McDonough's lower string action was a necessary prerequisite to this more legato style.

Two effects made McDonough's playing exceptional on this particular record; one was the use of a 'crushed note' which had often been heard on the piano by playing adjacent semitones simultaneously as a blue note, but now used effectively by fingering A on the first string of the guitar and G# on the second string, and picking them together with an up stroke as a fill-in against the orchestral phrasing. This effect soon caught on with other guitarists and became widely used.

The other device consisted of playing a minor chord in arpeggio form and, while holding the minor 3rd and perfect 5th on two strings, descend in the bars from tonic to minor 7th, major 6th, minor 6th, perfect 5th then up again to minor 6th, major 6th, major 7th to tonic. The notes were actually as follows:

```
 B  D  F#        A  D  F#        G#  D  F#
 G  D  F#        F# D  F#        G   D  F#
 G# D  F#        A# D  F#        back to B D F#
```

McDonough used them both as an accompaniment to a solo and as a solo for guitar. Considering that Gershwin did not use this progression until two years later in *Summertime* (1935), it was, to say the least, an innovation for guitarists.

Among guitarists Dick McDonough is remembered for his duets with Carl Kress (another famous figure of the era). These duets on

Brunswick were *Stage Fright/Danson* and *Chicken a La King/Heatwave*, featured on stage at the Imperial Theatre, New York, 1936.

It is not surprising that in his 7 or 8 years as a prominent guitarist his ideas inspired many other players. Unfortunately, he succumbed to pneumonia and died at the age of 34, only 5 years after Lang, leaving the musical world deprived of another major influence within a short space of time.

George Van Eps (b. 1913 Plainsfield, New Jersey)
George Van Eps, whose father Fred Van Eps was recognised as the leading banjoist of his day, was born in 1913 and naturally took up the banjo, but after hearing Eddie Lang, switched to guitar. Eddie (whom George knew well) lent him his first guitar in 1926 and in 1927 George bought his first guitar – a Martin.

When I first heard about him it was the middle 30s when he was a member of Benny Goodman's Orchestra. One little gem I still recall was an eight bar solo in a record of *Love Me or Leave Me* by Benny Goodman. The orchestral arrangement was very ordinary but the eight bars of gently swinging guitar playing a chord solo were more than outstanding. They were an innovation in changing harmonies.

A typical example of Van Eps' unorthodoxy can be heard in the 6th and 7th bars of this solo where he uses the notes of the B13th chord instead of the B♭7 in order to bring more excitement to the extemporisation.

He was reputed to have had differences with Benny Goodman because of his inventive flair for chords which were not written in the part and which irritated the sharp but orthodox ear of his employer. Probably because of this difference, Van Eps did not stay long with Goodman.

Van Eps later joined the recording orchestra of Ray Noble and when Noble went to Los Angeles, rejoined him.

George, unlike many orchestral guitarists of the day, played an Epiphone guitar when most played a Gibson, and I do not know whether it was this that made me switch from a Martin 'cello to an Epiphone de Luxe, but his style had a very strong effect on my playing. Later (in 1939) the Epiphone Company published a tutor by Van Eps which I immediately used as a basis for practice and I must confess, as groundwork for my own plectrum guitar tutor published in 1943.

It is safe to say that among guitarists, Van Eps has, from that period and throughout his eventful career, been considered the guitarist's guitarist and although, in 1974, he had not played for about a year, regard for his genius had never diminished. He has accompanied many famous artistes including Peggy Lee, Frank Sinatra and Jo Stafford and has often recorded under the baton of Paul Weston. It was with the co-operation of Paul Weston that he recorded the solo album *Mellow Guitar* on Columbia 929 and a further LP as well. His modesty and kindness are exceptional and he is the type of person who is capable of elevating one's morale by appreciating your talents and giving you confidence to aspire to better things.

Comparing himself to Albert Harris (who had been a pupil of his in New York and who now lives in Los Angeles where he is a leading film arranger and orchestrator), George considers himself a monotalent. During a short stay in L.A., we had a long telephone conversation during which he gave me so much food for thought that it was a tonic to talk to him.

He plays a 7-string guitar with the seventh string tuned to A below E one octave below the 5th string and in explaining his method one cannot help being inspired by his enthusiasm.

Whenever he has given a solo performance in Donte's in Hollywood, the club has been packed with guitarists, some of whom have even given up record dates to hear him. He is (as I mentioned) recognised by all professional guitarists as being the complete master of his instrument with a sense of harmony which remains ever fresh.

Allan Reuss (b. June 1915 New York City)
If ever a disciple's style resembled his master's it was the style of Allan Reuss, fours years junior to George Van Eps.

Reuss played the banjo from the age of 12, then in 1934 had a strong desire to play the guitar. He took lessons from Van Eps and, remarkable as it may seem, six months later when George vacated the guitar chair in Benny Goodman's Band, Allan filled it to Goodman's satisfaction. It is, therefore, not very surprising that when one compares his guitar solo of *If I Could Be With You* with George's solo of *Love Me or Leave Me*, it is impossible to miss the resemblance.

If I Could Be With You was recorded in 1936 on HMV N8480 and in bar ten of his solo, Reuss uses the semitone device by raising the melodic line a semitone from $A\flat 7$ to $A7$ before returning to $B\flat 7$.

Although the extemporised melody is different from that of Van Eps the idea is the same.

Allan Reuss was extremely popular in the New York recording scene and played with the jazz élite of the day, often being a member of Teddy Wilson's Orchestra, which included Harry James (when he still played jazz), Buster Baily (clarinet), Johnny Hodges (alto), Cosy Cole (drums) and John Kirby (bass), Helen Ward and the legendary Billie Holliday singing the vocal refrains in titles like *There's a Lull in My Life, It's Swell of You* (Ward) and *Sentimental and Melancholy, I'll Get By* and *Mean to Me* (Holliday) or *No Regrets* and *Did I Remember* with Billie Holliday and her Orchestra, all on the Vocalion Swing series.

In 1938 Allan Reuss composed seven pieces which were published in one folio illustrating both his fast chordal chromatic style and his slow sentimental style which guitarists favour so much. The seven pieces are all interesting and up-to-date even by today's standards.

In the 40s he, too, moved to Hollywood but during 1939 he wrote and recorded a swing plectrum guitar solo called *Pickin' for Patsy* with Jack Teagarden's Orchestra on Parlophone Super Rhythm Style series No. S4R.2836. This was a milestone in the use of the acoustic guitar in concerto form with orchestra.

I was playing with the Geraldo Orchestra when I heard it and immediately saw the possibilities of popularising the guitar by playing it myself; so I transcribed it from the record and broadcast it with the band many many times. Although I thought the solo was unamplified, I eventually discovered that Reuss's guitar was amplified on the session. It was considered such a remarkable achievement at the time that the *Downbeat* of 1 December 1939 wrote:

'Allan's recent work on Jack Teagarden's Brunswick record *Pickin' for Patsy*, his own number, proved to the record companies as well as to muscians and to public alike that as a solo jazz instrument the guitar is far from stillborn'.

Up to 1976 he was very much occupied with his Los Angeles studio dates, being a sight-reader and guitar player much in demand. Unfortunately, in 1976 his wife became ill and he retired from playing and sold his instruments in order to care for her. He did so for three years having himself had a stroke in the meantime, and, sad to relate, his wife died in January 1979 after having been married for 42 years. He told me he would never play guitar again thereby creating a gap in

THE GREAT GUITAR PIONEERS 149

the style of guitar playing of which he and Van Eps are the last living masters.

Teddy (Theodore Leroy) Bunn (b. 1909 – d. 20 July 1978)
Upon reflection I can honestly say that when I heard Teddy Bunn's solo guitar work in *Four or Five Times* with Jimmy Noone on Vocalion, I enjoyed it more than any other jazz guitar playing I had ever heard. Yet in comparison to Django, he was hardly ever mentioned in guitarists' company. Django has been dead more than 20 years and he is still a major influence among the leading contemporary jazz guitarists, but Teddy Bunn, who recently died and was, for almost 10 years, partially blind and partially incapacitated, is all but forgotten.

Today I have not changed my mind that Bunn's blues extemporisation constituted the very foundation of the art of jazz at its best, pungent with its every ingredient. Rhythmic, free flowing extemporisation, soulful feeling coupled with a happy lift, originality of harmonic conception beyond his times and variety of melodic phrasing. He played an acoustic guitar and, in my opinion, produced a greater depth of tone and swing than Django. I would have been happier to be creative in the style of Teddy Bunn rather than in the style of Django or anyone else of the period simply because I had a deeper feeling for the music I loved instinctively rather than because of its virtuosity.

Teddy Bunn's vital rhythmic performances which can be heard on any of the 'Spirits of Rhythm' records were deep yet happy jazz.

He was born in Freeport, Long Island of poor parents and never had music lessons. Due to his keen ear, he was able to play melodies on the guitar and learnt to accompany various blues singers until 1928 when he joined the Washboard Serenaders with whom he stayed for 18 months. He then joined Duke Ellington as a replacement to Fred Guy and confessed that memorising the Ellington book was just about the most difficult task he had ever undertaken.

But what brought Teddy Bunn to the notice of British jazz enthusiasts was his recordings with 'The Spirits of Rhythmn' whom he joined in Washington DC replacing Buddy Blanton. The leader of the group, Les Watson, otherwise known as Slam, played the bass and sang scat, the tiples were played by Doug and Wilbur Daniels and Virgil Scroggins produced wonderful rhythm by swishing a pair of wire brushes on a piece of brown paper stretched tightly across the top of an upturned suitcase. Fortunately, Joe Belbook in New York was on the look-out for a new talent to fill the bill at his Onyx Club, a famous intimate nightclub on 52nd Street, and 'The Spirits of Rhythm' seemed to fill the bill. They became famous enough to attract the attention of Claude Hopkins, who ran the Harlem Serenade radio programme where they became regular guests as well as recording artistes with Brunswick. It was on these records that Teddy Bunn's guitar, Les Watson's scat singing and the Daniel brothers tiple playing was first heard in Great Britain.

Teddy Bunn also recorded with blues singers for 'Race' records, forerunners of the 'Rock and Roll' craze. If one should have the good fortune to come across any of the following records, they will find Bunn playing *some* solo guitar:

I Got Rhythm—My Old Man	Brunswick 01715 Spirits of Rhythm
I've Got the World on a String—	
Way Down Yonder in New Orleans	Brunswick 01997 Red McKenzie with the Spirits of Rhythm
Bump It–Four or Five Times	Vocalion 5209 Jimmy Noone and his Orchestra
Melancholy	Vocalion 5207 Johnny Dodds Orchestra
Beale Street—Maura	Vocalion 5233 Bob Howard Orchestra
Home Cooking—	
Man with the Frying Pan	Brunswick 02691 Milt Herth Quartet
Tired of Fattenin' Frogs	Vocalion 274 Rosetta Crawford and Orchestra
The Washboard Get Together	HMV B6114 Washboard Serenaders
Ja Da	HMV B9236 Tommy Ladnier Orchestra
Just Another Woman	HMV B9261 Hot Lips Page

During 1970 he was working in a night club in Honolulu but later his health suffered a setback and he died in the Lancaster Hospital, Palmdale, California. He had lived in retirement because of several strokes and heart attacks from which he never recovered sufficiently to be able to play again.

Charlie Christian (b. 1919 Dallas, Texas – d. 1942)
Late in 1939 I bought a record of the Benny Goodman Sextet in which the beauty, simplicity, originality and invigorating lift of the electric guitar solos melted me and it was a case of love at first hearing. The titles were *Rose Room* and *Flying Home* on Parlophone R2917 Super Swing Music No. 50 recorded New York, October 1939 with Artie Bernstein (bass), Nick Fatool (drums), Fletcher Henderson (piano) and Lionel Hampton (vibes).

THE GREAT GUITAR PIONEERS   151

Flying Home I think, contains almost a basis of his whole style and *Rose Room* illustrates some of his other well-known phrases. One ingredient, however, cannot be imitated and that is the personal feeling with which one expresses oneself on a musical instrument. The warmth of feeling produced by Charlie Christian is inimitable.

Nevertheless, everything I played I hoped was based on his style of extemporisation. I was even able to buy a guitar like his – a black Vega non-cutaway with one pick-up which I used until such time as De Armond marketed their pick-up '1000' a few years later. Later he used a Gibson ES.150, a non-cutaway with one bar pick-up (since called a Charlie Christian pick-up).

Most of today's leading jazz guitarists confess to being influenced by the playing of Charlie Christian although his playing career with Goodman lasted about two years. Nevertheless during this time he made many recordings with Goodman.

Five years after his death the VOX recording label discovered the existence of several acetate recording discs cut by Jerry Newman, jazz fan and amateur recording expert, when he happened to have his recording machine at Mintons, a Harlem nightspot, one night when Charlie Christian dropped in with his guitar. This resulted in the Charlie Christian Memorial Album with chorus upon chorus of marvellous extemporisation by Christian on two tunes, *Stompin' at the Savoy* and *Charlie's Choice*.

In an article by Charlie Christian in the 1 December 1939 issue of *Downbeat* he writes: 'Guitar players have long needed a champion, someone to explain to the world that a guitarist is something more than just a robot plunking on a gadget to keep the rhythm going'. He then quotes Bernard Addison, formerly with Stuff Smith's Band: 'Guitarists are Goats. In the present day set-up it's the guitar player who gets the short end. Leaders don't appreciate the possibilities of the instrument'. Then Charlie Christian, after paying tribute to Goodman, ends by saying: 'With an appalling ignorance of the effective use to which they could put the instrument, most leaders, including those in the radio and movie studios, have demanded a guitarist who can fiddle, arrange or pick his teeth, walking a tightrope every other chorus. The fact that he might have been truly an artiste on the guitar was negligible".

He was born in Texas and raised in Oklahoma City, and the fact that his father was a guitarist probably helped in the choice of his instrument. By the age of 15 he was working his first steady job although he began to use a pick-up and amplifier in 1937. He was discovered by Mary Lou Williams who raved about him to John Hammond who made a special journey to Oklahoma City where he heard Charlie play on an old Spanish guitar with a pick-up hooked up to a primitive amp. 'Before an hour had passed' writes John Hammond (*Downbeat* 25.8.66) 'I was determined to place Charlie with Benny Goodman'.

Charlie arrived for an audition with Goodman in August 1939 at the recording studios in Los Angeles hugging his guitar and amp, dressed in a cowboy hat, tight pointed shoes and a purple shirt with a matching bow tie; but it wasn't until later that night when Christian was smuggled on to the stand of the Victor Hugo Club in Beverley Hills that he got the chance to play.

The first number Benny Goodman called for the band to play was *Rose Room*, and after the opening choruses Benny pointed to Charlie to take a solo. The number which usually lasted three minutes stretched out to 45 minutes and there could be no doubt that the most spectacularly original soloist ever to play with Goodman had been launched. The band returned to New York in October, and recorded *Rose Room* and some riffs by Charlie which became *Flying Home*.

From his previous weekly income of $10.00 to about $200.00 per week with Goodman was a big jump and Charlie enjoyed himself. In addition to working in Goodman's band he spent a good deal of time at Mintons and in the company of girls which may not have done any harm had he not had a tubercular history.

Charlie did not follow medical advice and after his final recording session in June 1941 he was sent to a hospital on Staten Island where he died on 2 March 1942. The jazz world was shocked! The man who had launched the electric guitar as a major jazz instrument and had become the main jazz influence for generations, was no more.

He made many records and played many solos including one complete concerto with Goodman's Orchestra – *Solo Flight*. I could not rest until I had put down some kind of musical appreciation and I wrote *In Charlie's Footsteps* as a dedication which I recorded with Geraldo's Orchestra on Parlophone.

There are many re-issues of Charlie Christian records including the original *Rose Room* and *Flying Home* as well as the music of *Solo Flight* and other transcriptions.

Carmen Mastren (b. 1913 New York)
Carmen Mastren to me, was a kindred spirit who was known for his excellent work in the rhythm sections and in accompaniments, but not for his solos. For some time he played with Tommy Dorsey's band at

THE GREAT GUITAR PIONEERS 153

the height of their fame, when Frank Sinatra was the band's crooner and Buddy Rich was the band's drummer; when Buddy not only clashed his cymbals but clashed with Frankie. Be that as it may, Carmen Mastren not only played guitar for Dorsey but scored those original arrangements of *Marie* and *Black Eyes* which were great favourites with all musicians.

Carmen later played at Hickory House on 52nd Street and recorded with the Delta Four consisting of Carmen, Joe Marsala on clarinet, Roy Eldridge, cornet, and Sid Weiss, bass, an unusual combination for those days. The titles were *Farewell Blues* and another blues *Swingin' on that Famous Door* (the Famous Door was the name of a nightclub) and his solos were executed rather like an arranger and not just single notes. During the war, to my surprise and pleasure, I discovered he was the guitarist in the American band of the AEF led by Captain (later Major) Glenn Miller, and we both broadcast from the London Casino in Old Compton Street which had been requisitioned for the duration, the name changed to the Queensbury Club, and served as a Forces Club.

We became close friends and we even played the same model guitar – Epiphone Emperor. It was also my first opportunity of seeing and hearing American musicians at close quarters and I must admit their tonal qualities were fantastic. The rhythm section was particularly brilliant with Ray McKinley on drums, Mel Powell (composer of *My Guy's Come Back*) on piano and the most agile bass player of the era, Trigger Alpert. This was certainly the best rhythm section Glenn Miller ever had.

Carmen stayed at my house whenever he could and one day showed me the score of a guitar solo he had written called *Two Moods* with an orchestral accompaniment and I took to it as a duck takes to water.

Soon I was broadcasting it as an alternative to my other solos and later recorded it as a backing for *In Charlie's Footsteps*.

After the war, Carmen joined the staff of NBC in New York and one of his regular functions was soloist and MD to a morning quiz and fashion show five days every week.

Whenever I go to New York we catch up on musical gossip over dinner and a visit to a musical event whether it is the 'Hickory House' (no longer in existence) '52nd Street' where he used to play with Wingy Manone or some other venue like Birdland on Broadway where one would never be disappointed.

Perry Botkin (b. 1907 d. 4 October 1975)
Another American guitarist whose musicianship brought him more fame than his solo performances was Perry Botkin, who came to London in 1959 as MD and accompanist to Hugh O'Brien (star of the TV Wyatt Earp show) during his season at the London Palladium. Perry, himself, was also featured in a solo spot playing guitar and ukulele.

He appeared at Wardour Street one day while I still had the Central School of Dance Music, and he was surprised to hear that he was no stranger to me, having heard him in a number of Crosby records. He had, in fact, been Bing Crosby's musical supervisor and accompanist for 15 years and was responsible for arranging and playing in the records of *Dear Friends and Gentle People* and *Ghost Riders in the Sky* as well as many other titles.

Although it is not a name that guitarists will remember, he, nevertheless, contributed the music for the TV Beverley Hillbillies which also contained some terrific playing by Earl Scruggs (banjo) and Lester Flatt, guitar.

Perry Botkin was born in Indiana, U.S.A. and began to play the ukulele at the age of eleven then changed to the larger tenor banjo which he found more stimulating but soon the tenor banjo became redundant and he changed to plectrum banjo. Suddenly, in 1926, he heard the Mound City Blue Blowers and (as readers will recall), this is where Eddie Lang made his debut as a guitarist. Eddie's guitar playing was a startling revelation to Perry who, at the time, was staying in the same New York hotel as Dick McDonough and they both agreed that this phenomenon spelt the writing on the wall for the banjo and called for a quick change to the guitar.

There were, of course, no printed methods so it was a case of self-tuition or bust.

Perry's next move was to play at Barney Gallant's Night Club in New York's Greenwich Village and freelance around New York with various radio shows. Two of these shows were directed by Victor Young and Johnny Green, and when they both decided to take their network broadcasts to Hollywood, they asked Perry to join them and go West. This, Perry considered his greatest stroke of good luck as it opened many doors in Hollywood and two years later he joined John Scott Trotter's Orchestra which then provided all the recording accompaniments for Bing Crosby.

This is where I heard the tasteful playing of Botkin which stuck in

THE GREAT GUITAR PIONEERS   155

my memory and in those far-off days there was not the remotest thought that one day he would call to see me.

He asked me to play and I did so, performing a new solo I had been broadcasting which I dedicated to Barney Kessel called *Personal Call* (*for Barney Kessel*) and Perry asked 'Why do you fellows dedicate your work to other musicians? It's good enough to stand on its own merits. Get your own name over!

In America *he* certainly did. In 1952 he recorded – as a novelty – a ukulele solo of *Lover* backed by an original composition called *Ukey-Ukulele* which became a best seller in the Hawaiian Islands where ukulele playing originated. In fact, it led to him being invited to Honolulu by the Royal Hawaiian Recording Company who set up the latest recording equipment on Waikiki Beach and – you've guessed – to record *On the Beach at Waikiki* which he backed with his own composition *The Duke of the Uke*.

I have heard his ukulele playing and it is truly amazing, no gimmicks, sounds like a musical instrument!

He loved to be involved in the commercial side of the profession and in this respect he owned a couple of publishing companies, which he ran very successfully or, as he remarked, 'The guitar has not been unkind to me'.

He was a large sized man with a large sized enthusiasm which may have been the cause of his death in 1973 aged only 66 and if you hear the name of Perry Botkin today, it will, no doubt, be that of his son Perry Botkin Jnr. who is a famous songwriter and publisher.

I am sure his father had a lot to be proud of.

Django Reinhardt (born Jean-Baptiste Reinhardt) (b. Liverchies, Belgium 12.1.10, d. Fontainebleau, France 16.4.53)
I first heard the playing of Django on an Oriole record somewhere around 1933-34 and the titles were *I Saw Stars, Lady Be Good, Tiger Rag* and *Dark Eyes* and in these recordings of the Quintette du Hot Club de France I had ears only for the guitarist whom I considered by far the outstanding instrumental performer.

The violin playing of Stephane Grappelly was, of course, excellent and the rhythm, consisting of his brother Joseph and Roger Chaput (guitars) and Louis Vola (bass) formed what became the characteristic background but I could feel that the strong influence belonged to the genius of Django.

By 1937 he had already made some impact on British fans but very little in comparison to Eddie Lang who had by that time been dead for

4 years; that is, if we are to believe that the votes cast for him by readers of the *Melody Maker*: Eddie Lang (1st) 1,737 votes, Django (2nd) 225 votes, truly reflected the extent of his popularity. But it must be remembered that there were not many professional guitarists in England and the general dance music listeners were more interested in bands or singers than in guitarists.

The Quintette first received public acclamation in England in 1935 when recordings were first issued on the Oriole label. It was not until January 1938 that the Quintette came to London and a small group of guitarists consisting of George Elliott, Jack Llewellyn, Sam Gelsley, one or two others and I, went round to his hotel to give him a warm welcome, and although greetings were rather mute owing to the language barrier, he was very pleased.

They opened at the Cambridge Theatre in London's West End. This was a Sunday concert and in this intimate, comfortable, newly built auditorium facing an audience of musicians and fans, excitement ran high.

It resulted in what must have been the most thrilling audience appreciation of their tour because the dates that followed were commercial bookings at suburban variety theatres.

They played at the Shepherds Bush and the Wood Green Empires to sparsely filled halls. I remember sitting in the stalls at the Shepherds Bush Empire watching the group, on a stage which seemed so far away and apparently not very artistically lighted, with the sounds echoing and remote.

I am sure they were not a financial success and certainly caused no musical sensation for the multitude. However, there were compensations. Whenever I could, I sat in the dressing room between shows watching Django wield his hard pick on his Maccaferri guitar. He used down strokes except in tremolo passages and hit the strings very near the bridge, not resting his fingers but working from the wrist and elbow. As most people know, the third and fourth fingers of his left hand were withered and could be used only for simple seventh chords and the like on the first two strings, but what he could do with the other two was, of course, nothing short of natural instinctive genius, chromatic runs, octaves *et al.*

His music fascinated me; he never played a wrong note. I enjoyed his music so much but I had no desire to copy it. I was probably so deeply immersed with the playing of the American guitarists that I did not think of Django's playing as jazz in the American blues sense but rather as his own gipsy style and, therefore, to me not as valid as the jazz of the great American jazz musicians.

But Django was ploughing his own furrow, his own melodic line, and it was not until years later that his genius was fully appreciated, to the extent that he is one of the three greatest influence among jazz guitarists, the other two being Charlie Christian and Wes Montgomery.

The fire which damaged Django's left hand plus other injuries to his side and leg occurred in 1928 and it was not before 1930 that he began to play again. When he became known outside France he used a Maccaferri guitar, but prior to that he played on what Stephane Grappelly describes as 'a piece of wood he calls a guitar. He shows no concern about his inferior instrument but poured his heart into the most enthralling improvisations'.

Nevertheless, the Maccaferri guitar is now a collector's item and although a copy is currently being manufactured in Japan for sale in Europe and the States supervised by Mario Maccaferri I doubt if this will produce another Django.

His tour with Duke Ellington in the United States is often spoken about by guitarists and is generally considered as having been a disappointment to all concerned except the few guitarists who heard him.

Harry Volpe, the guitarist who befriended him in New York, and was present at the Carnegie Hall concerts with Ellington, still talks about him with reverence. 'I invited him home after the first show and hoped he would play to us but on this occasion he refused to be drawn although he spent a relaxed evening after a meal, but the second night, Wow! It was entirely different. I had invited a few guitarists round to meet him and he performed musical miracles late into the night. He was absolutely wonderful and I will never forget it'.

It must be remembered that Django did not take a guitar with him to America and believed that Messrs. Gibson would be only too pleased to provide him with an instrument. However, this was not to be, and it was Ellington who, belatedly, had to find an electric acoustic guitar for him to use. I cannot imagine anything worse than for a guitarist to be handed an instrument just before the show and be told to get on with it. Even when using an electric guitar on recordings I do not think he sounds the same Django as when he pours out his soul in the warmth of sound he produced from his acoustic guitar.

He never returned to the United States and although he might have had a great effect on the style of guitar jazz had he done so, his influence has been such as to affect the style of players like Les Paul, Barney Kessel, Chet Atkins and Joe Pass, to name a few.

His early death was tragic. On the morning after returning home from a Swiss tour on 15 May 1953, he could not move out of bed. He was terrified to discover that he could hardly move his arms and legs. His wife called a doctor but before he arrived Django began to feel a bit better, got up and went to the door to see some friends across the street, but when he stepped out he collapsed and never regained consciousness.

The most singular phenomenon of invention and extemporisation of the guitar had died of cerebral haemorrhage at the age of 43.

Albert Harris
Albert Harris, my old friend and one-time partner on our Brunswick Record guitar duets, became the best British guitarist of the thirties but he started off as an accordionist. When he was about 17 he was engaged to play accordion in the band playing a summer season at the Dreamland Ballroom, Margate in 1931. He had lent a fellow musician some money which for reasons which now do not matter, the poor chap was unable to pay back. By some strange chance he was the possessor of a guitar which was of no use to him and he offered it to Albert in lieu of the money he owed and Albert, considering it as better than a dead loss, accepted it.

With his excellent harmonic knowledge for one so young, he quickly picked up the threads – or should I say strings – and discovered a liking for the instrument, so much so that returning to London after the summer engagement, he took a job playing guitar.

He became the guitarist in Stanley Barnett's Band at Madame Tussaud's restaurant and when I left Jack Padbury's Band late in 1932 to join Roy Fox, he took my place.

It was not very long before he became the most sought after guitarist in London joining Lew Stone at the Monseigneur, accompanying Jack Buchanan and taking part in many sessions. When asked to record the classical guitar solo *Homage a Debussy* by Manuel de Falla he did so on the plectrum guitar with the strings tuned down one tone in order to lower the tension of the strings, and at the time no one knew the difference!

He joined Ambrose's Band later on but when, in 1938, he could see no future for himself in England, he emigrated to the United States where they did not exactly give him a ticker tape welcome. However, with a little help here and there from Carmen Mastren and George

Van Eps from whom he received some tuition and for whom he sometimes deputised, he kept his head above water.

To be in steady work he joined Horace Heidt and went on a tour which ended in Los Angeles. Albert liked L.A. and decided to stay there. Being the musician he was he worked and studied, eventually becoming a Doctor of Music, arranging and composing really being his metier.

So he gave up the guitar around 1950 to become one of Hollywood's top arrangers for films, having also to his credit record albums by Sonny and Cher, and Barbara Streisand, for which he MD'd and arranged the music.

He is now a most sought after teacher of arranging and composition and has had some notable pupils namely Barney Kessel, the late Jack Marshall and Fred MacMurray, the actor.

His guitar compositions include a Sonatina and *Variations on a Theme* by Haydn which was recorded by Segovia, and *Homage a Unamuno* all published by Columbia Music in Washington.

In short, a happy well adjusted human being providing a musical service.

Josh White, Blues Artiste Extraordinary (b. 1908 d. 1969)[1]

It was during the war that I first heard a guitar with steel strings producing such an exceptional melting tone that I could hardly believe it.

It was the guitar of Josh White accompanying himself on a BBC programme, recorded in the United States, about a nation at war. The guitar was a small 00-21 size Martin and sounded neither percussive nor edgy. I never forgot it or the playing of Josh White on that occasion.

Fourteen or fifteen years later I had a call from Decca Studios at Broadhurst Gardens and when I arrived for the session the only other musician present was Jack Fallon, the bass player. Then to my surprise, in came Josh with his guitar to record a couple of titles for which I considered myself superfluous. Of course I was delighted not only to meet him but to be recording with him. As I listened I felt I wanted to be able to emulate his style of fingerpicking, so after the session I asked him if he would allow me to write down some of his solos and accompaniments, but he was dubious about this. As he explained, he played from memory and by ear and was neither able to read nor write music, therefore, it would be very time consuming coupled with a lot of effort. I was undeterred so he eventually succumbed and times for meetings were arranged.

Armed with my guitar and manuscript paper I presented myself at his apartment in Airway House at the back of the Haymarket and, what Duke Ellington would describe as a 'beautiful chick' opened the door and informed me that Josh was still in bed. Indeed he was, and did not seem very well, so I telephoned my friend and erstwhile pupil Dr. Sidney Gottlieb (a fan of Josh's) and gave him a rundown of the situation. Well, it was not long before he arrived, took care of Josh and gave him the necessary treatment to put him on his feet. And that is the way the work was done; a few hours a day for a week until I had transcribed sufficient material. There were no short cuts. We selected a suitable tune which he sang and played while I wrote down both the vocal melody and accompaniment which I then played back to him from my manuscript. His ear was infallible. I never heard him play a wrong note nor would he pass one. Everything he sang and played was Blues. Even an Irish folk tune like *Molly Malone* became a blues when treated with his chord progressions and vocal inflections.

He was a master of the art of linking chords by means of suspensions or passing chords. From A to E7 he would insert F#m7 and Fm7 or B7, B7–5 to E7 quite unlike the other folk or blues singers of his day who used no such sophistications. Perhaps that is one reason for his late acceptance by the masses.

Although he worked hard Josh never made a fortune, nor did he become popular until the 60s.

On 10 February 1956 Joshua Daniel White, of New York City, and I signed a copyright agreement with Messrs Boosey & Hawkes and later that year the *Josh White Guitar Method* was published. Author and BBC producer Charles Chilton read the proofs and wrote a foreword.

Josh was a great character and a great lover. My wife, always popular with my musician friends, is usually interested in their welfare and besides being very sympathetic can be an excellent counsellor during their trials and tribulations. Once, a few years ago, Josh was visiting and while talking to him about his wife, family and girl friends, she asked 'How many grandchildren have you?' Like a flash, Josh retorted 'Legit?' Actually, he admitted to 42 grandchildren. A prolific and creative artiste in more ways than one.

Josh died on 5 September 1969 while undergoing surgery at Northshore Hospital, Manhassett, NY for a defective heart valve after being professionally inactive for three years following a serious accident.

Between the ages of 7 and 12 the boy from South Carolina acted as a guide for blind blues singers including Blind Lemon Jefferson, and Josh himself introduced real blues and neglected treasures of negro folk music to a new audience. He also proclaimed in words and music his ethnic identity and social convictions long before this became fashionable. I sorely miss his occasional visits and warm friendship but let him say the last word with his own paragraph at the beginning of the book.

'I want to commend and thank Ivor Mairants for accomplishing what has heretofore been known as "the task impossible". In other words, to set into musical copy the actions of a completely unorthodox musician − one who, technically, can neither read nor write a single note of music as it is known to the world today. The remarkable part of all this is the fact that during the one week that we had to work on this book, I had to do four shows for the BBC with the George Mitchell Choir, rehearsing with them, writing with Charles Chilton and his girl Friday Sheila, not forgetting the dozens of telephone interruptions plus being overtaken by the 'flu all at the same time.'

Carmen Mastren

Charlie Christian 1939

Eddie Lang

Teddy Bunn

Django Reinhardt with Harry Volpe.

'MY FIFTY FRETTING YEARS'

Chappie D'Amato, Mario Maccaferri, Ivor Mairants.

Promoting Maccaferri guitars 1933.

Ivor Mairants Guitar Quartet (left to right) Ivor Mairants, Malcolm Lockyer, Alan Metcalf, Ike Isaacs, Jack Collier, Frank Deniz.

With Barry Galbraith, Elstree Film Studios 1954.

Roy Plummer with a 'Roger' guitar.

With Kenny Burrell, 1965.

With Herb Ellis, 1955.

With Josh White, 1955.

With Les Paul and Bert Weedon, 1952.

With Joe Pass, 1975.

Jamming with George Barnes, Frank Clarke (bass).

Barney Kessel giving an in store guitar clinic at the Musicentre.

With Perry Botkin, 1959.

Three rare D'Angelicos from Pete Townshend's collection.

Laurindo Almedia displaying his cutaway classic guitar.

Gibson's Nashville guitar factory.

The famous Harmony Stella 12 string guitar.

A 'Gibson' welcome.

Reception to launch Maurice Summerfield's book 'The Jazz Guitar'. (Left to right) Ivor Mairants, Herb Ellis, Joe Pass, Barney Kessel, Maurice Summerfield. October 1978.

Mario Maccaferri tells I.M. the secret of his success – or is it just a dirty story. British Music Trade Fair, London, 1977.

Chapter Fourteen

THE POST-WAR ELECTRIC GUITARISTS

The popularity of the electric guitar was sparked off by Charlie Christian who, according to the statements of nearly all the leading post-war players, was their first and main influence. He also influenced many arrangers and some composers although it will be understood that the talent of individual extemporisation played a greater part than actual composition, accepting that where a good player arose, his ability would be catered for by the arranger or composer.

In England after the war, London became the home of many featured players who devoted much of their time to the electric guitar, outstanding amongst them, Dave Goldberg, Pete Chilver, Roy Plummer, Ike Isaacs, Jack Llewellyn, Denny Wright, Terry Walsh, Judd Proctor, Bert Weedon, George Elliot, Billy Bell, Roland Harker, Archie Slavin, Alan Metcalf, Lauderic Caton, Ernie Shear and the Deniz brothers (Joe, Frank and Laurie).

In recognition of the rising popularity of the instrument, the BBC presented *Guitar Club* a half hour weekly Saturday broadcast in which they featured all varieties of players including John Williams on classical guitar, Antonio Navarro, flamenco guitar, Freddie Phillips, acoustic guitar, Dorita y Pepe, Latin-American folk playing and singing, and Wally Whyton, Folk, the whole being compered by Ken Sykora, a Reinhardt disciple whom I had discovered in the relief band when I was playing a May Ball at Cambridge with Geraldo. Diz Disley (who, with Stephane Grappelly, revived the Hot Club of France in the '70s) was also one of the programme's soloists.

In the words of Rock Island Line 'Skiffle King' Lonnie Donegan, 'You couldn't *buy* a guitar' (guitars were in short supply). Naturally, the guitar attracted youngsters in all parts of the country culminating in the birth of the Beatles and another wave of guitar adherents.

American jazz records began to trickle over to England but due to the dollar restrictions, the trickle was limited compared to today's huge output, but in spite of these limitations, a formidable array of jazz guitarists was heard in the '40s and '50s.

To name but a few dozen, here are some who have played something worth remembering:

Laurindo Almeida, Bernard Addison, Don Arnone, Irving Ashby, Chet Atkins, Billy Bauer, Dave Barbour (ex-husband of Peggy Lee), George Barnes, George Benson, Dennis Budimir, Billy Bean, Kenny Burrell, Charlie Byrd, Al Caiola, Al Casey, John Collins, Bill D'Arango, Herb Ellis, Tal Farlow, Barry Galbraith, Grant Green, Arv Garrison, Hank Garland, Tiny Grimes, Jim Hall, Bobby Hackett (the trumpet player who played guitar with the new Glenn Miller band), Al Hendrickson (Jerry Gray band), Charles Jagelka (Chuck Wayne), Barney Kessel, Mundell Lowe, Tony Matola, Wes Montgomery, Johnny Pisano, Les Paul, Howard Roberts, Tony Rizzi, Jimmy Raney, Sal Salvador, Johnny Smith, Toots Thielemans and Attila Zoller.

Chuck Wayne (b. 1923, New York)
The first post-war record to reach me from the U.S. with some outstanding guitar playing was one of the Joe Marsala Sextet playing *Cherokee* and *Melancholy Baby*, recorded 1.12.45 on the Black & White label, 18A. BW74. Chuck Wayne was then playing with Joe Marsala at the Hickory House in New York where the band performed on an elevated bandstand in the centre of the restaurant, above the oval bar which surrounded it.

On this record he was in the company of Dizzie Gillespie who inspired Chuck to great heights. In *Cherokee* Chuck demonstrated his phenomenal technique and fast jazz invention at a tempo of $\rfloor = 144$.

In 1946 he joined Woody Herman and made a number of recordings, one with the Woodchoppers on the American Columbia label, where he was featured in *I Surrender Dear* at double tempo and given credit under the identity of Charles Jagelka.

Charles or Chuck, was fortunate in serving a band which employed excellent arrangers, one of whom was Ralph Burns, who composed an orchestral suite for the band called *Summer Sequence* recorded on Columbia DB257819. Here is a case in point where the composer wrote one of the themes as a guitar solo and another in harmony with the woodwind thereby using the instrument attractively as another orchestral voice.

After leaving Herman and a period of freelancing, Chuck joined the original George Shearing Quintet which was responsible for the 'George Shearing' block chord sound and began a new fashion. They recorded many gems like *East of the Sun* and *Lullaby of Birdland* in a style which sparked off many similar groups, but in 1952 Chuck left George Shearing (who had by now adopted a more commercial policy) and spent about 6 months practising about 6 to 8 hours a day in order to be able to emulate the sound and technique of a blowing instrument. Ever since he had first heard Charlie Parker his ambition had been to advance his own style and in order to do that he gave up work for regular methodical practice.

I learnt something about Chuck Wayne's work and ambitions after a surprise telephone call in June 1955 when he was in London prior to a fortnight's provincial tour with Tony Bennett for whom he was acting as MD and accompanist. He needed an amplifier and asked if I could lend him one. Fortunately, I happened to have a spare one available and was able to oblige, while at the same time becoming more closely acquainted with his history and his method of practice.

Charles Jagelka was born in New York on 27 February 1923 and his father was a cabinet maker from Czechoslovakia.

Although Chuck began to play the guitar when young he had no formal tuition but taught himself through the old method of trial and error. He was of the opinion that no established school existed for the plectrum guitar so it was up to each player to improve his own playing. 'Physician, heal thyself' as it were. He divided his practice into scales and arpeggios so as to become absolutely familiar with the fingerboard. Scale practice was based on the major and minor chord shapes from which as many as eight different scales could be played in each position (as described in my handbook *Play the Guitar* – Foyles).

Arpeggio practice consisted of fingering a system of four string chords and their inversions from the lowest to the highest, commencing on the lowest four strings then transferring to the middle four and top four strings, using different types of picking, *i.e.* all down, all up or alternate down and up. His own ability to use any kind of picking in very fast ascending, descending or cross fingerboard runs, with perfect ease, proved the advantages of his research and he was good enough to permit me to add this arpeggio system to my *Book of Daily Exercises* (EMI).

His guitar was made by John D'Angelico, fitted with medium gauge strings, and he used a drop shaped pick of an inch in length with a very rounded point. So much for his technical details.

At the time he expressed the hope of making a solo LP as a vocalist and a guitarist, but actually a record was issued the following year of the Chuck Wayne Quintet on Savoy LZ–C14014 which included

Zoot Sims and Brew Moore, tenor sax, Harvey Leonard, piano, George Duvivier, bass and Ed Shaughnessy, drums, for which Chuck contributed four original titles.

During the early '60s he worked at CBS and later teamed up with another guitarist, Joe Puma, with whom he performed at the 1973 Newport Jazz Festival and hoped to do some interesting things. It had always seemed somewhat strange to me that a guitarist of such great ability and talent had never figured in the *Downbeat* Polls.

The solos he plays in *Cherokee* and *Melancholy Baby* should be of interest to guitarists if only to prove that the mainstream of jazz style has not advanced that much in the intervening years.

A short biography of all 36 guitarists I have so far mentioned could provide enough material for a whole book. Therefore, I will limit myself to those who have innovated new styles or those with whom I am personally acquainted or both

Arv Garrison (b. Toledo, Ohio, USA 17 August 1922 d. Toledo 30 July 1960)

First, I would like to mention Arv Garrison who today is probably completely unknown, although according to his playing in the period of 1946/7 he should have made a great name for himself. He showed a distinct individual and up-to-date style in a recording with George Handy (pianist and arranger with Boyd Raeburn's Band) of *These Foolish Things* and an original by Handy *Tonsillectomy* in the bop idiom.

Arv employed substitute chords to very good effect in *These Foolish Things*, his substitutions, in a way, being almost a standard blueprint of this type of substitution for a commonplace harmonic sequence.

For example the simple sequence of *These Foolish Things* beginning with
$||$ I vi $|$ ii V7 $|$ which is equal to $||$ E$\flat$ Cm $|$ Fm B$\flat$7$|$
becomes $||$ E$\flat$6 Cm $|$ Fm7 E7+9 $|$ E$\flat$ $^6/_9$ Cm$^7/_9$ $|$ F9–5 E9–5 $|$
and so on.

These harmonies allow the extemporisation of the melody considerable freedom which Garrison, with absolute calm and certainty, used in a most attractive rhapsodic way simply by adding the 6th, 7th and 9th to the major and minor chords.

If you could hear the 16 bars of *These Foolish Things*, they would act as a fine exercise in phrasing in the slow-free-flowing rhapsodic style.

A pity that Arv Garrison disappeared into the limbo of forgotten men.

Mundell Lowe (b. 21 April 1922)
When I first met Mundell Lowe in West 48th Street, New York during October 1964, he cut a handsome gentlemanly figure and, true to his demeanour, he took my wife and me to lunch in the nearby Italian eatery.

I was known to him and he had seen my guitar tutor. He had, in fact, been instrumental in selecting my first Gibson L.5 when I changed from my Epiphone Emperor.

Mundell was then a staff musician on NBC both playing and acting as musical director for the Merv Griffin Show and he also freelanced. However, his ambition was to compose and with this object in mind, he left the New York 'rat race' in 1965 and went off to Los Angeles to become a runner in the Hollywood 'rat race'.

He became quite successful writing for TV and films and, in fact I saw his name recently included among sub-titles of a Starsky and Hutch TV instalment.

In Hollywood Mundell enjoyed playing on jazz dates, organising Monday nights at Dontes as special guitar nights, including the special night in commemoration and in appreciation of the late Jack Marshall.

Mundell Lowe has on occasion been called 'the forgotten man of jazz' because of his lack of influence on guitarists internationally. Nevertheless, his playing and arranging show talent and very tasteful application on an LP he made for HMV GLP.1084 with his own *Mundell Lowe Quintet*.

The personnel is worth mentioning because there are two excellent session boys on one or other of the titles, Sal Salvador and Don Arnone (very well known New York studio musicians). There is also my old friend Trigger Alpert (late Glenn Miller Army Air Force Band) on bass, and Ed Shaughnessy, drums.

Mundell plays languid, luscious jazz and pretty fast jazz with a delicate tone. He also took part in the *Music Minus One* record, Vol. 3, which is well worth getting for the guitarist who wants to improve his playing to the accompaniment of a fine rhythm quartet.

He visited London for a holiday in 1974 and we carried on where we had left off nearly eleven years earlier as if there had not been any time lapse.

Although he spends a lot of his professional time writing, his greatest pleasure is in playing jazz with other guitarists. When we met again (February 1979) it was in Hollywood and he was playing guitar on the Merv Griffin Show – now based in Hollywood. How the circle closes!

Barney Kessel (b. 17 October 1923, Muskogee, Oklahoma)
One player who has stayed the course is Barney Kessel, the guitarist with the evergreen fingers and the fertile mind; musician, guitarist and philosopher. Born in Muskogee, Oklahoma of Hungarian-Jewish parents who were not very keen on their son becoming a musician, he, nevertheless, had a guitar at the age of 12 and by the time he was 14 was playing in an all-Negro band. He left school in the 9th grade after his question 'How will schooling help me to become a musician?' remained unanswered.

He met Charlie Christian when Christian came to hear him play during a visit to Oklahoma City in 1939 when they met for the only time and spent an evening together.

In 1942 Barney made his way to Hollywood and settled in Los Angeles playing in the orchestra with Ben Pollack and later became the leading guitarist on the radio networks and in the bands of Artie Shaw, Hal McIntyre, Benny Goodman and Shorty Rogers. It was in 1947 that he joined Norman Granz's 'Jazz at the Philharmonic' and toured with the Charlie Parker group and Sarah Vaughan. It was through this combination that I first became acquainted with his playing on an Esquire record 10-031 (D1072) of *Cheers* and *Carvin' the Bird*. The combination was called 'Charlie Parker's New Stars' with Howard McGhee, trumpet, Wardel Gray, tenor, Dodo Marmarosa, piano, Red Callender, bass and Don Lamond, drums, and was a prime example of cool basic bebop.

In *Carvin' the Bird*, Barney's solo was quite boppish but in *Cheers* it sounded positively like an extension of Charlie Christian. After that introduction I always kept an ear open for his playing, which was not a difficult task because of his association with the Oscar Peterson Trio whom he joined in 1952, and which brought him to the notice of jazz fans.

Listening again to Barney playing *Stompin' at the Savoy* and the *Astaire Blues* with the Oscar Petersen Quartet on Columbia 33C/1038 confirms Barney's attachment at the time to the Charlie Christian style.

The Vogue LDE085 (recorded in November and December 1953 in Hollywood under an exclusive contract with US Contemporary Records) which included Kessel's *Salute to Charlie Christian* still tied him to Christian's style, and it was not until 1954 on *Barney Kessel Volume 2* on Contemporary LDC 153 that Barney seemed to develop his own style with arrangements such as *Love is Here to Stay*, recorded in June and July 1954, although in Volume 3, Contemporary LAC 12058, he again lapsed into Christian. *Julie is her Name* (London Records HAU 2005) created great interest among guitarists as an example of a vocal accompanied by guitar and bass. Remember *Cry Me a River* (London Records HAU 2007)?

Then in 1956/7/8, Barney, in company with Shelly Manne, drums, and Ray Brown, bass, won the popularity polls of *Downbeat, Playboy* and *Metronome Magazines*, and to commemorate the occasion made an LP called *Poll Winners Three* on Contemporary LAC 12237 which heralded the winning of the 1959 *Playboy, Downbeat* and *Melody Maker* polls.

Barney's playing on this disc showed a distinct refinement of phrasing compared to previous records.

I first met Barney Kessel during the interval of a JATP show at the Gaumont, Hammersmith when we had a lot of fun singing and playing Charlie Christian choruses, but he soon out-distanced me with his extensive knowledge. Needless to say, we took to one another as if it were a reunion rather than a first meeting. That was in 1968 when George Benson and Larry Coryell were on the same bill. Coryell, the rock/jazz feedback innovator with the Gary Burton Quartet made his English debut at that time.

The following year Kessel returned to London as the star attraction at Ronnie Scott's Club and wrote to me before his visit offering to do anything he could to help guitarists. So I suggested that he gave a guitar clinic at the Musicentre. The event was a terrific success. The place was full to the ceiling. The audience was thrilled by Barney's artistry and he was very happy with their appreciation. His opening remarks began with:

'Although I have been playing the guitar a long time, I certainly don't know the answers to all the questions. There are a lot of things I can't do although I've tried to do them and given it up as a bad job. But inasmuch as I have been playing for 32 years, been blessed with a crazy kind of life and wide experience... I'm not being presumptuous or trying to give the impression that I'm the Great White Father and I've got the answers.... Many of you may ask questions that I've not even thought about.'

He is, nevertheless, a thinker who, after a great deal of deliberation, came to realise that for many years he had been entrapped in the session business. No sooner had this dawned upon him than he set about freeing himself by learning more about music. He became a composition and arranging pupil of Albert Harris and gradually emerged as a solo performer of distinction, concertising around the world Truly a musician of intelligence, vision, modesty and talent. A perennial performer who has endeared himself to guitarists all over the world. For the past eight years Barney has presented his annual guitar seminar 'The Effective Guitarist' in Britain, under the sponsorship of Musical Instrument Distributors, Summerfields of Gateshead. In May 1980 he gave his first master class for jazz guitarists in Britain. His dedication to the education of other guitarists is quite unique.

Tal Farlow (b. 1921)
When I was fortunate in getting hold of some copies of recordings of the Red Norvo Trio and first heard Tal Farlow it was clear that things would never be the same. Farlow had broken through the Charlie Christian barrier and moved guitar style into the 1950s which was singularly unusual considering that Christian had exerted a tremendous influence on Farlow.

According to Talmage Holt Farlow, born in Greenboro, N.C., he played a sort of North Carolina style – until he heard Charlie Christian. He was then about 20 and working in a sign shop when he listened on the radio to a broadcast of Benny Goodman's Band which, at the time, featured Christian on a rather extended solo. Later he recalled:

"First, I couldn't figure out what kind of instrument it was. It was a guitar of some kind, but at that time electric guitars were mostly all Hawaiian guitars. It had a little of that quality, but it was not that slippin' and slidin' business of a Hawaiian guitar. That was the first time I had heard an electric Spanish guitar. I copied his choruses – I learnt how to play them.'

Then he began to listen to other jazz groups and since he designed and painted the signs for the special locally held dances, he was able to obtain passes to the dances which were otherwise limited to only coloured audiences. In this way he heard Hampton, Basie, Andy Kirk and the Trenner Twins' Band which played like Lunceford. He also met Irving Ashby when he was playing guitar with Lionel Hampton.

In the early 40s Farlow played in dance bands in the Greenboro district, then he met pianist Jimmy Lyon stationed at a nearby air base who had a magnificent harmonic sense which stimulated his interest.

While playing with the trio of vibraphonist Dardenelle which moved from Philadelphia to the Copacabana Lounge in New York, he would go to 52nd Street every Monday where Charlie Parker was playing, hoping to hear him, and sometimes he was lucky. The music of Charlie Parker seemed so new and so different from what was previously being played. Farlow then returned to Philadelphia and worked at clarinetist Billy Krechmer's club in a trio with the owner on clarinet and Freddie Thompson on piano; since there was no bass, he would, at times, play bass lines on guitar. All good practice but no help in music reading to the natural musician who never took any lessons and did not read music.

When he returned to New York in company with Jimmy Lyon pianist and bassist Danny de Franco (Buddy de Franco's brother), the trio had hoped to get club dates while waiting the three months for their local 802 cards, but although piano and bass were easy enough to fix up, nobody required a guitarist who could not read or sing for gigs, so it was back to the sign shop.

Tal then took Mundell Lowe's place in vibist Margie Hyams' group at the Three Duces where he worked opposite Charlie Parker for two weeks and was really able to listen to him at close range.

In 1949 Tal was living in West 93rd Street with fellow guitarists Jimmy Raney and Sal Salvador, and the only one who was working was Sal whose father had a shop in Massachusetts from whence, every now and again, a food parcel arrived for Sal which was shared by all. They called it the 'Care' package. Jimmy and Tal played together a great deal because they both seemed to be the last to be called for work, but at the end of the year Tal became part of the Red Norvo Trio with whom he went to California, and the problem of work was solved.

When I first heard the records of the Trio (with Charlie Mingus on bass), I was doing regular broadcasts with my guitar group comprising Joe Mudele, bass, Dennis Wilson, piano, Billy Bell and Jack Llewellyn guitars and immediately wanted to throw my arrangements away. But instead, with the help of Dennis Wilson, wrote down some of the pieces and tried to adapt them for the group. We did *Zing Went the Strings of My Heart*, *Move*, and *I've Got You Under My Skin*.

I had only recently been to Paris where I had had my first concentrated earful of Charlie Parker and Miles Davis and I was well under the spell.

The Red Norvo Trio also recorded *God Child* (Davis), *Good Bait* (Parker) as well as the standards *I'm Yours*, *Night and Day*, *This*

Can't Be Love, If I Had You and *Dancing Cheek to Cheek*, and I think that these were some of the best recordings of Farlow, to me at any rate, that they were the heralding in of a new style of jazz guitar.

Farlow left Norvo in 1954 to work with Artie Shaw's new 'Grammercy Five', returned to Red Norvo, and finally left in 1955 when Sy Barron, owner of the 'Composer', a club in New York, persuaded Tal to play at the club with pianist, Eddie Costa and bassist Vinne Burke where he worked until his marriage in 1958. Since then he has given up professional work apart from a concert at the 1968 Newport Jazz Festival with Johnny Knapp, piano, Jimmy Booth, bass and Mousey Alexander, drums. Two of his most avid listeners were fellow guitarists Jim Hall and Barney Kessel both of whom had performed the previous night.

Tal Farlow was voted new star guitarist in the 1954 *Downbeat* International Jazz Critics Poll, similarly in 1956 for Leonard Feather's *Encyclopaedia of Jazz*, and in the *Downbeat* Critics Poll 1956/7, but apart from one recent LP he had removed himself from the arena but I was sure that he had not forsaken his interest in the guitar. No guitarist ever does, as I discovered in June 1977. He was supposed to have come to the NAMM Show to demonstrate a new guitar, made specially for him by Philip Petillo, but hurt his ankle in a fall at the dockside (where he permanently parks his boat), so once again I left the States without meeting him.

Jimmy Raney (b. August 20 1927, Louisville, Kentucky)
When I first visited New York in 1964, West 48th Street was the street of musical instrument stores. When the big liners docked at Pier 59, they disgorged a few dozen musicians who invariably made a beeline for W. 48th St., and probably to 'Mannys', who gave large discounts on musical intruments.

Next to Mannys, a cafe, 'Jim and Andys', was frequented almost exclusively by musicians, some who came down from the A&R studios on a floor above, from the Broadway theatres round the corner, band contractors looking for musicians, musicians meeting musicians, radio producers and musicians expecting telephone calls or making telephone calls. You could meet anybody and everybody there, and that is where I first met a not-too-happy Jimmy Raney, who at that time was working in the pit orchestra of *Hello Dolly* on Broadway.

Over his gin and tonic he related how hard times were for a jazz musician. If a jazz guitarist wanted to eat, he had to play in a regular job and since he was 'fed up' being hungry, he was working in the theatre in a job that any pro guitar player could do, but there was a silver lining. He was about to record an LP with Jim Hall, one of his favourite guitarists, the other being Tal Farlow. He had always wanted to do an album with two guitars and, he told me, it was soon to come about, especially when he found that Jim Hall was available. The record was called *Two Jims and Zoot* with Ossie Johnson, drums, and Steve Swallow, bass (Fontana TL 529Z), in which there are compositions by Jimmy Raney, Jim Hall and Gerry Mulligan.

In 1954 and 1955 Raney won first place in *Downbeat's* International Jazz Critics Poll, but never received the acclaim of their readers who, after all are only aware of the most publicised personalities. Jimmy Raney did not fall into this category, being of a rather reticent nature. He disliked touring and in fact he backed out of the 1964 Benny Goodman Russian tour after rehearsing with the band.

My first introduction to Raney's inventive and lyrical jazz was from a recording of the 'Stan Getz Quintet's Jazz at Storyville' with Al Haig, piano, Stan Koteck, bass and Tiny Kahn, drums, recorded in 1951 in which they play *Parker '51* at the breathless tempo of ♩ = 178 about 90 bars to the minute, in which everybody plays with great freedom, flow, and no sign of faltering.

Another thing I noticed about Raney was his subtlety which made him a guitarist to appreciate but not easy to emulate, *i.e.* for listening but not copying, and I must say that with Stan Getz and Al Haig he was in perfect company.

Unlike his contemporary and friend, Tal Farlow, Raney had lessons in music and guitar and was still a great jazz player. The reason I point this out is to contradict those who say that the ability to read music is detrimental to good jazz playing. Much depends on the individual; some can do both and others can do neither.

Jimmy Raney was the son of a journalist, and his mother, who played the guitar a little, showed him some chords when he took up the instrument at the age of 10, but after a few months he took first of all class lessons then individual from the same classical guitar teacher. By the time he was 13 he knew he wanted to play jazz and therefore went to a jazz guitarist named Hayden Causey, who taught at a music school attached to a music store, and in the course of learning, met other pupils with the same ambition. He was also informed about Charlie Christian. 'When I first heard *Solo Flight* (a Benny Goodman record featuring Charlie Christian) I almost fainted' said Raney.

In 1944 his teacher recommended Raney as his replacement in the Jerry Wald Band then playing at the New Yorker Hotel. During the couple of months he was with the band, the 17 year old Raney took many opportunities of going to 52nd Street and to Harlem to hear Charlie Parker, Dizzie Gillespie, Art Tatum and Chuck Wayne who, he thought, was one of the few guitarists playing close to the modern style.

Al Haig, who was the pianist with the Wald band, found Raney a kindred spirit in the admiration of the Parker-Gillespie school and they often practised together – and one can trace the Haig connection in Raney's development. Haig was to play and record with Parker and Gillespie the following year while Raney returned to Louisville for six months in order to listen and practise.

Raney's next move was to Chicago where he first worked with pianist-vibist, Max Miller, and met Lee Konitz, Lennie Tristano, and Lou Levy (piano) with whom he played in gigs with Jay Burkhart's band.

It was while the George Auld Sextet was playing in Chicago that two of the musicians, baritone player, Serge Chaloff and drummer, Tiny Kahn, heard Jimmy Raney and in January 1948 the latter recommended Jimmy to Woody Herman. They were strongly supported by Chaloff and Stan Getz, so Raney joined Herman in January and stayed till September in the superb band that recorded *Four Brothers, Four Others* etc. But, superb as the band was, it did not suit Raney who did not like spending most of the time playing rhythm. It was during this period that Getz, Haig, and Raney, made some records for the now defunct 'Sittin' In' label. In late 1949 he was living in a house in 93rd Street (as mentioned in the previous section) where the other tenants included Tal Farlow, Sal Salvador and Phil Woods (alto) and worked intermittently with Artie Shaw.

When Stan Getz returned from Sweden in the autumn of 1951, Raney joined his group and recorded the *Jazz at the Storyville* disc which has been previously mentioned.

In March 1953 he joined Red Norvo and enjoyed his year's stay which included a European tour in 1954, and while playing with Norvo made his first 10" L.P. under his own name on the 'Prestige' label in which Stan Getz played under the pseudonym Sven Codson.

In 1955 he made another 10" L.P. under his own name with a quartet which included Hall Overton (piano), John Wilson (sax), Teddy Kotick (drums) and Nick Stabulas (drums). This was issued on 'Esquire 20-054' and includes the titles *Spring is Here, Tomorrow*

Fairly Cloudy (Raney), *What's New?, One More for the Mode* (Raney), *A Foggy Day, Someone to Watch Over You, Cross your Heart* and *You don't Know what Love is*.

In order to be able to settle down with his wife, he took a job in the Jimmy Lyon Trio in the lounge of the Blue Angel Supper Club and took time off to play in a couple of Broadway productions in 1959 and 1960. He did not like to play overlong solos which he thought began to sound like a string of sausages; he never wanted to be a leader and was sometimes a reluctant soloist. He took up the 'cello as a second instrument in 1959 and studied for nearly three years in order to broaden his musical outlook. He liked the playing of Bob Brookmeyer and Lee Konitz but as for his own style he said he based it on 10% this, 10% that, 40% Parker and the rest Bartok. He uses a celluloid pick because it breaks-in in a day. A tortoiseshell pick, he said, never breaks in, it is always like new.

In the early 1960s he recorded *For Guitarists Only* on Music Minus One Guitar MMO4009 which he arranged himself and took part in MMO Vol 8, *The Rogers and Hart Song Book*, sharing honours with Joe Puma. He is quoted as saying:

'I have an ideal in music. I know I'll never reach it – it's not stationary – it changes like I do. An ideal is a sum total of your conception at the moment. It's a synthesis of the difference between what you can do and what you want to do'. Very wise words from a sincere and great musician.

In April 1977 he did a concert at the Shaw Theatre (London) in which he was accompanied by his son Doug. Jimmy was now fifty and his playing was more fabulous than ever.

After the show and supper, a small group of us including Maurice Summerfield and Ike Isaacs went over to Ronnie Scott's Club to see the 'Complete Jazz Soloist' Joe Pass who was drawing in fans from all over the country (Pete Chilver had come from Edinburgh).

This was the first meeting between the two talents and they had plenty to talk about. Joe had very much wanted to hear the Raney concert but pressure of work did not allow this pleasure. Jimmy's opening remark after the initial delight at meeting was: 'Mr. Pass I presume?' 'Yes, Mr. Raney' or would it be the other way round.

Billy Bauer (b. 1915 New York City)
If Tal Farlow was the first jazz guitarist to break through the Charlie Christian barrier, Billy Bauer was the only guitarist of the period to deviate from the bebop road.

My first awareness of Billy Bauer was through a 10" 78 disc on Keynote K-647B recorded in New York, 8 October 1946 in which he played with Lennie Tristano (the jazz avant-garde pianist of the era). One side was *I Can't Get Started* and the other *Out On a Limb* by Tristano, aided by Clyde Lombardi on double bass. It was clear from the start that Lennie Tristano was the master and Billy Bauer the disciple. It was also clear that the guitar style was unaffected by either Charlie Christian or Charlie Parker. The melodic line (if it can be termed melodic) was based on moving harmonies played in quaver and triplet phrasing in what might be termed free phrasing torn asunder from the robust rhythmic feel of jazz.

The piano playing in *Out On a Limb* proved that Tristano could play extremely rhythmic chordal jazz but it still left the guitar meandering rather than bouncing. Nevertheless I suppose Bauer's fresh approach brought him into prominence which resulted in the *Downbeat* Awards of 1949 and 1950, and the *Metronome* Awards from 1949 to 1953. He also became a member of some famous bands, namely Woody Herman and Benny Goodman, and played with Charlie Parker, Miles Davis, Lee Konitz and Lennie Tristano.

But the other musician whom I always associated with Billy Bauer is Lee Konitz, also a Tristano disciple, with whom he recorded in the 1950s. In fact, by the time Billy Bauer recorded *You Go To My Head* and *Palo Alto* with the Lee Konitz Quintet on Esquire 10-205, he had absorbed some of the characteristics of Lee Konitz. He did an excellent job of 'comping' (that is chordal gentle rhythmic accompaniment) using rich chromatic harmonies and passing notes, while *Palo Alto* shows his ability to play in duet with the alto saxophone at a fast smooth tempo.

On the Esquire disc No. 10-280 recorded on 7 March 1951 with the Lee Konitz Sextet with Miles Davis on trumpet, Billy Bauer's playing showed the additional influence of the Miles melancholia and the Charlie Parker intervals, although in *Duet for Saxophone and Guitar* it is in rather free form or, as Lennie Tristano sometimes called it, 'collision type' playing.

Around the 1950s the Tristano/Konitz/Bauer school had quite an influence on the jazz players of the period and both Tristano and Bauer recorded with 1948-49 Metronome All-Stars conducted by Pete Rugolo. Other famous players in the band were Dizzie Gillespie, J. J. Johnstone, Charlier Parker, Buddy de Franco, Fats Navarro, Charlie Ventura, Shelly Manne, Kai Winding and Eddie Safranski.

Billy came from a poor uneducated family, as he relates. His father was a 'half-baked vaudevillian' who left school in his seventh year of schooling and left home to go to work. 'It's like a history of unsuccessful people, not in living or dying or being happy, but, as far as leaving any great wealth, at least, in an artistic way. My mother was another half-educated type of person. I don't mean stupid. She just didn't know how big the world was. So she was content to play church organ. I got bought a little organ when I was 14'.

When Bauer was 15 and playing banjo, his father put him into a local radio amateur show where he performed for 15 minutes once a week. Then in 1931, he worked in a club seven nights a week and began to double on guitar. This was followed by a job in a tavern in the Bronx where he stayed for two years, giving up the banjo for electric guitar which he claims he was one of the first to play. 'A year or two later' he says, 'Remo Palmieri was playing it on the West Side and I was playing electric guitar on the East Side'.

Later he joined Abe Lyman's Band and when he applied for tuition at the Juillard School of Music, he was refused because he did not have a high school diploma. He regarded this as very intolerant on their part, and to prove it he had the satisfaction of giving a recital there ten years later in the company of Lennie Tristano.

Today, Billy Bauer's main interest in life is teaching people how to play guitar. Not just how to play a few tunes but how to be a musician who plays guitar.

New Yorkers are, indeed, fortunate to be able to learn the guitar from the Billy Bauer Guitar School, Willis Avenue, Albertson, Long Island, NY 11507 where he has also founded a guitar playing club where pros and semi-pros can get together. Occasionally there are special clinics attended by leading lights like Barry Galbraith, Jim Hall and Barney Kessel.

Johnny Smith (b. 25 June 1922, Birmingham, Alabama)
What has made Johnny Smith's name a byword in electric guitar playing? It was not his jazz extemporisation because as far back as 1952 I heard him taking a chorus on a Benny Goodman Sextet record and although it sounded technically brilliant, it was not outstanding jazz. But later he recorded *Moonlight in Vermont* which I first heard on the US Royal Roost label 1108.1953 and that whole conception of arranging for the guitar threw a different light on his musicianship and originality. (This record was later issued here on Vogue 2137). What had he done that was so different? Well, he closed some of the

gaps in voicing, which generally other guitarists had not considered. Although both Tal Farlow and Billy Bauer did use some close harmony in their chordal playing, they did not make a feature of it. Sixth chords on the guitar sound surprisingly different when the sixth is placed next to the fifth as, for example, the first chord in *Moonlight in Vermont*, voiced C E G A on the 4th, 3rd, 2nd and 1st strings.

When I published a transcription in the *Melody Maker* of 6 February 1954, many guitarists doubted that this stretch spanning from the 10th to the 5th fret was possible, and I often had to demonstrate that one could hold the first finger down on the 5th fret at the same time as fingering the 8th, 9th and 10th frets of the 2nd, 3rd and 4th strings with the 2nd, 3rd and 4th fingers.

It was Johnny Smith's close harmony playing that led me to arrange *8 World Famous Melodies* as a solo guitar album. Voicing apart, Johnny Smith produced the most luscious rich round tone ever heard.

When some of my musician friends met him during a visit to Birdland in the fifties, they remarked about his modesty and friendliness apart from having been thrilled by his playing.

His first inspirations were Segovia, Django, and his father who played a 5-string banjo. During the 50s Johnny Smith won most awards for jazz; *Downbeat* Jazz Critics' Award, *Metronome* Poll; *Downbeat* Best Jazz Guitarist; and the Award for the Best Record.

He retired from the session business and opened a musical instrument store in Colorado Springs also concentrating on guitar clinics. He has also written some arrangements and a two-part tutor published by Mel Bay with the title *The Johnny Smith Approach to the Guitar*.

It is worth noting what he says about the advent of the umpteen watt amplifiers. 'The loud sound was dishonest to begin with. I have never been able to get on the bandwagon of selling these kids on the big amplifiers because it was really dishonest. Some of the big manufacturers would take the same components and put them in a bigger cabinet and although they improved the sound a little, they would mark up the price a lot. And these people who bought all this junk are back at the dealers trying to unload it. This puts the dealer in a bad spot because if he doesn't take them back, he's going to make an enemy'.

And them's my sentiments.

Life is full of surprises. During 1976 Johnny Smith came to London as part of a small jazz group accompanying Bing Crosby for a short season at the Palladium. When they opened I was away in Sweden (visiting Levins, the guitar makers who had been taken over by C.F. Martin) and had no idea that a guitarist who had been such an influence on my style was actually within calling distance.

On the Monday of my return home a fellow came into the shop and said to me 'Do you know Johnny Smith's in town?' to which I replied 'So is Ivor Mairants'. But it transpired that he had a message from Johnny Smith to say that he would like to meet me. Rather surprised but happy, I telephoned him and invited him and his wife to lunch.

When he arrived at the shop I was testing a new electric device and told him that he was the guitarist who had had a most profound effect on my playing. He is very shy and quiet with many talents, including that of a professional airplane pilot and instructor.

He brought me regards from Mel Bay who had come to see me during his two-day visit to England a few years back and who publishes his *Johnny Smith Approach to the Guitar*. The few hours we spent together were all too short but I was able to demonstrate the different excellent guitars we stocked; I would much sooner have heard him doing the playing.

A year later he returned to London, again with Bing Crosby and I had the pleasure of seeing them at the London Palladium, sadly, as it turned out, less than a week before Bing died on the golf course in Spain.

About Johnny Smith's playing, I can say without fear of contradiction that he has *the* cleanest fastest plectrum technique of anyone I have ever seen or heard. His performance with the Joe Bushkin Jazz Group was impeccable, demonstrating a relaxed right hand co-ordinating with a perfect left hand fingering technique.

I hope that my new guitar tutor *Perfect Pick Technique* conveys what Johnny Smith does in practice.

Jim Hall (b. 4 December 1930 Buffalo, New York)
Every guitarist who has heard Jim Hall perform affirms to his unique jazz talents. It has been said of him that he is self-effacing and almost deprecating in assessing himself, but be that as it may, the construction of his jazz, solo or counterpoint, is uncluttered, perfectly formulated, as carefully constructed as a Bach fugue, and played with warmth, certainty and conviction.

When he played at Ronnie Scott's Club in the late '60s, he insisted on turning his volume down to the extent of retaining the natural sound coupled with the rich timbre. The audience simply had to keep quiet if they wanted to hear the subtle changes of harmony. One particular incident well illustrated his sincere and honest character. He had just finished his first performance and came up to my table for a chat, when a musician who had attached himself to him almost dragged him away with the excuse that there was little time between shows to have a meal. Jim, looking embarrassed, allowed himself to be pulled away and that was that. I did not see Jim again before his departure from London, but on the day he left, he telephoned me to say good-bye and to apologise for the rude behaviour of his companion that night at Ronnie's. Ever since, he has shown his sincere friendship.

I first heard him in the the Chico Hamilton group during 1958, then with Jimmy Giuffre Three, and in the early '60s that remarkable LP with Sonny Rollins called *The Bridge* (RCA Victor 2527), to be followed by *Undercurrent* (United Artists 15003) with Bill Evans. Each one of these albums is exceptional for its originality.

Whenever a musician proves himself to be exceptional, people interested in the subject wonder what influenced him; in fact, on a recent BBC broadcast, John Taverner, the composer, was asked this very question to which he answered Messien, Boulez, Cage and Stockhausen, with one anti-influence, Schoenberg.

How about Jim Hall?

His first introduction to the guitar was by his uncle who played 'folk', and he had lessons at the age of ten. By thirteen, he was working professionally and became interested in jazz. The first jazz record to come his way was *Air Mail Special* by Benny Goodman with Charlie Christian, whose playing in *I Found a New Baby* was one of the most perfect things he had ever heard.

When he was sixteen, Jim Hall's family moved to Cleveland where he was again lucky to have a good teacher *and* a job playing with a band in which some of the members were a great help to him, introducing him to the playing of Lester Young (tenor) and the styles of Lennie Tristano. He also studied arranging with Joe Dolney and took a music degree from the Cleveland Institute of Music.

At the same time he was studying privately with a teacher who introduced him to the playing of Django Reinhardt. Nevertheless he felt that he could not get much further in Cleveland and therefore went to Los Angeles to pursue his studies at the UCLA, but was introduced to Chico Hamilton who was looking for a guitarist so he accepted the job.

Hall stayed with Hamilton for eighteen months, then joined the Jimmy Giuffre Trio, but in 1960 left to join Ella Fitzgerald for European and South American tours, to be followed by a ten week tour with Yves Montand, the French actor and singer. On his return to Los Angeles, he formed a trio which developed into a quintet and included Ben Webster, but he had an urge to return to New York, against the advice of his friends.

After working with Lee Konitz for about four weeks, Jim Hall said 'Everything got very cold – the weather, the chances of jobs, everything'. Then came an inexplicable absence of work – a position only too well known to musicians. Jim got so far into debt that he thought he would never extricate himself.

I can confirm this, not that it needs confirmation. In the autumn of 1964 I went to see Eddie Bell at his West 49th Street Guitar HQ. We were talking about Jim Hall when he told me that he gave Jim spare guitar strings for a recent tour because he was unable to pay for them. A terrible situation. Also, coincidentally, Mundell Lowe, then one of New York's leading session men, confided to me that there was no future for him in New York, and he was going to set up a TV Jingle Agency in California, which he did in 1965.

It so happened that he left a vacancy in the New York based Merv Griffin TV show, and Jim Hall jumped at the chance of a steady job. It was also in 1965 that Jim Hall married. Eventually the Merv Griffin show moved to Hollywood after three years, the guitar chair to be filled there by Herb Ellis. Nevertheless Jim Hall, his marriage, his fame and fortune, have continued to progress favourably.

On one of my visits to the NAMM Show in June 1973, Jim Hall sent me a letter via Jimmy D'Aquisto to tell me that my old friend, Bill Finegan, was a close friend of his and would like me to contact him in Long Island.

Jim Hall's dream is to use the guitar as a complete solo instrument, and one can be sure that his musicianship will not be wanting, but ever changing, ever growing.

Kenny Burrell (b. 31 July 1931 Detroit, Michigan)
Kenny Burrell comes from a musical family which, in another way, means that other members of his family are musical.

His father plays banjo and mandolin, his mother played piano and sang, and both his brothers (who are his seniors) play the guitar, the older one being the pioneer guitarist.

Although Kenny wanted to play the saxophone, there was not enough money to buy one, and since a banjo was not considered an instrument of sufficiently serious content, the guitar became the chosen instrument. As an afterthought it was something which might attract the girls.

Kenny is generally a serious minded person, and even when he had only been playing a year (at the age of 13) he was keen on becoming a jazz player.

During the following 10 years he played in local groups and in the Miller High School Dance Band, later entering Wayne University. He then took lessons in classical guitar from Joe Fava (a teacher and guitarist of some note) which helped him with his reading and other facets of playing, and at the age of 25 majored in music. 'That does not help me with my work on the bandstand' he told me in 1969 when he was in London playing at Ronnie Scott's, 'but the education has helped me as a person to understand the world around me more than I could otherwise have done and to understand my problems, musical and otherwise'.

He financed his further education from his own earnings as a professional musician from the age of 16. Said he 'How else can one's education be paid for if your parents cannot afford to do so?'.

His first main influence was Charlie Christian, then Oscar Moore and Django Reinhardt as well as Art Tatum, Charlie Parker and Segovia. He has a great admiration for Segovia who 'has done more than anybody else to bring about respectability for the guitar'.

Kenny worked with Dizzie Gillespie in Detroit during 1951 and made his recording debut with him, later joining Illinois Jaquet (tenor) and worked in Detroit until he graduated in 1955. He left Detroit in 1955 to go for a six months' tour with the Oscar Petersen Trio which took him to New York where he was engaged by Hampton Hawes (the piano modernist) for a further tour.

Returning to New York, he worked with organist Jimmy Smith and even joined Benny Goodman at the Waldorf Astoria staying with him for about a year.

Besides being able to extemporise, Kenny, being a good sight-reader, did well in the session business with Kenny Dorham, Gene Ammons, Jimmy Smith, Paul Chambers and Frank Wess, and led his own group on Blue Note and Prestige labels.

I had first heard of him in 1962 when I came upon his work in a title called *Winners Circle* on Esquire Records and when I was in New York in October 1964, I heard he was working in a bar-restaurant called 'The Nag's Head' in uptown New York, leading his own quartet of guitar, piano, bass and drums. I sat enthralled listening to this well-knit group, playing just the type of free jazz improvisation I liked, and later asked Kenny why he was playing in such an out of the way spot. His reasons were quite clear; he had been working in two Broadway shows for a couple of years which was followed by sessions and wanted to free himself from the rigour of orchestral work or written arrangements, so he formed his quartet and was free to play whatever he pleased and to develop some of the ideas he had been bottling up during the previous few months.

This policy was beginning to pay off, because he was about to record a solo session with a big band, to which he invited me. I believe the title of the LP was *Guitar Forms* on MGM's Verve label.

Kenny cuts a handsome figure as he stands up and plays his D'Angelico or Gibson L.5 guitar confidently and without histrionics, allowing his rich tone and smooth phrasing to speak for him. His technique could be termed traditional by today's standards and he uses a firm pick varying his strokes as we all do and using his fingers whenever suitable. His one outstanding characteristic is his orientation to the blues. 'Blues' he says 'is a valuable ingredient that is providing the world with popular music today. It is like gold which can become debased until its adulteration makes it worthless. I feel obligated in promoting the natural beauty of the blues. Credit should justly be given to the Negro musicians of America for having brought this about; especially now, because there are not many young people who are old enough to understand this'.

Kenny takes a rather aloof intellectual stand about the music he plays and, in a quiet firm way, is a torchbearer for the music of the American Negro. That he has delivered his message is clear, if his success can be measured by his topping the *Downbeat* Poll for a number of years since 1968 and his continued output of LPs.

He again visited England in the early '70s as solo accompanist to Sammy Davis Jnr, a brilliant artiste who doesn't suffer fools gladly. I've worked for him! And I do not think there is a performer with a higher artistic and musical IQ than his.

Kenny's last visit to London was in January 1976 when he repeated his successes at the Ronnie Scott Club.

George Barnes (1921-1977)

The United States is rich not only in the number of its jazz guitarists but also in the variety of different styles produced by a number of performers born within the same five year period.

The years between 1919 and 1924 saw the birth of Barry Galbraith, Sal Salvador, Jim Marshall, Bill de Arango, Arv Garrison, Chuck Wayne, Barney Kessel, Tal Farlow, Johnny Smith, Herb Ellis, Chet Atkins and George Barnes, all of whom have distinctly recognisable degrees of similarity or individuality.

George Barnes however stood apart from all the rest in terms of both tone and style.

To quote a choice morsel from my friend Benny Green's review of the Ruby Braff, George Barnes Quartet in the *Observer* of 9 March 1975 'If the members of the group had just been loosed on the world after spending 30 years in a hermetically sealed compartment, they could not present more sweetly anachronistic delights than they do'. The news that the chunky, cheery George Barnes passed away aged only 56 shocked and upset me very much; we were both chunky chappies with great affection for one another.

In New York recording studios, he used to be known as 'The Organiser' but, alas, the studios are poorer for his passing. He died of a heart attack on 5 September 1977 in a hospital in Concord, California where he had been living, working and teaching since 1975, and had made an LP to be released on a Concord Jazz label.

He was born about 20 miles outside Chicago, Illinois, in Chicago Heights on 21 July 1921, and began to play the piano at the age of four, but a few years later when the depression hit the United States, the piano had to be sold to provide food for the family. A keen musician, even at that age, he found an old guitar which he learnt to play and by the age of 14 was sufficiently advanced to join a professional group. He told me that although he was then earning only $26.50 per week, he was the sole breadwinner of the family.

Although the club 'Spina's Casanova' was owned by the Al Capone Syndicate, gangsters used to treat the musicians very well even though one of the musicians was accidentally wounded by a stray bullet.

Musically, George's influences were mainly blowers rather than pluckers and he learnt a great deal from jazz clarinettist Jimmy Noone. In fact, he was able to play the blues so well that he was a regular featured member on many Race Records, accompanying some of the leading black blues singers. Reviewers often credited his work on these records to some unknown coloured guitarists.

Due to the Race Record connections he used to be asked to join other musicians in playing at 'rent' parties which took place after normal working hours. 'Rent parties' were set up to help poor black folk to pay their rent and everyone who attended contributed what they could afford and so saved the unfortunate tenants from being evicted. Few guitarists have had such an exciting and eventful career. At the age of 17 he joined the staff of the National Broadcasting Corporation in Chicago where he not only played the guitar but arranged the music and conducted his own group.

Then the war came and he was drafted into the US Army Intelligence Service where he became an Intercept Operator. Due to his hobby which was amateur radio and helped by a keen ear, he was good at morse code and intercepted and decoded enemy messages.

He was discharged in February 1946, and returned to Chicago where he joined the American Broadcasting Company, this time as Musical Director and Conductor which gave him many creative opportunities.

For five years he led an octet which, between them, played clarinet, bass clarinet, saxophones, oboe, cor Anglais, flute, piccolo, piano, vibraphone, bass and drums and he not only experimented by arranging for various combinations of instruments but also regularly wrote new compositions.

In 1951 a disc jockey friend of George's advised him to have a crack at the New York broadcasting and recording world and George did so, never looking back. He joined Decca as conductor, arranger and soloist as well as working on Grand Award and Mercury labels. In fact it was his extensive freelance connection, during which time he worked with most of the leading recording stars of the time that 'won' him the name of The Organiser.

In 1963 he formed a guitar duo with Carl Kress, playing concerts at places like the New York Town Hall and in 1964 fitted in a season at 'Birdland' on Broadway.

A highlight came to the duo when they were invited by President Johnson to perform at the White House Christmas party on 17 December 1964 and it is hard to imagine two guitar players alone providing dance music for 1,500 guests.

On one of my visits to George's apartment in New York he showed me the painting which was presented to him by the President together with a letter from Mrs Johnson which ended 'Please know how much the President and I appreciate your kindness – you made many people happy. . . .'

I can recount many interesting coincidences happening in my time but here is one concerning George. During 1966 I was asked to record a jingle for TV and the producer had heard a piece called

Something Tender which he wanted me to arrange; I discovered that *Something Tender* was a George Barnes composition recorded on United Artists with George, Carl Kress and Buddy Freeman on tenor sax (Jazz LP UAJ14033), and I duly taped it for TV using Judd Proctor on second guitar and Tubby Hayes on tenor.

Unbeknown to me, at that time George (whom I had never met) had been on a strenuous tour of Sweden and Czechoslovakia with Paul Anka and stopped over for a few days holiday in London. While in London he accepted a concert engagement and I was called in to play second guitar. Naturally I was pleased and when we met to talk over the programme, I asked him to play *Something Tender* and surprised him by playing Carl Kress's part, while he played the melody.

From 1969 to 1972 he teamed up with Bucky Pizzerelli and one of the results was a terrific duet record which received many airings in England.

Many readers will remember the Ronnie Scott season in 1975 when he appeared in the George Barnes-Ruby Braff quartet.

I well recall one night when John Williams was there, and George, his wife Evelyn, Wayne Wright and myself were discussing the music that had just been performed and John expressed his admiration for George's guitar playing.

I feel that the theme of *Something Tender* made a fitting requiem to this appreciation so I arranged it for two guitars in his memory. It was published in *Guitar* magazine of November 1977. The last time we met was in New York in July 1975.

Here is a list of some recordings:
George Barnes Living Guitar Method. LP (Chappell); *Ten Duets for Two Guitars*, with Carl Kress – Music Minus One 4011; *Town Hall Concert*, United Artists, VAL3335; *Guitars Anyone?* Carney LP M202; *Ruby Braff-George Barnes Quartet*, Chiaroscuro Records CR.121; *To Fred Astaire with Love*, RCA, APC1,1008.

Chapter Fifteen

WALKING WITH WES

If I were to include potted biographies of all the good jazz players I have heard it might become as interesting as a Musicians Union Directory so I will conclude these chapters with the dozen or so great jazz guitarists I have met or whose playing have made a special impression on me.

Bill de Arango (b. 20.10.21 Cleveland, Ohio)
One of the latter is Bill de Arango who played in the recording of the *52nd Street Theme* by Dizzie Gillespie's band, a very popular tune of the 50s at very fast tempo. The outstanding solo of this exciting and exhilarating bit of fun is the absolutely even and non-stop phrasing by De Arango executed in a very cool manner with a tone which can be described as round as a circle. It is absolutely distinctive and worth mentioning if only because, like a firefly, he disappeared at dawn (from the recording world at any rate) and has a music store in his home town of Cleveland, Ohio.

Herb Ellis (b. 1921 Texas)
Not so with Herb Ellis whom I met when he played at the Kilburn State in London with Oscar Petersen and Ray Brown in 1954. He confessed that when he took over in the Oscar Petersen Trio from Barney Kessel, he was not used to the inversions he was required to play, but after a little time and a lot of hard listening, he developed a wonderful 'comping' style of accompaniment which is well illustrated in his book *Herb Ellis Guitar Styles*.

He plays with an incisive attack and his blues style is easily recognisable. Guitarists in London who heard him imitating a conga drum or bongo effect, soon pricked their ears up and tried it for themselves by pressing the strings lightly, high up on the fingerboard, so that they did not touch the frets or fingerboard, and picked the pitch required.

For a boy who was born in the country near a town called Farmersville, Texas, and raised on a farm, he built a very fine reputation with musicians and has played with Jimmy Dorsey, Ella Fitzgerald, Dizzie Gillespie, Roy Eldridge, Stan Getz, Della Reese and Jazz at the Philharmonic. He also made a fine duet record with Charlie Byrd on CBS.MONO BRG.62552, recorded in 1965, and since 1961 he has lived in Los Angeles and until very recently worked as a studio musician, taking part in the Merv Griffin and Johnny Mann TV shows. Today he realises his musical freedom is more important than regular studio work.

Herb is one of those who never took lessons on the guitar, but when he was at the North Texas State College he met other jazz players including saxophonist Jimmy Giuffre and with him introduced jazz to the music class of the College.

His biggest guitar influence is Charlie Christian and he was also influenced by Lester Young and Charlie Parker. He and Joe Pass, formed a group featuring this unique two-guitar sound. Also with Joe Pass he has written a book of jazz guitar duets.

He used a Gibson ES.175 which he called an 'honest guitar', meaning that whatever is put in comes out. He does not like solid guitars which he sometimes has to play.

We met again in October 1978 when he came to London in company with Barney Kessel and Charlie Byrd (a group known as 'The Great Guitars') and he looked young and healthy and played beautifully. There was an added maturity to his phrasing, and his rendering of *That Rainy Day* was masterly.

Charlie Byrd, who partnered Herb Ellis on the CBS record I mentioned, carved out quite a different career from Ellis. His claim to fame is his adaptation of the nylon-strung guitar to the jazz field and his story will be found at the end of this section.

Barry Galbraith (b. 18.12.1919)
During the late 40s when I was playing with Geraldo, we used to salute a different American band each week on the programme *Tip Top Tunes*.

One week came the turn of Claude Thornhill's Band and this particular recording had a marvellous jazz guitar chorus (in *Anthropology*) which I played as part of the salute. I discovered that the guitarist was Barry Galbraith.

During 1954 or thereabouts I was in Dusseldorf, Germany, at the Musical Instrument Fair when I heard that Stan Kenton was on a European tour, and that the nearest he came to Dusseldorf was Dortmund, where he was performing at a late night concert.

Knowing that Barry Galbraith was playing in the band, I prevailed upon a German friend (Freddie Wilfer of Framus) who had a car, to take me to Dortmund at the end of the day's work, and after a mad dash, arrived to hear most of the concert which featured some sensational jazz saxophone playing by Lee Konitz, Frank Rossalino (trombone), Neil Hefti (trumpet), Zoot Sims (tenor) and Stan Levy (drums). In short, it was an absolute 'knock-out' and I was thrilled, especially as I could not have heard them in London where they played exclusively for the US Armed Forces.

After the show, I introduced myself to Barry Galbraith and showed him a piece of manuscript I had prepared with his solo from the Thornhill band and asked him if he recognised it. He was very puzzled but admitted ignorance and it was not until I played it to him and told him where it came from that he began to recognise it as his own solo! Of course, it caused a good laugh after which he introduced me to the other musicians and to Kenton who seemed to have a cool, tolerant personality tinged with sardonic humour.

The next time we met was in London where we and our wives became a little more friendly. He wanted to swap me his Stromberg acoustic 'cello guitar but my family would not allow me to dispose of my Epiphone Emperor which I had been using since 1938.

Barry returned to New York and to his lucrative session connection, and the next time I heard him was in the Sauter-Finegan band – I knew he was one of Bill Finegan's favourite guitarists.

On 16 January 1959 Barry recorded an L.P. for Brunswick (L.A.T. 8273) known by the title *Guitar and the Wind* comprising a rhythm section with Ed Costa, on piano, and Ossie Johnson, drums. In addition there was Bobby Jaspar, flute, and four trombonists including the outstanding Urbie Green. Inspired by some very interesting arrangements written by Billy Byers, Barry stepped out of his usual important but relatively unheralded presence and became the principal speaker.

Barry's earlier influences were Lonnie Johnson, Eddie Lang and George Van Eps, but later it was Charlie Christian. 'If you hear Charlie Christian in my playing, it is no accident. I would feel a sense of fulfilment when and if my way of saying things took on the artless spontaneous feeling that was Charlie's calling card'. So says Barry Galbraith who, today, has vacated the bustle of New York to live a quieter life in Vermont and to-date has written two study books on Jazz Guitar, arranged and recorded 15 Bach Inventions and has become one of the most sought after teachers in the New York area.

Attila Zoller (b. 1927 Hungary)
During September 1957 an International Guitar Congress was held in Erlangen, a university town not far from Nuremberg in South West

Germany at which I was invited to play at a televised concert, and a surprise awaited me.

While I was watching the proceedings during one of the concerts a guitarist walked on to the stage and accompanied by the German house band proved himself to be the best jazz player at the Congress by producing some Tal Farlow style jazz with absolute ease and panache.

His name was Attila Zoller of Hungary whose father was a music teacher in the Budapest Conservatoire of Music He did not waste any time before teaching his son the violin at the age of four. When he was ten he had had training in harmony, violin and trumpet and became a member of the school symphony orchestra. The German invasion of Hungary put an end to his schooling. In April 1945 the Germans were expelled, by which time Attila was attracted to the guitar and making quick progress, found regular employment.

Hungary being limited in more ways than one, he found work in Austria, Turkey, Germany and Sweden, playing with dance bands and his own group but it was not until 1954 that he began to concentrate on jazz. Living in Frankfurt in the American Zone of Germany had its effects and he was influenced by Billy Bauer, Lennie Tristano, and Lee Konitz.

He found his way to the U.S. in 1956 where he was lucky enough to work with Max Roach (drums) and Clifford Brown (trumpet).

He returned to Germany where I first heard him and wrote of him that 'he plays as good jazz as the best'.

During 1959 Oscar Pettiford (bass) was working in Europe and persuaded Attila to emigrate to the U.S. and once again, he had the good fortune to find work with Chico Hamilton, replacing Jim Hall who had just vacated his chair. He did some work with Kenny Burrell and after six months joined flautist Bobby Jasper's Quartet, then he spent three years with Herbie Mann.

He recorded an LP for Mercury Records entitled *The Horizon Beyond* in an avant-garde style. His talents in composition have brought him work for three films one of which *The Bread of our Early Years* won the Bundes prize in Germany. He has also played a concert at the New York Carnegie Hall which, according to Ira Girtler, *Downbeat* critic, 'showed a couple of Django touches and a lot of inventions of his own along the way'.

It's a long way from Budapest to New York both in life style and music style, but it seems the bridge can be crossed if one has the ear and the talent. Zoller has still another talent and that is for electronics in the pick-up field where he excels. He is a bubbling person, always ready with new ideas and with a smile, and has figured high in many *Downbeat* polls. On 26 May 1976 he recorded an avant-garde piece called *Dream Bells* with bass and drums on ENJA 2078. This lasts nearly 19 minutes and takes up a whole side. Two more of his compositions are heard on the other side. I saw him again in 1977 in Atlanta when he, George Benson and I were trying out George's new guitar (the Ibanez Benson model).

During 1979 Attila recorded *Jim and I*, an L.P. (L.R.40.006) with Jimmy Raney consisting of almost free extemporisation apart from Raney's *Hommage a Bach*. Two more L.P.'s on ENJA label followed; *Conjunction* (3051) solo guitar and *Common Cause* (3043) with Ron Carter, bass, and Joe Chambers, drums. In the title *Meet*, Attila particularly displays his advanced jazz musical thoughts.

Jack Marshall (b. 1921, El Dorado, Kansas, d. 1973 California)
In enumerating guitarists who have helped to develop the guitar in jazz as known and practised by the players I have mentioned, there comes to mind a man who has innovated or introduced the guitar as a background to film music.

Before Jack Marshall wrote his exciting arrangements for the TV series *The Deputy* starring Henry Fonda, backgrounds were more or less orchestral, but when Jack Marshall (himself a good guitarist) had startled everybody with his quartet of guitars, 2 electric, 1 rhythm and 1 bass guitar, things were never the same.

He had a Masters degree in engineering but due to his love of guitar, took a staff job for MGM playing the instrument. Then he began to take lessons with Albert Harris (my old friend) and was amazed at what could be done.

When I met him in Chicago during the NAMM Convention in 1973, he told me that after his first arranging lesson with Albert, he was so excited that he could not sleep, but sat up working at his lesson all night and ready for more instruction.

Jack was the inspiration and mentor for the guitar development of his cousin, Christopher Parkening, America's most popular classical guitarist, and his arranging and conducting engagements went far and wide. Incidentally, his lead guitar on all the quartet work in the films was, whenever possible, Howard Roberts, one of Hollywood's busiest sessioneers.

It is not generally known that Jack Marshall was compiling, producing and editing a recorded history of the guitar for *Time and*

Life magazine under the title *The Wonderful World of the Guitar*, and, in fact, he asked me to contribute the duets recorded by Albert and myself when he heard about them, but, alas, this was not to be. Later that year – in September to be exact – Jack Marshall was sitting at home watching the tennis 'match' between Billie-Jean King and the challenging amateur, when his wife came into the room to ask if he wanted a drink or something and found that he was no longer alive.

A bitter blow to the guitar world and to everybody who knew him. The amount of energy and bonhomie that radiated from this one man was phenomenal, and although I had met him just once, I felt a real personal loss which hurt. It still hurts when I think of him as he was in Chicago – full of life, energy and ideas.

Wes Montgomery (b. March 6 1926, d. 1968)
The last in the line of great jazz guitar innovators was fated to follow in the wake of Lang, McDonough, Christian and Reinhardt and die before his time. And although there are some great players on the scene today (and my own favourite is undoubtedly Joe Pass) no new guitarist has taken the big stride that moved guitar style into the 1960s such as the playing of Wes Montgomery demonstrated.

He had done what the great guitarists mentioned here had been unable to do – play in an instantly recognisable way. Not another Charlie Christian or, to some extent, another Tal Farlow.

The LP *The Incredible Guitar of Wes Montgomery* on Riverside was the starting point of Wes's fame, and by 1962 he had become the acknowledged leader of jazz guitar style, or as Ralph J. Gleeson had labelled him in 1960, 'the best thing to happen to the guitar since Charlie Christian'.

He was born in Indianapolis and for some time worked in a steel mill, playing the guitar after work. He was, in fact, a hard working married man with a family of 6 children, who developed this highly personalised style over a period of 10 years or more, before anybody outside his home town heard of him, although he played with Lionel Hampton between 1948 and 1950.

It was Cannonball Adderley who brought him to the notice of Riverside Records for whom he recorded *Wes Montgomery Trio* (RLP.1156), *Incredible Jazz of Wes Montgomery* (RLP.1169). He is also featured on *Work Song* Nat Adderley (RLP.1167). then on 2 October 1960 Wes recorded *Movin' Along* (with Britain's erstwhile boy wonder drummer Victor Feldman on piano) (RLP.342) and is featured on *Cannonball Adderley and the Poll Winners* (RLP.9355) with Ray Brown.

On 3 January 1961, he recorded *Groove Yard* (RLP.362) with the Montgomery Brothers, Buddy (piano), Monk (bass) and Bobby Thomas (drums). Later, he recorded many discs for Verve and AM Records. Among some of the best are *The Best of Wes Montgomery* and *A Day in the Life* (AML.2001) showing how to be commercial and hip at the same time, playing with an orchestra of piano, bass, drums, 3 percussion, flutes, woodwind, French horn, 12 violins, 2 violas, 2 'celli and harp, arranged and conducted by Don Sebetsky and recorded 6, 7, 8 and 26 June 1967. This record reached the top pop charts.

On a technical note, most guitarists probably know that his method of right hand motivation was by means of his thumb alone, resting his fingers on the body of the guitar to the right of the top (1st) string. In fact, Messrs Gibson made him a special L.5.ES with a heart shaped mother-of-pearl inlay below the cutaway section as a finger rest.

Wes did try changing to plectrum in order to help him play faster single note runs, but he could not get on with it to satisfy himself, so he reverted to the thumb which he says brings him closer to the strings and produces more of the tone that he likes. As he adds 'You don't have to play fast!'

Although he was known for his octave playing which became almost a commercial feature, he did not, of course, invent it; but his great use of octaves brought them to all guitarists' notice to the extent that most jazz players included octaves to be fashionable. Wes was not only an innovator of style using single strings and octaves, but with chordal solos as well. In fact, when he came to London in 1966 to appear at the old Ronnie Scott Jazz Club for a month, he played such phenomenal solos that it more or less seemed miraculous for one human being to be able to invent so much music and play it with such rhythmic lift and heart without being able to read music at all. I have, personally, never derived the same measure of amazement since my first Segovia concert in 1937.

He came to the shop a few times and played on various guitars and asked me to demonstrate some of our excellent concert guitars which seemed to please him. He confessed that he felt absolutely lost when trying to play with the fingers of the right hand and to show how honest he was about it, he tried hard to play finger-style but made such a dismal display that we had a jolly good laugh about it.

Although he could not read music he could remember any new piece of music after hearing it once, no matter how intricate.

He was straightforward, natural and an easy companion to be with, and always ready to show you anything you wanted to know about his playing.

His playing inspired me to write a new guitar solo I called *Walking with Wes*, a study in octaves and jazz which I played to him for his delectation. He gave me permission to put his photograph on the cover.

During a meal of spare ribs (his favourite food) I asked him if I could write a treatise on his style with his collaboration but he said that it was not possible because he had promised Ray Brown (the bass player) the rights for any such publication. *The Wes Montgomery Jazz Guitar Method* illustrating his style and including a number of his recorded solos was, in fact, published in 1968 by Robbins Music Corporation with music edited by Jimmy Stewart but, unfortunately, he did not live to see it.

Whoever would have dreamt that this excellent father, husband, companion and generous human-being, full of life and vigour, would be stopped in his tracks by a failing heart at the age of 43? First Lang, followed by McDonough, Christian, Reinhardt, then Montgomery, all falling far short of their three score years and ten, but all leaving great legacies in their short span of professional life.

Hank Garland (b. 11.11.1930, South Carolina)
Wes Montgomery exerted a great influence on jazz guitarists during his short reign of about 7 or 8 years although, apart from his innovation of octaves which became standard, his general style had more of a subtle effect, in contrast to Charlie Christian whose phrases are more easily recognisable.

One might say that Joe Pass's relaxed phrasing and tonal qualities bear some resemblance.

There is however one almost forgotten guitarist who, in the normal way, would certainly have been recognised as one of the best but, due to a bad car accident, was unable to, continue his very short brilliant career. His name is Hank Garland, born in Orangeburg, South Carolina, who began his professional career by playing in *Grand Ol' Oprey* then in Nashville, and became the busiest session guitarist of his time being featured behind all the singers playing Country and Western. But in 1961 he made a long playing record issued on the Phillips label BBL.7475 with the title *Jazz Winds From a New Direction* in company with Gary Burton (vibes), Joe Morello (drums) and that great bass player, Joe Benjamin (who died in 1973).

Hank Garland's playing was really like a fresh jazz wind but with strong influences of Wes Montgomery and more subtle ones of Tal Farlow, Charlie Christian and a sprinkling of Barney Kessel. Garland's *Three Four Blues* particularly has very close connections with Montgomery's *West Winds* his signature tune, but Garland in contrast to Montgomery uses a little reverb which brightens the tone but at the same time softens the attack of the pick in contrast to Wes's thumb.

Garland sustained damaging injuries in an automobile accident and, try as he might, was unable to continue professionally, but I have been told by another American guitarist that Garland's sessioneering friends were so shocked by his inability to continue working that they took it in turns to sign their recording slips with Garland's name in order to help with his livelihood. True charity indeed.

George Benson (b. 22 March 1943, Pittsburgh, Pa.)
If proof be required that Hank Garland had an effect on other guitar players, let us hear what George Benson (whom I met in 1968) said about the subject. He said he was a great Charlie Christian fan himself, but he liked the modern boys too, but it was when he heard an album by Hank Garland that he realised all the possibilities of the guitar.

Benson left school at the age of 17 and formed a little Rock & Roll group in which he sang. At 18 he was engaged by Jack McDuff to play in his group and here he discovered how far behind he really was. He said:

'Grant Green made the greatest impression on me. Before he went out on his own, he got his first recognition with McDuff, too'. About Wes Montgomery: 'He's a wonderful musician, a kind of virtuoso, but that wasn't the groove I wanted to get into. As a matter of fact, I felt I could never get that far!'

Those are some of the impressions of a player who achieved fame in the early 70s, adopting a fast driving style, but in 1977/8 he became a superstar playing and singing on some of the fastest selling LPs in the history of jazz guitar. At the end of 1967 there was a great gathering of American guitarists in London playing the concert circuit in a show known as 'Jazz Expo 67' and among those on exposition were Barney Kessel, Jim Hall, George Benson and Larry Coryell (born in Galveston, Texas 1943).

Larry Coryell made the most startling (explosive) impression for his mixture of jazz, rock and use of feedback effects which was certainly the main talking point among the guitarists in the audience, and Coryell was the guitar bombshell with the Gary Burton Quartet of vibes, guitar, drums and bass. This was the first time Barney Kessel and I met and it was like a reunion of old friends. George Benson was new to me so I wanted to know all about him.

'Well', he said, 'five years ago I tried to improvise. I never thought I'd be able to fit in; I was too clumsy. They told me never to use my thumb. Then Wes Montgomery came out. I was using the diminished chord but they told me that was incorrect. But these were guys who didn't know what they were talking about.... my challenge was trying to improvise – when I got with a group that was playing jazz. You know, I figured other people do it, why can't I? I never, never thought about technical facility. I always thought 'What's the music?' You should be able to play any tempo, any song'.

In answer to another question he said, 'Well, it's possible for other musicians to hold back a player's individuality. Like they told me never to use my thumb. I found out because Charlie Christian showed Grant Green how to hold his thumb and Grant showed it to me'. (Grant Green, according to my information, was born 6 June 1935 and Charlie Christian died in 1942 so this point seems a little doubtful. *I.M.*)

Question: Charlie Christian showed him? How old is Grant Green? Benson answered: 'He's close to 40. My father (actually, stepfather) taught me to play.... He never thought that there were any guitar players after Charlie Christian. Of course there were but he doesn't recognise them.... I've been learning for the past 10 years and I have made good headway. But not compared with what I could have'.

George Benson did make more headway and to prove it he returned to London in 1974 for a season at Ronnie Scott's Club, full of confidence.

When George Benson and I met again it was in quite different circumstances. The place was Atlanta, Georgia, USA where the American Music Trades held their annual fair in 1977.

George, who had by now become a millionaire due to the sales of his LPs (and it couldn't have happened to a nicer person), had also won every award going. He was there demonstrating the qualities of Polytone Amplifiers and the Ibanez George Benson model guitar.

He performed a concert in the Omni Auditorium and his playing was masterly. I had never heard him sing before and I was amazed at the fluency and jazz feeling he poured into *Georgia on My Mind*. I found it thrilling. The previous day we had met at the Polytone stand and he asked me to try his new guitar. I took it and happened to select a fairly fast jazz piece called *Jordu* which must have caught his ear as he was talking to somebody, for he stopped and watched me, never having heard me play before. When I had finished he said to me 'I wish I had your right hand technique'. Since his technique is superb I was nonplussed and asked him what exactly he was referring to. He said he was referring to my right hand freedom in picking across the strings in comparison to his rather awkward, angled position resting his hand on the pickguard.

Attila Zoller (a mutual friend) had also been watching and agreed with him. I was overwhelmed at the compliment coming so spontaneously, and later on, giving it some thought, could not bring to mind a published method specifically dealing with right hand picking and decided to write one. When I mentioned the incident to Mr. Hansen, my publisher, he agreed that a book of this kind was timely and the upshot was *Perfect Pick Technique* which I dedicated to George Benson and Attila Zoller. Good company is hard to beat or, as it is said, 'By your friends ye be judged'.

Howard Roberts (b. 2 October 1929, Phoenix)
One of the busiest studio musicians in Hollywood is Howard Roberts whose name I first heard in 1957 from Bobby Troup (the composer and pianist) when I was working with Julie London, accompanying her in the film *A Question of Adultery*. A little later in the year I again heard about his activities from Robert Farnon and his brother who was on a visit to Bob. He was, they told me, a great all-round guitarist and making a big name for himself in Hollywood. Therefore, when his first record was issued here I was very anxious to hear it. It was entitled *Mr Roberts Plays Guitar* on Columbia 10″ LP 3309038 and was recorded under the personal supervision of Norman Granz.

Oddly enough the sleeve portrays Mr Roberts sitting on a long piano stool with his ES.175 guitar in an upright position with the florentine cutaway on the left side, thereby falsifying the evidence, making it appear that he is left-handed which he is not.

His tone on this record was rather hard and cold, his jazz good and his technique excellent.

He received the New Star Award in the *Downbeat* magazine for 1955 and since then has become recognised as the leading studio man in Hollywood.

When I was in Los Angeles in 1969, Albert Harris, one of Hollywood's leading arrangers, told me he always used him as lead guitar and that he was a phenomenal reader. I finally had the pleasure of meeting him in 1973 when he was demonstrating guitars for Gibson at the Chicago Music Fair.

Howard Roberts took music seriously and began to study its problems and those of the guitar at the age of 17 and is a past product of the Schillinger School. He has become one of the great names in electric guitar playing more due to his regular studio work and connection with arrangers and conductors than to his jazz records and appearances and it would be hard to detect more than general jazz influences in his playing. I met him again in Chicago in 1975 demonstrating Gibson guitars accompanied by Bruce Bolen (English born all-round guitarist, who is an important person in Gibson's executive team). Roberts' performances then had a distinct rock, avant-garde flavour, proving that since leaving the Hollywood session scene he had developed enormously.

He has also written some excellent jazz tutors and has embarked on a career of advancing the music of the guitar.

Joe Pass (real name Joseph Passalaqua b. 15 January 1929, New Brunswick, New Jersey)

It is my opinion that Joe Pass produces the most effortless jazz played today by any guitarist, and listening again to one of his first solo records *Catch Me* (on Fontana Pacific Jazz 6881372L), I would say that he has done so at least since 1963 when this LP was recorded.

In 1962 he was unheard of by most guitarists yet by 1963 he was voted in first place in the 11th Annual *Downbeat* International Jazz Critics Poll.

Where was he before then? It's a long and sad story but one that can bring hope to those unfortunate enough to find themselves in like circumstances.

When he was nine years of age, he thought he would like to have a guitar and his father (who worked in a steel mill), bought him a cheap Harmony flat top, but what is more to the point, recognised some musical talent in his son, and tried to help him along the road. Helping a child in music means keeping his nose to the grindstone whether he likes it or not. Joe would have preferred to go out in the street and play ball but instead he became a good guitarist, so that when he was thirteen years of age he was sufficiently competent to play with groups. Later, he went to New York where Harry Volpe had made quite a name for himself both as a performer and as a teacher.

Harry Volpe told me that Joe was a youngster when he came to him for tuition, but after two lessons he stated he was not going to continue. When Harry asked for the reason, young Joe replied that he thought he knew more about the guitar than his teacher. Such is the brashness of some teenagers.

However, being away from home and strict parental guidance, Joe was sucked into the drug habit. Having read about past difficulties I asked Joe 'What set you off on the road to Synanon?' (the narcotics rehabilitation centre in Santa Monica, California). He replied frankly and thoughtfully:

'It all started when I split from home. I got the opportunity to go on the road when I went off with groups and trios. And I got introduced to drinking and all that. I was rebelling really and although I wasn't influenced by knowing that other jazz players were on to it, there was a point where there was a definite identifying with that because it was part of the whole scene. It's just part of the environment and still is; but I thought that was the way to go and I went from one thing to another and that's how I got started. I got heavily involved and people were saying "You'd better cool it, you'd better stop" but, I mean, I couldn't hear anything they said. Everybody, people close to me, my family, I didn't hear them, you never do.

'Well, after a certain number of years, everybody that gets involved starts to realise and see that this is not it, so you look for a way out and the difficult thing is that you can't find that way out, and it can be right there in front of you, but you can't utilise it; you can't do anything about it. Well, I'd been through a lot of other places looking for a way out; you see, you have to be ready for it or you won't get out. So I was ready and I was looking for years. And in one of the places I was in, I heard about this self-help group place and it's funny because I didn't plan on going there; I just stumbled on it when I was in Los Angeles. I even ended up in the same town and there it was. So maybe it was an accident but I'd planned at the back of my mind to find a way out. But that's how I got to it, I just walked up to the door and said "Here I am". I was there for $2\frac{1}{2}$ years. I didn't do a lot of playing then. In fact, when I got there the guitar had absolutely no meaning for me and they said "OK the guitar, put it in the corner and forget it".

'Like you don't play the guitar because that's something that stands in your way. So I didn't play the guitar for a long time. I did other things like straighten out my head and my person. Later, I maybe played the guitar on Saturday and then perhaps Friday and Saturday. But the most I feel I've accomplished has been after that scene. Using drugs didn't help me to play, all it did was to hang me up for about 15 years.'

Joe Pass came to London in 1974 as part of a European tour with the Tommy Flanagan Sextet accompanying Ella Fitzgerald. During their fortnight at Ronnie Scott's Club there was standing room only, but the most spoken of feature was Joe Pass's solo accompaniment to Ella's singing. Joe, in his quiet unassuming and unobtrusive manner had demonstrated his unique artistry, so much so that in the autumn his visit to Ronnie's was as soloist accompanied by Tony Crombie on drums and Lennie Bush on double bass. He was absolutely tremendous. He tried to show other guitarists how he 'did it' in a clinic which I arranged and the hall was packed with enthusiastic guitarists. It all seemed so easy but then great technical ability never looks difficult.

Joes says he loves the guitar but his first love is his wife and family, then comes the guitar. A great artiste and a simple human being who has developed into a wit with no mean sense of humour. He has also become the complete guitar soloist, quietly and confidently performing without accompaniment.

Joe has a number of tuition books published, the first one being *Joe Pass Guitar Styles*. When I asked him what made him write it, he replied that he used to teach a guitarist named Bill Thrasher who suggested that since the exercises Joe prescribed would be so valuable to guitarists, why not put them down in the form of a book and tape? This seemed a good idea and with the help of Bill Thrasher the book was compiled.

I am pleased to say that I discovered this book early on and immediately presented it to British guitarists. His latest creation is entitled *Chord Encounters for Guitar* illustrating the blues chords and their substitutes and in my estimation it is the clearest exposition of chord substitution ever published. Anybody interested in the subject should easily be able to grasp the principles from the book and two records. Published by Charles Hansen, it has already been translated into German and is assured of world sales. It deserves all the success it will surely have.

Tommy Tedesco (b. 3 July 1934, Niagara Falls, New York) Tommy Tedesco became well known a few years ago as a studio player in Hollywood and then through his articles in *Guitar Player*, the American guitar journal.

In his *Studio Log* (published monthly) he gives details of the music he plays, time taken and amount earned. For example the log for 24 to 26 October 1978 lists: *Project:* Movie 'California Suite'. *Leader:* Claude Bolling, *Hours Worked:* 15, *Wages Earned:* $1,236.15, *Instruments Played:* Ramirez Classical.

In the musical example, he illustrates the method he uses for simplifying the actual written part so that it can be sight-read with little practice and more certainty. Furthermore, since it's written for classical guitar and Tedesco uses a pick (even on a nylon-strung guitar) alteration of the original score is necessary for smooth playing.

I cite this example in order to give the reader a picture of the Hollywood pressures – where time is money and more important than music played exactly as written by the composer.

I had the good fortune to hear Tommy play at the booth of a music publisher during the NAMM Fair in Anaheim (Southern California) during January 1979 and I was struck by his fluency of phrasing and relentless drive. He was being accompanied by 32-year-old Ted Greene on an old Fender Telecaster, and although Ted is not a studio musician, he is one of Hollywood's most original practitioners of jazz guitar. His style is a mixture of chord voicings and single string lines and he is the author of some very good books on jazz guitar playing.

But to return to Tommy Tedesco, who works as a studio musician from 30 to 40 hours per week. We were able to have an hour together while he was waiting to record some music for Elmer Bernstein in one of the studios at the RCA building on Sunset Boulevard. He told me his first recollection of the guitar was at the age of nine. 'I heard a guitar player at a party and I knew I always wanted to play guitar. I told my dad, (who was an insurance salesman), and he was happy to pay for my lessons on plectrum guitar with John Morrell. Although I had lessons for three years and learnt to read music, I hated studying. So I did not practise and consequently was a bad student'.

At the age of 12 he ceased playing altogether and apart from sporadic bouts, left any serious connection with the instrument until he left school at the age of 16. He then joined different groups who were playing in the district and again developed an interest which has never ceased.

Eventually, he joined 'Ralph Marteri and his Orchestra' and went on a three-month tour which ended in California in 1953. California, its sunshine and its musical prospects are difficult to leave behind so he decided to stay there. But studio work was not easy to obtain; it was a long slow process of pushing through in the face of competition from other guitar players.

Today he is considered the number one, which means that he has first call on many of the film and record sessions that take place in the local 47 area of the American Federation of Musicians which incorporates Los Angeles.

Tommy is, of course, a terrific sight-reader, and my old friend Albert Harris tells me that some of the guitar parts are so frightening that he himself would be unable to tackle them. Albert is a friend of Tommy Tedesco and has a very high regard for his ability.

While Tommy was talking to me, he was playing a Mexican-made classical guitar with a plectrum and it reminded me of myself when I have a guitar in my hands. Now I know how the other person feels when he or she is speaking to me 'through a guitar'.

The great influences in his formative years were guitarists Tal Farlow, Jimmy Raney and Barney Kessel, but he was too young to have appreciated the work of Charlie Christian who died when Tommy was only eight.

Not only is he on constant call but never knows what instrument he may be required to play until he arrives at the studio. He therefore travels with a complete selection of fretted instruments housed in a fitted cabin trunk about 5' long by 4' high by 2' deep plus a large amplifier and speaker which are taken from studio to studio by a transport company and charged to the employers.

On this particular occasion, after waiting for over an hour, he was called upon to play the banjo for about two minutes in order to provide atmosphere for an 1863 street scene in a bustling Western town. Tommy provided the music on a four-string Vega plectrum banjo tuned D G B E (like the top four strings of the guitar) and busked an appropriate tune. Although the session was booked from 4 to 7 pm the work lasted about 10 minutes.

Although the work is sometimes of little musical value, the high calibre studio musician is treated with respect by the musical director who, in some cases (as, for instance, this one), treats the musician more as a musical collaborator than an employee.

'Mr. Tedesco' says Elmer Bernstein (composer of the theme for the movie *Exodus* and many other films), 'would you play some music giving an impression of hustle and bustle going on in the busy street of a mid-nineteenth century Western growing city. As if there were somebody playing behind an open upper storey window', and Mr. Tedesco almost immediately puts pick to banjo and produces a melody in two-four time with eight-sixteenth notes to the bar which more or less captures the atmosphere. But to make sure, Mr Tedesco is asked to come into the control room where the scene is shown on a TV screen so that it can be soaked in before the music is recorded.

This time it is a 'take' while Elmer Bernstein, head lowered, sits next to Tommy Tedesco, listens and assesses. A playback follows, the music fits, and the session is over.

The musician gets paid not just for his ability to play but also for his ability to use his imagination and his store of musical knowledge. And now Tommy has some time to spare before his 7 o'clock studio call. This leaves him time to go home to his wife, three sons and a daughter (aged from 27 to 10). One can see that he takes a responsible attitude to his family as well as his work.

He has two record albums to his credit both on Discovery Trend Record label, namely, *When do we Start?* and *Autumn* in which he demonstrates his ability on both electric and acoustic guitars. He has also written a book entitled *For Guitar Players Only* which is a worthwhile addition to the jazz guitar literature and contains a full list of his credits. As for that ever increasing problem 'sight-reading', there is no short cut. He says "You just go on reading everything that comes your way, and the more you read the more recognisable the notes. It's tough but it pays well".

Les Paul (b. 1916 Waukesha, Wisconsin, U.S.A.)
Les Paul is unique in the world of electric guitar playing. He is an innovator of a style of playing, of a recording technique and a pioneer of electric guitar construction. He has had many honours bestowed upon him in the United States and today he is active both in playing the guitar and improving pick-ups and recording techniques – in fact, *a living legend.*

I became intrigued with his playing as early as 1946-1947 when I wrote in the *Melody Maker* about his recordings for Brunswick with his trio. In analysing the style of his solo in *Blue Skies* (Brunswick

3656A), I wrote that it was reminiscent of Django Reinhardt, but it was not until about 1973 that I discovered that Les was one of Django's greatest admirers. In fact, Les made a special pilgrimage to Paris in order to meet Django, but when he arrived there Django was nowhere to be found. In desperation Les found a co-operative taxi driver, told him to try and locate Django, and gave him part of a five dollar bill which he tore in half with a promise to give him the other half when he came back with the information. The taxi driver returned to collect the other part of the bill and took Les to Fontainbleau where Django greeted him with open arms.

While I was working with Geraldo, Robert Farnon, the composer/arranger, asked me if I had heard Les Paul's multitrack record of *How High the Moon* which Bob thought absolutely great. Of course I had heard it as I had heard most of his others including *Brazil, Lover, Caravan* and *Vaya Con Dios* backed by *Deep in the Blues*, a guitar solo.

When Bob Farnon spoke to me about *How High the Moon* he had no idea that in later years he was going to be involved with that piece, for Bob had saved the day for Les when Les Paul and Mary Ford performed at the Royal Command Performance at the London Palladium in 1952. Bob happened to be conducting the band, and only half the band parts had arrived from America for his signature tune *How High the Moon*. 'Don't worry' said Bob. He took the few orchestral parts that were available, wrote out a new set of parts for the rhythm section, and added the parts for the brass section, all without the aid of a score. It had never sounded so good and Les prevailed on Bob to re-orchestrate the rest of the show, with the result that the American musicians who used the parts later on went wild about the sound.

I first met Les in 1952 when he topped the bill at the London Palladium, and I threw a party for Les and Mary at my Central School of Dance Music, to which I invited my guitar colleagues. For a superstar (and he was one even then), he was very modest and being in a foreign land I think in retrospect that he was rather quiet. Having since met him a few times in his own country as well as in London, I realise what a great entertainer and raconteur he is.

Although I first met him in 1952 and we had some correspondence, our next meeting did not take place until 1973.

It was at McCormick Place, Chicago, venue of the Trade Fair of the American National Association of Musical Merchandisers. As I have previously mentioned I was on Jimmy D'Aquistas's stand playing one of his guitars. Someone stood casually by and when I'd finished playing, he looked at me and said 'Hi, don't you remember telling me not to hook my strokes!' I had not recognised him, but recognised his voice and the audacious advice I had been presumptuous in offering during a technical discussion twenty years or so earlier in London.

I was both delighted to meet him again and flattered to think that he remembered me. Later that week, I saw him during my visit to the Gibson guitar plant at Kalamazoo, where he was working on some new electronic guitar project in connection with the Les Paul guitars for which he acts as consultant.

By 1975 he was again playing, and when I heard him at the Pick Congress Hotel in Chicago he was absolutely on top form, giving two or three shows a day at the Gibson display. The man's energy was boundless and he travelled to Europe later that year doing solo concerts, sometimes accompanied by his son Bobby on drums. As Les said 'I've got 50,000 dollars' worth of guitars around the house and he's got to be at these damn drums!'

We met again at the Excelsior Hotel, London Airport where he agreed to do a concert on the way back from Paris to the States. As he was coming down the aisle to climb on to the stage, he spotted me and such is his friendly nature, that he stopped to say how glad he was to see an old friend like me in the audience.

His concert, during which he had live accompaniment, and for which he used a normal Les Paul guitar with low impedance pickup and his special Les Paulveriser guitar which he used in conjunction with a pre-recorded tape, was inspirational.

It inspired me to write a guitar solo dedicated to him, namely *A Bundle of Blues*.

After the concert we went up to his room where I switched on a tape recorder and we just chatted. Well, what he had to say covers almost the complete history of the plectrum and electric guitars. The fruits of my labours appeared in two issues of the *Guitar* magazine dated November and December 1975.

There are always new guitarists coming to the fore in the world both in Great Britain and particularly in the United States, but to write of all of them would take a whole book.

I must, therefore, leave new trends like John MacLaughlin's move to esoteric East-West-jazz-rock-plus electronics and a further development to a flat-top six-string guitar with sympathetic strings stretched diagonally under the 6-strings, to another occasion.

Perhaps one day I will delve into the flock of great British electric guitarists like Alan Holdsworth, Jimmy Page, Martin Kershaw and the many others who can perform almost any style to order.

Chapter Sixteen

THE NYLON STRUNG GUITAR IN POPULAR MUSIC AND JAZZ

Three guitarists must be placed in a special catagory, *Chet Atkins*, who plays jazz and country music on electric acoustic guitar and classical music and arrangements of the classic guitar pieces on a classical guitar; *Charlie Byrd*, who plays jazz, Latin-American and classical music on an amplified classical guitar, and *Laurindo Almeida*, who is really a classical player but is adept at any style, from *Bachianas Brasilieras* to *Tea For Two*, via his own Latin-American compositions. His marvellous sight-reading ability and his versatility have made him a prime favourite for guitar backgrounds in Hollywood films.

These players have had a great effect in inspiring guitarists to develop the range of their finger-style playing, both technically and rhythmically.

Chet Atkins (b. 1924)
I once wrote a survey about jazz guitarists and only mentioned Chet Atkins in passing. The result was a small storm of criticism from his devoted fans and followers who considered him the greatest of all guitarists.

Chet Atkins is an extraordinary guitarist whose neat and tidy swinging picking is sufficiently unique to have inspired a myriad of followers. It is a cross between country music, ragtime and jazz and is absolutely free and uninhibited in its performance.

I had, of course, heard him on records, but had never seen him perform or met him until June 1977 when, after a special performance in the Peach Tree Plaza Hotel, Atlanta, Georgia, I was introduced to him by Les Paul and, being the country gentleman that he is, said 'Oh, I know about you, I have one of your books!'

After seeing his performance, I began to understand why this highly entertaining personality and innovator of his own style of picking has received so many awards, including being honoured with a permanent plaque in the Country Hall of Fame in Nashville. Nashville is the extraordinary city in the state of Tennessee where a whole district is devoted to the music industry, and in the section known as Music Square, Chet Atkins has his office in the RCA Building. Besides his millions of record sales, he is also an important figure in the artistes' administration side of the RCA Company.

To return to the Atlanta concert, where Chester was keenly watched by Lester (Les Paul) who was sitting near me; Chester sometimes engaging in entertaining cross chat with Lester (they made a hit LP entitled *Chester and Lester*). The first half consisted of a solo performance on a nylon-strung guitar including *Falling Leaves*, and an equally fascinating version of a camouflaged *Just a Song at Twilight*, making a feature of harmonics.

He thanked a guitarist named Tommy Covington for making him aware of harmonics, but the way Chet incorporated them into his arrangement was both remarkable and enchanting. Such clarity demanded not only neatness and tidiness but absolute accuracy and definition.

Listeners to the classical guitar are used to hearing the usual changes of tone colours but Chet also added many rhythmic variations to the tone changes – rock, blues, bossa nova, boogie and two separate melodies intertwined at the same time in *Lady Madonna*.

He has a great admiration for the classical guitar and its repertoire, and to prove his words he played the Sor Variations on *O Cara Armonia* from *The Magic Flute* by Mozart. The difference happened to be his swinging bass notes in a strict tempo version, that is, until the last three variations. I do not think I will ever be able to play this again without expecting someone to 'take the mickey'.

After a few more pops he swung strongly into *Black Mountain Rag* before changing to his acoustic electric Gretsch guitar aided by piano, electric bass guitar and drums. With the electric guitar in his hands he assumed, what is known from Nashville to Nizhni Novgorod, as the Chet Atkins Style, and it is this style which has influenced a complete section of the guitar playing world. His complete command of the independent bass and melody lines interspersed with chord and arpeggio self-accompaniments is as fully orchestrated as the playing of a solo pianist. If there is any shortfall, it is in the single string jazz improvisation. Not having previously paid much attention to his recorded output, his arrangements of *Oh, By Jingo, You'd be so Nice to Come Home to* (both in constrasting styles), his pleasant singing, *September in the Rain, Jack the Knife, Oh, Mr. Sandman (Bring me some Sand!!!), Freight Train*, a medley of titles recalling Elvis Presley, Jim Reeves, Perry Como and Donovan, were all like a new discovery to me. So was the fascinating carillon call way of arranging *Mission Bells are Ringing*; while the comedy effects in a vigorous performance of *Yakety Yak* as a square dance gave me more than an inkling of the many faces one guitar, in the hands of an original artiste like Chet Atkins could provide.

And one can understand why he was nominated for the *Grand Ole Oprey Hall of Fame*. It couldn't happen to a nicer guitar picker.

Charlie Byrd (b. 16 September 1929, Chuckatuck, Nr. Suffolk, Virginia, USA) Charles L. Byrd has played the guitar since childhood when he began under the tutelage of his father. It was folk music then, followed by joining local bands during his high school college days at the Virginia Polytechnic Institute. When the war came he served in the 424 AEF Band, touring Europe, then settled in New York after his discharge.

Byrd had the good fortune to meet Django while in Paris towards the end of the war, and Reinhardt's enormous skill amazed him.

Django, he told me, not only had a terrific ear but the best pick technique of any player living, which Charlie thought was a balancing factor against his crippled left hand. He was also the only completely identifiable non-American jazz player he had ever heard, an opinion I thoroughly endorse.

In 1950, after his first marriage, he moved to Washington DC in order to devote his full-time to the study of classical technique, as a pupil of Sophocles Papas, to whom he was introduced by classical jazz guitarist, Bill Harris.

Papas, a well-known teacher and friend of Segovia, who gave Byrd tuition for about three years under the aegis of the Bill of Rights (open to ex-servicemen) arranged an audition with Segovia and in 1954 Byrd went to Siena and studied in the Summer Music Academy sponsored annually by Count di Cigi.

Byrd considers Segovia 'the greatest guitarist ever on the face of this earth. He has helped me a great deal, in his own way he is a good teacher although he doesn't teach technique. He teaches interpretation .... I came back from Italy with a lot of confidence in my own ability and a clearer idea of how music should sound'.

He spent some years playing with the trio at the 'Showboat' Club in Washington, playing every type of music. There Woody Herman heard him and thought that 'Byrd was the complete answer'.

In 1959 he came to London with Woody Herman's Herd and did a small solo spot, playing something like the *Villa Lobos Prelude No. 1*, and during that time discovered that I had a guitar by Ignacio Fleta which was for sale. He came up to Wardour Street (where I then had the Central School of Dance Music and had just established the Musicentre), introduced himself, and sat down and played for me, displaying a very good sense of harmony and chordal technique. (I had previously heard his playing on *Jazz Recital* on SAVOY MC.12099 and did not know exactly how to categorize it, some of his 'classical' compositions being somewhat unclassical, and his jazz standards rather staid and ponderous.)

However, back to my narrative. Charlie Byrd played the Fleta for a little while, asked me how much it was (£150.00!!) and said he would like to buy it. He then went across the road to the bank and returned with £150.00, and left. He has since been quoted as saying that it was the best guitar he had ever had, and he still thinks so.

During this period Byrd had two Hauser guitars, but found the Fleta had a 'bigger and better tone' because of his (Fleta's) individual ideas about guitar construction, particularly in regard to the inside ribbing and the bottom bar which is 'as big as my thumb'.

Charlie Byrd later soared to new heights of popularity when he recorded *Desafinado* with Stan Getz, which led to his winning popularity polls. His pioneering with the classical guitar in the spheres of rhythmic music and jazz placed him in a unique position, which he confirmed by his excellent performances with the combination *The Great Guitars* (Barney Kessel and Herb Ellis). His performance of Latin-American music and jazz on his amplified nylon-strung guitar was masterly.

When I met him in London in 1978 after 19 years, he had developed musically and socially into a mature personality, married an English girl from Sheffield, Yorkshire, named Maggie, as well as being the happy father of little Charlotte.

Laurindo Almeida (b. 2 September 1917, Santos, Sao Paulo, Brazil) Today many guitarists reach the road to fingerstyle guitar after they have become proficient on the steel-strung instrument, following the pattern of Charlie Byrd and Chet Atkins.

But Laurindo Almeida began on the gut-strung guitar, playing a variety of styles, and stayed on the same instrument, thereby, tonally, having the edge on his younger contemporaries. His is a unique talent combining performance and composition in a variety of styles.

'When did you first learn about the guitar?' I asked him, to which he replied 'In my mother's womb'. And you cannot begin earlier than that. Actually, he liked the sound of the guitar from early on and although it was his mother's wish for him to play the piano (she herself being a pianist), and he began at the age of five, he switched to guitar at seven after fooling around with his sister's guitar. He attended the Villa Lobos Orfeon at Santos until he was nine when the family moved to Sao Paulo. He came from a musical family, his father being a building contractor with a love for music.

Life became difficult after his father died, and at the age of 12 he joined a group known as the 'Conjuncto Regional' consisting of two guitars, flute and bass, which mainly accompanied singers. But then Laurindo discovered that if he played in a jazz group he could earn $15.00 more, but he received a rude shock when he discovered that he had to read chord symbols instead of music.

Not easily put off, he set about analysing the chord symbols, and in a week learnt the system and earned the extra $15.00.

A further task was asked of him when some Italian singers had to be satisfied, but as this meant a further $15.00 he learnt to play the mandolin as well, gaining extra experience.

When he was 16 he left Sao Paulo and studied at the Escola Nacional de Musica, in Brazil's capital city, Rio de Janeiro, for one year, until he was 17. Like other musicians he got the wanderlust, and wanted to discover what was happening on the other side of the Atlantic, so he signed on as a musician on a passenger/cargo boat going to Portugal, Spain, France, Belgium, Holland and Germany. This was the proverbial Showboat, but the advantage was fairly long docking periods for reloading which enabled him to go to Paris and meet Django Reinhardt and his brother Joseph. Laurindo's only regret was that the boat made no stop at an English port. However, he had become very attracted to the music of Django and had at least heard *some* jazz, but, for the rest, he was disillusioned, and when the boat returned to home base, he decided to stay in Brazil, and from 1936 to 1947 became Brazil's most famous guitarist, having first played and arranged for Radio Mayrink Veiga.

An earlier composition of his, *Johnny Pedlar*, had become quite a hit, and after much recording and radio work (and a fair amount of touring) he decided to try his luck in Hollywood in 1947. Hollywood was still a busy film factory in those days, and his first job was to play in the film *A Song is Born*, which included jazz stars Louis Armstrong, Tommy Dorsey, and an arranger named Joe Reso. Joe Reso knew that Stan Kenton was looking for new ideas and that Pete Rugolo (his arranger) wanted to write a work for guitar and orchestra, so he mentioned the Brazilian guitarist who had worked on the film. Almeida had been in Hollywood for about six months when he was asked to see Kenton, but when they met they hit the language barrier and nearly reached a stalemate. But Pete Rugolo, being Italian-American, spoke Italian which Almeida could also speak quite well and so negotiations resumed with a sight-reading test and a solo called *Insomnia*, which he later performed at the Carnegie Hall, New York. Meanwhile, Peter Rugolo finished *Lament* for guitar and orchestra, which was first performed early in 1948.

Lament was recorded on Capitol L13270A and caused quite a stir when we first heard it in England. Everybody wondered what kind of an electric guitar produced such a clear electric sound. We also discovered Laurindo Almeida, and that the clear sound was due to his delicate, firm touch, accurate technique and sensitive musicianship.

It is strange how my interest in this piece later led to my playing it with Ted Heath's Band on a TV show in which *Lament* was used as the music for a ballet. So, when I first met the man himself, he was no stranger to me.

Laurindo came to London with the Modern Jazz Quartet, and was featured playing the slow movement from the *Concerto de Aranjuez* by Rodrigo, with rhythm backing from the quartet. Roland Harker (who had already met him and was a great admirer of his playing) took me round to his dressing-room after the Festival Hall concert.

To return to Kenton and 1948, at the end of the year Laurindo wrote *Amazonia*, which he orchestrated for the orchestra and performed as a further feature. By 1950 Laurindo had had enough of touring and returned to Hollywood and the film business, where his first film with Dmitri Tiomkin was *High Noon* with Gary Cooper. Once again coincidence plays a small hand, because a few years later Dmitri Tiomkin came to London to record the music for the film *The Sundowners*, and I happened to be the guitarist. He told me all about Almeida, who was his favourite guitarist, and Tiomkin would have no other. In fact, Laurindo Almeida was *the* No. 1 guitarist in the Hollywood film studios, working with all the leading conductors including Victor Young and Alfred Newman. He himself has about 200 compositions to his credit, has written the music for over a dozen motion pictures and an equal number of TV films. He has recorded many solo albums, some with groups, some with singer Salli Terri, and later with lyric soprano Deltra Eamon, whom he married in 1971.

When he was in London with the Modern Jazz Quartet he played a Ramirez guitar on which he produced a tone of great delicacy, but a few years later he changed to a Felix Manzanero whom he popularised in Los Angeles, but now, to my surprise, he has a cutaway classical guitar made by Julius Gido, a nature-loving neighbour from Burbank. The string action suited me down to the last fret, the 21st, and the tone was very rich and sonorous.

The walls of the studio in his sumptuous, spacious, artistically furnished house in Sherman Oaks overlooking Los Angeles are hung with a score or more of his LP covers, while the shelves display at least ten Grammy Awards dated between 1958 and 1964. Modern recording equipment is neatly stacked. As if these talents are not enough, he cooks gourmet style, (as I have tasted), is a collector of wines (a hobby we share) and there is no more hospitable host or generous person.

But, like any other mortal, he has his moments of doubts and low spirits, and on these occasions he tells his troubles to his favourite saint, St. Francis of Assissi, whose small statue is to be found in an arbour in the corner of his garden, near the pomegranate and persimmon trees.

Chapter Seventeen

ARRANGERS AND THE GUITAR

The success of a 'pop' composition often depends upon the way it is arranged. A first-class arrangement also helps to bring success to the musical director and to the individual musicians who are spotlighted in the arrangement. Therefore the arranger plays a very important part in the field of popular music.

In the early jazz era, when the banjo and the guitar were considered just a part of the rhythm section, arrangers wrote guitar charts of simple major, minor and seventh chords copied from the right hand stave of the piano part. This led to two weak areas in the guitarist's musical ability: sight-reading of notation, and recognition of correct chords and inversions. But, as the guitar became more popular, the better arrangers, with or without consulting the guitarist, not only did a great deal to remedy the situation, but forced the guitarists to improve. The process has continued, so that session guitarists have to be as complete in their all-round ability as their co-instrumentalists. It is to these arrangers that I would like to pay tribute for their share in popularising the guitar.

In certain instances the guitarist influences the arranger, and this was clearly the way after Charlie Christian joined Benny Goodman's Orchestra. Christian not only effected a change in Goodman's clarinet style but also in the form of the band's arrangements, such as *Solo Flight* which centred round the guitar, and *The Sheik of Araby*.

Without the brilliant originality of Wes Montgomery there would have been no inspiration for the orchestrations in *A Day in the Life of Wes Montgomery*, which features string backgrounds. *Summer Sequence*, composed and arranged by Ralph Burns for Woody Herman's band and played by Chuck Wayne, is an example of a composition using the guitar as a solo and orchestral voice. *Lament* by Pete Rugolo is a perfect example of the marriage of the classical guitar playing of Laurindo Almeida and Stan Kenton's orchestra on Capital CL.13270A, in which the arranger/composer knows his musicians.

For example, Lew Stone's signature tune *Oh Susannah* gave an opportunity for the guitar to be heard as a background to the clarinet

ARRANGERS AND THE GUITAR

melody – a small beginning but a change in tone colour from the piano. There were a few arrangers in the Fox days who helped the guitar along a little bit. Stan Bowsher, the house arranger for Peter Maurice Music, used the guitar effectively as a background to *South of the Border*, and in the film *On The Air* I had the opportunity of standing up and playing a completely unaccompanied solo passage!

Film music often provided backgrounds to scenes which were enchanced by the sound of a guitar and Ben Frankel never missed an opportunity for doing this. Friends are a good thing to have and Jack Nathan who scored many Fox arrangements, did a little pen pushing in my direction where appropriate, as in *Rhythm in my Nursery Rhymes* with the vocal by Mary Lee, in which I used a National (Dobro) guitar to obtain a slightly amplified blues effect.

Phil Green, in his records of *Joe Paradise and his Music*, wrote duets, solos, and required extemporised guitar solos in his arrangements.

Stanley Black

Stanley Black really knows and understands the guitar, and has included it in many of his records. The sleeve notes of the LP *Spain* by Stanley Black and his Orchestra (Phase 4 Stereo PFS 4017) in which I play, are so musically accurate and descriptive that I think two are well worth repeating as examples of how an arranger works:

Ay-Ay-Ay

'The introduction is touched off sumptuously by the richly shaded Spanish guitar (left) and is brought to a close by the sharply punctuated pizzicato figures of the violins (right), cellos (left) and a silken run on the harp (right). The guitar sings the melody on the left and finds itself answered on the right by the softly speaking harp. Bringing the first statement of the song to a close are the dark pizzicato figures sounding from the left. The pastoral English horn (*cor Anglais*) then speaks with singular lyrical beauty as the guitar is heard in a soft commentary on the other side, and as the strings shimmer softly in the background. Later the strings bring to the melody a luxurious quality; the title is brought to a close when the guitar (left) plays figures recalling the introduction.'

Almost a blue-print for a guitar orchestral arrangement! Stanley Black conceived *Estrellita* (another track on the same LP) as a duet, as described in the short sleeve note:

'Woven with touching tenderness and mellow sonorities, the full warmth and beauty of this moving song is softy spoken by the guitar (left) and accordion (right).'

Bob Sharples

My experience of Bob Sharples exemplifies the influence of the guitar on the arranger. When he arrived with his first arrangement for Geraldo's orchestra he was still a captain in the army, but his enthusiasm and confidence came through as he took us through his arrangement of *Blue Skies*. He eventually became one of the band's regular orchestrators and used to write almost impossible guitar parts which he insisted on my playing. Never giving up without a struggle, I eventually found them playable. In this way, both my sight-reading and technique improved, especially when he wrote for a small group of seven or eight in which a missed note showed up.

It coincided with the period during which chords of a more complex character were introduced and Bob and I had many discussions on how best to give them symbols which would accurately describe them.

Wally Stott

Wally Stott was probably the band's most prolific arranger and was given the largest share of the up-to-date dance music and jazz orientated scores, not forgetting the opening orchestral piece of *Tip Top Tunes*, a programme which gave the arranger a lot of scope with tempo and instrumentation. Again the question of new chord symbols came into play and by the time Roland Shaw and Bob Farnon joined the array, we had it all worked out. Wally, who had found it impossible to combine playing and writing, left the band as a player and continued as a regular arranger in a freelance capacity. He went from strength to strength, becoming MD for Phillips Records, and I remember an occasion when he wrote a very stylish solo introduction for me to a Mel Tormé recording for Phillips.

I must mention that a phenomenal thing happened to Wally who had been married for some time and had two children. He underwent a sex-change and became a woman, now known as Angela Morley. Professionally, this did not affect his work in the slightest. He is still a prolific arranger and composer, a recent example being his music for the film *Watership Down*. Angela Morley recently settled in Hollywood.

Robert Farnon

The composer of *The Jumping Bean*, the music for the TV series *Colditz* and *The Secret Army*, TV jingles and many film scores, is an arranger who makes a very strong impression with all musicians.

During the war, he was in England conducting the Canadian Band of the AEF and later became MD for the Canadian Broadcasting Company. Gerry, in what was probably one of his best musical scoops, engaged Bob on a year's exclusive contract, giving him as one of his first assignments a mammoth arrangement of a selection from the film *Blue Skies*, which we broadcast in the programme 'Milestones of Melody' on 26 September 1946. In the broadcast, Irving Berlin, the composer, was the guest artiste, and the following day we repeated the performance with an orchestra of 70 from the Carlton Theatre as a prologue to the Film Premiere.

On 16 October 1946, the 'Queen Elizabeth' sailed on her maiden voyage to the United States with Gerry (who supplied musicians to the Cunard Line known as 'Geraldo's Navy') hopping aboard for the ride, leaving Bob Farnon in charge. Bob, being very popular with the boys, was certainly the ideal man, but there was one snag. Since Maurice Burman had left, we had not found a permanent drummer, and this left the rhythm section weak. Prior to this a bright young cockney sparrow named Eric Delaney (lately with the RAF) had been playing with Stephane Grappelly's Quintet – while Ray Ellington sang the vocals. He really sparkled and was a first class sight-reader too. I asked him if he would like the Geraldo job. He jumped at the chance and Bob agreed to give him an audition. From then on we were again swinging.

I say 'swinging' with reservations. Although the band did have its moments, it sometimes sounded, according to Phil Cardew, 'like a beautiful corpse'.

One of the most attractive pieces of solo guitar I have ever had the pleasure of playing came from Bob Farnon's arrangement of Duke Ellington's *Sophisticated Lady*, and besides sounding exquisite it fell under the fingers. This is an example of how well this orchestrator studied the technique of the instrument. Besides his tremendous musical ability and easy but firm manner of taking a score through, he could never resist pulling a gag.

When Gerry returned from his US trip we were assembled, rehearsing for a broadcast from the Fortune Theatre, when Bob brought along an arrangement of *Green Eyes*, a Latin-American tune, but with no guitar featured in it. Suddenly, as we reached the end I noted a solo arpeggio following the band's final chord, but since the band ended on B♭ and my arpeggio written ff contained the notes EADGBE (the open strings), I pulled up short and did not play, knowing that the effect would be disasterously discordant. Gerry, baton in hand, looked up at me and asked 'What's the matter? Why don't you play the chord?'. Trying to be diplomatic, I answered that it was probably a copyist's error, and explained that it would clash with the band's last chord. 'Should it be in?' Gerry asked Bob. 'Oh yes!' replied Bob, with a bright twinkle in his eye but giving me a wicked wink on the side. We ran through *Green Eyes* once more and this time I picked the arpeggio fortissimo! There can be no worse disconnected sounds than a chord of B♭ followed by EADGBE but Gerry did not bat an eyelid. Having had his fun, Bob, after apparent further consideration, said 'On second thoughts perhaps the arpeggio ought to be omitted'. Gerry agreed with him.

I was once on a film session with Bob Farnon, consisting of the cream of the dance and symphony players including the great clarinettist, the late Frederick Thurston. Suddenly, in the middle of a clarinet solo, an odd gurgling series of ascending and descending runs were heard from Mr. Thurston, which dried up the orchestra. Bob asked him what he was doing. 'Playing the part' said the mystified clarinet player. 'Let's try it again' said Bob. It sounded a little more halting, probably because of the self consciousness of the instrumentalist. Bob asked to see the part, altered a few notes and the music reverted to normal.

It was all taken in good spirit without detriment to the music.

Woolf Phillips

Woolf Phillips was the next one to join the band as a trombone player and arranger, and although he was an excellent musician and instrumentalist, his arrangements were never as smooth running as Bob's, were more difficult to play, and often sounded 'fractured'.

They certainly took longer to rehearse although the results, when we finally arrived at them, were quite interesting.

Bill Finegan

One of my most interesting and exciting experiences in music was in connection with Bill Finegan and, in a different way, with Tad Dameron, pianist, arranger and composer of *Ladybird.*

In his letters, Barney Spieler (one time bass player for Benny Goodman, later in the US Navy Band stationed in London) mentioned that Bill Finegan was temporarily living in Paris taking a composition course (under the US Veterans Bill) with Nadia Boulanger, and this piece of information gave me an idea.

Why not ask Bill Finegan (who had scored some of the music for *Sun Valley Serenade* and *Orchestra Wives* for Glenn Miller and had recently resigned as Tommy Dorsey's arranger in order to study) to write some scores for Geraldo's Orchestra?

I begged Gerry for his permission to contact Bill Finegan, and having received reluctant agreement to my request, I also suggested recruiting Tad Dameron, who was performing at the Paris Jazz Festival with Miles Davis in a group which included Barney Spieler on bass and Kenny Clarke on drums.

Gerry was very doubtful about committing himself further but was, no doubt, swayed by my enthusiasm. Now I had a mission to fulfil, as well as to enjoy the music, and soon after my arrival in Paris, Barney and I set out to locate Bill Finegan.

We climbed to the heights of Montmartre where he lodged and were admitted by his wife Kay into a large room (typical of the 'La Bohéme' era), a suitcase on top of the wardrobe, and the screened-off corner for washing and cooking.

Bill was asleep, stretched out on the divan, and when awakened, asked what was going on. After introductions and coffee, I outlined my hopes, but it took me quite a time to convince him about the musical qualifications of Geraldo's orchestra, a band unknown to him. And in any event, he explained, why should he jump from the frying pan into the fire? He had, after all, just left the most lucrative arranging job in New York in order to study for three years, thereby escaping those frantic conditions as Tommy Dorsey's arranger. Why should he interrupt his studies for an unknown quantity – at cut prices. (I had informed him that the average rate for a score was £15.00 in London). However, I continued with my pleas which his sympathetic nature could withstand no longer, and he suggested that we go out 'on the town' and get better acquainted. It turned out to be a cafe-cum-club crawl, partly drinking and partly taking over the musical entertainment with Bill playing piano (or trumpet) where we found one, Barney on bass and myself on a battered guitar when available.

By about 3 am we were on very friendly terms and he half agreed to consider writing a score. For three days and nights, during which we hardly saw our beds, we had lots of discussions, went to see the concerts, met the great musicians and, all in all, my time was fully occupied and my head was crammed with the new ideas I had amassed. But I also obtained Bill's promise to do some arrangements providing Gerry paid him £35.00 per score, his expenses to come to

London, and to rehearse the band to his own satisfaction. This demand for extra rehearsals was necessary to a musician of his sincerity, whose arrangements required a great deal of understanding.

When I returned to London I related the salient facts to Gerry and added that Bill Finegan would like to hear the band first, to which Gerry agreed. Eventually Bill came over, and was very impressed with the band, especially with Jack Collier, bass, Laddie Busby, trombone and Eric Delaney.

The first arrangement for the band was of *The Continental*, which blew a wave a rarified air into the band's playing. Every single part was a gem, and the guitar had become not just a rhythm or solo instrument but part of the orchestral tapestry, intertwining with the other parts. *The Continental* quickly became one of our standards, and Bill was commissioned to write some more. He chose *Comin' Through the Rye* which turned out to be a masterpiece of rhythmic counterpoint resulting in a musical ensemble we never thought possible. The circumstances of Bill's visit in connection with this are worth relating.

It was during our annual seasonal engagement at the Winter Garden Ballroom, Blackpool, that I received a letter from Bill informing me that he was 'on his way with an arrangement of *Comin' Through the Rye*'. Thereupon I hastily provided for his accommodation at the private hotel where I was staying and awaited his arrival. He turned up in the evening, found his way to the Winter Garden, and while waiting for the band to play their last hourly session, sat in the front row of the balcony opposite the stage, listening to our performance. Eventually we played our last number, followed by the National Anthem. The ten thousand or so dancers stood to attention while we played, but, glancing up in front of us, we spied a long figure with head resting peacefully on his arms – fast asleep. The brass almost dried up, finding it impossible to control their mirth.

That night Bill and I stayed up to about 3.30 a.m., talking about music; for me, a very valuable lesson in the art from a patient teacher.

The next day the rehearsals were so exciting that the musicians would gladly have paid Gerry for the privilege of the musical education they received in the course of rehearsing *Comin' Through the Rye*. When the BBC broadcast our recording of this arrangement on 6 May 1974 (after the sudden death of Gerry on the night of 4/5 May) it sounded more outstanding then ever. It was unmistakably Bill Finegan.

The next arrangement, or should I say 'variations on the theme of *The Arkansas Traveller*', was an even greater masterpiece, and took many rehearsals before it reached broadcasting standard; one miscount and you were in trouble. The guitar part included bass figures, long arpeggios based on perfect 4ths, bell notes, harmonics, solos and duets; every instrumentalist had to count or he was lost. Bill had written to the furthest extent of the players' ability and they rose to the challenge. Other arrangements were *Strike Up the Band, Piccalilly Dilly* and the *'Polovtsian Dances from Borodin's Prince Igor.*

Unfortunately, Gerry did not think the British listening public was ready for these orchestrations and, coupled with the cost of the scores and hotel bills, Gerry was cooling off Finegan arrangements. Rather than tell Bill directly, he left me to be the man in between, and some of Bill's letters to me were masterpieces of hilarious English invective – unrepeatable to Gerry, of course.

When Bill returned to the States, he joined forces for a time with Eddie Sauter and produced those fabulous LP's of the Sauter-Finegan Band.

We are still in contact and he has never forgotten his friends in England, the country he would like to live in, and occasionally he sends me wonderful guitar arrangements, which are as inspiring and original as his orchestral arrangements.

Tad Dameron
On the morning of my second day in Paris, Barney took me to the rehearsal of the Miles Davis/Tad Dameron Group, and I was able to get some idea of their methods.

For example, Tad at the piano would suggest some phrase to Miles Davis by singing it in a high falsetto voice and Miles said 'You want me to go right up there?' 'Sure' answered Tad, 'You can make it!' 'No', exclaimed Miles, and proceeded to play it, a look of amazement in his eyes. The whole scene appeared to be so casual but was so intense and inspirational.

Their performance that night at the Salle Pleyel was exceptional. Miles's trumpet playing was a complete innovation in tone and style and his limpid tone and introspective performance almost resembled a 'walk across a path of eggshells' as one critic described it.

The mercurial Charlie Parker and his group were positively electrifying; Max Roach was master of all he surveyed, Al Haig played the piano delicately and brilliantly, Kenny Dorham was excellent in the Gillespie style and John Lewis carefully selected his tuneful bass notes.

At the party after the show, Charlie Parker insisted on signing my programme as 'Sir Charles Parker' in deference to the English, and this tickled him immensely.

The following day I went to see Ted Dameron at his first-class hotel where I found him in his bath attended by his beautiful girl friend Margot. Again I explained the purpose of my mission and, as with Bill Finegan, he said he had never heard of Geraldo.

I related to him that I had played the Dizzie Gillespie Big Band record of Dameron's *Our Delight* to Gerry and the band and, though they considered it a bit 'way out', Gerry was prepared to accept some arrangements from him. He was rather pleased with the idea of coming to London and agreed to bring along his arrangement of *Our Delight*.

Some weeks later Tad Dameron came to London with Margot, and settled in a nice little flat in Shepherds Market, but his first appearance in front of the band at the Maida Vale Studios caused quite a disturbance. The boys had never seen him before, and the brass section had never heard of him, so when he came into the studio dressed in a light powder blue suit that positively shrieked, took his stand on the conductor's rostrum, and gave the command to start the band, the brass section bristled with resentment. *Our Delight* was scored in the most advanced 'bop' style, containing very close chromatic harmony especially for the brass, as well as a written out 'Gillespie' trumpet solo, which did not make them any happier. Although the saxes and rhythm section were very eager to get on with it, the brass clearly showed that they cared neither for the arranger nor his arrangement.

Gerry, always willing to give new music a fair trial, was cautious, even though he saw that the brass were out of sympathy with the advanced harmonic progressions.

We soon mastered *Our Delight* and broadcast it, but it was hard going and crises occurred at future rehearsals.

For myself I greatly admired the music of the composer of *Ladybird* and he often played his inventions to us at my home and at his flat. He was in my opinion, a great jazz innovator, and although he was quite envious of my daughter's ability to sight-read and her keyboard dexterity, he need not have been. His genius for inventing original melodies and setting them to lush harmonies was a much

ARRANGERS AND THE GUITAR

greater gift; although he was very fluent at writing a score, his music reading was very poor.

However, his great musicianship did not compensate for his incompatibility with Geraldo's orchestra so, after a month, I accepted defeat, and recommended his talents to Ted Heath who was happy to play his arrangements and original scores.

Tad was very anxious to settle in London so I put his name forward to the BBC with the suggestion that he be employed in a freelance capacity; but there were obstacles. The big hurdle to overcome was a work permit, which could only be applied for from abroad, and for this purpose Tad left England to stay in Paris.

I heard from him on 3 July 1949 to tell me that he had written to the Ministry but a letter dated 18 July informed me that there had been no progress. Here is part of that letter:

'Margo and I are hoping to see all of you soon. I've been very busy since I've come to France but can't get the good sounds of English bands out of my ears. I wrote to the Ministry as you can see, so now it's left in the hands of Jim Davidson (Head of BBC Dance Music) or Ted Heath about this matter for me. Thanks a million!

I haven't forgotten your guitar leads. I'll send them to you next week. Your friendship was very precious to us during our stay in London; I don't quite know how we can ever repay you....'

He didn't really wish to return to the United States but he could not stay in Europe any longer and returned home to New York, alas, only to die from drug addiction a few years later. I am convinced that had he been able to work in London he would have lived a more normal life and British musicians (including myself) would have been well repaid by playing his musical creations.

Roland Shaw and Denny Vaughan

Two more arrangers played an important part in the shaping of Geraldo's Orchestra; they were Roland Shaw and Denny Vaughan.

Roland had been in the Middle East during the war, playing piano in the band directed by Frank Cordell. When he was demobbed, Basil Jones, one of Geraldo's trumpet players (who had been in the same band) recommended him to Gerry as an arranger, and he was asked to bring up a score. We tried it over, and it sounded quite up-to-date and stylish and Roland, standing by, waited for the verdict. But there was no verdict. For some reason there was little reaction from the band, and no comment from Gerry, so that Roland thought he had failed to impress the maestro. But he need not have worried; I think the band had decided to refrain from expressing their opinions which Gerry was waiting for. Roland went on to arrange many scores for Gerry and a very fine one of a Latin-American composition of mine called *Cuban Heel*.

He was very impressed by Finegan who had a great influence on him for a time as his orchestrations for *Tip Top Tunes* showed. Roland became one of the country's leading orchestrators and developed into a film MD. He scored and conducted the music for the film *The Great Waltz* as well as writing for Mantovani and Decca Records.

Denny Vaughan was a protégé of Bob Farnon and came to London from Canada to join Gerry as a vocalist and arranger, also playing piano occasionally to his own vocals. His arrangements were very smooth, of rather a delicate texture, and extremely musical and tasteful, and he added his talents to a very strong arranging team. After returning to Canada he became a kingpin of Canadian TV music.

It is no wonder that every musician playing in the band felt he had the finest opportunities to improve his musicianship, and not surprising that most players in the country would have cherished being a member of the Geraldo Orchestra. But no matter how enjoyable it was to have the benefit of the arrangers who created the style of music we played with Gerry, one had to move outside that enclosure and sample the work of other musicians in other fields.

Film work was such a field and Stanley Black, whom I have already mentioned, did some very slick work as MD of Associated British Picture Corporation at Elstree. As a film music fitter, there was no one faster, and not a minute was ever wasted. One film that required musical background was called *The Sundowners*, directed by Fred Zinneman with music by Dmitri Tiomkin. Although Stanley Black's office fixed the orchestra, Fred Zinneman would not do the film unless Tiomkin was there directing the music. Tiomkin was very painstaking, very funny, got just what he wanted out of the music and never hurried – which was fine for the musicians.

Dmitri Tiomkin (d. 1979)
I was one of the musicians who were nagged by Tiomkin for eight full days working on *The Sundowners* at Elstree, during which time I played 'too soft'; 'too slow'; 'too fast'; 'not together'; as well as 'wonderful, I love your playing', in the opinion of the unihibited Mr. Tiomkin. Of all film conductors in the US, he is one who has featured

the guitar whenever possible. So during that week's recording, I took the opportunity of having a chat with him about the guitar.

Dmitri Tiomkin is a very relaxed, large, assertive, critical and to some extent, boastful man. He has conducted the music for many films and written some commercial hits, *High Noon* being a prime example.

Tiomkin studied music and piano at the Leningrad Conservatoire and knew Rachmaninov, Paderewski and Busoni. Later, as a concert pianist in France, he made the acquaintance of Ravel, Stravinsky and Debussy. In 1925, he emigrated to the United States and five years later travelled to Hollywood, where he began to write for films.

His Russian accent and phraseology never left him, and he loved to tell relevant stories against himself. To illustrate his point he told me that in the 50s he met Gregory Ratoff who said to him 'How long you bin in United States?' Tiomkin replied 'Twenty-five years' to which Ratoff, with disdain, exclaimed 'An you spik sooch lousy English!'

Tiomkin's lousy English fascinated me so much that I made notes of his more pithy idiosyncratic remarks, and asked if I could print them. He did not have the slightest objection and, furthermore, allowed me to ask him many questions relating to the use of the guitar in his films.

In *High Noon* he used two guitarists – one, his favourite, Laurindo Almeida (for whom he had lots of praise) and the other, Barrosso – Tiomkin could not remember.

The Warner Bros. film *Sundowners* was a movie about the Australian outback and sheep farming, and was directed by Fred Zinneman, a quiet, clean-cut, small man for whom Tiomkin had worked on many films, being permitted absolute control of the music with unlimited recording time so as not to skimp on quality. No matter how trite the subject, Tiomkin liked to have the music well performed or, as he succinctly put it, 'I like to make from stink, something'.

In one case, a slightly grotesque effect was required from the trumpet but the player, known for his sharp wit and 'mickey taking' exaggerated the lip slur to produce a very comical sound which resulted in some sniggers from the orchestra. 'I love that', Tiomkin exclaimed expansively 'but Mr. Zinneman will throw me in the river in Petrograd. I am for good laugh. Ha! Ha! Ha! Ha!'". The music for this film, composed and conducted by Dmitri Tiomkin, consisted of two folk tunes *The Lime Juice Tub* and *The Overlander* linked together to form dramatic background music, and an original theme, *Sundowners*.

The guitar was included because of the instrument's general use in the backwoods and ranches.

'Sometimes', explained Mr. Tiomkin, 'it is necessary to introduce a secondary colour in a film score to add certain character to the film. In this film, although the guitar plays a secondary role, it is, nevertheless, this sound that provides a certain folksy simplicity'.

For the major part, the music was played by four flutes, three clarinets, bass clarinet, two oboes, cor anglais, two bassoons, contra bassoon, harp, accordion, guitar and harmonica. The harmonica was often featured and wonderfully played by Tommy Reilly whom D.T. always called 'Tony' until it was useless to correct him.

The guitar chords were voiced to sound the way the arranger imagined them, and were probably practical when played on the piano, but almost impossible to finger on the guitar. However, I did my best and when I was able to twist my fingers round the required frets, the chords sounded very effective, thereby extending possibilities so far unexplored.

Tiomkin Reminiscences

When I asked Mr. Tiomkin if I could chat to him about the guitar, he replied 'Naturally, I love the guitar and all the different kinds of music played on the instrument'.

The formidable list of his films that feature guitar music proves the truth of that statement.

In *Rio Bravo* he arranged the music for trumpet and six guitars, two of whom were Joe Carioca (who always played for Carmen Miranda) and Morales. George M. Smith, author of *Modern Chord Method for Rhythm and Chord Improving* (phew!) was a favourite of Tiomkin who often used him in his films.

Filmgoers who saw *Duel in the Sun* will have heard the guitar of Vicente Gomez who was brought over from New York by Tiomkin to record the music for the film. (*Blood and Sand*, which Gomez also recorded for the Brunswick label brought him more fame.)

Dmitri Tiomkin also mentioned Bill Coleman, a country and western and hillbilly expert who was one of the guitarists in *The Alamo*, a story of the war between Texas and Mexico and, naturally, the music is 'Texican' (if I may coin a word).

One piece in 'jota rhythm' is called *D'Equello* (The Cut-throat) featuring Laurindo Almeida and José Barrosso in addition to Bill Coleman. *The High and the Mighty, The Old Man of the Sea, Friendly Persuasion* and *Giant* all have music written by Tiomkin who mentioned that he had recently written the music for *The Unforgiven* which was recorded in Italy. Both D.T. and his assistant spoke very highly of the wonderful Spanish guitar playing of the orchestral guitarist, but, unfortunately, neither of them could remember his name.

Tiomkin's autobiography is entitled *Please Don't Hate Me* because it is a phrase he uses with relish and the first time I heard him use it, it was to the harpist, Maria Korchinska, who had confided to us that some of the harp parts were impossible to play. It must have got to the maestro's ears because one day, looking down from his rostrum he said to her, 'I hear you have been spreading rumours that I can't write harp parts. I know you hate me. . . .'

Later in the afternoon we reached a section where the xylophone and harp had a unison passage, but, probably because they were placed a long way from one another, there may have been a time lag. Anyway, the passage did not sound quite together.

Tiomkin addressed the xylophonist, Steve Whittaker, with the words, 'If you don't look at me we won't be together – but when you look at me I see you hate me'.

In spite of his exacting requirements, it was easy to play for Tiomkin with the utmost relaxation because of his excellent sense of humour and self-deprecating remarks. How can you be serious when the conductor says 'So help me, gentlemen, the woodwind, the best what I have heard; music (his own) it stinks!"

To the trumpet player whom he accuses of being behind the beat: 'I love your playing but I must follow *you* and the film don't follow *me*. So, *I* follow the film and *you* follow *me, then* will be good'.

He took much longer to fit the music to a film than any other conductor I know and the reason was very clear. Most of the sections were arranged for the full orchestra but often the effect he desired required only a few instruments, therefore his procedure was as follows:

First, he rehearsed the segment of music with full orchestra, then instructed certain players to remain tacit. He repeated the rehearsals until he heard a balance that he considered suitable, then began to record. Once after much alteration, and instructions to the musicians to remain tacit resulting in most of the orchestra having nothing to play, he consoled them with 'Don't be insulted. I think about the *film* not about the *music*.

As I have aready mentioned, he could be hypercritical and after one bout of nagging concerning the phrasing of a few notes he calmed us down with 'Maybe nobody in audience will hear, but I am born different'.

Tiomkinisms
To produce the right musical spirit in the performance he often explained what the scene was all about.

One scene portrayed the hero (Robert Mitchum) an inveterate gambler, gazing purposefully at a beautiful racehorse, the outcome of which was described by Tiomkin as follows:

'First will bring fortune, then losing' and after a shrug of the shoulders, he added 'like with horses'.

Instructions on the alteration of a note:
'Can you don't make the A natural?'
Comment on playing too softly (pianissimo):
'I don't heard you!'
Comment on playing too loudly:
'Too much was'.
Comment on playing behind the beat:
'Too late was!'
Comment on the wrong tempo:
'Too much slow!'

When he spoke to the tympanist he referred to 'the precawshun' and he *always* spoke of the side drum or snare drum as the 'snore' drum. Whatever his odd methods, the musicians loved working for him for although the playing had to suit, they were never rushed or overworked, and working on a Tiomkin film meant at least twice as many recording sessions as with any other musical director, and no charge for entertainment.

Phil Green
Phil Green not only arranged and conducted the music for many films, but often played in the orchestra as well. A very mercurial character, he was a sharp critic who could be very satirical. The only way to deal with him was to win him over by your playing and gain his respect. You were then safe from invective.

In the heat of his excitement during large orchestral film sessions, he could terrorise a musician who was guilty of an imperfection, but he did not get any change out of the brass leads who sometimes gave as good as they received, and Phil loved it, even apologising for his rudeness.

ARRANGERS AND THE GUITAR 239

It was he who arranged for me to take part in the film *A Question of Adultery* to accompany Julie London in her song and he even arranged a piece of duetry between George Malcolm on harpsichord and myself on guitar in the film *The Singer not the Song*.

Louis Levy
Louis Levy was not such a jovial individual. He was a stern taskmaster. His criticisms would often be directed at the line of second fiddles and at times this area became so vulnerable that it was known as 'Bomb Alley'. But he admitted he knew little about the guitar or jazz, so he allowed me to interpret the parts my way and even accepted advice from me on the subject.

I played for him as long as he was musical director, mostly for Gaumont British, and his technique in fitting the music to the screen action was perfect. In the early days when the music had to be recorded onto film at the same time as the live action, timing was critical, and in the event of retakes, the scene and the cameras had to be reset each time; a situation enjoyed by the musicians while the pay clock ticked on.

Small-statured though he was, Louis Levy was larger than life as a conductor, but I enjoyed the sessions with him as well as his musical howlers like 'If it's marked 'morendo' (dying away) then let's have more of it!'

Ben Frankel
Ben Frankel was a brilliant musician and composer, a meticulous conductor and a patient teacher (in fact, he later taught composition at the Guildhall School of Music) and it was a privilege to work under his baton and to play a part in his musical creations. Besides that, we became friends in the social sense and it was in one of his compositions that I first made the acquaintance of the alto flute (sometimes incorrectly called the bass flute).

My last meeting with him before he died was when we sat together at the Festival Hall for the first performance of his *Seventh Symphony*, conducted by André Previn. Intellectually Ben was in the top class.

Muir Matheson
The atmosphere at a Muir Matheson film session was very formal and so was the music in which the guitar was often used to create atmosphere. The music was often played by a symphony orchestra of

dignified schooled musicians which the conductor liked to match with rather high class sardonic humour when the opportunity arose. In one film, *The Vessel of Wrath*, starring Charles Laughton, when I found I had to play a solo in $\frac{7}{8}$ time, I became a little apprehensive about being able to follow the beat. The conductor himself admitted he was unsure of the way in which to get the best results, and after some discussion with the leader, decided to conduct it in two, dividing the seven quavers into one down beat for four quavers and an up beat for the remaining three quavers. That taught me not to worry too much: I was not the only one who didn't know!

Mantovani (d. March 1980 aged 74)
Mantovani always took an interest in the guitar, and because of the tremendous sales of his records throughout the world, any solos that were arranged for the guitar became more prominent than they would have been in a lesser known ensemble.

When I first joined 'Monty' as a regular member in the early 1960s, the guitarist was expected to play all the written solos and background fill-ins on an acoustic unamplified guitar which had to battle to be heard, especially on a tour of concert halls, without the aid of studio amplification.

So, I took the bull by the horns and introduced my amplifier and convinced Monty that an electric acoustic guitar would sound as warm and natural as an acoustic but with a smoother voice and smoother phrasing. From then on, I was able to use the electric guitar, or, in recordings the classical guitar, whenever I considered it suitable.

The orchestra was known to the public for its singing strings, but on closer examination it was an orchestra in which the guitar was heavily featured. Monty had been a concert violinist but he obviously loved the guitar because whenever he wrote a score for the orchestra (and he did quite a number) the guitar was not forgotten, sometimes to the point of weaving through the whole arrangement.

Due to ill health Monty retired in 1977 at the age of 71. He died in March 1980. As the reporter of the *Sunday Mirror* (12 February 1977) wrote 'They will never silence those singing strings' but as Monty said: 'I'm all right in myself – just getting old and forgetful'. Alas, that was the end of the world's most popular light orchestra.

Working for Monty in contrast to Tiomkin was like coming from the sunshine into an electric storm, from relaxation to tension. He could at times be a prickly character, and although he knew exactly what he wanted to hear from the orchestra he always caused a certain amount of tension because of his own unease which I usually sensed. Therefore I reacted in the only way I knew how, that is to relax and play my part to my own satisfaction, which would set him at ease.

Matyas Seiber (b. Budapest 4 May 1905, d. 1957)
Of all the musicians I have worked for, Matyas Seiber must be regarded as the greatest. He studied composition with Zoltan Kodaly and 'cello with Adolf Schiffer at the Budapest Academy of Music from 1919 to 1924 and had written many compositions for orchestra, choirs, films (including the music for *Animal Farm* by George Orwell) and solos for violin, 'cello and piano.

His chamber music had often been performed and he had published Four French Folk Songs for high voice and guitar (1959) and Eight Dances from Thesauras Harmonicus (1957) which he arranged for guitar from the original Lute tablature by Jean-Baptiste Besard (1603).

He was very much influenced by Kodaly, Bartok and Hindemith and took a great interest in both jazz and 12-tone music.

Groves Dictionary of Music and Musicians devotes three pages to him and says in one paragraph:

'Seiber's inquiring mind, seeking comprehension of transcendental values by analytical understanding of physical realities, is clearly reflected in his music. This mental attitude is the explanation of his interest in problems of musical technique and his superior craftsmanship is due to his preoccupation with these matters in his capacities of composer and teacher of composition.'

'Superior craftsmanship' describes his arrangements perfectly, for to play in any combination for which he wrote was an excursion into the wonders of musical sounds.

During the war the BBC used to broadcast an Arab propaganda programme beamed to the Middle East and in order to make it attractive, included suitable Arabic music which was played by a combination of guitar, violin and percussion. The guitar part that Matyas wrote was so authentic that it could not have sounded better on an Ud (an Arabic lute) and as an exercise in sight reading was both exciting and enjoyable.

I think that must have been the first time I played for him and after that I did most of his sessions that included a guitar.

"Superior craftsmanship" could also be used to describe the music he wrote for the Hallas & Batchelor cartoon films, one series of which concerned the bewildering exploits of Flook (Mr. Average Man). The combination consisted of violin, flute, double bass, tuned percussion and acoustic guitar, and there was surprise, suspense and romance in every section of music. The five-piece sometimes sounded like a full orchestra and at other times like a contrapuntal joke depending on Flook's moods.

The violin was usually played by either David McCallum or Louis Stevens, flute by Geoff Gilbert, double bass by Jack Collier, percussion by Jimmy Blades with myself on guitar.

We used to record the music in a first-floor conference room at the Windsor Hotel in Bayswater Road opposite Hyde Park and I always remember a small slight figure entering the room holding a little plastic box containing lunch of raw vegetables. Even in those far-off days he was a vegetarian.

He was a modest, mild man with a gentle sense of humour and it was an education to play under his direction.

I was hoping to take lessons from him in harmony and counterpoint but, alas, he was killed as a result of a car accident while on a visit to a South African game reserve in 1957 thereby dashing my hopes and leaving England poorer by the loss of a leading composer, teacher and most knowledgeable musicologist of the work of Bartok and Kodaly.

Frank Cordell (d. 6 July 1980)

During the war Frank Cordell served as Musical Director for the MEF in Cairo and later became a freelance arranger attached to Parlophone Records, where I often played on his recordings.

His arrangements were always on an advanced musical level and his film scores were extremely interesting, adventurous, and often avant-garde. It was probably his reputation on that score that brought his work to the notice of film producers in other parts of the world and brought us face to face again after a period of almost a year.

It was in Kyoto during our tour of Japan with Mantovani in 1963 that I was about to step out of the lift in the lobby of the New Kyoto Hotel when there was Frank waiting to enter. It transpired that he had been in Japan for six months or more writing and directing the music for a famous Japanese producer known for his new-style movies.

Prior to that time I used to take part in many of the sessions he conducted for Parlophone Records and one of the artistes we accompanied was Alma Cogan who will always be remembered for her record of *Love and Marriage*.

But on one of these recordings the guitars did not cover themselves with glory.

Wally Ridley, Parlophone's Artiste and Recording Manager, had chosen a Rock type of pop tune for Alma which Frank had arranged for a small group including two guitars. Wally had heard the song on an American record and asked Frank to score it for us to record.

Frank, who was able to write well for any instrument was well versed in the intricacies of the guitar, and wrote accordingly, giving the guitars prominence, somewhat on the wild string-bending semitone clashing style, with Roy Plummer and myself on the two electric guitars.

We played the arrangement but it did not resemble the looseness and ring of the American group despite my using a Les Paul guitar and no matter what we did to imitate that loose sound the result remained too stiff. We turned up the treble, played near the bridge but still it did not happen and Wally had finally to accept the best we were able to simulate.

What, I later asked myself, was the secret of that raunchy Rock attack, and, much later, I discovered it was the gauge of the treble strings. In those far off days English guitar players were not using an .010 first (which was actually the gauge of a first banjo string), an .013 second and an unwound third string, nor were these gauges available in Great Britain.

Being more interested in a good jazz sound, neither Roy Plummer nor I gave that (Rock) sound more than a passing thought and we were supposed to be the experts! Years later, I failed to give complete satisfaction on an Alyn Ainsworth TV show but that was on bass guitar and this time it was not just the sound of the strings but the type of bass guitar which was unsuitable.

Alyn Ainsworth
We have seen, in an earlier chapter, the many routes guitarists take to becoming leading lights in the musical profession, and every branch of the profession has its stories to relate.

I met Alyn Ainsworth while with Geraldo. He had joined the Geraldo office as a copyist and brought the parts round to the studio for us to play. What I particularly remember was his nice copying of the parts from my scores for the Swing Septet, especially from my hurried scribble.

Well, we both left the Geraldo-cushioned establishment in due course and, to my surprise, the next time I heard Alyn Ainsworth mentioned was (and quite often) on BBC Radio. He had become Musical Director of the BBC Northern Dance Orchestra operating from Manchester (he is a Northener) which also demanded much orchestrating work.

Eventually he returned to London as a freelance Musical Director and very often directed the orchestra for the BBC2's International Cabaret show which included many world famous artistes.

Although I worked regularly for Harry Rabinowitz on his many and varied TV shows, I was not normally included in Alyn's combination which was booked by Alec Firman (Harry Rabinowitz's fixer or contractor). One day, I had an urgent telephone call from Alec asking me to help out and to come along immediately to the BBC TV Centre to play electric bass guitar. I wasn't keen, not having played bass guitar for some time, and then only using a six string bass guitar. However, Alec was a very nice fellow, a good friend and one for whom I regularly worked, so I agreed to be there as soon as I could. I was in the shop at the time, and looking round I saw that there was a Rivoli bass guitar and an Ampeg bass guitar amplifier available so I grabbed them and went.

I must explain here that both the Rivoli bass and the Ampeg amplifier were designed to produce a round mellow tone which I personally liked because of its greater similarity to the string bass than, say, a Fender bass.

When I arrived at the studio the session was in full swing. The orchestra, comprised the top freelance musicians, with Joe Mudele on string bass and Dave Goldberg on guitar, but some of the orchestrations included bass guitar. These were specially written for beautiful petite vivacious French heart-throb Mireille Mattieu who demanded the inclusion of a bass guitar. Alyn Ainsworth, the Musical Director, therefore had to provide one and that is where I came in. I set up my equipment and the rehearsal proceeded without any fuss with Mireille singing very emotionally and the band playing very rhythmically. After a few songs a request came from the control room for more treble from the bass guitar and I altered the controls on both the amp and the guitar, but it was still not exactly what the French manager wanted, and no matter which way I tried to simulate the Fender tone, it did not seem to satisfy him.

A five minute interval was called while Alyn and the others conferred and a decision was reached. I had to go. Alec was called over and was instructed to pass on the verdict. So, with great regret and embarrassment, he handed me my cheque and told me to pack up, and with egg splattered all over my face I had no option but to do so.

The bass guitar man that was later brought in did not have a Fender guitar either and therefore could do no better, but the show had to be recorded so there was no more time for further finesse.

I certainly have not forgotten the incident and I am sure that when Alyn sees me, he too, thinks of Mireille Mattieu and the French Connection.

Geoff Love

Today Geoff Love has become widely known for his TV appearances with Max Bygraves, his orchestra, and for his combination known as 'Manuel and his Music of the Mountains'.

Although he was once a mere trombone player (*and* dancer) with Harry Gold and his Pieces of Eight, his dancing feet have never left him and his bright, cheerful, relaxed and jovial nature has always been part of his personality during the 20 years or so I have enjoyed working for him.

In the fifties he was also Musical Director for the Winifred Atwell Radio Luxembourg programme (advertising Curry's stores) which we used to record in front of the public in various halls around the country, and besides conducting the small band he would also occasionally sing *Joshua Fit the Battle of Jericho*.

I have attended orchestral accompanying sessions where Geoff musically directed and scored the arrangements for Eddie Fisher, Andy Williams and Connie Francis.

It was Geoff who conducted the orchestra for one of Maurice Chevalier's later recordings of an LP including *Louise* and *Thank Heaven for Little Girls* and I can still see Chevalier standing facing the microphone, his thumbs tucked into the armholes of his waistcoat sounding as great as always, recording his songs effortlessly with the same facial expressions he used on stage and screen.

But Geoff always had a love for the guitar, and in the early sixties he and Norman Newell struck upon the idea of recording with a combination called 'Manuel and his Music of the Mountains'. The idea was due to the 'Honeymoon Song' featured in the film of the same name which was set in Spain and among others featured the great flamenco dancer Carmen Amaya.

The combination of the orchestra consisted of strings, percussion, sometimes voices, plus four guitars playing rhythm, with gaps in the orchestration for solo ensemble passages, dubbed separately by four guitars and mandolin as a section.

From that little single seven inch record, the recordings have increased to scores of LPs in which I have taken part as leader of the guitar section, sometimes playing solo passages on classical guitar. On one of these sessions Geoff had made a special arrangement of the slow movement from the *Concierto de Aranjuez* by Joaquin Rodrigo and, as usual, I played the solo guitar part on classical guitar and this was issued on an LP on the Studio 2 label of EMI under the overall heading of *Carnival*. More than a year later the Rodrigo piece was issued as a single and imagine my surprise when Geoff 'phoned to tell me it had reached No. 1 in the charts! When I arrived in Studio 2 at Abbey Road for the following recording session, Geoff Love and his wife Joy were in the studio and greeted me with a gift. It was a gold wristwatch with the words 'To Ivor. Muchas Gracias. Manuel'. Generous with it, too! What more can one expect than payment *and* appreciation for doing what one loves to do?

So much for the people who arrange and conduct the music that guitarists play to earn their daily bread and as one can realise, there is a very strong bridge between some arrangers and guitarists.

SHAKE, RATTLE AND ROLL

Apart from taking part in recordings and performances of Rock 'n Roll in the early 50s, being a member of Tony Osborne's Band for the BBC Six Five Special during the Twist craze and my attempts at the Rock idiom with the Mairants/Langhorn Big Six followed by a rather stillborn recording group which I called the Dawnbusters, my interest in the idiom has been rather peripheral. The Mairants/Langhorn Big Six actually shared an A.T.V. spectacular with Cliff Richard and The Shadows. The latter (which included Hank Marvin) turned out to be on their first rung of the ladder to perennial fame while the Big Six were stillborn.

We had a young guitarist working at the shop whose idol was Eric Clapton. Eric Clapton was then unknown but when my assistant brought me a recording of him, I was amazed at the long sustain and note bending such as I had never heard before. But my taste in music could only accept that as something for occasional listening not for personal performance.

Although The Beatles and The Rolling Stones in their ways were very clever, attractive and exhilarating and I sometimes heard the Beatles recording at the Abbey Road studios, I never went out of my way to see them perform as I always did to see live performances of great jazz, classical or flamenco guitarists.

I appreciated the guitaristic talents of Pete Townsend and sold him a 12-string Rickenbacker electric guitar which at the time he was too poor to pay for. His style, for me, was more of a novelty than something I wished to emulate, and I guess his father Cliff (an old friend of mine with whom I used to record when he played lead alto for The Squadronaires) used to think the same way. I do not, therefore, propose to include these developments in my story. There are many books on the subject of Rock and Country music particularly *All You Need is Love* by Tony Palmer.

However, many of the Rock players are very interested in the classical and flamenco guitars as instanced by my selecting a flamenco guitar for Paul McCartney or helping George Harrison with a classical guitar. Steve Howe, a very versatile rock guitarist equally loves the classical guitar and so, of course, does Mike Oldfield as I have mentioned earlier.

There are many famous Rock and Country players who have spent hours trying to select a classical guitar for their own pleasure and I, too, have spent much time studying the classical guitar and the flamenco guitar, its music, its players and constructors as I will try to describe in Part Three.

'MY FIFTY FRETTING YEARS'

PART III

THE CLASSICAL GUITAR

PART 3

THE CLASSICAL GUITAR – INTRODUCTION

The guitar in sixteenth century Spain was not exactly the same as the instrument we know today and there is no doubt of its popularity, as is confirmed by the wealth of music published for it.

Several kinds of guitar were then current in Spain, differing in the size and the number of strings. Guitars were made with four, five or six strings or pairs of strings, and were known by the term 'vihuela'.

The vihuela provided entertainment for the Spanish Court, in aristocratic circles, and among the people, and the music for the instrument was written and played by a talented group of vihuelists born between the end of the fifteenth century and the first part of the sixteenth century.

These musicians not only performed but published music and instruction books. Fortunately, these publications have been preserved and many of them have been transcribed for the classical guitar, making it possible to establish their names and the dates of publication, as follows:

Luis Milan *(El Maestro 1536)*
Luis de Narvaez *(Los seys Libros del Delphin de Musica 1538)*
Alonso Mudarra *(Tres Libros de Musica en cifra para Vihuela 1546)*
Enrique De Valderábano *(Silva de Sueños 1547)*
Diego Pisador *(Libro de Musica de Vihuela 1552)*
Miguel de Fuenllana *(Orphenica Lyra 1554)*

A a result of the Spanish rule in Naples, the instrument's popularity was not confined to Spain, but spread to Italy and continued on to the nineteenth century. In fact, in 1596 a book was published by Juan Carlos Amat describing how to finger all the chords, with drawings – a sort of pictorial chord encyclopaedia for the instrument which was tuned Aa, Dd, gg, bb, ee.

Museums in many countries display fine examples of guitars made by the artisans of the seventeenth century onwards, and in the middle 1970s I had the pleasure of closely examining a wonderful piece of craftsmanship by Jacob Stadler (of Vienna) who had made this particular Battente in 1625. (It later sold for £10,000.)

France, too, succumbed to the charm of the vihuela and in 1551 music was published by Adrian Le Roy. Diplomatic relations still existed between England and Spain, so one should not be surprised to discover that a description of King Henry VIII's effects listed 'four gitterns or Spanish violles'.

The two virtuosi/composers of the seventeenth century who helped the Spanish guitar to rise to new heights were Gaspar Sanz who, in 1674, published his famous book *Instruccion de Musica Sobre la Guitarra Española*, and the Italian master, Francisco Corbetti, Corbetta or Corbett, the combined Segovia/Villa Lobos of his time.

He taught Louis XIV of France, he was invited to the Court of King Charles II after the Restoration, he wrote a collection of guitar music, the first book of *La Guitare Royelle* dedicated to the Kings of England, published in 1671, and he wrote a second collection in 1674 which he dedicated to Louis XIV of France.

The height of guitar popularity must have been reached about 300 years ago when Francisco Corbett was employed by the Duke of York, and one can still read the entry for Christmas 1677 which reads 'Lady Anne's (the future Queen Anne) guitar master, Mr. Francis Corbet £100 p.a.'.

Fortunately, Robert de Visee was a pupil of Corbetta's and after Corbetta died in Paris in 1681, de Visee helped the guitar to survive at the French Court. But this period marked the beginning of the general decline, although the guitar was being played by some talented amateurs in Spain well into the eighteenth century.

One of these talented amateurs was Fernando Sor's father who, naturally, influenced his young son, Fernando.

Fernando Sor was born on 13 February 1778 in Barcelona, and twenty years later reactivated the popularity of the guitar for a few decades, during which period there arose a number of virtuosi/composers whose influence has never ceased. Among these great players were Dionisio Aguado (1784-1849) (to whom Sor dedicated *Les Deux Amis* before he died in Paris in 1839) Napoleon Coste (1806-1883), one of Sor's pupils, whose playing career was brought to an end when he broke his right arm in an accident.

One of the other leading virtuosi was Mauro Giuliani (1781-1829), born in Italy but moved to Vienna in 1806, who played before an audience in 1806 which included Beethoven. Two other Italians who also played in Vienna, Paris and London, were Matteo Carcassi (1792-1853) and Fernando Carulli (1770-1841).

Nicolo Paganini (1782-1840) must have been very impressed with the instrument because he took it up and wrote for it. But after that, in the middle of the nineteenth century, the guitar again went into a decline.

In Spain, however, the guitar continued to be favoured by good musicians and continued to be improved by good luthiers. One such combination led to a great improvement in guitar construction – the systemisation of fan strutting, the increase in the body width and speaking length of the strings. The great luthier, Antonio de Torres, advised by his friend the Spanish virtuoso Julian Arcas (1832-82), became the first maker of the modern Spanish guitar, whose design has been used as a basis ever since.

Julian Arcas also met Francisco Tarrega (1852-1909), and may well have inspired him to take up the guitar and it was Tarrega, who, by means of logical study of technique, helped to lay down the foundations of modern technique.

There surely cannot be one guitarist who has not attempted to play one of Tarrega's romantic compositions. Two of his pupils also did a great deal to keep the flag flying; Miguel Llobet (1878-1938) with his transcriptions of Albeniz, Granados and Catalonian folk songs, and Emilio Pujol (b. 1886) through his tutors and compositions.

But it is to Segovia that the twentieth century owes its fantastic guitar explosion. It was not until his Paris recital in 1924 that leading musicians and critics admitted that the guitar was an instrument worthy of serious consideration. It was then that composers began to write works specially for the guitar, many dedicated to Segovia.

Truth is indeed stranger than fiction and no one, least of all Segovia, could have forecast the musical results of his single-mindedness.

But, enough of history and now to my first encounter with the classical guitar.

Chapter Eighteen

SEGOVIA

Andres Segovia (b. 28 February 1893, Linares, Jaen, Spain)
The most important event for some guitarists in this country during 1937 must surely have been the Segovia recital at the Wigmore Hall on 22 October. It was certainly so for me who had, by chance, discovered the Segovia GA arrangements of Bach and Scarlatti in my early search for practice material.

Discovering the fingerings given in the original works of Turina and Torroba as well as in the Segovia transcriptions, set me on the right path of fingerboard technique, and I still think his fingering is the most logical for smooth phrasing.

Fortunately, some of the music was available on 10" and 12" 78 rpm discs and tonally they are still unique. But, not yet aspiring to play a classical guitar, I practiced them with a plectrum.

So there I was in the dressing room or at home, picking away at the music of *Recuerdos de la Alhambra* by Tarrega, *Courant* and *Gavotte in E* from the Bach *4th Lute Suite*, the Sor Variations of *O Cara Armonia* from *The Magic Flute*, and *Fandanguillo* by Turina.

Although I could not get the contrapuntal separation some of the music required, the practice really built up my pick technique.

One can therefore imagine my anticipation when I heard that the Master was coming to London to play in person. The only other classical guitar recital I had ever heard was by Mario Maccaferri before he emigrated to the United States.

Segovia's programme, *Chaconne* (Pachelbel), *Allemande* (Bach), *Bourrée* (Bach), *Andante et Menuet* (Haydn), *Canzonetta* (Mendelssohn), *Prelude, Allemande, Capriccio, Ballet, Sarabande, Gavotte* and *Gigue* (Weiss), *Sonatina Meridional* (Ponce), *Tarantella* (Castelnuovo-Tedesco), *Serenata* (Malats) and *Torre Bermeja* (Albeniz), his performance, his tone, his expression and wonderful gradation of dynamics were so supreme that I have always tried to cling to the feeling of amazement and pleasure which enveloped me.

I walked out of the hall after the concert in a daze, and when I later arrived home and played my plectrum guitar, it sounded like rusty nails over a piece of corrugated tin. This comparison stayed with me for about six months but, gradually, the memory of his playing inspired me to produce a better tone and made me believe that one day I would ask Segovia to teach me the rudiments of classical guitar playing. I was of the firm opinion that *he alone* possessed the secret of how to apply the hands to a guitar and produce great music.

It was not until 10 years later that he showed me the correct hand positions. The 1937 Segovia experience was traumatic for me simply because of the realisation that never would I be able to attain such musical perfection. Nevertheless, it gave me a goal to aim for in spite of my having to go out into the world to earn my living.

It is interesting to note that when Segovia returned to London in 1938 for a Wigmore Hall recital on Saturday 3 December, his programme was quite different and equally demanding:

Folias d'Espagne Diferencias and Finale (Ponce), *Six Little Popular Songs of Catalonia* (Llobet), *Capriccio-Hommage to Paganini* (Castelnuovo-Tedesco), *La Frescobalda* (Frescobaldi), *Menuet* (Rameau), *Andante* (Mozart), *Prelude* and *Mazurka-two* (Chopin), *Choros* (Villa Lobos), *Guitarreo* (Pedrell), and *Trois Pieces* (Granados).

Nearly ten years later, with the world just beginning to recover from its most terrifying upheaval, I sat in a circle seat of the almost empty Camden Theatre (then serving as a BBC studio) while Segovia, a lone figure on the stage, broadcast a programme of music which, for me, bridged the gap of that last unsettled decade, and once more reminded me of my desire to play the classical guitar.

After his broadcast I was introduced to him as a professional guitarist and I told him of my desire to learn the technique of the Spanish guitar, and much to my surprise, he invited me to his hotel where he promised to give me a lesson the following morning.

I did not have a Spanish guitar, so I borrowed one (hardly fitting for the occasion) also taking my own Epiphone guitar. I made my way to the Stratford Court hotel in Oxford Street, parked the car, and walked along to the hotel entrance. Suddenly, I felt completely numb with fright and almost turned back. But having come so far, I decided to keep the appointment and went up to Segovia's room, knocked at the door, and was invited in.

Firstly, he asked me to play something for him but, never having played finger-style, I begged permission to use the plectrum guitar and proceeded to play the pieces that he had broadcast the previous day, finishing with *Recuerdos de la Alhambra*. He sat and listened until I had finished the tremolo study, i.e. *Recuerdos de la Alhambra* (with a plectrum), remarked that it was incredible, went across the room, opened a communicating door to the next room and called to someone. His friend (a famous folk singer and guitarist, once a pupil of Segovia's) then appeared, and after introducing me (as some sort of curiosity I think), the Maestro asked me to repeat *Recuerdos* which I did. When I finished the friend had a good laugh at my novel rendering and thought it was very remarkable for the tremolo study to be played with a plectrum.

Segovia then seriously advised me to throw away the plectrum guitar. 'The guitar' he said 'is a polyphonic instrument with separate voices and these voices can only be made to move in different directions by means of the independence of the right-hand fingers, so throw away your plectrum guitar and take out your classical guitar'.

And here beginneth lesson 1.

First, he showed me how to hold my right hand and apply my fingers in apoyando and arpeggio picking. Then, to illustrate his point, he took the guitar from me and played a scale, producing that inimitable tone.

It must be remembered that my guitar was a very poor instrument, yet the tone that I heard was full and pulsating and it was then I realised that this was due not only to his right hand apoyando but to the strength he exerted in pressing down each finger of the left hand, adding life to each note using vibrato. I know it sounds incredible to use strong vibrato on a scale passage; it takes great effort, but there it was.

He handed the guitar back to me and when I placed my thumb in the usual position, for plectrum playing, he took me severely to task. 'Your thumb' he said 'should be placed in a position behind the neck so that in a single note run it is between the second and third fingers. This ensures that the angle of the hand is square to the fingerboard and the fingers do not point towards the lower or higher ends but straight across, thereby enabling them to press firmly behind the frets with freedom of movement'.

During the course of the lesson, he pushed my thumb into the correct position many times and was very precise about the right hand position showing me exactly how to play an apoyando (a rest or down) stroke with the tip of the finger backed by the nail, all in one movement.

Segovia expected quick responses to his instructions and I did my best to grasp everything he taught me. Although 30 years have elapsed I have retained practically total recall of every movement and word of advice Segovia offered.

I would, of course, have paid any fee for this initiation into classical guitar playing, but when I broached the subject before being dismissed, he would not hear of it; in answer to my protests that his refusal would prevent me from asking for any further lessons, he replied that when he returned to London I was to be sure to contact him for another lesson. The next time he came to London, a year later I *did* contact him and, true to his promise, he invited me to come for another lesson, this time at the Piccadilly Hotel.

When I arrived he asked me to sit and wait in his room while he was instructing a young man who was deep in the middle of playing *Fandanguillo* by Turina, and playing exceptionally well, but not good enough for Segovia who took him to task at one certain point.

Perhaps you have guessed that in 1948 there was only one young lad who could play *that* well – namely Julian Bream.

I followed Julian (rather lamely) for my lesson but Segovia was very patient with me this time; perhaps because I had been practising, studying all the music I could, including the Pujol studies. I asked Segovia to advise me about study music and he immediately recommended the Aguado Method. When I mentioned that I had been studying the exercises from the Pujol books, he became quite angry. Perhaps it was because of his (Pujol's) right hand method (i.e. bending the thumb and no nails). I am sure it could not have been his exercises or compositions, which I have always found very musical and well constructed. Actually, when I asked Segovia if he bent his thumb, he played something first before confirming that he did not. He told me about the importance of good fingernails and an unbending thumb.

Today, it may be interesting to hear that when I asked him for advice about buying a guitar, he recommended two names, both equally inaccessible to me at the time, Viudez of Geneva, Switzerland, and Casa Nuñez of Buenos Aires, Argentina. Segovia himself was then playing on a Herman Hauser, who had been constructing instruments for him since 1933 (until he, Herman Hauser, died in 1956). This one he was playing at the time, had a particularly high action, but what a sound!

When Segovia returned to London the following year, we conversed on the telephone a few times but I could not get time off for a lesson to coincide with his available free periods so that was the end of the lessons.

After that I did not feel justified in taking up his time, as I did not think I had devoted sufficient practice to the instrument which I would dearly have loved to master.

Up to the present time I have not heard any guitarist produce the spectrum of sound, beauty of tonal nuances or expressive phrasing to equal that of Segovia, without whom the present development of the classical guitar and guitarists would have been impossible.

Although both Francisco Tarrega (1852-1909) and Miguel Llobet (1878-1937) were pioneers of the Spanish guitar early in this century, the former writing a whole library of compositions and establishing the apoyando method, and the latter leaving some superb transcriptions, I must assert that neither could have been the major world influence that Segovia himself became from the early part of his career.

His transcriptions of J. S. Bach (which are today considered rather individually romantic) were a revelation to me, and had it not been for his performances, which I considered a perfect balance of polytonality, I might not have become acquainted with one of my favourite composers.

Today Segovia has become a legend in his own lifetime, and, now at 87, he is still able to demonstrate the musical finesse and tone colours unemulated by any of today's excellent guitarists.

He proved his ability in *The Song of the Guitar*, a film made in Granada, Spain and produced and directed by Christopher Nupen for the B.B.C. At the preview of the film in London, Segovia did not look his age and was quite charming, also proud of his six year old son whom he had brought along together with his wife.

In conversation with Christopher and myself, he again voiced his dissatisfaction with the weakness (in sound) of the first string of his guitar, this time a Fleta, but a year later at the Festival Hall, the sound of the first string projected clearly in perfect balance with the other strings. It was also worth noting that, age notwithstanding, there remained abundant strength in the left hand to finger firmly the big barré chords whenever necessary.

Chapter Nineteen

THE LADIES

It was not until a few years later that London was graced with two lady guitarists. Both had been child prodigies in their time; one was in her early twenties and was later to form the greatest guitar duo ever to perform, and the other, in her middle forties, had been part of the famous Miguel Llobet duo.

The first one to appear was Maria Luisa Anido, born near Buenos Aires in January 1907, of whom Miguel Llobet said in 1919, 'Maria Luisa Anido is for me something of a revelation'.

She made her debut at the age of ten, and later became a pupil, companion and partner of Llobet in a guitar duo.

She appeared at the Wigmore Hall in March 1952 playing to a half-filled hall, a small shy figure about to perform in a country where little was known of the classical guitar and still less of the artiste.

I found her first three pieces rather dull musically with much forcing of tone, from an instrument which was capable of beautiful sounds, as demonstrated by her 'piano' passages.

Her interpretations of Handel and Mozart were rather exaggerated, but the *Impromptu* by Llobet proved her to be a mistress of the art of rhythmic guitar playing.

In the second group of pieces, her own *Suite Argentina* was most outstanding and gave her scope to exploit her natural aptitude for folk rhythms. The audience really warmed up to her.

Of the third group, Llobet's arrangement of Spanish Dance No 5 by Granados commenced at great speed and a little wildly but settled down; *Asturias* (Leyenda) by Albeniz was phrased extremely well and rhythmically and *Sueño* which followed demonstrated her mastery of harmonics and general technique as well as feeling for the music. For an enchore she played Tarrega's *Gran Jota* in which she used a good deal of showmanship, left hand legatos, harmonics, *et al.*

Some members of the audience did not have a good word to say for Madame Anido's playing but then these 'experts' derive more pleasure from criticising than from enjoying a performance.

I spent a few hours with her and she taught me a great deal about co-ordination. In particular, the importance of practising scales, alternating between the ring, middle, index and middle fingers; that is to say, when playing runs or scale passages, to use a m i m; a m i m; instead of alternate i m i m; m i m i; a m a m; or m a m a.

This was very good advice and does more to create speed and independence than any other single note exercises for the right hand. Her hands were very small and the tips of her right hand fingers were ball-ended from constant use. Being a pupil of Llobet's and a product of the pre-Segovia school, she did not use her nails for picking the strings.

She has not made a repeat visit to England but has continued to give concerts in other parts of the world. I found her a very kindly person and, of course, dedicated to the guitar.

The late Dick Sadleir, well-known for his work in the music industry and in educational promotion, also saw the concert, and I find his review a confirmation of my own and quite descriptive:

'Five foot Maria Luisa Anido covered seven centuries of music in a bewildering display of guitar technique at the Wigmore Hall on 1 March ... the recital attracted the most representative guitar audience seen in these parts for many a day and proved beyond doubt that guitarists have, at last, started to study the guitar. . . . Señora Anido was at her best in her own idiom, the music of Spain and Argentina. My second hand recorded the longest applause for her own suite *Argentina* and her elaborate arrangement of Albeniz' *Asturias*.

As a feast of musical memory alone, her playing of 18 numbers was remarkable. Points of technical interest were that Señora Anido does not use her right hand fingernails and has exceptionally small hands. Her mastery of the artificial harmonic technique, too, aroused great interest.'

Ida Presti (b. 1924–1967)
The young French girl needed no extra consideration from critics or reviewers. She had made a brilliant debut in Paris at the age of 14 and played in as masterly a fashion as Segovia himself; tone, feeling, technique – the lot. Incidentally, from the age of 7 till 9, she had lessons from Mario Maccaferri and later with Emilio Pujol. Women's Lib would have been proud of her no-nonsense attitude to life, music and the battle for equality. She later married Alexandre Lagoya, an excellent guitarist, and with him formed the most musically perfect guitar duet team that is ever likely to exist. It was nothing short of a major tragedy to the guitar world when she died from cancer at the

age of 42, leaving a desolate husband who, with great fortitude, continues to play and teach.

I have always thought of Ida Presti as *the* exceptional female player in the way that Segovia is exceptional. Her appearance at the Wigmore Hall did not draw a very much larger audience than the Anido concert a month earlier, which I thought was regrettable, since it was the London debut of one of the greatest classical guitarists of all time. However, the loss was theirs.

It was the first time I had heard her play, and was struck by her complete devotion to the music, which cast a magic spell over the listener. One was enfolded into the music one heard without the realisation that it was actually being produced on an instrument. Her tone was full and her vibrato intense (although not quite as strong as Segovia's) and it was not possible to find any technical fault, in spite of the breaking of the third fingernail early in the programme, and the worn condition of the other fingernails due to overwork.

I remember comparing her performance of some of the same pieces with Anido's and had some uneven reactions. For example, I was thrilled by Ida Presti's playing of the Bach *Chaconne* but quite unmoved by her rendering of Ponce's Variations on *Folies d'Espagne*'. Anido's *Asturias*, I recalled, was more rhythmic than Presti's but lacked her technical brilliance or serenity. Many would-be players, male and female, offer the excuse of small hands for weak or bad playing, but the hands of both Maria Luisa Anido and Ida Presti were tiny. Despite her small but well proportioned hands Ida Presti was able to perform enormous left-hand stretches on the fingerboard. The usual spread of E's from the seventh to twelfth fret was quite easy for her and there was great control and strength in her right hand.

I saw her again a couple of days after her Wigmore Hall appearance at a private recital to which I had been invited. Her artistry was then even more evident and the select audience regarded her with awe. Although I had some conversation with her (in my broken French) during which she obviously radiated dedication to the guitar, I was unable to learn more other than by close observation.

It is generally known today that her right hand application differed from Segovia's by picking the strings more with the right hand corner of the nails (hand flat facing down) than the usual left hand slope. The Presti-Lagoya summer school was later established where this method was taught with various degrees of success although most of today's leading soloists, Bream, Williams, Diaz, Ghilia, and many others base their right hand technique on Segovia's example.

The 1970s have witnessed the blossoming of quite a number of young ladies who are able to perform very well and perhaps one will reach the rarified heights of an Ida Presti. There is no reason to think otherwise.

The same is happening to both the male and female of the species but among the males there are, of course, a number of internationally recognised leaders apart from Segovia, who is still unique. It is this handful of internationally recognised classical guitarists that I would like to include in this part of my story.

Siegfried Behrend

Andres Segovia

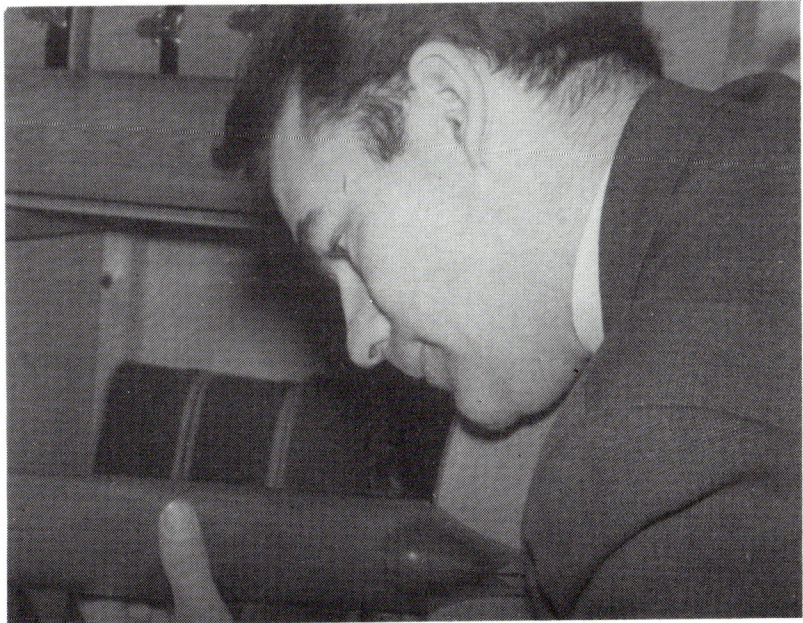
Julian Bream at the Musicentre, 1958.

With Narcisco Yepes and his wife, 1960.

Alirio Diaz

Jose Luis Rodriguez, 1970.

Panel of pictures, Ramirez's old shop.

Paco Pena, Sabicas and Ivor Mairants.

Antonio's Flamenco Company (left to right) Francis Chagrin (conductor/composer), Ivor Mairants, Joaquin Baena, Sabitas, Manolo Moreno (Moraito de Jerez).

With Pepé Martinez, recording 'The Lyrical Guitar', for Philips Records.

Serranito's London debut. (Left to right) Ian Davis, Ivor Mairants, Peter Sensier, Serranito, Dorita, Juan Martin, Ike Isaacs.

Carlos Montoya

Mario Escudero

With Pedro de Lunar, Rosa Duran and Perico el del Lunar.

Mariano Cubas Martin and his collection of guitars.

Ignacio Fleta, 1966.

Ignacio Fleta, bending a guitar side, 1966.

Paulino Bernabe, 1971.

Faustino Conde with Nino Ricardo, founder of the modern school of Flamenco.

Marcelo Barbero

Arcangel Fernandes and Marcelo Barbero Hijo.

Manuel Contreras

Jose Ramirez III

Felix Manzanero

Edgar Monch

Hernandez y Aguado

Luis Maravilla and his son, 1963.

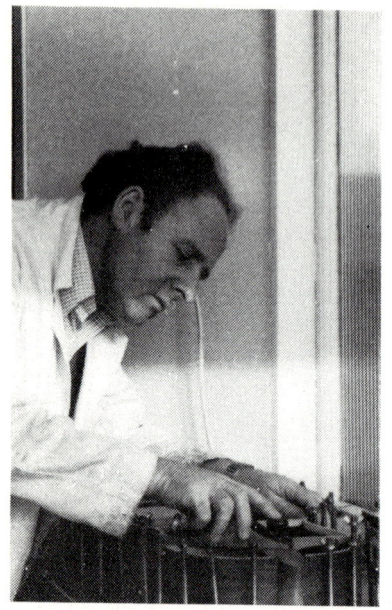
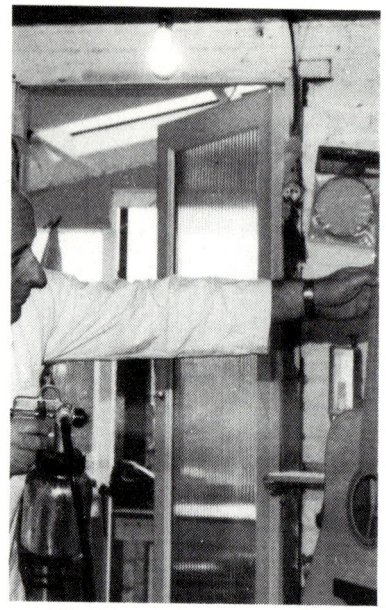

Ray Spain at work.

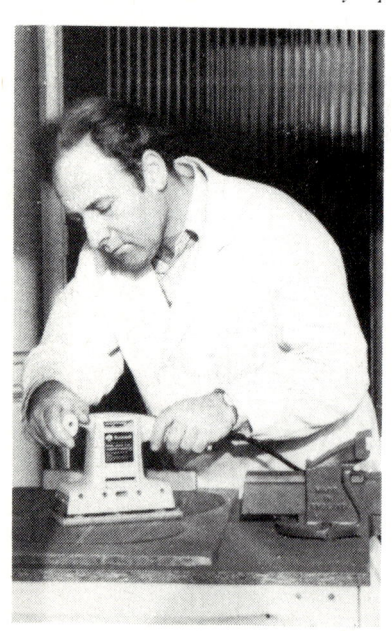

Rose Augustine and Lily Mairants.

The D'Addario family (left to right) John Jnr, Charles, John, Jimmy.

Trying out new Barcus Berry pickup at Frankfurt Music Trade Fair.

The Fleta family (left to right) Ignacio Fleta, Francisco Fleta, Ivor Mairants, Gabrielle Fleta.

David Rubio

Pepé Martinez (left) with Ramon Montoya.

Chapter Twenty

MY FRIENDS THE RECITALISTS

Julian Bream (b. 1933 London)
I have known Julian since he was about 11 or 12 when he played *Recuerdos de la Alhambra* on the BBC Children's Hour as a novelty.

When he was about 16 I asked him to teach classical guitar at the Central School of Dance Music which he did for a period, during which time his father died, and he was left with a void in his family life.

When he was 18 he was conscripted, and good use was made of his talents in the Royal Household Cavalry. He was later awarded a scholarship to the Royal College of Music but not on guitar since there was no guitar chair. In fact, he took up the 'cello.

His enthusiastic personality is reflected in the intensity of his guitar playing on which instrument his musicality and performance have grown greatly in stature. But it is with the lute that I think he has made his most individual and most far-reaching impact. On this subject I would, with permission, like to quote from a letter to V. Bobri by Segovia, published in No 39 of the *Guitar Review* asking if the addition of strings (i.e. the 10 string guitar) improves the guitar as a musical instrument. Stating that the guitar should be left as it is, he makes the following observation.

'As for guitarists who wish to play before the public compositions originally written for vihuela or lute, let them take the trouble to learn to play those instruments. Let them revive the ancient sonorities of distant epochs and everything will remain in its place. That is what, happily, Julian Bream, notable English artiste of our time, is doing. Listening to the works of Dowland, Ferrabosco, Besard, etc recorded by him on the lute is a pure delight. And we must thank him that he respects the guitar when he plays them on this instrument.'

This is what Julian himself had to say to me in 1960 about the guitar and the lute:

'I have played the guitar for 18 years and have played the lute for 10 years. I began with guitar and after 8 years picked up the lute. The reason is that first and foremost I was interested in the music of the lute and while you can play the music on the guitar, you can't play it exactly the same way. The sound of the lute is more apt and has greater clarity than the guitar. It is more abstract for contrapuntal composition. The guitar has almost too much character. For instance, in the guitar each string has almost a different character whereas the strings of a lute are much more uniform in character. It is lighter in texture. It has less possibility of colour than the guitar but the lute has a more touching quality of sounds; a little more ethereal. Whereas the guitar has more of the quality of sound of this world – you know what I mean? Also, the abstract polyphony of the sixteenth century masters was built up by linear composition in which each part is as important as the other.'

I asked if the guitar and the lute complement one another in a concert.

J.B. 'Yes, I think they complement one another. You see, the great thing with lute and guitar together, is that you can play the music right from the fifteenth century to the present day. Now you could say you could play that on guitar. But the quality of the early guitar music is of a different quality and it is this quality of early lute literature that helped me to decide to play the lute, because the lute has a much finer literature than the guitar. But the guitar as a contemporary instrument has a great deal to offer because it can play romantic music and contemporary music, *and* it can play eighteenth century music very beautifully.

But in actual fact, the two instruments, to my mind, make a very good programme because you've got the earliest music on the lute and then I play some Baroque music on the guitar. Then you've got the Bach pieces for the lute and have an adequate modern literature like Villa Lobos and Turina, the best tunes of Sor and together with a few nineteenth century transcriptions, you've got a very fine programme.'

I.M. *'What are your perspectives?'*

J.B. 'What I want to do? I don't know, I just want to give concerts and play better and better.'

I.M. *'How about composing?'*

J.B. 'Well, I like to improvise but have very little talent for composition and although I have written one or two compositions, which are not bad, it takes me a long time. No, they are not published. It takes me so long to compose that I get discouraged. I find it difficult to find a style which I want to compose in because what I compose is nearly like something I've found before. That's why I get discouraged, because in order to create you've got to create new things and if I can't do that I'd rather spend time practising the guitar. I would also rather spend the time delving into the old museums for old lute music.'

I.M. 'What music did you play in your last tour?'

J.B. 'Well, I've just returned from a tour and in the first half I played music by Luis Milan, Dowland, Jean-Baptiste Besard, Simone Mishinamo (these are, of course, all Renaissance music) then I have an interval, get on the guitar and play some pieces by Weiss, Prelude then three pieces called *Tombeau on the Death of Count Logy*, the final piece of three called *Fantasia*. Then I did a few parts from the *3rd Lute Suite* by Bach, three studies by Villa Lobos and then Soleares and Garrotin by Turina – not often played.'

I.M. 'Which country boasts most lovers of guitar?'

J.B. 'I find that very difficult to answer. I find Germany – well, perhaps not Germany – the United States is terrific. Marvellous audiences there. Very good audiences in England. Very good audiences in Italy – well, perhaps not all that good. They are good in Germany – I'll come back on that. America and England have very fine audiences. I've only played in Paris a couple of times and audiences have been very fine – also in a couple of other places, but there has never been all that much interest.'

I.M. 'Do you think that the lute will become popular again as the guitar has done?'

J.B. 'Well, given time there will be a renaissance in lute music, chiefly because more and more music is being delved into in museums and more is being published. But the great drawback is instruments, but I've found (particularly in America) there is a terrific interest in the lute and even the critic of the *Washington Post* wrote that the lute was the right thing and I think there could be a revival. There is a terrific revival in early music and I think in many ways the lute is the queen of instruments of old music and providing enough good musicians (I mean, not frustrated guitar players) get on the lute and really make beautiful sounds and play the music beautifully, otherwise there can't be the same renaissance as there is on the guitar. In fact, if it did come about, it would have a more universal renaissance because, whereas the guitar relies on its following to a large extent on addicts (as it were) – on enthusiasts – the lute relies much more on its music for what it is, not so much for the instrument.'

I.M. 'Then are you of the opinion that if they could play the lute, *more musicians would take up the lute in order to interpret the music?'*

J.B. 'Yes indeed, but not only that. The present problem is instruments and finding makers. The lute I use, the Tom Gough lute, I think the best, but, of course, it's a matter of preference as to what kind of instrument you like.'

I.M. *'Do you consider you're more of a guitarist or a lutenist?'*

J.B. 'Well, I don't know, because I am primarily interested in music; I mean all sorts of music, but I happen to play the guitar and lute. It seems my fingers happen to fit these instruments better than others and I love playing the instruments.

What I am interested in is not so much the instruments as what can be got out of them. And not only that. I think the power of plucked instruments in these days of noise and bustle very important and I think that they have very unusual powers, providing that the right people are behind the 'machine' – (i.e. behind the instrument), and I think they are very arresting instruments and very personal. They affect people when they listen to it – you know, very spontaneous. And that is what interests me with these instruments, too. The contact – the power of contacting people.'

I.M. *'Do you think it is possible to engender as much audience enthusiasm from a guitar or lute solo as by a virtuoso violin concerto?'*

J.B. 'Yes. I found that you can. I think it's another approach. You bring the audience to you. The instrument is intimate. You don't go out to them, you only give the feeling that you go out to them, but in actual fact through some cunning devices and some artifice and also by the very nature of the instrument it brings the back rows of the hall to the front.'

I.M. *'But if they don't want to listen you can't shout it out to them.'*

J.B. 'Oh, no! But the art of playing a concert is to convert them. They might find the instrument tiresome at first but you have got to make them enjoy it.'

I.M. *'Then wouldn't you say that you have to be a much better player on your instruments than a violinist on his in order to get as enthusiastic a reception?'*

J.B. 'Not necessarily a player, but you've got to have a great deal of sensitivity to the audience and also in the choice of material you play, as well as the way in which you arrange your programme.

For instance. if you play in Blackpool, you don't play the same programme as you play in Jesus College, Oxford. I think one's got to be careful. I think you can bore people with a programme which may have wonderful musical potential but does not quite have the universality of a programme a little bit lighter where the layman (who has never heard the instrument before) can appreciate it. I don't believe in bowing down to one's public – never – but I do believe in being sensible about arranging a programme.'

I.M. *'What are you preparing for the New Year?'*

J.B. 'I hope to be going to Russia in the autumn and then I'm doing a tour of India for two months in the New Year, Australia, back to the States and also work very hard at the little ensemble I started – the Consort – looking up manuscripts and editing music for this group and that's taking quite a lot at the moment. And, as I say, you never know what is in store for the future.'

Narciso Yepes (b. Lorca, Spain 1927)
At the beginning of 1961, some months after I had had that most interesting and enlightening chat with Julian Bream, a small studious-looking man, wearing thick spectacles, and bald for one so young, came to the shop to buy some music. I recognised him as Narciso Yepes, who had recently arrived in London after a Japanese concert tour. I had seen him playing at a recital for a specially invited audience at the Spanish Institute at Eton Square and remembered that concert particularly for his rendering of the Sor *Variations on O Cara Armonia* a theme from Mozart's opera *The Magic Flute*. Having cut my classical guitar teeth on Segovia's recording of this under the title *Theme Varie* I hadn't altogether taken to Yepe's phrasing.

In 1959 he had recorded the *Concierto de Aranjuez* by Joaquin Rodrigo (b. Valencia 1902), (SXL 2091 Decca) but was still fairly unknown outside his own country in spite of the fact that he was the first guitarist to have recorded the Concerto (which had not yet gained great popularity but has since been recorded by nearly 30 players).

Narciso and I talked, became friendly, and after his Wigmore Hall concert on 17 February 1961, my wife, son Stuart, Narciso, his wife and I, went out to dinner, and became much better acquainted socially and I learnt more about his dedication to the guitar.

But the concert (which was very well attended) resulted in factions being created among the audience, where opinions regarding his phrasing differed widely.

Jack Duarte reviewed the concert for *BMG* with such critical severity that in the correspondence that followed in the columns of the magazine one letter congratulated the reviewer on 'his lucid and constructive criticism' while another described the review as 'this odorous diatribe' and 'an attack of unbridled viciousness'.

I have already mentioned that his phrasing was individual and, even to me (who takes the view of one professional to another), not wholly to my taste. Therefore, in view of the controversial atmosphere engendered by him, I was interested to hear his opinions.

When I asked if we could discuss this, he was most cooperative in spite of what must have been my very frank probing.

First, about his background. He was born in Lorca, South East Spain in 1927 and when I asked him to tell me the story of his life, he laughingly replied 'There is not much of it as I have not yet lived long enough'. There were no musicians in his family, but he began to study the guitar at the age of four taking lessons from a guitar teacher in Lorca and then, to be brief, he went to Valencia where he studied harmony and composition, continuing with his studies in Paris.

He described this period in the following way. 'I studied interpretation with George Enesco, and with Walter Gieseking the high problems of technique of the instrument. Not only of the guitar but every instrument.

I.M. *'But did he help you with the technique of the guitar?'*
N.Y. 'Yes, very much. He told me of the high problems of an artiste not only the high problems of a guitarist. Not only the fingering of the guitar but the ideas behind the instrument which is very different.'

I then asked him about whether he used nails or the tips of his fingers in string picking to which he answered he used both nails and tips of fingers.

During the concert I noticed that he sometimes bent the right hand thumb from the middle joint and asked him about it.
N.Y. 'Yes. I have several positions for the thumb. In fact, I have several positions with all the fingers not only with the thumb. Also, with the other fingers, I play with one position or with another position – depending on the nature of the music; depending whether I play an Andante or an Allegro. I also use them in a different way when I play with a very metallic sound or when I play with a sweet sound. It also depends if the melody line is being played with the thumb or the other fingers; whichever it is, the melody must be strong. I cannot give you a general system because this is not possible.'

When I asked the reason for holding the guitar in an unorthodox position, this rather mystified him until I took the guitar from him and demonstrated, i.e. (a) *Yepes position*. Left foot on footstool, shoulder

of the guitar on left thigh, lower bout of guitar resting on right thigh.
(b) *Segovia position.* Usual position, concave waist of guitar fitting into left thigh, lower bout between thighs.
N.Y. 'Because the right hand is more free if I have the guitar in the middle of the two thighs; and if I have the guitar on the left thigh (b) my position is *so* and not *so.*' – and here he demonstrated the difference. 'furthermore' he added, 'the position of the left hand is more comfortable'.

It is difficult to explain these positions in a hurry and would take a good deal of time and demonstration to prove this.

He confessed he used to hold the guitar in the same way as Segovia but changed for the following reasons:

Traditionally the forearm rests on the wide bout so that the hand hangs over the strings. Narciso, on the other hand, brings the elbow over the edge of the bout which he claims gives the hand more freedom for a variety of hand positions. He then proved his point by playing chords with his hand square to the strings then at various angles from square to almost parallel.

When the hand squared to the strings, the sound of the chords was sharp to the point of string slap, but as the hand was brought anti-clockwise, the tone became less sharp and more round until the point where the sides of the fingers as well as the nails picked or sounded the strings. In this manner it was possible to use more force and produce a fortissimo without distortion or string slaps.

Concerning his nails, the edges were filed at an angle slanting up from right to left, palm facing.

'As you see' he remarked, 'every nail is different'.

He then played various passages of single notes, triads, thirds and grace notes, all of which sounded very rich and full. To continue he demonstrated a number of very fast scales on the top three or four strings during which he rested his thumb on the 6th string.
I.M. *'Do you always rest your thumb when playing runs?'*
N.Y. 'No, not always. I only do that to prevent the harmonics (overtones) of the basses from interfering with the runs.'

He then played some notes on the treble strings without damping the bass string and, of course, the overtones mingled with the notes causing a great disturbance; immediately the bass string was damped with the thumb the treble notes projected clearly without interference. In short, he advocated picking the strings with the fingers at various angles depending on the kind of dynamics required.

I then broached the sensitive subject of phrasing in which Narciso Yepes differs from Segovia, Bream and Williams to name but a few. For example, Segovia plays *Theme Varie* between 126 and 138 = ♩.

'Well' said Yepes, 'it is marked 'andante'' and proceeded to play it at about 116-120 = ♩.

He not only played it slower but held the G♯ and E in the first section while playing the B on the 3rd string instead of the written way, by producing the B with a pull-off from E to B on the second string.

N.Y. 'It is quite incorrect to pull off the E to the open B because it is then impossible to control the harmony note (E) which should sustain as long as the melody note. Nor can you control the open B as well.'

Continuing on phrasing, I asked 'Why in *Recuerdos de la Alhambra* (Tarrega) do you make a tenuto (hold up) at the end of the 12th bar and again almost a break at the end of the 16th bar?'

N.Y. 'Well, consider the melodic line. The four 4-bar phrases from bars 13 to 16 are a repeat of 8 to 12 but in a lower pitch.'

'If you hear this piece played by a violin with piano accompaniment you will notice that there will be a fresh bow between the G♯ at the end of the phrase and the B at the beginning of the 13th bar; likewise, between the F at the end of the 16th bar and the E melody at the beginning of the 17th bar.

If you sing the phrase you must take a breath in these places. It is both necessary to imagine it this way and to play it this way.'

I then continued relentlessly by criticising both his halting performance of the first movement of Prelude No. 1 by Villa Lobs and the big hold-ups in the second movement after the large chord of B and the F♯ followed by a B harmonic. Whereupon he played it producing a full glorious tone the way he liked it and then the other way (more steadily) which he did not like. After he had played the second movement, I exclaimed 'Do you think it necessary to play that section as slowly as you do?' 'Why, yes' he said, 'Look at the paper (music) and you will see it written that way'. When I again mentioned that Segovia did not play it that way, he had no doubt had enough of my comparisons and answered, somewhat heatedly 'I have a great admiration for Segovia and everything he has done for the guitar and its history, but I do not have to put on a record of Segovia and play the music exactly as he does. No, I don't think so!'

I apologised for making the questions so personally controversial, but he said he did not mind. He was very happy about the enthusiastic reception he had received at the Wigmore Hall and in answer to my question said that the guitar was now popular all over the world. 'It is the same in Spain and in every country because now the guitar is not Spanish, it is Universal.'

I.M. *'What form of practice do you advocate?'*

N.Y. 'Of course scales are the most important and to *hear* the sounds: also playing of chords and other left-hand exercises. But it is impossible to explain in a few minutes how to practice scales. It is not enough just to have the guitar and begin to play scales. *How* to make scales, that is very difficult. *How* to make them sound 'molto legato'. You can make scales 'molto legato' or 'molto staccato' or 'mezzo legato-staccato (here, he demonstrated the legato or staccato way by playing the single note bass passage on the 5th string from Torroba's *Fandanguillo* from the *Suite Castellana* first played molto legato then molto staccato). 'For example, I play scales with three fingers – never two' (and did so at terrific speed [a.m.i.m.a.m.i.m.]). One should study good music, always.'

I.M. *'What is your opinion of the instruments made by present and past luthiers?'*

N.Y. 'For me, the best ones are Ramirez and Fleta for the present. I cannot say whether there are any better because any other guitarist can have *his* opinion. But for me the best are Ramirez and Fleta, and the proof is that I play a Ramirez or Fleta. Of the past masters, I think the best one was Santos Hernandez. Marcelo Barbero was different from but a continuation of Santos Hernandez. But Ramirez and Fleta are of a different school.'

A few years later Yepes decided to have a 10-string guitar made with four additional bass strings which he says help to strengthen (by their overtones) certain weak treble notes. I have played the 10-string guitar which one can, of course, get used to, and found it quite manageable after a quarter of an hour, but personally, I am quite happy with the 6-string version and leave the Renaissance and Baroque music to be played on the lute which produces a lighter tone more suitable to the spirit of the music.

Here is how I was introduced to the 10-string masterpiece. It was early Spring 1964, the time was past eleven, rather late for cocktail time at Jose Ramirez' flat in Madrid, and Pepe, not in the slightest bit perturbed by the time, was busy on the telephone. When he rang off, he announced that, first, we were going to visit Narciso Yepes, then, all going to the Coral de la Moreria to eat and see Lucera Tena (the leading flamenco dancer of the era) perform. When we arrived at the

Yepes' flat and disposed of pleasantries and drinks, Pepe said 'Show Ivor the new 10-string guitar'.

I must say Narciso accepted the challenge gracefully. He not only explained the reasons for the ten strings but gave a concert of works by half a dozen composers from Mudarra to Villa Lobos which he played with dazzling technique, producing a tremendous tone and volume.

The body, incidentally, was the same in size as the six-string, but with a wider fingerboard to accommodate the extra four strings. These were tuned C, B♭, A♭, G♭ and, theoretically acted as sympathetic vibrators helping to lengthen all the hitherto weaker notes.

However, due to the weaker notes becoming stronger, they also produced stronger overtones which required to be damped, a process which Yepes has developed successfully with his right hand. It seemed that 'improvements' had brought their side effects.

By 1975 Narciso Yepes had become much more famous than in 1961, had made many recordings and had filled many concert halls all over the world.

In Spain he is extremely popular and while we were all having supper at the Coral de la Morreria in Madrid, Lucera Tena the star of the flamenco show, announced that they were honoured to have with them the famous artiste Narciso Yepes, who acknowledged the audience's acclamation and thanked Lucera Tena and 'Serranito' (who was accompanying her) for the special castanet solo she performed to the tune of *El Colibri* by Sagreras played at breakneck speed by 'Serranito' (Victor Monge).

Alirio Diaz (b. 12 November 1923 in Caserio la Candelaria near Carora, Venezuela)

Alirio Diaz is a guitarist in a class of his own, a master of relaxed playing who can play at a tempo sometimes faster than his contemporaries in a most unassuming manner. In fact, he is at times criticised for playing the Venezuelan Waltzes by Lauro too fast, although he denies that they are faster than the tempos he thinks suitable.

Both Diaz and Antonio Lauro were pupils of Raoul Borges, to whom Diaz introduced himself by letter in 1945 when he went to Caracas where Borges taught at the Escuela de Musica. Prior to commencing lessons with Borges, he played a steel-strung guitar (by ear), but after hearing records of Segovia he decided that he must seek advice from the creator of the School of Venezuelan guitarists, who died in 1967 aged 79.

Now it happened that in 1961 a countryman of Alirio Diaz living in London took part in the annual BMG Rally which was that year held in the Seymour Hall (of all places), too vast for a guitar, rally at which two Latin Americans performed; one, Manuel Lopez Ramos from Mexico on classical guitar, and Freddy Reina (then living in London) playing Quatro (a small 4-stringed Venezuelan guitar). He was fantastic and I told him so, and we soon became good friends. It transpired that Freddy had met Alirio Diaz when he (Freddy) was a pupil of Borges, and, according to Diaz, a brilliant one (which I do not doubt) so they were no strangers.

It seems that everything was happening that Spring as well as the two concerts at the Wigmore Hall by Diaz. Of course, I went to see the concerts, and was so enthralled by his performances that, after I had been introduced to him, I begged him to give me a lesson, although I felt rather guilty at having imposed on his good nature. However, I felt it was in a good cause, i.e. furthering my knowledge.

During his stay in London he was sharing an apartment in New Cavendish Street with John Williams and Christopher Nupen, and it was there that I went to receive my instruction. However, I am not sure if there were positive results. I played some pieces that I knew and some that I was not quite sure about, while he listened and smiled reassuringly, but without comment. So I began to ask questions about my fingering, hand positions, phrasing and so on. 'Is this correct?' 'Yes.' 'Is there nothing wrong with it?' 'No, you are playing it the correct way.' 'How about my technical application or method of tone production?' 'I can't see any fault with it.'

He may have thought that I did not display any bad habits, or perhaps my phrasing did not irritate him, I cannot really say. But I felt rather frustrated at not having been criticised or corrected, like the old dear who has nothing wrong with her health but is disappointed if, when visiting the doctor, he fails to prescribe *some* medicament.

However, back to our main subject. Diaz has a natural talent for the guitar, proved by the fact that he changed to classical guitar at the age of 22 and after five years played his first public concert in Caracas. He then won a scholarship given by the government to study at Madrid Conservatoire with Regino Sainz de la Maza (who has turned out many good guitarists) and, most important of all, went to join a master class with Segovia, which opened up a new vista, or, as he puts it, 'a new vocabulary of sounds'; but unlike Segovia, he also loves flamenco music and, of course, Spain – an affection which I share. That is where we met again later that Spring.

Spain is full of history and beautiful relics of the good and the bad – particularly Toledo with its Alcazar and its gruesome relics of the Civil War, its famous Jewish Quarter with its fourteenth century synagogue, the house of El Greco, previously the abode of Reb. Solomon Levi, financial minister to the Islamic ruler of the time, and other historic treasures.

I was just about to park my car near the church of St Tome when I saw a familiar figure walking along the pavement beside the car. 'He looked at me and I looked at him and when he bent down to put his head through the open side window I recognised Alirio Diaz. He was just about to visit the church to see the famous painting of *The Burial of the Count Orgaz*, one of the greatest masterpieces by Domenico Teotocopulo, otherwise El Greco (The Greek), born in Crete 1541.

Alirio had been to Madrid to record some broadcasts before going to Siena for the Summer School he was to supervise in July and August.

Alirio Diaz (who lives in Rome) continues to amaze audiences with his relaxed playing and delights them when using his special talents in playing the music of Venezuela and Latin America.

John Williams (b. Australia 1941)
The fourth member of my International quartet of concert guitarists was born in Melbourne, Australia of a half-Chinese mother and an English father. His career from childhood can only be described as pre-ordained by a set of circumstances directed to one goal; to become the world's most natural executant of the concert or classical guitar.

His father, Len Williams, was a plectrum guitar player in the 30s who had taken lessons on the classical guitar from Mario Macceferri. He used to work at Bessons in London assisting Jack Abbot, Snr. in the making of Aristone guitars before emigrating to Australia where he now devoted himself to the classical guitar. In 1952 he returned to London with his small son John, and established the Spanish Guitar Centre in Cranbourne Street, London, a couple of years or so after I opened the Central School of Dance Music in Cambridge Circus. He at one point suggested some kind of tie-up with me which I firmly avoided. But all that is beside the main point which is to describe the talents of his son John.

As a small boy John could pick out melodies on the plectrum guitar and he was what we older people with children call 'a good boy'. He was receptive to his father's tuition, a condition which rarely prevails between father and child. John did not mind practising and must have shown (especially to an experienced musician) great natural talent; in fact, when he was seven he made a solo recording.

I first heard John in the Kensington Town Hall in 1953 at a BMG Annual Rally at which I performed with my guitar group. A small bespectacled boy came on the stage, played four pieces including the Villa Lobos *Etude No 1* at breakneck speed and accepted the tumultuous applause without any particular show of emotion. It was a foregone conclusion that we had been present at the debut of a future great guitarist.

Len, his father, introduced him to Segovia for whom he played. Most of the rest is known. Segovia invited him to go to Siena where John studied with Segovia and after a number of student concerts he was the first student to give a public concert in Siena with Segovia in the audience. That was in 1963 when Segovia said about him 'A prince of the guitar is born'.

John, besides having the ability to play anything that is written for the guitar, is, as a person, a product of contemporary youth; a nonconfirmist in relation to the 'establishment'. In fact, he broke the dress barrier by not playing in tails, he broke the concert barrier by playing at Ronnie Scott's Jazz Club, and the music barrier by playing different music from the usual programme material.

He came to see me in 1973 and asked me to find an electric guitar for him and to keep the information confidential because until he had experimented and perhaps recorded what he proposed to play, he did not wish it known that he was messing about with an electric guitar. There were various snags to finding a suitable instrument. First of all the fingerboard of a classical guitar is at least $2\frac{1}{16}''$ wide at the nut but the usual Gibson electric or electric/acoustic is more like $1\frac{5}{8}''$. Fortunately, however, I had a Gretsch acoustic/electric and they make the width of the fingerboard at the nut more like $1\frac{3}{4}''$.

John tried this guitar for about an hour on an amplifier using the fingers of his right hand and after a number of adjustments found it sufficiently comfortable to work on.

Watching him and listening to him perform feats of pyrotechnical brilliance without effort become so customary that one simply comes to accept it as normal. Try as I did to discover some secrets from this display, I could only come to the conclusion that his co-ordination was tuned to the fine perfection which only nature could provide. It was such that no amount of practice by ordinary mortals could equal. John, in fact, does not regiment himself to regular practice periods, but only to learn new pieces or refresh his memory on works he has not played for some time and which crop up to supplement a concert. Eventually, John took the guitar and, after getting used to it, recorded *The Height Below* by Brian Gascoigne in which he uses both electric guitar and classical guitar. (I reviewed this record HIFLY 16 in the *Guitar*) and proved that he was free of snobbery or musical prejudice, a quality he had already shown in his *Fly* record conducted by Stanley Myers on which he recorded an arrangement of the Bach *Preludium in E* from the *Lute Suite* with a rhythm background. *Cavatina* which was composed by Stanley Myers, and which he played on classical guitar became a major hit with guitarists, and the printed copy has had very good sales. So has his recording with Cleo Lane.

John Williams is not only versatile, he is a thorough professional without any apparent awareness or 'side' of the high regard people have for him.

I have played guitar for Mantovani's Orchestra since about 1961, and on one recording session John appeared with his guitar. I was surprised because I was usually assisted by another guitarist (the parts have often been written for two guitars). However, he was called in by 'Monty' to play guitar in an arrangement of *Ay-Ay-Ay* in which we played a duet, he, of course, playing 1st guitar. The LP was *Mantovani Olé* Decca SHL 4712, but as one expects in commercial orchestral records, neither of us was mentioned. I wasn't surprised because I had played hundreds of solos on his LPs without being mentioned. It is always expected that a 'session' musician plays whatever music is placed on his music stand without fuss, and if it is a feature, he must be capable of rising to the occasion.

Although all session players in the orchestral field are very good sight-readers, John Williams is phenomenal for a guitarist. I saw him reading the guitar line in a score written by Stephen Dodgson which included harp and orchestra. He not only just played the notes, he produced the notes with understanding of the subject at the correct tempo. He has extended the range of the guitar by working with composers such as André Previn and Stephen Dodgson.

Since 1963 he has, of course, done many concerts but he says 'I hate travelling, but it's not just the travelling. You just have to go at a certain date and this does not appeal to me musically. The set-up of our lives is too organised. Composers don't work like that. They write music when they want to'.

I saw him recording some of the electric guitar background to Patrick Gower's *Concerto for Guitar* which consists of a classical guitar solo over a background of electronic organ and electric guitar. It was, of course, recorded in stereo where each few bars of electric guitar had to be taken on a separate track played facing a different microphone and starting and stopping at very awkward places. Some of the short sections had to be re-recorded many times before perfection was achieved, but John complied very patiently and turned out a perfect job.

Watching him at the same studio with the English Chamber Orchestra and Sir Charles Groves recording Stephen Dodgson's *2nd Guitar Concerto* proved that he could play through any required section perfectly or almost perfectly during every take. This proved to be a great advantage to the final orchestral performance as, for example, the balance of the bongo, when in duet with the harp was not quite perfect, or when the tempo was not quite to taste. As far as John was concerned there seemed to be no additional tension because of retakes.

He says, 'Playing with other instruments is very enjoyable. The most enjoyable recordings I've made have been with Julian Bream down in the country. We both play differently, like chalk and cheese, but somehow it works. It was taken for granted that I would take guitar as a career because I was good from a young age, but I wish I had had some jazz experience!'

I wonder if it is the longing for jazz that drew him to play a Les Paul Solid Electric guitar for a new composition by Stanley Myers, although he is currently using an Ovation acoustic-transducer-fitted guitar with his new group 'Sky'.

And that's the rub. Whatever one has, one wishes for something else. Let it be a consolation to mere mortals that even the 'greats' do not have everything.

Siegfried Behrend

Now we come to a guitarist who revels in the most way-out *avant-garde* music. One almost needs to learn a new musical language to appreciate it.

In spite of not having had any formal training or perhaps because of it, I have been able to keep an open mind, therefore never ceasing to listen to new musical phenomena. In this respect I first heard an amazing guitar player during the Erlangen (Germany) Guitar Concourse held there in 1957. I have already mentioned Siegfried Behrend who, while sitting on a settee in the lounge of the hotel, played the Bach *Chaconne* on the guitar while carrying on a conversation with me at the same time. On another occasion at the Festival, I went to see him perform an *avant-garde* guitar concerto of tremendous virtuosity which he executed with complete aplomb. He was then twenty-four, and in the ensuing years has become the most celebrated guitarist in Germany, internationally known for his ability to perform way-out music whether it is written in notation, fly swattings, blobs, squiggles, circles or diagrams. I think it is fitting, therefore, for a guitarist of our time to have the last word about the guitar music of our time.

As a guitarist, he is a controversial player whose tone production and phrasing have always been considered unorthodox to the ears of English guitarists. While they do not find his rendition of traditional music always acceptable, they take great interest in his *avant-garde* music. On the other side of the coin, he himself has seemed to appear more interested in his own performance when playing modern music than when playing classical music which he brushes off nonchalantly with indifference. In fact, quite an enigma, and, because of that, I felt that guitarists would be interested in his thoughts on the music of the guitar, which were bound to be controversial as well as enlightening. Prompted by my questions, he more than proved himself a formidable guitar-intellect of our time.

First of all I asked him what had created his interest in modern contemporary music and recorded his answers.

Siegfried Behrend Speaks about Music and the Guitar
'I am a man of the twentieth century and am very interested in knowing what is going on in my time. While I admire the old music which I love and perform, I live with the new music because it is my music. It is the music of my time.

Actually, of all the people who are active about the renewal of the guitar today, there are Julian Bream, who commissions music to be written for him by modern English composers, while on the other side there is myself who commissions new works from modern *avant-garde* composers in other parts of the world.

Why do we do it? Because we need new elements, musical elements for our instrument. Works which are beautiful and which contain many possibilities and many colours.

It has been the same throughout musical history. Take Mozart for instance. Why did he not write anything for the guitar? Because there were no guitarists around him who commissioned music to be written for the guitar. It was ever thus and similarly in our own time (era) we must interest the composers of our time to write for our instrument.

I.M. *How do you judge the quality of an* avant-garde *piece? Don't you think that often it is frivolous and unworthy?*

S.B. That is quite right! Especially when a composition appears to be fantastic and excellently notated, but really they are completely dilettante pieces. It is a question of experience. If you have no knowledge of the works of Johann Sebastian Bach then you cannot discern the difference between good and bad counterpoint, but if you know a little bit about it then you are able to tell immediately which is good and which is bad. Similarly, with modern music, if you have knowledge of this type of music then you can clearly tell whether this is a good piece or that is a bad piece.

I will give you an example. Last year I organised a festival and held a music competition for guitar music in Brazil at which I received about 25 entries. At least six compositions were completely dilettante and I am sure there was no schooling behind their works. It was just something done without any background. Of course, none of the jury knew the identities of the competitors, nevertheless all the judges (six composers and myself) came to the same conclusion, i.e. that there was no music behind it. So you see, that there is a way to judge good work in modern music.

Now comes the other thing. It takes at least one or two generations before audiences discover their preference from the selection of good *avant-garde* pieces which they hear. But this is not our (the performers) problem. We have no problem. Our job is to perform the good music which is written in our time. The composer must compose, the performer must perform, so that the audience becomes informed and can then say whether they like it or not. But at least in this way the audience is informed and can choose. The main thing is that it has to be done. That is very important.

I.M. *Do you play the music of unknown and completely unproved composers?*

S.B. Old or new?

I.M. New.

S.B. I would say yes. There is also a great deal of old music written by composers whose names have never appeared in any programme. For instance the famous Italo-German Kapsberger and the great

Italian Piccinini. There are, to my knowledge, some Italian composers one in particular, Brascianello, whom I recently discovered had written about 35 Sonatas for guitar no one had ever heard. Of course they were very similar but two or three of them were very nice. The same applies to new music. I am not only interested in established composers but in students. I have asked some of our composition students to write something. These young people are able to discover their own new way of writing for a new instrument. Sometimes the results are immediately evident and sometimes the results come many years later, but they come.

I.M. *When you play new compositions, do they have to be atonal?*

S.B. They can be tonal, they can be atonal, they can be punctual, free tonal or graphical, but that does not mean anything.

I.M. *What kind of standards do you apply to a piece of music?*

S.B. From the point of composition, there has to be a clear statement (auszage) in the work. If there are some complicated 'struggled' things, they are things which I don't like personally. So for me it has to be a very clear statement in the score and when I like it, I try to formulate it the best way I can. The young composers try all kinds of experiments, for instance, take the competition last year in Brazil. The Brazilian composer Jorge de Freitas Antunes who won the first prize with his composition *Sighs* used two guitars, one for the 1st and 3rd movements and another for the middle movement in which the whole instrument is tuned in B. He got fantastically nice sounds out of it but had to use two guitars and change guitars for the 2nd movement, but it was worth it in the end as it aroused tremendous interest. Likewise in Japan, they too try new tunings but they do it for a different reason. They are saddled with the pentatonic scales and probably desire to break this tonality of major minor, prevalent on the guitar due to the E minor tuning, and that is why they began experimenting with the tuning. Although I do not go in for it myself, I think it adds to the possibilities of finding new sounds.

And that is always the question. You try to discover new sounds, sometimes you are fortunate but at other times it is just a big mistake. It can have merit without new sounds. Do you rememeber the John McCabe piece I played on Sunday? This Canto is one of the most excellent pieces written in the last ten years and it is completely tonal with even a bit of Spanish flavour. But it was written in our days (1968) and I think is one of the most excellent pieces. *Nocturnal* by Benjamin Britten is a totally tonal piece and it is wonderful, therefore it does not have to be experimental for its own sake, just a good statement.

If you take the graphical scores of Roman Haubenstock-Ramati, (*Credentials* published by Universal Edition AG, Vienna partly illustrated in *Notation in New Music* p 102) of Anestis Logothetis, you will see that there are few written notes but the statement is so wonderful that it stimulates your imagination to play and make music out of it. It is the same if you see the paintings of Paul Klee. They are completely musical. If you are a musician you can immediately see what sound it should be. I think that all types of art belong together. There can never be a true musician who is ignorant about painting and the history of fine arts. All arts are unique and an artiste can only be a good guitarist if he is knowledgeable about these things.

That is to say, knowledge of the arts which have existed in past centuries in order to have some perspective and knowledge of what exists around him so that he is informed about the other fields of art.

For example, the *avant-garde* movement in painting existed long before it came to music and even then most musicians were not interested. They were very backward and did not exist in their time.

Take (the United States) America, although it is a very young country, only 200 years old, it is a point in their favour. Many talented artists in America have open minds because they have no tradition. That is one of the problems with the people in Europe. They have too much tradition so that their minds are too closed because of their tradition; that is another problem in itself.

Schönberg's influence, after he settled in the US, may have been slow at first but before long, they quickly understood what he wanted to say because their minds were open to everything. But it is difficult. Schönberg himself had his bad times in Vienna as well as Webern because nobody wanted their music.

I.M. *You yourself seem to be a different person when you play a traditional piece and when you perform an* avant-garde *piece, playing most of the traditional music with nonchalance, almost boredom; as if you don't care if you impart any feeling or otherwise. Just notes. But when you played the duos for voice and guitar you really appeared to enjoy that.*

S.B. I would not say enjoy it, it would not be the right word. You see, there is a misconception in the way guitarists think of the guitar as a beautiful instrument. The guitar is indeed a beautiful instrument but it is only a musical instrument, no more. And if you take music by Sor and Giuliani for instance, it has nothing to do with depth of feeling (deepness, SB). It is just virtuosi play really as the word describes it 'play' virtuosi and enjoy it. A lot of finger movement, R,r,r,r,r, ... forget it! nothing else, just be happy to listen to it, but there is no depth in it.

I.M. *And that is exactly the way you played Sor and Giuliani, also faster than necessary.*

S.B. Take Rossini. An orchestra with average ability haven't the technical ability to play Rossini as fast as it should be played, but when you hear Toscannini with the NBC Orchestra, you will discover it is played faster and with much greater precision – ra-pa-pa-pa – because they are able to do it – and it is fun. Nothing more, it's just fun. I don't know if Giuliani would have approved of the tempo I played the *Grand Concerto Op 61*, but I see it from the point of view of the music. If I were to conduct this piece for an orchestra then I would take that tempo. As far as I am concerned I visualise the score and try to instrumentate (orchestrate?) it as it would be played by an orchestra and try to perform it the same way on the guitar.

I.M. *How is it that you were able to play the Giuliani almost as a throwaway with great ease and encountered great difficulties with the English Suite by John Duarte?*

S.B. Mmmm, yes. There is no reason at all. I just did not have enough time to work on it – ha ha ha ha ha ha. Very simple. Therefore I also played it with the music in front of me. I had just come from Hong Kong and thought that if I played it without music I would forget it. I got into some difficulties with the second movement, of course, but then – it's not important. It did not bother me very much (hearty laughter).

I.M. *When you played the German folk tunes for an encore there was authenticity in the performance, but when you followed it with a Carcassi, it sounded trivial. It is these contrasts which make you an enigma to your audience. There is a certain unaccountability about your playing. You play most difficult and complicated music with understanding and yet you fail to invest the familiar works with any dynamics or tone colours.*

S.B. It is a question of thought, a question of mind. Such a little piece is of little importance as far as interpretation is concerned. It is just a little thing that passes away. If you make it important I think it is dilettante.

Now comes the other thing (familiarity). You may often hear (and I say this as a guitarist myself, but I always try to say) that I just use the guitar as a vehicle for transmitting music not from the point of guitar. There are many examples. *Fandaguillo* by Turina, the *A major Minuet* by Sor, and I could mention at least one hundred pieces. I have often heard them but I can assure you that I have never heard them PROPER (presumably played properly or interpreted properly) NEVER! Because if you take a metronome and hear *Fandaguillo* (play it with metronomic precision) you find that it becomes a wonderful piece and always enables you to have in your ears the one complete idea of it. Take any recording of it, set the metronome and play the record and you will find out what I mean (he then proceeded to sing and conduct the introductory movement of *Fandanguillo* at a fastish 3 of about 1 3 2 beats to the minute). It becomes a completely different piece from the one you know (*Fandanguillo* is marked Allegro Tranquillo ♩ = 72).

I.M. *Therefore, you are criticising, let us say, Segovia's interpretation.*
S.B. Any, any, any!
I.M. *Yet it was dedicated to Segovia whose interpretation has set the pattern.*
S.B. I am not criticising. I merely wanted to say that the feeling of the audience is sometimes like this. Very often because they have in their ear some interpretation which they think has to be like that. But it should not be like this. Music is scored and timed to a metronomic reading. This gives you the timing, then comes the phrasing within the timing and only then the music starts going (begins to become alive) and if this is wrong it is not the correct interpretation.
I.M. *In spite of the fact that the listener derives more enjoyment from a performance that is not an exact metronome reading?*
S.B. If it is not a metronome reading, it is no longer the same piece. Why play the piece at all. Why did the composer insert bar lines when there is no more purpose in it?
I.M. *If Turina had not cared for Segovia's interpretation of* Fandanguillo, *might he not have mentioned it to him?*
S.B. I would not like to say nor can I explain this. I just have the music and read it and hear it the way it has been written. If it were otherwise, I would hear it otherwise and Turina would have written it otherwise, but I like to hear it the way it is written. For me the music score is the only proof (authentic) material of the way it should be played because the composer is a composer and is able to write his notes into the bars so that they fit.

If you take the *A Sor Minuet* and play it at ♩ = 126 beats to the minute, it has life and vigour, but when it is taken down to ♩ = 96 beats per minute, it is no longer the same piece. It becomes completely and totally dilettante. If guitarists cannot accept this because they have been conditioned by other performances then they cannot, but things are changing.

The young people not only learn the guitar today. They learn, as well, also piano and harpsichord. In Germany it is compulsory to have one main instrument besides guitar and one more secondary instrument and what they don't learn with the guitar teachers they pick up with the others.

These things are changing all the time and I see this during my master classes. Many many students and good guitar players from all over the world discuss these matters which many of them have never thought about before. But when they start thinking of it, they discover how much beautiful music is written for the guitar if the music is performed properly. Phrasing and expression always go with the tempi especially in classical music. In Romantic and late Romantic music, you can often over-phrase in one bar but you must restore it in the next bar. You can make it gipsy-like in the slow movement of the *Concierto de Aranjuez* by Rodgrigo but in classical music, never. The phrasing goes within.

It is not a question of tempo, it is a question of perfection.

It can be half tempo, it can be double tempo; this has no meaning, but the exactness of the tempo, that is important, otherwise there need be no bars.

I.M. *About your techniques. You have always had the ability to find your way around the fingerboard without effort. Did you acquire that facility at a young age?*

S.B. Maybe because I studied the harpsichord and the piano so for me this was no problem. I still believe that moving the fingers (and every typist moves the fingers as well as any musician and anybody can do this) has nothing to do with art and nothing to do with music. It is just a question of practice; it is very easy to learn.

But to organise musical understanding, music in the mind by phrasing, is a difficult thing.

I don't think that the solfeggio system is used in either England or Germany which is a pity. Before taking up a musical instrument one should just move the hands in conjunction with the musical sounds in order to clarify the music not to take an instrument and collect a few notes.

The basic education of the guitar is wrong all over the world ... very wrong. When people take up an instrument they start taking the notes on their fingers and by doing this they have one problem organising this hand; the second problem is organising the other hand; the third problem is understanding the music and the fourth problem is reading the music and relating the music to the hands.

These problems can never be covered together only one by one – this is the main problem.

I.M. *But does one need a special talent and technical facility to be able to do what you do?*

S.B. This is another question. When you become a virtuoso on your instrument, you are not yet necessarily a musician. That is a different question. Now comes the talent and artistic ability which have to be educated and many other things; a knowledge of historical things. If you play sixteenth century Italian lute music, you should know what was going on in Italy in the sixteenth century. If you play that kind of music with force using great spread arpeggios, then it has nothing to do with it.

I am not a purist at all, but you have to have knowledge of the period in order to give a proper performance.

The good thing about music is that every good performer has his own way of understanding and interpreting the music. Therefore, people go and listen to different violinists playing the same piece, which is a very natural phenomena and should be like this.

I.M. *How would you advise one to start on the guitar?*

S.B. Only methodical work. Simple methodical work – even before taking an instrument. Educating one hand, educating the other hand, educating the brain and putting it all together before taking the instrument as illustrated in *Gitarre – mein Hobby* Books 1 and 2, published by Zimmerman, Frankfurt (by Behrend).

I.M. *How did you start?*

S.B. I did not start this way, therefore, I had a long way to go. I did it all wrong as well as everybody else but I had the good fortune that because of my technique on the harpsichord I was quickly able to analyse the mistakes I was making and discover what was wrong.

At the time I started there was nobody around who could offer any advice to a beginner so I had to learn from my mistakes. Musical history led me to the guitar. The books available for the lute and guitar which I had never previously heard of and which aroused my interest.

Then I took up the guitar, examined the transcriptions and became fascinated so that I came nearer to the guitar and further away from the harpsichord. I really taught myself to play the guitar. I treat it more like a harpsichord and not from the romantic point of view; more as a vehicle for producing the music than as a romantic instrument.

Advice on technique is rather difficult to offer and it is global. You cannot give any advice because it always depends on the human body. One person has long fingers, another has thick fingers or short fingers; one good fingernails and another bad fingernails, therefore you cannot lay down any regulations for that. And it also depends on the body which has to be completely relaxed. If one suffers from cramps then there is something wrong. Of course, in general, one can say something (i.e. give advice) but it always depends on each person. (A recent concert had included *Duo* for voice and guitar by Behrend and *Ultima Rara* (Pop Song 1969) by Sylvano Bussoti sung by his wife Claudia Behrend.)

I.M. *I would like to ask you about the declamatory vocalising frequently heard in modern works. Is this vocalising to attract, to enervate to excite or to relate a story?*

S.B. None of these things. Like other phenomena in music, it is just a new development. There are so many songs and pieces composed for singing voice that our composers are looking for new possibilities, new musical elements. There were already some things by Luciano Berio and his wife, Cathy Berberian.

Things like disturbing the voice in order to rebuild it from another angle, that is making quarter tones out of these noises and out of the tone and so on.

It is very easy with the pieces we performed because Claudia (his wife) has studied the theatre. She was working in the theatre and after we were married she was unable to continue in the theatre because we wanted to travel together. So I ordered (commissioned) compositions by composers to write new music for *acting* voice not singing, not talking but acting voice, to use the voice as musical material together with the guitar.

One of the first pieces we received was the Sylvano Bussoti *Ultima Rara*, then we got very interesting pieces by Anestis Logothtis and Haubenstock-Ramati and I myself wrote a couple of pieces for voice solo or for voice and guitar using the voice as voice making, breaking the quality of the sound and using this material as musical elements.

There is some talking and sometimes singing, not the average type of classical singing. It is supposed to be a type of art never previously presented so we can only call it acting voice not singing voice or talking voice.

I call it 'acting voice', Bussoti calls it 'Human Voice' – 'Menschlicha Stimma' and it should affect people the way Ligetti's orchestral pieces do. Take it whichever way they want to. What the composers wanted was to transmit the feeling of our time to the audience. And if you examine our era you will agree that it is NOT conspicuous for the beautiful noises one hears. It is rather full of bad noises, also full of bad things. This is the kind of era we are living in and the music has always reflected the period in which people lived. In Mozart's time people danced with graceful movements. All music of that period was influenced by the surroundings of its era and *our* music is influenced by *our* surroundings. Some people try to run away from its surroundings. I try to use it. This has always been a composer's problem. When Tchaikowsky's violin concerto was first performed in Vienna, the critics wrote that it sounded like three different music boxes playing three different melodies at the same time when, actually, it is a most romantic piece. So, it is always a problem.

A composer works with musical material and a painter works with ideas and in each instance they are a little ahead of the audience but the people prefer to get away from the new connotations which, for them, are more on the bad side than on the good side.

The problem of being a creative artiste is that one always stays a little aside, make experiments which one hopes are not too distant from the audience. You find the same in jazz or in entertainment music like Manesdorf or Doldinger (Previn or The Beatles?). They use electronics and there is no particular reason; no more reason, no more melodies. Just collages of noise. Funnily enough, young people like it but in my opinion they like it too much although they do not really understand it.

It is a fact that when one works with one type of material one becomes so familiar with it that it becomes boring in the same way as when you hear the same old jazz phrases and aim to extend the improvisation and harmonies but to the general listener, the extemporisation seems quite unrelated to anything they have heard.

I.M. *How do you break the new music to large audiences when, in general, they are more interested in the familiar, although Julian Bream had two full houses when he recently played a new guitar work by Henze. Where do you find the best audiences for* avant-garde?

S.B. In Japan. The people in Japan are very open-minded. You can play Bach today and *avant-garde* tomorrow.

I performed a couple of *avant-garde* concerts recently in Tokyo to big audiences who were tremendously enthusiastic, a thing which could not have happened ten years ago. It is something that has recently developed and it is also happening in Germany but only recently, and it has become a source of steady work.

It is in the traditional countries which take longer to accept the new music. It is a battle today and it has always been a battle to attract people to a concert of music they have not heard before. It is a familiar situation but it is necessary to continue trying to induce the listening audience to acquaint themselves with the new as well as the old.'

Siegfried Behrend is undoubtedly an important figure in the world of the classical guitar and while one does not have to agree with what he says or does in regard to performance or the creation of its music, he has the great gift of not only talking about what he does but of doing it. And without the doers of this world, there would be few new exciting horizons.

Chapter Twenty-one

MAINLY SPAIN

The first flamenco 'tableau' I saw took place at the Palace Theatre in Cambridge Circus during 1952 and that is when I met Angel Iglesias the guitarist who was accompanying Teresa and Lusillo, the dancers who were performing there for the season.

Angel was a technical virtuoso who was equally at home both with flamenco and classical music. His arrangement of Liszt's 2nd Hungarian Rhapsody (which he played at a tearaway tempo) was a 'tour de force', and he gave me some very useful exercises including the well known scale in arpeggios of Aguado which I include (with variations) in my *Simplicity* tutor (B. & H.).

He also sold me a rather exceptional Esteso guitar with a one-piece back of Rio rosewood with the label *Viuda y Sobrinos de Domingo Esteso* (made in 1948) *7 Gravina, Madrid* (illustrated in *The Story of the Spanish Guitar* by A. P. Sharpe).

Domingo Esteso himself lived from 1884 to 1937 and when he died his nephews Faustino, Julian and Mariano (who had been his assistants) took over.

The season by Angel Iglesias was followed by other excellent flamenco guitarists all of whom taught me and became my friends. Rosario's ballet (at the Saville Theatre) was accompanied by Juan Garcia de la Mata (b. 1928) who had assisted Regino Sainz de la Maza as professor of guitar at the Madrid Conservatoire; Pilar Lopez at the Cambridge Theatre, brought with her Luis Lope Tejera (b. 1914) or Luis Maravilla as he was professionally known. His scrap book was his constant companion and before long he showed it to me, pointing out that when he was 11 and in short trousers (as the newspaper cutting and picture proved) he was so brilliant that he was christened Luis Maravilla or Luis the 'marvel'. He played a Santos Hernandez guitar which he valued at £600.00 although he said he would never sell it. He now has a guitar shop in Madrid. His son Luis followed in dad's footsteps and is a professional flamenco guitarist.

Then came the fiery legendary Carmen Amaya and her fiery guitarist José Motos who had had a legal training while studying classical guitar but was bitten by the flamenco bug. A very articulate and technical player.

The best of the bunch was, of course, Manolo Moreno (Moraito de Jerez), a gipsy 'natural', who always accompanied Antonio at his greatest. Manolo was the perfect foil for the dancer or singer and he could anticipate every extraneous move Antonio made – toe-heel-taps or finger snaps; one of the undisputed 'top ten' of the art.

These visits to London in the early 50s aroused my curiosity about flamenco music and, having had lessons from the visiting guitarists, few of whom could read music, I decided to delve deeper and set down my findings in a tutor, written both in musical notation and cifra or tablature.

I mentioned this to David Platz (then in charge of Latin-American music and now head of the large pop-orientated Essex Music) and he was very interested. 'If you agree to let us publish it' he said, 'I can help you to get a lot of information on the subject.' It seemed logical, so I agreed. David introduced me to Manuel Salanger, chief of Musica del Sur in Barcelona, who had studied flamenco music for over 20 years and was, himself, an orchestrator and gave me a pressing of *Introduction to Flamenco*, with guitar by Paco de Aguilera.

Tommy Ward Snr., director and legal adviser to Southern Music, gave it his blessing and, of course, financial support, and all I had to do now was to write the book!

My friend, the late Dr. Alex Martinez (probably the most knowledgeable flamenco aficionado in Great Britain) said that although I had undertaken an impossible task he would, nevertheless, give me all the assistance I required when necessary. Coincidentally, because of the occasional interest shown for fingerstyle guitars in England, and aware that I was going to Spain, Geoffrey Hawkes asked me to accept a roving commission to find some suitable Spanish guitars for British distribution.

Thus began my many working holidays around the world, and the first to Spain. It also began my close involvement at first hand with classical and flamenco guitars, their players and their makers.

San Sebastian

The time; June 1955. The travelling party: my wife, son and daughter and an aficionado friend who was also a courier and an Hispanophile. First port of call San Sebastian in the Basque region (NW) with its sandy beach, Royal Summer Residence, and large enclosed market, but not a guitar to be seen or heard – on the surface.

Henri (the courier) of course knew better and soon we found ourselves in a little glove shop in the Avenida di España where we were introduced to a grey haired balding man with aesthetic intelligent features and high domed forehead, sitting behind the cash register.

This was the man Henri wanted us to meet. His name was Sancha Granada and before inheriting the business from his father he had been a regular concert performer and, unbeknown to me, had given concerts in England. As soon as he heard I was interested in guitars, he got rid of the customers and had the shutters pulled down. When the shop was closed, he disappeared behind the dividing curtain at the back of the counter and returned with a handsome guitar made by Manuel de la Chica (b. 1908, still living in Granada), sat on a stool and gave a dazzling display of classical and Spanish music – an unexpected pleasure in 1955. But that was just the beginning. We returned after dinner and there on the counter, guitars had taken the place of gloves. Six or seven guitars, all made by Manuel de la Chica, which I found to be light on the treble and a little tubby in the bass, although the first string in one or two of the better sounding guitars produced excellent resonance.

After I had made my comments, out came the prize guitar of the collection, a Santos Hernandez (Madrid 1873-1942) which was indeed a masterpiece, with a firm brilliant tone and a particularly clear and resonant 1st string. It was, in fact, this clarity which gave the Santos its unique quality of sound and it became obvious that De La Chica was trying to emulate that sound. (Retail prices for the Chica of course, 3,500 to 8,000 ptas.)

It is interesting to note that Santos Hernandez (who had been an assistant/pupil of Manuel Ramirez) sold his first few guitars for 350 ptas each (less than £3 at today's rate of exchange). Today, one would have to pay thousands of pounds for a genuine Santos Hernandez and in 1957 his widow was asking £400 for a renovated one.

Sancha Granada and I finished the night off with some duets and solos before I left for a few hours sleep prior to motoring on to Madrid.

Madrid

We made a stop at Burgos on the way to Madrid just to see the magnificent cathedral, the centrepiece of this medieval city of El Cid, before continuing to Madrid which has really been the centre of the art of guitar construction in this century. With a few notable exceptions (Fleta, Hauser and of course Antonio Torres), the leading makers have risen to fame in the city of the Prado and flamenco tablaos, where social life began at midnight.

Our first appointment took us to Madrid's leading guitar collector, Mariano Cubas Martin, then reputed to own the finest collection of modern classical guitars in the world.

Señor Cubas, a charming courteous man of middle age, welcomed us enthusiastically and led us to a richly furnished room with a glass fronted cabinet displaying a number of guitars with a history between them of unequalled interest for guitarists. I examined them and played them in the following order.

The Cubas Martin Collection
1) Guitar by Antonio de Lorca made in 1885, fitted with a resonator or sounding board (tornavos) inside the sound hole. It had been played by Francisco Tarrega, and when I played it, it produced a rather refined delicate tone.

The Lorca family consisted of three generations of guitar makers commencing with Antonio Lorca Snr., born in Malaga in 1803, who founded the guitar workshop and worked there until he died in 1870. He was succeeded by his son, Antonio Lorca Pino (date of birth unknown) who had been his assistant as well as a distinguished guitarist, and had, in fact, made the guitar upon which I was playing. Lorca Pino died in 1909 and was succeeded by *his* son Antonio Lorca Ramirez who continued to make guitars until he died in 1925 and brought the dynasty to an end. This 1885 guitar was unique insofar as I have not seen or heard of another guitar made by any of the Lorcas.

2) Made by Santos Hernandez in 1924 and said to be the favourite guitar of Miguel Llobet. I could well believe it, since I considered it to have the cleanest, clearest tone of all the guitars I had handled up to that point.

3) Made by Antonio de Torres Jurade, born in the parish of San Sebastian, Almeria in 1817 and died in 1892. Recognised as the designer of the modern classical guitar, using the system of bracing to the top known as fan strutting and establishing the sounding length of the string (scale length) at 65 cm. The label read Antonio de Torres 1887 and according to my host it was Segovia's favourite.

4) Another Torres made in 1867 known as 'La Famosa'. La Famosa bore its name because it had been played by Julian Arcas, the most famous guitar executant of his day, a player and composer who collaborated with Torres in his work of improvement.

5) A third guitar by Torres made in 1888, also in perfect condition.
6) A guitar made by Domingo Esteso (Madrid 1887-1934), a pupil of Manuel Ramirez, who worked there at the same time as Santos Hernandez and Modesto Borruguero. The guitar, dated 1925, had a slightly lighter if broader tone than the Torres although a little larger in the body measurements, but more of Esteso and his nephews later.
7) A guitar made in 1897 by Enrique Garcia Castello (born in Madrid 1868 died in Barcelona 1922) in particularly good condition, and one which I especially admired. Garcia was an apprentice of Jose Ramirez I who established his shop in Geronimo No 2, Madrid in 1882, and, if he made this instrument in 1897, then he must have been a brilliant pupil, but then, so was Jose Ramirez's younger brother, Manuel, who also learnt his trade from Jose I.
8) Made by Manuel Rodriguez, a young man who was at the time working for Jose Ramirez II, and made the guitar in his own time outside official hours. The novel thing about it was the solid head with machine heads similar to a steel-strung guitar. It was new but sounded quite good (more of Manuel Rodriguez later).
9) A guitar made by Franz Neuman 1941, had neither the aesthetic appearance nor the tonal beauty of any of the others but I think Señor Martin bought it because it was the nearest he could get to Hauser. The label said 'Franz Neuman 1941, a pupil of Herman Hauser' and it was thought that some of Hauser's guitars were made by Neuman when Hauser was unwell. Be that as it may, the tone was 'boxy' and lacked the resonance of the Spanish made guitars.

The estimated value of the collection (at the time) was, I was informed, about £6,000 but I do not know what amount they fetched when they were sold to guitarist Manuel Cano of Granada, who bought the collection after the death of this charming gentleman aficionado who demonstrated to me how to play using the *four* fingers of the right hand – a method for which he had published a treatise.

Handling and playing the guitars in this collection had afforded a wonderfully enjoyable and valuable experience.

Our next task was to find Marcelo Barbero (1904–6.3.1956) whose workshop was situated in a block of apartments in Old Madrid in the narrow back street of Ministreles. We found the number, entered the dark stone hallway behind the heavy wooden door, groped our way up to the first floor landing and rang the bell of the door with the plate bearing his name, but there was no reply, so we made our way down again. As we retraced our steps we saw a light beaming through an opening in the staircase wall looking into a well, and, putting my head out of the aperture, I saw a lighted window to my right. The window was open and a young man was standing at a bench working on an unfinished guitar. It seemed unreal; too typical to be true, until I broke the silence with a greeting and, smiling, he invited us in to the apartment which I thought was very friendly of him considering the lateness of the hour (10.30 pm).

The flat consisted of a small bed-sitting room, a small workshop, a kitchen and an alcove in which a young woman (his sister) was looking after a slumbering baby.

Manuel Rodriguez

We introduced ourselves and he told us his name was Manuel Rodriguez who was employed as the leader of a team of luthiers at the workshop of Jose Ramirez II and the guitar he was making had been commissioned by a private customer; that is, not connected with Ramirez, who would not have been very happy with his employee's extra home production.

It was my first experience of seeing a constructor at work, made more interesting by his detailed explanations of how a good spruce top had to resound like a bell when suspended between forefinger and thumb and tapped lightly. He then showed us how the top was fan braced with carefully cut wooden struts of well seasoned light tone wood, followed by the stronger cross bracing of the back which had to withstand great pressure. He then turned to the neck and heel block showing us how the curved sides fitted into the slots cut into the sides of the heel block, and type of resin glue he used. Finally, but equally as fascinating, was the delicate work of building up the sound hole mosaic from strips of coloured wood. We wished him success and before leaving, I said I was sure we would be hearing more about him in the future, unaware that our next meeting would take place in Los Angeles, California, almost 15 years later.

Manuel Rodriguez eventually left the Ramirez workshop and shared premises with another young luthier named Arcangel Fernandez, and when an opportunity arose for one of them to emigrate to Los Angeles, Manuel Rodriguez seized that opportunity.

When I visited his very Spanish styled shop and house in Los Angeles he had a very flourishing business, two cars, was married to a girl from Madrid, the father of two children and the inventor of a special adjustable bridge.

He remembered me, and was delighted to see me again. I, too, was pleased with his success in Los Angeles, where he was receiving 800 dollars to 1,000 dollars for one of his guitars.

By 1972, however, Rodriguez had had enough of living abroad, having had for some time a longing to return home, and this he did. He sold out and became re-established in Madrid at 32 Calle Hortaleza, where he has a shop 'manned' by his wife when he is busy in his spacious well-aired workshop making superb guitars of distinction.

Marcelo Barbero (Madrid 1904-1956)
The morning following our interesting and instructive meeting with Manuel Rodriguez, we returned to Ministreles where Marcelo Barbero was happily working at his bench, making his apologies for not being present the night before, since he now lived away from his workshop.

He was a mild looking, small, round faced, quietly spoken man, and, when he heard that I had been using a Barbero for about 9 months, he was eager to hear my opinion of it. Needless to say, he was not disappointed when I described it as having a velvet tone and a beautiful appearance. It had, in fact, won a prize at an exhibition.

Marcelo was still working for Ramirez when Santos Hernandez died in 1942, leaving a widow and a shop with no one to tend it (he had no apprentices) and when the Viuda de Santos offered him the job, he took it. In the course of his work, he repaired guitars, some of them made by Santos, and so became acquainted with the master's manner of construction.

Marcelo made the first guitar which bore his name between 1945 and 1946 labelled 'Viuda de Santos Hernandez, Calle Aduana, Madrid, Constructor Marcelo Barbero'. It was made for Pepé Martinez who paid 800 ptas for it.

This is how Pepé Martinez (who was a favourite of Marcelo's) describes the telephone conversation informing him of the completion of the new guitar: Marcelo (in Madrid) 'Pepito?'

Pepé (in Seville) 'Yes, this is Pepé'.

Marcelo: 'Good! I have your guitar ready and I will send it by train so listen while I tell you what to do. The Stationmaster is a friend of mine, so I will take the guitar round to him; he will give it to the guard who will keep it safe until the train arrives in Seville. You will be there to meet the train; give the guard your identity and tip him 25 pesetas for a drink – OK?'

Pepe: 'OK Marcelo'.

In due course Pepé met the train and collected the guitar — cost, 800 pesetas including carriage.

In 1973 Pepé had a Barbero flamenco guitar for which he was asking £500. Today, the price has gone up considerably.

During our visit in 1955 Marcelo demonstrated how to bend the rosewood sides round a portable heated metal cylinder and explained his complete method of construction. Here (if I can explain), is his method of strutting the top. Two lateral cross struts, one above and one below the sound hole; one vertical centre rib running from the lateral strut below the sound hole well past the bridge position, two tapered ribs on either side of the centre rib slightly fanning out, reaching past the bridge position; two more struts fanning out and tapering past the edge of the bridge; finally, two shorter ribs (not touching the lateral strut) about the same distance from each other as the other struts ending about two inches from the bridge. Seven ribs in all.

Dimensions:
- Scale length: $25\frac{1}{2}''$
- Width at nut: $2''$
- Width at lower bout: $14\frac{3}{8}''$
- Upper bout: $10\frac{7}{8}''$
- Depth of body: $3\frac{5}{8}''$ to $3\frac{7}{8}''$.

Despite his enviable reputation, Marcelo was a simple, unsophisticated, charming person, but who was, unfortunately, fated to die less than a year after our visit (6 March 1956).

Arcangel Fernandez (b. 1931) then 25 years old, had been Marcelo's only assistant, and in accordance with custom, took over. He finished the instruments already begun, labelling them with both names, and wound up Marcelo's affairs.

Arcangel himself, who had been a flamenco player, was for a time undecided about his future career. He came to London and even contemplated settling here, but eventually returned, and took premises at Calle Jesus y Maria in the old part of Madrid off Plaza Santa Anna, which he shared with Manuel Rodriguez.

Naturally he used his own name, and eventually achieved a tremendous reputation both for flamenco and classical guitars. The present waiting period for one of his guitars is at least five years, and he has ceased to take orders.

Marcelo left a widow, a daughter of 20 and a son of 12. When the son grew a little older, he expressed a desire to become a luthier, and so another link was attached to the Barbero chain.

Marcelo Barbero Hijo

Marcelo Barbero Hijo (Jnr.) was born in Madrid on 26 December 1943 and before he reached the age of 13, his father succumbed to pneumonia and died and young Marcelo was left an orphan – a poor orphan at that.

In fact, he had to leave school and find a job; where else but at the Jose Ramirez workshop where his father had worked before him.

He stayed for three years and joined his 'Uncle' Arcangel to become his pupil and his assistant, thus ensuring the continuity of the Barbero – Arcangel school of construction.

Marcelo completed his first guitar during 1960/1 and up to date, his guitars still bear the label 'Made for the House of Arcangel Fernandez by Marcelo Barbero (Hijo)', in spite of the fact that his instruments are sought after almost as much as Arcangel's. The Japanese buyers offered to take his whole output, but fortunately for the rest of the world's players he preferred to remain free to select his own customers.

Marcelo was married in 1970, has two children and seems quietly content to share the workshop of his friend and master. Two more straightforward talents would be difficult to find.

Conde Hermanos

Domingo Esteso born Domingo Esteso Lopez, 12 May 1882 in the village of San Clemente in the province of Luenca, was apprenticed to Manuel Ramirez (1865-1916) younger brother of Jose Ramirez I, where he (Esteso) worked alongside Santos Hernandez.

In 1917, one year after the death of his late master, he established his own shop and workshop in Calle Gravina No. 7, and it is interesting to note that of the three Manuel Ramirez assistants, Esteso, Hernandez and Borruguero, the two former have become legends and their instruments collectors' items.

Esteso was fortunate in having three nephews, Faustino, Julio and Mariano Conde, who worked and learnt his craft, and who continued to work on the same premises after Domingo Esteso passed away in 1937.

The name on the label was then changed to Viuda y Sobrinos de Domingo Esteso, and when we arrived at Gravina No 7, the shop had the appearance of a guitar club meeting, with people standing around chatting or playing guitar. I had ordered a guitar from Faustino Conde and had arranged to meet Angel Iglesias there, so that he could help me check it. I found Faustino in charge, large expansive and jovial, and Mariano, shorter and quiter, happily working at the bench, while the old Señora sat quietly enjoying the scene.

My guitar had been completed, and I handed it to Iglesias who showed off his prodigious technique, then handed the box over to me for my approbation. There was no way out; I had to obey the challenge and was soon immersed in my own test session. As soon as I began to play, everyone stopped talking to gaze at the foreigner, but after a little while, having apparently passed my audition, they continued with their conversations, and I was very happy to have taken delivery of my new bauble.

Having settled my personal affair, I then outlined my request for a range of commercial guitars for Messrs Boosey & Hawkes, but Hermanos Conde (Conde Brothers) had not yet commenced producing guitars, and recommended me to Ricardo Sanchis of Masanasa near Valencia, who was then providing the shop with cheaper instruments. Later, after many hours of negotiating with the wiley Faustino, we formulated an agreement for the delivery of Sanchis guitars to London (checked by Conde Hermanos) which actually began later that year.

As for the continuing history of Hermanos Conde, after the old Senora died in the 1960s, the name of the firm was changed, a guitar factory was opened in the country and another branch of Hermanos Conde was set up in Calle Ancha, while the best hand-made guitars were still being constructed in Gravina No 7.

Now the few custom-made guitars bear the label:
SOBRINOS DE DOMINGO ESTESO, HERMANOS CONDE
Gravina No 7.

The factory made models have different labels, varying from
Hermanos Conde, Gravina No 7
to
Hermanos Conde, Calle Ancha
or
Hermanos Conde, with the address of the factory, depending on the grade of instrument.

Although the best of Conde concert guitars are not fashionable today, the best of the flamenco guitars are still exceptional, and in 1979, I selected the whole range of Hermanos Conde classical and flamenco guitars for the Musicentre. Faustino and Mariano were delighted to introduce their wives and families to us. Faustino looked older and smaller, but his eye and wit were just as sharp.

Valencia

The following day, we made our way to Valencia where, every Sunday in summer, the long wide stretch of sandy beach is full of humanity, sunbathing, or eating in one of the many seafood restaurants. But the town is dry and dusty, made more so by the shavings from the furniture and guitar factories. Twelve miles out of town there is the one street district of Masanasa, the home of Sanchis guitars.

Vicente, Ricardo Sanchis' eldest son, greeted me with the sad news of his father's recent death. In fact, the workshop had not yet started to re-function.

Vicente, was then taking a postal course in English, but had never heard it spoken, so we communicated through written bits of paper *and* negotiated future deliveries of guitars for Boosey & Hawkes, without saying a word!

Telesforo Julve

The name of Telesforo Julve (pronounced Ch(hard)oolvay), had fascinated me ever since I had seen a cheap guitar bearing that label, so I took the opportunity of going to his guitar shop and factory in Calle Americano.

Both Julve and his workshop were a little small and Victorian, with rather dim lighting in the workshop, particularly in the room where the girls were buffing up the polish on the guitar backs. I happened to remark about the dim lighting and am pleased to say it did not fall upon deaf ears, for during a later visit Senor Julve proudly invited me to see the improved lighting and the new white tiling on the walls.

The guitars were tonally quite good, but in common with other Valencian makes, the finish was poor, so I tried to convince him that if he could present them with a better finish I would order a number of instruments. I suppose he did try to improve them but like all the other makers in Valencia, was not keen on exporting to England. Proof of this was the large file of unanswered correspondence I was permitted to read from wholesalers in Europe and America requesting deliveries of guitars.

Tatay

No visit to Valencia would have been complete without a 'tour' of the 'Vicente Tatay' factory. The name of Tatay was famous everywhere as the makers of the lowest priced, best toned guitars in the business, particularly for beginners and students.

We entered the factory through a corridor stacked on either side with guitars in various stages of completion, and pointing to one dusty pile our guide informed us that this was reserved for delivery to Rose, Morris & Co. of London (exclusive importers of Tatay guitars at the time). The corridor led to a large, very lofty, area of about 35′ square where the sun streamed through an opening, high up on one wall, throwing a slanting beam of dust-filled light on to a large band saw being operated by two men. It was a sight reminiscent of a 19th century prison yard. We ascended a score of stone steps alongside a brick wall and passed through an opening into the main factory where a big fire blazed in the open grate and a number of operators were going about their tasks.

A boy of 14 with a multi-coloured strip of wood purfling in one hand and the top of a guitar in the other, fitted the glued purfling round the sound hole and bound it with tape in the time it takes to describe it, and repeated the process; in fact, all the operators did their jobs quickly and efficiently without hurry or fuss. Bodies were fitted and taped, fingerboards were glued and taped on to the necks with extraordinary speed, proving their high degree of skill despite the primitive conditions. When the guitars reached the customer, the lowest priced one (No 2) sold for £9 ranging to £30 for the next half a dozen models. When the Japanese guitars with their excellent finish reached Europe it took about five years before they pushed the Tatay guitars right out of the British market.

Jose Mas y Mas (translated Joseph More and More) did not actually make guitars himself, but owned a small factory producing a fair range of guitars. At the Musicentre I was able to introduce two models for young beginners; one for the up to 12 year olds, and a smaller Requinto or half size guitar (with a shorter scale length) for children of six to nine years of age, priced £12 and then £13. But that ended in 1974/75. Now, a large modern factory directed by Mas Jnr. produces guitars and exports them all over Europe.

There are, of course, a number of other guitar factories in Valencia including the firm of Vicente Tatay Tomas, another member of the Tatay family.

So much for the thriving city of Valencia, famous for its mass production guitars, but even more famous for furniture, electrical equipment, car manufacturing and, of course, oranges.

Majorca or Mallorca

Commercial flying was, as yet, unheard of in Valencia, so we took the night boat to Palma, Mallorca, and it must have been on a night like this that Jonah was shipwrecked in the calm Mediterranean before he was swallowed by the whale.

Palma was not yet a city of tourism but of noisy trams, poor islanders, cheap taxis, Tito's and 'Jacques el Négre' night clubs with their flamenco shows.

But I also discovered a guitar player and teacher named Bartolomé Calatayud (who recently died at the age of 80) who, by his work, kept the guitar flag flying in Palma and who later taught two talented youngsters who are now known internationally and will, no doubt, be famous one day. Their names are Gabrielle Estarellas (the younger of the two) and Diego Blanco, who both gave recitals in London during 1974.

Having discovered him, I arranged for him to give a concert for the guests of the hotel and, in those days, this was quite an event. We met later on a few occasions and he always reminded me of this pleasant evening.

The day boat to Barcelona was full of excited Majorcans making their first trip to the mainland with their luggage of baskets, bedclothes and some livestock, and the scenes as we docked at Barcelona rivalled those of the Russian refugees arriving at Ellis Island, New York, USA at the beginning of the century.

In Barcelona, Manuel Salanger was my guide to the inside entertainment scene. Manuel Salanger was, on the face of it, head of Musica del Sur, but he was not just a 'pretty face'. He was a pianist, arranger, publisher, A&R man for Belta Records and an expert on flamenco. He knew where every player of note was performing and there were at the time a few excellent players including some very fiery gypsies. I still carry a vivid memory of a 16 year gypsy girl holding the floor *and* the audience spellbound with her wild barefoot flamenco dancing. Her name was 'La Chunga' (gypsy for The Ugly One although she was extremely attractive), a niece of Carmen Amaya. She danced in the ancient true flamenco style. This was her first break, but she soon became very famous, appearing in Hollywood, New York and Mexico.

Later, I was given a charcoal drawing of her little sister 'La Chungita'.

Niño Ricardo

Manuel also introduced me to Niño Ricardo, who 'happened' to be appearing in a variety show at the old music hall on the other side of Catalunia Square. El Niño Ricardo (Manuel Serrapi) was born in

Seville 1904 and died in 1972 and to see him performing at that time was a rare treat.

I have never heard more spontaneous, more suitable or more accurate accompaniment to a flamenco singer. Niño Ricardo's ear was equal to his technical ability and his originality of invention placed him in a class of his own – a class of *one*.

I saw him backstage and he took me into his tiny dressing room. When he heard that I was a guitarist seeking information, he wasted no time and although he had just finished his show, he demonstrated his tremendous barrés, most difficult variations, all over the fingerboard. After his display of virtuosity he handed me his guitar and laughingly asked me to show him what I could do. I was forced to accept his request and tried my hardest to repeat some of the rasgueados and falsetas I had just heard, encouraged by his breezy enthusiasm, but I must confess that inwardly I felt as desperate as a scalded cat, scampering up and down the fingerboard, hoping to cool off.

I met Niño Ricardo many times during the ensuing years and he always greeted me with a big hug and a breezy hullo in his low gravelly voice, before passing an interesting few hours at Conde Hermano's shop at Gravina No 7 in Madrid. He always played an Esteso guitar and was a close friend of Faustino Conde.

I usually broached the subject of a short British tour and he finally agreed. However, between the concert agent's scepticism and Niño Ricardo's hesitance, the tour did not take place – and the agent never did return the records I lent him.

Manuel Serrapi (Niño Ricardo's real name) was always immacuately dressed no matter how hot the weather and when he died in April 1972 the flamenco world lost one of its all time 'Greats'.

His son, Niño Ricardo (hijo) is also a flamenco guitarist and can be heard on the LP *In Memoriam* on Polydor Stereo 2385047.

Chapter Twenty-two

THE FLAMENCO GUITAR TUTOR

Casting my mind back to 1955 and realising how little I knew of flamenco music (especially after the revelation of hearing the founder of the contemporary virtuoso style, Niño Ricardo), I should have zipped up and admitted ignorance. Instead of which, I felt I could not rest until I had unravelled some of the forms, rhythms and deeper meanings of a music, which up till now had merely brushed past me. When I returned home from Spain I began to look around for a player who could provide the fundamentals. I found Joaquim Gomez, a very good guitarist and a good work horse, who was prepared to play for me day after day and answer my probing. Aided by my daughter Valerie (who can do with music dictation what a shorthand writer does with aural dictation), I began to write down what we heard.

I then played the passages from the written musical notation and checked every note with Joaquim. It was not just writing notes but unravelling the compas (beat), compartmentalising and differentiating between the subtleties of similar rhythms.

Carlos Sanches and one or two other flamenco players who passed through London gave me a helping hand, but the guardian angel of the project was Dr. Alex Martinez, a medical doctor, who, because of his love for flamenco, was the physician to all the flamenco troupes who visited London. He happened also to be a guitar player, whose knowledge of flamenco music and its traditions was encyclopaedic as well as discerning – a top flight aficionado.

While demonstrating Bulerias and Seguiriyas to me, he tried to explain why my undertaking was impossible and seriously advised me not to embark on such a hopeless task. However, the more he spoke about it and the more he played it the clearer it became, until gradually I was able to analyse some of its fundamental modes and syncopations so that even a beginner could, if keen enough, commence on the right lines.

Eventually, I collected sufficient material for nine full length solos of Soleares, Tanguillos, Allegrias, Tientos, Farruca, Seguiriyas,

Bulerias and Granadinas as well as a section devoted to learning the guitar as geared to flamenco music.

Alberto Velez was then playing flamenco guitar at Margarita's Spanish Restaurant in Cork Street, W1 and he was kind enough to check over the Granadinas which was one taken from a disc recorded by Mario Escudero and himself.

Finally, Manolo Moreno (Moraito de Jerez, Antonio's regular guitarist who was then in London) came over to my house after the show bringing Sabitas and Joaquim Baena, the other two guitarists in the show who, between them, stayed until early morning checking the music, which I played from end to end.

Now I had sections 1 and 3 finished but still had to transcribe the LP of Paco Aguilera playing 25 short examples. The reproduction was rather scratchy so I enlisted the help of Eric Gilder (then sub-Principal of the Central School of Dance Music, a musician with a most phenomenal ear) who wrote down what he heard so that I could transpose it to the open guitar position, at the same time adding cifra.

Eventually, after more than two years devoted to a music which was really right outside my professional sphere, the manuscript was ready for the printers.

At about this time, my daughter (who is a barrister and a member of the Bar Musical Society) invited me to hear a recital Segovia was giving for the members of the Society. It happened to be an outstanding concert (even though the Temple bells struck ten right in the middle of a Bach Sarabande) and at the reception afterwards I did a most unprofessional thing. I took along my manuscript and asked Segovia to comment on it. Considering the circumstances I think he was very kind in his answer which I quote. 'I was born in Andalusia where the guitar is played and has always been known as a flamenco instrument. All my life I have striven to lift the guitar to higher musical levels, therefore I am not interested in a flamenco book and do not want to see it.'

The reply was certainly honest and it served me right for not being more perspicacious.

The book, *The Flamenco Guitar*, was published in 1958 after it had been reviewed by Federico Moreno Torroba (prolific composer for the guitar, now President of the Spanish Society of Composers and Authors) who wrote the following foreword.

'The learned and sensitive Ivor Mairants has succeeded in moulding into a practical musical form the harmonic and rhythmic feeling of the flamenco guitar', Madrid 1956.

Nearly 20 years later, a small grey-haired dapper man was ushered into my office and to my surprise I recognised Torroba himself. He happened to be passing the shop, saw my name and remembered the flamenco book. I was thrilled to meet this sprightly young man in his early 80s. I played one of his pieces to him and he autographed the latest edition of the book with 'Con mucho carino y admiracion a despues de 1956' – 'With much affection and admiration after 1956'.

The flamenco story does not quite end there. In October 1969 I visited Washington and met Sophocles Papas who had been selling many copies of the tutor. He suggested that Part 3 should be recorded in addition to Part 2, so that students could hear exactly what had been written. It was certainly an idea of which I was in favour, and after a great deal of persuasion, the publishers agreed to issue it on their SPARK label.

There was only one player capable of undertaking the task – Paco Peña (b. Cordoba) England's foremost flamenco exponent, and needless to say the resultant recording was clarity itself.

Although, because of contractual difficulties, it was recorded under the pseudonym 'Pepe del Sur', it nevertheless became a steady seller both on disc and as a cassette, while the book has been translated into Spanish and Japanese.

Pepe Martinez and other Flamenco Players

A number of years ago I wrote a piece for the magazine, *BMG*, about my meeting with Niño Ricardo, and in it I wrote that Ricardo had told me that Pepé had been a pupil of his. Not having heard Pepé at the time, I innocently repeated what I was told. Well, one day I received a telephone call from an English friend of Pepé, asking me to meet him, because he was very upset about my publishing false information concerning him – so, meet him I did, and he turned up with about four henchmen as if for a duel, and over a drink we sat down to iron things out.

Not only had Pepé been informed of my article by his English friends (of whom he has many since he annually spends October to December in England teaching and giving concerts), but the 'Pepé Martinez' fan club of Seville had sent a long and strong letter of refutation about Pepé ever having been a pupil of Niño Ricardo, but that he was, in fact, a disciple of Ramon Montoya (as his playing proved). Of course, they were right and I was wrong, but never having heard Pepé, I took Niño Ricardo's word, but I can confirm that even if Pepé had listened closely to Ricardo it could not have been as a pupil. Pepé did, in fact, listen to Ramon Montoya to the point of playing a tour with him when he was a young teenager.

'One Night' relates Pepé, 'Ramon was tired, so he told me to carry on without him while he slipped offstage for a smoke. I was delighted and, as you know, I loved his playing. Having a pretty good ear I quickly learned his falsetas and only that afternoon Ramon had invented a new 'toque' which I picked up and secretly practised before the show. Now was my opportunity of trying it out and I did, loud and clear. But, unknown to me, Ramon was standing at the back of the stalls and when, suddenly, he heard his new falseta he involuntarily shouted 'You thief, you have stolen my falseta!'

Pepé and I soon became good friends and the error (or should I say my original sin) was washed clean by my publishing the letter from Seville together with an article about Pepé. I also discovered that no records of Pepé had ever been issued in Great Britain so I engaged him to record an LP which I called *The Lyrical Guitar of Pepé Martinez* issued on the Fontana label T.L.5207 and later another LP for CBS under the title of *Pepé Martinez in Old Seville*.

The pieces were so genuinely flamenco that I transcribed some of them, and these were published by Belwin-Mills in three albums. Album No. 2 contains a really beautiful *Soleares con Bulerias* and Album No. 3 the *Rondeña* in correct compas and notation.

Pepé tends to underplay rather than over attack and his right hand picking is as light as the proverbial feather, each note sounding with perfect clarity and seemingly little effort. I have some tapes which he recorded at my home on an old beaten-up Julve guitar and even on this instrument and on a home recorder it sounds crystal clear.

Pepé is a great character (he taught himself English in a few years), a wonderful raconteur, and a very good friend who signs his letters 'Con fuerte abrazo' (with a fierce hug!).

Put a cigar in his mouth and he will play till the cows come home or should I say until sunrise. But he is also very astute, is a business man, knows the value of money, loves lots of it, and knows how to earn it.

Ramon Montoya (b. 1880 d. 1949 Madrid), of gypsy parents, undoubtedly laid the foundation of the modern style of the flamenco guitar. Niño Ricardo (Manuel Serrapi 'El Nino Ricardo b. 1904 Seville, d. 1972), was the inventor and creator of the fast virtuoso style (adopted by the leading younger players) who lived and breathed flamenco until the day he died.

I was also privileged to meet Perico el del Lunar (1894-1964) who came to London and played in London with Rosita Duran and the show from the 'Zambra'. His knowledge of flamenco 'cantes' was unsurpassed as I discovered from his detailed explanations, and his playing was forceful, exciting and primitive. His son Pedro who was with him in London took the lead in the 'Zambra' after Perico died and continues in his father's footsteps.

Carlos Montoya who was born in 1905, is a nephew of Ramon and must have picked up a great deal of style from his uncle. But let me begin from the first letter I received from him. He, or I should say, his American wife Sally, wrote to me informing me of his forthcoming Wigmore Hall concert and his desire to make my acquaintance. Well, we met, oddly enough in the same suite where I had had my first lesson from Segovia. Carlos is a very jovial personality and while talking to me he practised with a handkerchief hung over the strings near the bridge in order to damp the sound.

He told me that his aunt (Ramon Montoya's wife) was very jealous of him because her own son was unable to make headway on the guitar in spite of his father's tuition, while he (Carlos) lapped it up and quickly learned to play.

After Carlos Montoya's concert (which I reviewed for *BMG*) we went out for a meal and I told him that the stuff he played was quite bewildering and showed off a vast and flashy technique but had left flamenco far behind. He did not mind and explained that although I was probably right, it nevertheless brought him full houses everywhere in the world (except in England the first time round) and, in fact, sold vast numbers of LP albums.

In the past he was, of course, one of flamenco's leading accompanists and travelled to America with La Argentina and La Argentinita. But, he said, the guitarist always had small billing which went with humble pay and he decided to alter that by bringing the guitar to prominence and so innovated the flamenco guitar as a concert instrument. He has an apartment in New York and a sumptuous flat in Madrid (which can't be bad) and continues to earn a lot of money in spite of the disdain in which aficionados hold his playing which, as Liberace said 'makes him cry all the way to the bank'. I am pleased to number both Carlos and Sally among my friends. When he came to London in 1979 for a QE Concert he drew a larger than ever audience many of whom had never seen him before. It must have been an exhilirating experience for them.

Victor Monge (Serranito)

On my subsequent visits to Madrid I made the acquaintance of Jose Ramirez III and introduced his guitars to Great Britain. Although there was a big language gap between us which was bridged by his wife, Angelita, he always wanted me to meet the new and up and coming guitarists who came into the shop. One day, a young boy with a long coat and fair curly hair came in for a chat and I was introduced to Victor Monge known as Serranito.

Serranito was asked to play something, and he demonstrated his tremendous skill on the flamenco guitar, rather as a shy schoolboy shows respect for his elders.

Since that time he has become Spain's leading flamenco guitarist only to be overshadowed by Paco de Lucia (not to mention Manolo Sanlucar) who gave up accompanying to devote his skill only to concert playing.

Serranito taught me quite a few new 'toques' some of which I wrote down and published, and he has since given a concert at the Queen Elizabeth Hall in London in 1970. But I can truly say that of the players who have dazzled me with their ability, 'Serranito' has displayed the most phenomenal inventiveness, technique and excitement. I recall how a couple of years ago Serranito left an experienced well-known professional open-mouthed when he met and heard him for the first time in Paulino Bernabé's workshop. He has now toured the world and played with many famous bailores especially Lucera Tena the petite and beautiful dancer and castanet player from Cuba, with whom he recorded *El Colibri* at high speed.

Born about 1940, he was a prodigy at 14 and though getting on for 40, he still pays me much respect and regard.

Mario Escudero

Out of the blue I received a letter from New York written to me by Mario Escudero (b. Alicante 1931) one of the top flamenco guitar technicians of today. It was a long letter reviewing and comparing my *Flamenco Tutor* with all other written flamenco music, and freely complimenting me on having written the truth. Imagine my feelings at being accepted by one of my favourites. Incidentally, the Granadina in my book is a transcription of his solo on Esoteric Records which also contains songs by El Pili and duets with Alberto Velez, so his letter really confirmed the correctness of my transcription.

Mario has always striven to present the flamenco guitar in a more sophisticated manner including more advanced harmony, following in the footsteps of his master, Niño Ricardo.

We met in New York in 1965 and had a lovely time socially and musically, with his charming wife (a flamenco dancer) and his children, and I had also an opportunity of examining his teaching methods at his school where he was assisted by Juan Grecos (or Juan David as he was known). He had also recorded duets with 'Sabicas' entitled *The Fantastic Guitars of Sabicas and Escudero* on Brunswick STA.3019. I did not meet Sabicas until his Queen Elizabeth Hall debut in London during 1968 and after hearing him on record where his tone came over with tremendous strength, I was disappointed by the small delicate tone he produced on his Ramirez flamenco guitar with La Bella Black trebles.

Sabicas

Sabicas was born in Pamploma and his name is Augustin Castellon, but because of his early virtuosity he was known as the 'pea', Niño Sabicas, and he mentioned that his mother used to call him by that name. Whichever it was, Sabicas is still one of the most famous names among, flamenco guitarists. He is one of the great creators of flamenco 'toques' along with Ramon Montoya and Niño Ricardo and before them Javier Molina (1868-1956).

His appearance, including his wig, as well as his playing, are immaculate and when I asked him his age he tried to chop off 10 years, not that it matters. I think that of all guitarists, as a group, the flamenco breed are more touchy and sensitive about opinion than any of the others. But about his playing Sabicas was completely detached, wearing the mantle of greatness with complete equanimity.

In his concert he rather under-estimated the knowledge of the British aficionados and ran a Seguiriyia into a Saeta and omitted to play his well known introduction to *La Garrotin*. When I taxed him with this, he said that he played it that way to make a change but had no objection to performing it the way I preferred next time.

Madrid Flamenco Clubs

There have been many instances both in London and Madrid where flamenco music has enthralled me both in private juergas, and public tablaos like The Corral de la Moravia, Cafe Chinitas, Las Brujas, Torre Bermeja and the Zambra, all in Madrid.

I remember on one occasion taking Dennis McCarthy, a percussionist colleague of mine, to the Zambra in company with my wife, Jose and Angelita Ramirez and guitarist Stan Watson, and towards the end of the show about 2.45 a.m. Dennis was so emotionally charged with the evening's fabulous singing, dancing and playing, he hugged the female artistes and handed out 100 peseta notes to each of them. One of them was La Quica, one of the greatest castanet players of our time.

I would advise flamenco aficionados to read *Lives and Legends of Flamenco* by D. E. Pohren if they want more detailed information on the subject, but the man who draws the biggest crowds today is undoubtedly Paco de Lucia who has become the most popular flamenco guitar phenomenon wherever he appears. His attack, rhythm and airé are tremendous. He also plays for the crowd, who love his tango flamencos which he presents either with his brother playing second guitar or with a rhythm group.

Paco de Lucia
Perhaps it would not be amiss to recall his first London concert at the Wigmore Hall, Friday 15 February 1976.

The foyer of the Wigmore Hall was full of guitarists mingling with aficionados in a hum of humanity, before filling the auditorium where they settled down to await the slightly late entrance of the almost unannounced debut recital of today's young king of flamenco – Paco de Lucia.

He came on, holding his Conde Esteso 'Black Flamenco' (rosewood back and sides instead of cypress), sat down, crossed his right leg over his left and in an unsmiling, casual manner (holding his guitar as most of us do when we are playing to ourselves), began with a melodic introduction which eventually led into an Alegrias in the minor before developing into the major key. The tempo was easy but some of the runs were taken at lightning double speed which shot up the temperature of the performance although not of the duende. This was no ordinary run-of-the-mill flamenco style. If you have based your flamenco on Sabicas, forget it. Everything about this style is different as evidenced by the Tarantas which followed.

The traditional trills and legatos were there, very clearly defined but in a different level, played with a finesse and freedom that should have been highly charged with emotion but somehow weren't; perhaps the mask-like expression of the player with eyes shut did not help. There was no helpful programme nor did the soloist announce the titles of his offerings, the next of which was a Guajira which, as everything else he played, was recognisable by its strong compas or beat.

The variations and the rhythm sailed along freely, incorporating some popularly recognisable melodies like Leonard Bernstein's *America (West Side Story)* and *Canarios.*

Then, changing the cejilla from the 1st to the 2nd fret, he went into an exciting and somewhat original Bulerias. Paco de Lucia certainly does not play traditional flamenco; perhaps it is an offshoot of flamenco, but whatever it is, it is played with complete mastery, abandon and freedom and makes some of the older masters sound very square. And yet it does not emit the deep emotion and great excitement of Niño Ricardo – the founder of this school.

Paco has the great gift of playing a clear melody so that the rhythm accompaniment is perfectly balanced, even to the interpolation of Falla's *Miller's Dance.*

For his fifth offering, he returned the cejilla to the 1st fret, and gave an outstanding rendering of a *Medio Granadina* in which he showed his artistry by relegating the accompanying arpeggios to their rightful position and balance, thereby allowing the melody to ride freely and clearly. Then, to my surprise, he 'rasgueadoed' into the old *Panaderos Flamencos* note for note like the 25 year old record of Vicente Gomez but a few notes faster, and I must say it was nice to hear one of the first flamenco pieces I had ever transcribed and played, but, I may add, with fireworks!

The second half began with a Rondena in very Moorish mood and developed with many sweeps and flourishes but with no great attempt at any dynamics. When he grabs a chord he grabs it, and when he plays a double speed run it is like a supersonic dive bomber, relentless until the bottom is reached.

The Zapateado which followed was a perfect exhibition of the triplet form of dance. If only a fleet-footed dancer could have made it a perfect duet.

One cannot say that the *Soleares* which followed illustrated what its name traditionally means. There was nothing lonely or forlorn about it, but a search for the new, although some of the falsetas were recognisable and well used. The *Soleares* changed to a faster tempo and finished with a flourish of alzapua – fascinating thumb work.

Again a change of compas, this time to a *Fandango* which was played excellently and in perfect tempo. He was then joined by his brother Ramon de Algeciras, who seemed to bring out Paco's lighter nature and actually produced some reserved smiles. He should do this more often!

His brother's guitar (also a Conde Esteso) was made of Palo Rosa (a lighter type of Brazilian rosewood used for strictly non-classical work) and Ramon played effectively and lightly, well versed in his job of accompanying – in this instance a guajira followed by a high speed rhumba flamenco which allowed the lead guitar a free rein to extemporise on the chords. Pyrotechnics without limit. After one of his phenomenal extra long single note passages, some of the audience spontaneously rose to their feet galvanised into action, and by this time the atmosphere had built up to great excitement.

The two guitars were brilliant in the *Bulerias*, the first encore, and although Paco had suffered some nail injuries during the evening's playing, he ended with another encore, a *Verdiales*, which interpolated Lecuona's *Andalusia* and *Malaguena* with the regular cadenzas. Although one can say that Paco de Lucia's tone production is at one level, and there is little finesse of emotional depth, he must be recognised as one who plays guitar with freedom from inhibition and with a complete mastery of technique. One of the 'Greats'.

For those who wish to know more about him, he was born Sanchez Francisco Gomez in Algeciras, the port town next to Gibraltar and opposite Tangiers in North Africa. The date was 2 December 1947 and he, his father and brothers all either play or sing flamenco.

Paco de Lucia seems to have made a relentless bee-line for solo performance rather than playing in groups for singers and dancers. I wonder if Sabicas's statement holds good when he says 'One should play with singers and dancers for 25 years before embarking on a solo career'.

An Interview with Paco de Lucia and Friends

In a frank interview I had with Paco de Lucia, he agreed with me when I remarked about the unsmiling casual manner he displayed during his first concert. He said he was much more relaxed and happier during his second concert at the Wigmore on the 15 February. He plays as he feels and can do it no other way. 'I feel nervous' he said, 'when I play in front of a concert audience as at the first Wigmore Hall concert and because no audience wants to see a performer in a nervous state, this has to be covered up with calm. Frankly, I don't like to play for the public. When I feel good I play better than when I don't. The high spots just come and go. They are transcendent'.

Paco is the youngest of four brothers and at the age of six or seven his father introduced him to the guitar which he then found quite easy to pick up but the more he plays it the harder he finds it becomes.

His brother, Ramon de Algeciras continued Paco's guitar education where dad left off, and he played to his first audiences at about the age of 11. Local charities and broadcasts mostly, but a little later, at the age of 12, he made an LP with his brother Pepe, a record which was, at the time, recommended to me by a friend in Madrid. The name of Paco de Lucia comes from his mother, Lucia, although his full name is Sanchez Francisco (Paco) Gomez. At the age of 13 he turned professional and left home for a year's tour of North and South America with flamenco impressario, Jose Greco.

Don't ask me what happened to his formal education but he returned to Spain after his American tour, and played with many singers and dancers amongst them the great Antonio Gadez, Antonio, and Manuela Vargas. He also toured with artistes appearing in Festivals, gaining a wealth of experience. When he was 18 he, his brother Ramon and Enrique Jimenez, toured Germany giving a number of concerts.

Although he considers Ramon Montoya the fountain-head of flamenco guitar playing, he was first attracted to the style of Niño Ricardo and listened to his records avidly but although he later met Ricardo many times, he never actually received formal tuition from him.

Paco does not devote his time to formal practice nor has he ever learnt to read music, but like other famous players of free form playing like Les Paul, Django Reinhardt and, say, Wes Montgomery, his practice consists of the new phrases he wishes to perfect. The pattern seems to be the same, when they invent a phrase they really like they keep playing it with many variations until it becomes cast-iron, and thereby they build up their own special technique.

When I asked Paco to name his proudest moments, he found it very difficult to do so because those moments were fleeting. 'Transcendental' as he so correctly puts it in his limited but intelligent English.

One occasion he was rather proud of occurred about 12 months earlier when he gave a solo concert at the Teatro Royal in Madrid, the very first time that a flamenco concert was performed on that stage.

His ambitions, he said, did not lie in his guitar playing. 'Actually', he said, 'I am a frustrated singer and when I play I really do not play from the fingers but from the head which guides the music. My ambition is to feel and live with great intensity and to understand people.

And as to my future, it does not really matter. My future is every day; one does not predict the future'.

'How then', I asked, 'do you prepare those long phenomenal high speed runs with that tremendous drive?'

'As they say in Spain', he answered, 'I play from my bottom, that is, by tightening the cheeks of my bottom and driving my way through', or, as it is said in the bible, 'by girding his loins'.

Whatever it is, it has made him, at the age of 28, the flamenco players' most highly regarded guitarist. When I broached the subject of whether one should play flamenco guitar as a solo instrument rather than as part of the flamenco group, he said that he does both, 'why, only three days ago I made a record with singer Camarron'.

Of course, I examined his right hand fingernails which were of normal length not trimmed in any particular way and were never coated with any strengthener, glue or hardener. Just natural.

Off stage Paco is a warm, enthusiastic fellow, with a good sense of humour rather like the ironic English humour which he enjoys. He constantly strives to do better and his wish is to retain his creative enthusiasm.

Chapter Twenty-three

FROM GUT TO NYLON

Much has been written here about guitar making in the USA and in Spain but since the advent of the international popularity explosion, guitar making has developed in many other parts of the world including Great Britain.

Geographically these countries transcend all political barriers and read like a mini-United Nations. In alphabetical order they are as follows: Argentina, Australia, Brazil, China, Canada, France, East and West Germany, Finland, Holland, Israel, Italy, Japan, Korea, Mexico, Spain, Sweden, Romania, Taiwan, UK, USA and USSR.

I am in no position to comment on the guitars of all these countries, but in my travels as a buyer, etc. I have met many luthiers and guitar manufacturers, played their instruments, and have had many detailed discussions with them. Many are friends of long standing and I am privileged to be so accepted and to be able to relate matters of interest to players, makers and aficionados of the guitar. Before I do so I would like to preface Spanish guitar making with the story of string making – to be specific, the nylon string.

The advent of the *nylon* string for classical guitars instead of the *gut* string, which had reigned for a millenium, was, in my opinion, a major factor in helping the guitar to become accepted during the 1950s. The difficulties in maintaining correct pitch with gut strings, together with other attendant hazards, would have detracted considerably from the instrument's popularity. Therefore, let us see how necessity acted as the mother of the nylon string invention.

Guitar history has little to say about the materials used for making strings, therefore this little gem (from the *Art and Times of the Guitar* by Grunfield) is relevant.

It is taken from a conversation reported by the historian Ibn Hayan writing about the first audition of the Persian minstrel Ziryab (the Blackbird, eighth-ninth century) before the Caliph Harun al Rashid in which Ziryab compares his lute and strings with that of his master's Ishaq.

'Ziryab: My lute weighs about a third less than Ishaq's and all my strings are made of silk that has not been spun with hot water which weakens them. The bass and third strings are made of lion's guts, softer and more sonorous than those from any other animal. These strings are stronger than any others and withstand better the striking of the plectrum.' (The Arabian lute or Ud is still plucked with an ostrich quill which Ziryab is credited to have introduced as an alternative to a wooden plectrum.)

Through the history of the lute, vihuela de mano and Spanish guitar, gut trebles and wire-wound spun silk bass strings were used, and it was not until after the termination of World War II that another material was introduced.

The development of the string story, however, began at the end of 1939 when World War II had already commenced. Silk was scarce or not available and Messrs. DuPont in New York were developing nylon as a substitute to be used in a variety of ways; for textiles, floss for parachutes, lengths for fishing lines and short cuts of various thicknesses for brushes. DuPont were also very interested in developing nylon strings for violins and other stringed instruments and with this in mind approached the Kaplan String Company of Connecticut (makers of the famous Red Oray violin strings) and E. & O. Mari, the makers of La Bella strings.

I am told by Daniel Mari that these mono-filament strings were actually tested by them and fitted to the violin and kindred instruments but they proved to be too smooth for bowing. In fact, when a bow was applied, the nylon twisted as it did not have the gripping surface of gut. However, when the strings were played pizzicato the sound was clear and in tune, which gave rise to the idea that while mono-filament strings were unsuitable for bowed instruments, they might be suitable for plucked instruments such as the guitar.

But few people played classical guitar in the United States around 1940 so the idea was shelved. There was, however, a demand for strings for the Venezuelan Quatro and after experimentation, during which the nylon mono-filament was treated and gauged to suit the instrument, the nylon strings were sent to South America under the Señorita label.

After 1940, Messrs. Mari must have gone further and manufactured nylon strings for guitar because, according to Juan Arozco Snr, now in his seventies, he first saw a set of nylon strings in March 1943. As he recalled to me, he was sitting in the Madrid café Riesgo at the corner of Alcaca and Peligro chatting with his friend, the late Ramon Montoya (the originator of modern flamenco guitar music), when in came guitarist Pepe de Badajos. Pepe had just returned from a tour of Mexico, where he had bought a set of La Bella nylon strings which he presented to Ramon Montoya. Montoya immediately restrung his guitar with the new strings and tuned them up to pitch very tentatively, expecting the trebles to snap with the frequency of gut strings, but to everybody's surprise they stretched without breaking, held their pitch, and sounded louder and clearer than gut.

It must therefore be assumed, according to this personal account, that La Bella nylon strings were, in fact, used by guitarists in Latin America and to a much lesser extent in Spain, during the early 1940s, although the world's leading classical guitarist, Andres Segovia, was quite unaware of their existence until a few years later. Segovia discovered nylon guitar strings in quite different circumstances and I am indebted to Rose Augustine for relating to me the first hand account of how her late husband, Albert Augustine, and Segovia pioneered the early development of nylon guitar strings.

Albert Augustine, who was born in Denmark in 1900, emigrated to the US in 1926-7 to pursue his trade of guitar making, marrying Rose in 1928. His guitar-constructing business also entailed his making some experiments with strings, but no more than that.

Nearly 20 years had passed when Segovia, who was then in the United States, happened to be a guest at a function, and there, in conversation with some diplomats, deplored the shortage of good guitar strings, mentioning that he had almost run out of his Pirastro gut strings.

General Lindeman, a member of the British Embassy, asked Segovia which strings he needed most urgently and he replied 'the gut strings, and especially the 'prima''.[1]

They met again a month later and the General, true to his promise, presented Segovia with some nylon strings which he had obtained from some members of the DuPont family who were his friends. Segovia fitted a string to his guitar and when it reached the correct pitch, it produced a clear sound but with a faint metallic accent which distinguished it from the sound of a gut string, a fault which he hoped could eventually be corrected.

Then during 1946, Vladimir Bobri, editor of the *Guitar Review* and a friend of both Segovia and Albert Augustine, introduced them to one another and at the meeting, the guitarist asked the luthier to make

---

[1] In his 'Illustrated History of the Guitar', Alexander Bellow states (p 193) 'They (nylon strings) were first tried by Olga Coelho in January 1944 in New York'.

him some nylon strings. Mr. Augustine, seeing the nylon first string on Segovia's guitar, remembered that two years previously he had found some nylon thread in a bundle of war surplus, and had, in fact, experimented with the nylon thread, using it as a substitute for gut, but, as a guitar maker, he was not at all keen to give up valuable time for string making.

In the meantime Segovia received the information that although DuPont could not be persuaded to undertake the manufacture of guitar strings for the trade, they promised to supply the necessary plastic material to anyone who would seriously undertake the task of making the strings. Well, at the second meeting between Segovia and Augustine, Albert, with the support of his wife Rose, agreed to make the strings for Segovia; and thus began a long uphill struggle in which he did not submit to any dissuasion from the sceptics who included the DuPont experts.

After about three years of work, Augustine was, at last, satisfied with the results, and requested DuPont to assemble three players to hear the difference between the original nylon, the gut, and Augustine's specially treated nylon first string. The experts had no difficulty and their judgement was unanimous – the treated nylon made a big improvement to the tone of the guitar. DuPont, too, were very impressed and from then on Augustine strings have received DuPonts unstinted help.

Now to send them to Segovia for his opinion. He was then in Washington and received the strings in the afternoon before a concert. As luck would have it, he broke a first string, which he eagerly changed in order to be able to use the newly-arrived strings for the concert. He became so excited at the sound that, after the concert, he immediately returned to the house at which he was staying as the honoured guest of two old ladies, and made a beeline for his bedroom so that he could continue exploring the pleasures of the sounds produced by the new string.

Having made good progress with the treble strings, Augustine struggled hard to produce bass strings but the wound strings continued to be a great problem. They were either unstable, toneless or their windings would loosen; they also squeaked. It took Augustine four hours to wind the first bass string and eventually, after changing the metal thread many times (using successively copper, silver, 14-carat gold, aluminium and stainless steel) and smoothing and polishing the silver strings until his hands literally bled, he produced his first successful nylon-wound strings.

Segovia's gratitude to Albert Augustine for this achievement 'reflects that of all guitarists today', and it is not for nothing that the strings have always received Segovia's endorsement.

There is also another endorsement which hangs in the Augustine office. It consists of a specially selected spruce guitar top with the inscription 'This guitar masterpiece of Albert Augustine belongs to me. I will praise it with loud speaker through the world', signed A. Segovia, March 1956; and thereby hangs the tale of the unfinished guitar that Segovia had requested Augustine to make, but which only reached the first stage. In 1948 Albert Augustine suffered his first heart attack, but recovered to see the fruits of his labour, then succumbed to a second attack from which he died in April 1967.

The business was continued under the capable direction of Rose Augustine who was no newcomer to strings, guitars, or hard work. Besides undertaking the string-making responsibility she recalled the assistant who used to work for her husband and had learnt the craft of guitar construction from him.

His name is Frank Haselbacher, an American of Austrian parentage now in his 50s who works on his own producing only a few guitars a year. I had the privilege of comparing three of his guitars, made respectively in 1971/2 and 3. I was so favourably impressed that I asked for my name to be added to the waiting list. It is the favourite guitar of Carlos Barbosa-Lima, the brilliant Brazilian concert guitarist, who used it at his London recitals.

One of Albert Augustine's most prized possessions was a classical guitar made by Herman Hauser in 1941 and one which Segovia would have dearly loved to possess, but with which Augustine would never part company. I can honestly say that I have never played on a guitar with the unique tonal qualities and perfect string action of that most exceptional instrument. More than that one cannot say in praise of it.

Incidentally, my wife and I intended to pay a short visit to the Augustine factory, but there was such immediate rapport between Rose Augustine and ourselves that we stayed for six hours (with a break for lunch) being fed delicious hot corned beef sandwiches on rye – and no salt-beef sandwiches ever tasted better.

There are many guitar makers in the US whose instruments reach various degrees of excellence but with guitars as with other things, beauty is in the eye of the beholder.

In New York there is Manouk Papasian; not far away is Michael Gurian, and Manuel Velasquez, is now back again in New York from

Puerto Rico. Apart from the Big Three manufacturers, i.e. Martin Gibson and Guild, there are many private makers dotted around the US, but very few of their guitars have come across to Europe or have been heard on the concert platform. Mention must be made of the *Guitar Review*, the most artistic and informative of all guitar magazines. Its contents are an encyclopaedia of information about the guitar both historical and musical.

Chapter Twenty-four

THE RAMIREZ DYNASTY

This survey of Spanish guitar-makers mainly concerns those whom it has been my pleasure to know and includes some of their thoughts and experiences about the past and present which they related to me.

Other information from books on the history of the guitar is used only where it is connected with the people in my story.

The most important influences on classical guitar construction during the present century came from three generations of one family of José Ramirez and their pupils which I call The Ramirez Dynasty. When ten years old José Ramirez (1857-1916) was formally apprenticed to Francisco Gonzalez (1830-1880) in 1867. Spain was a country comparatively isolated from the rest of Europe but a country from which famous composers like Tchaikowsky, Bizet and Rossini found inspiration for music in the Spanish idiom.

Madrid was colourful, somewhat picaresque, vivid and palpitating, with its leisurely habit of long mid-day lunch breaks and café life going on till the early hours.

But the position the guitar occupied in music was that of a 'popular' instrument not the classical or concert instrument of today.

Despite the work of the sixteenth and seventeenth century vihuelists, the late seventeenth and early eighteenth century guitar virtuosi composers or the efforts of the young Tarrega and his pupils, the place of the guitar was then in the café Contente, as an accompanying instrument to the song and dance, in the drawing room, and the instrument of the amateur to be found in many homes.

El Baile (The Dance), an early tapestry designed by Goya, depicts two couples dancing in the open accompanied by three guitar players; *El Jaleo*, a painting by John Singer Sargent, is the epitome of the classic Flamenco tableau showing two guitarists and others accompanying the dances, and a song illustrating the leisurely times which goes: 'I remember, sirs, when I used to sing Tonadillas a solo with my guitar' also illustrates the point. Therefore, the types of guitars that were being made during the last quarter of the nineteenth century were not, in the main, what we would term 'concert' guitars.

337

Many had peg heads, with the wood for the body consisting of cypress, maple or mahogany, but not essentially of rosewood.

Antonio Torres had already established a scale length of 65 cm. and stabilised the body dimensions so that when José Ramirez was formally apprenticed to Francisco Gonzalez the modern principles of guitar construction had recently been established.

Francisco Gonzalez was a man with natural mechanically-orientated talents, which ranged from building a lever-operated car to constructing guitars and was, at the time, Madrid's master luthier, working at his shop at No 25 Calle de Carretas. A fine example of his work can be seen on display at the Museum of the Paris Conservatoire.

Fifteen years later (1882) José, now aged 25, set himself up in business, first at No 24 Calle Cava Baja, later moving to the Plaza Santa Ana before finally settling at 2 Conception Jeronima in the heart of old Madrid, ten minutes stroll from Plaza Mayor and Puerta del Sol.

José had a younger brother named Manuel, born in 1866, who became interested in his brother's craft, eventually becoming apprenticed to the now famous José.

It was at Calle Cava Baja that José taught his young brother Manuel. Other pupils at the time were Julian Gomez Ramirez (no relation) who later established himself in Paris, and Enrique Garcia who became famous when he returned to his native Barcelona and set up his own workshop.

José I later taught two other pupils, Antonio Viudes (whose guitars were recommended to me by Segovia in 1949) and Rafael Castaña. Viudes successfully settled in Buenos Aires while Castaña went to Cordoba, where he committed suicide in 1905 and is reputed to have taught Miguel (Rafael?) Rodriguez.

Meanwhile, back at the Ramirez workshop, Manuel (who was beginning to disagree with his teacher, about construction), expressed the desire to follow Julian Gomez Ramirez to Paris and José helped him with the preparations. However, Manuel seemed to have had no intention of going to Paris and soon set up a shop nearby at the Plaza Santa Ana and later at No 10 Calle Arlaban.

Well, this caused a great rift between the two brothers who never spoke to each other again. Technically, Manuel (like so many brilliant pupils) had disagreed with his teacher's ideas on guitar construction and, now free to pursue his own independent ideas, began to make guitars which were considered better than José's.

Perhaps because of working on the principles of Antonio Torres, Manuel's guitars became very popular so that he eventually became official luthier to the Madrid National Conservatoire.

Everyone who has read Segovia's autobiographical articles will have heard the story of his visit to Manuel Ramirez' shop when he was 18. Segovia relates how he asked to see a guitar, but scorned those on view, whereupon Ramirez brought a guitar from the back room and handed it to Segovia, who played it, fell in love with it – but had no money to pay for it. Manuel, however, was so impressed with the young man's playing that he made a present of the guitar to Segovia who played it and cherished it for many years – and, by all accounts, still has it.

But, according to José Ramirez III, there was another reason for the gift and here I quote from Pepé's (José III) letter to me on the subject:

'The guitar which, after others, Manuel Ramirez showed to the maestro 'Segovia' was not newly constructed but one that had been finished several months before and commissioned by Manjon, a blind teacher and soloist who was well-known at the time, but who, so I have heard, had the habit of haggling over price. Every time he went to Manuel's workshop, he would try the guitar and would begin by saying that it wasn't bad, but not what he had hoped it would be. . . . The guitar would then be put away. This happened on several occasions until Segovia visited Manuel and the latter clearly saw the chance of obliging Segovia on the one hand and on the other, of preventing Manjon from carrying on trying to acquire the guitar at a lower price.'

It was in the shop at No 10 Calle Arlaban that Manuel Ramirez was fortunate in having as assistants and pupils, Santos Hernandez (1873-1942), Domingo Esteso (1884-1937) and Modesto Borreguero the youngest of the three who, for a time, assisted the other two. There was also a very clever pupil named Pepillo who did not stay with guitar-making (because of his inability to earn a living at it) and became a chauffeur for the municipality of Madrid.

Santos Hernandez and Domingo Esteso both became famous and Borreguero eventually set up a shop in Atocha, the thread continuing with one of his sons, at present working in the Ramirez shop.

When Manuel Ramirez died in 1916, his widow (as is customary) took over the business and changed the name on the label which now read 'Viuda de Manuel Ramirez, Arlaban No 11, workshop for violins and guitars'.

For a time both Santos Hernandez and Domingo Esteso stayed on, either finishing their late master's guitars or constructing their own, but their guitars bore their initials on the corner of the label – SH or DE, and I have seen one in the Ramirez Collection bearing that very label with the initials 'SH'. Soon, however, both guitarerros left the Ramirez fold and set up on their own, as I mentioned earlier.

Santos was known to be reluctant to teach his methods of guitar construction and this precluded him employing anyone other than a helper to sweep up, and when the helper, Alejandro Fernandez, grew old enough to learn about guitar construction, he was dismissed. Despite the fact that Santos worked on his own, he produced a fair number of guitars, a number of which have been offered for sale, both by his widow and by others for very high prices.

When Santos died in 1942 leaving his widow to continue the business, Marcelo Barbero (who had learnt the craft both from José I and Jose II) left the Ramirez workshop and made a bid for the job of running the shop for Santos's widow. The opportunities that Marcelo had to complete the unfinished guitars left by Santos must have given him fresh ideas and, no doubt, the reason for any implication that Marcelo's guitars were influenced by those of Santos. Nevertheless, before he opened on his own in his workshop in Ministreles, Marcelo had learnt a great deal about Santos Hernandez guitars through repairing them and working with the templates left by Santos.

Domingo Esteso, Santos's colleague at the Manuel Ramirez shop, established himself at Gravina No 7 and, as we have seen, was fortunate in having three gifted nephews, Faustino, Julian and Mariano Condé, who became worthy disciples and continued to develop the business. When Domingo Esteso died in 1937, the business became known as Viude y Sobrinos de Domingo Esteso (Hermanos Condé).

In the meantime, José Ramirez I had continued to prosper, retaining his own methods, and when his son José Simon (José II), born 1885, was 13 or 14, he, too, began working in his father's shop. About five or six years later José Simon set out on a tour of Latin America, and ended up by staying there for 19 years, establishing his own guitar shop in Buenos Aires, and getting married. However, upon the death of José I in 1923, José Simon returned to Madrid and took charge of the business. His son, José III, was born in 1922, and when he began to work in his father's workshop, Marcelo Barbero was one of the master builders and it was he who gave José III his first lessons. When Marcelo left, José began to study with his father as well as with

THE RAMIREZ DYNASTY

Alfonso Benito, another master builder, who had been there at the time of José I, and who was more or less responsible for the continuity of the work.

By 1941 José III (whom I will call Pepé), had made two flamenco guitars, both of which are in his collection, and one is dated 1946 and numbered 7. But, according to Manuel Rodriguez, Pepé started to work in the family shop in 1945 which then included (also according to Rodriguez) Alfonso Benito, Pepé, Rodriguez, two apprentices and a finisher.

In any case, Pepé was always more interested in study and research than in just production and there was plenty to study in producing guitars for the changing times and styles, particularly in flamenco style.

During the late forties the fierce accompanying rhythms of the thumb and index finger players like Melchior de Marchena or the more melodic hard hitting style of Perico el del Lunar (which required a normal string action) gave way to the lighter fingered faster players like Ramon Montoya, Niño Ricardo and Sabicas, who required a lower string action, and it was Pepé Ramirez and Marcelo Barbero who worked on these lines, Pepé eventually developing the sharp sounding low action Ramirez Flamenco guitar.

Although Pepé took his Master Luthier's certificate in the late forties, he was not yet able to effect great changes.

In 1953 Paulino Bernabe (born in 1932) the son of a stonemason, joined the Ramirez shop. Paulino learnt how to use tools as soon as he was able to sharpen a pencil, and became a cabinet maker upon leaving school. But he fell under the spell of the guitar, studied with Daniel Fortéa, and became curious about its construction. Of all the guitars he had handled he admired those made by Ramirez and so, when he began to work alongside him, he took to making guitars like a duck takes to water. In fact, after two years he was allowed to make a guitar of his own, and eventually became the foreman of the workshop, where he stayed happily for 16 years.

Manuel Rodriguez (having learnt many of Pepé's theories and very experienced in his own right), left in 1955, to share a workshop with Arcangel Fernandez while Paulino brought in his friend Manuel Contreras, who was originally a renovator and constructor of antique furniture. Somehow or other however, after just two years Contreras became unsettled and left, having fallen out with his friend Paulino.

Although Contreras had a very tough struggle to make a living when he first went solo, he was later able to establish himself with the help of a partner, and has had a very fine business in Alcala for many years. His guitars are renowned all over the world, and much sought after. Steve Howe of the *Yes* would not part with the one I selected for him.

Felix Manzanero
During the later 50s, Ramirez was looking for someone to finish the instruments and Felix Manzanero's father helped Felix to get him the job at the age of 14. But Felix was no finisher and had to start at the beginning under José II's stern eye, before he was allowed to make even a banduria. He became a craftsman under Pepé Ramirez and stayed for 12 years before establishing his own shop in Calle Santa Ana near the famous Rastro flea market. Felix admits that José II was a tough master and a perfectionist, and so was Pepé in a more advanced way.

José II died in 1957 and Pepé took over the running of the business, putting his own ideas into practice. I was first introduced to Pepé in 1959 by guitarist Stan Watson, a good friend of mine, who was then living and studying in Madrid, and over the years my wife and I have seen his two children, José IV (Pepito) and Amalia grow up and become guitar-makers. Pepé's wife Angelita, who came from Manila, of course, spoke English and was able to act as interpreter for us, helping both in business and becoming friends of the family.

In 1959 I began to import Ramirez guitars and spread their fame in Great Britain when little was known about them or any other except Tatay. Pepé Ramirez, in my opinion, is the greatest innovator of new constructional ideas among the twentieth century luthiers, and even coming into the 80s, he is as keen as ever on effecting original improvements.

The making of a Ramirez guitar begins with the selection and buying of the trunks of rosewood, ebony, cedar and all the other types of wood required for the struts, and the process of development from the logs of wood to the finished guitar is apparent from a tour of the four-storey building where the guitars are constructed.

When Paulino Bernabe vacated his position in December 1969 there were 20 craftsmen employed. Ten years later the number had increased to 30, 17 of whom are master builders who, between them, produce over 1,000 concert guitars annually.

The innovations introduced after Pepé took charge of the business have affected the whole world of guitar construction, from the introduction of scientific improvements in the finish to the change of Torres' dimensions.

Innovation No 1 was the increase in the size of the box in proportion to the increase in the scale length (scale length = distance between nut and bridge saddle). Instead of using the 65 cm. of Torres he increased it to 66.3575 cm. These measurements may be compared to Hauser 65.357 cm. and Fleta 65.143 cm.

Innovation No 2 was to use a special varnish applied with a spray instead of with a brush or French polished. The polyurethane is quite individual to the Ramirez guitars and numerous attempts to analyse it have failed to produce an exact copy.

At the same time he introduced an electric wood drying machine to produce controlled humidity, as well as other machine tools for accurately cutting the wood and routing the fret grooves.

Innovation No 3 (1965/66). He began to use Canadian Red cedar for tops (instead of spruce). I first saw this on his flamenco guitars, and when I taxed him about these reddish very even-grained tops, he explained that because of the shortage of first class old seasoned spruce, which was fast disappearing from the European forests, he had experimented with cedar, which he found more consistent and more responsive.

This innovation was so widely imitated that there is now a world famine of suitable first class cedar for tops.

Innovation No 4 A wider fingerboard with a strip of ebony through the centre of the neck to ensure stability.

Innovation No 5 A heavy diagonal strut running from behind the bass side of the sound hole towards the treble side at an angle of about 25 degrees, so that the fan bracing on the bass side is longer than the treble side, producing an even balance between bass and treble.

The theory behind the change is to produce clear trebles with the necessary force to project when needed.

Innovation No 6. Because of rosewood sides (rims) sometimes undulating, Ramirez reinforced the inside of the rims with a thin layer of cypress wood which holds the rosewood firmly in place. This expedient gives rise to the criticism that the sides are made of plywood which is, of course, untrue.

Innovation No 7. A special way of fitting the end block which allows the top to vibrate more freely.

The international fame of Ramirez really grew from 1960, after Segovia having seen and approved the new design and, after having played a Herman Hauser for about 20 years, began to use a Ramirez for his concerts.

I remember trying Segovia's Hauser guitar, and noticing at the time the extremely high string action which must have required great strength from the left hand. Although his 1960 Ramirez had a lower string action, examination showed that the height of the 6th string above the fingerboard was also rather high at 4 mm. Another innovation by José Ramirez III was the 10-string guitar made especially at the instigation and with the co-operation of Narciso Yepes, and later of an 8-string guitar often played by José Tomas.

For some years Pepé (José III) had been talking of the inadequacy of the small premises established by his grandfather in 1882, and when premises in a small arcade opposite the old shop became vacant, he siezed the opportunity and bought it. The result was a replica of a nineteenth century shoppe with timbered joists, wrought iron, blown glass windows, hanging lamps and fittings to match. The final artistic touch is a guitar museum with a fine collection of about 30 old instruments.

The new shop was opened in 1972 and, as if to put the seal of approval to the extension, Pepé was awarded the State's Gold Medal as the best artisan; an example to the guitar constructors of Spain.

Pepé has a daughter, Amalia, and a son whose name is of course José IV (Pepito) who, at the age of 22, was studying physics and acoustics at the University. He, too, has now made guitars. His first one, traditionally a flamenco guitar, was made in 1972 and numbered 1.

Pepé (José III) has continued to improve his instruments, and has been experimenting with a shorter scale guitar which has a scale length of about 65 cm. ($25\frac{1}{2}''$) and a deeper body than the $26\frac{1}{8}''$ which compensates for the shorter length of the sound box. I played two of them, and considered that they, too, produced an attractive sound, and were perhaps easier to finger.

One interesting model was made completely of ebony which made it rather heavy and not as lively.

After much consideration and testing by various players Ramirez decided that although the shorter scale guitar may have been easier to play, it would have been to the detriment of the sound capacity and quality.

It may be of interest to note that in 1964 the price of a Ramirez concert guitar was £185.00. Ten years later the price at the Musicentre was £485.00 and in April 1979 many increases in the cost of labour due to higher wages and the super inflationary cost of raw materials, particularly the shortage of excellent tone wood, shot the price up to £975.00.

Although Pepé employs about 30 craftsmen at the time of writing, and does not work at the bench himself, his No 1 guitars are unmistakeably and distinctly Ramirez: as Paulino Bernabe comments, 'He is the maestro!'

Three generations of Ramirez have devoted themselves to making and improving guitars and passing on their craft to their pupils, and now this continues to the fourth generation, male and female.

When I saw them in 1979, both father and son were extolling the talents of Amalia, now 23, who may well become one of the first women to build guitars. A truly fine record of which the Ramirez family may be proud.

THE RAMIREZ DYNASTY

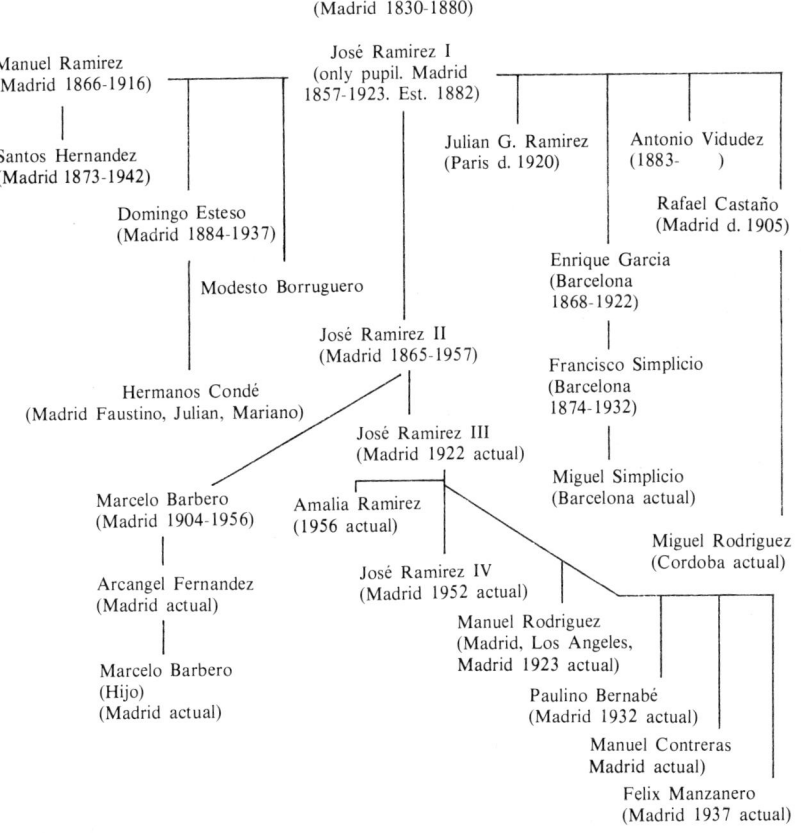

Famous Spanish guitarreros of three centuries

In 1963 José Ramirez gave me a little booklet written by Vidal Benito Revuelta published in 1962 entitled
La Guitarra, su Historia y su Industria
which has a section naming the most highly admired Spanish luthiers of the eighteenth, nineteenth and twentieth centuries up to that time.

However, in spite of the author's and advisers' research, there are many details about the makers which are unknown. Therefore, there is a preface to this section which says that there were usually family connections or working connections between many of the makers.

It also appears that after the eighteenth century when guitar-makers occupied small workshops situated in the back alleys of Cadiz or Málaga, the craft shifted in the nineteenth century to the capital Madrid where most of the best makers gathered and, learning from one another in their close proximity, developed the art to a brilliant standard.

The dates after their names probably denote the dates of the guitars that are in existence.

Eighteenth cnetury
JUAN GUERRERO – Málaga, 1750
(I.M. – Credited with having invented the 6th string in 1801)
DIONISIO GUERRA – Cadiz, 1750
FRANCISCO SANGUINO – Sevilla, 1760

Nineteenth century
FRANCISCO MIR – Cartagena, 1805
FRANCISCO ESPAÑA – Cadiz-Barcelona, 1810-50
JOSÉ PAGÉS – Cadiz, 1814 (1794-1819)
JUAN RUIZ – Almeria, 1815
JUAN MUÑOZ – Madrid, 1820
ANTONIO LORCA – Málaga, 1825
(I.M. – The workshop of LORCA was founded in 1803. Antonio Lorca died in 1870. The shop continued under his son LORCA PIÑO (d. 1909) then LORCA RAMIREZ (d. 1929). Nothing further is known.
RUIZ DE LEON – Zaragoza, 1823
ANTONIO LLORENTE – Granada, 1830
FRANCISCO GONZÁLEZ – Madrid, 1830
AUGUSTIN CAMPO – Madrid, 1840
(collaborated with Dionisio Aguado)

THE RAMIREZ DYNASTY

MANUEL GUITERREZ – Sevilla, 1850
JUAN ALCARAZ – Valencia, 1855
AUGUSTIN ALTÁMIRA – Barcelona, 1855
VICENTE ARIAS – Ciudad Real, 1870
JOSÉ RAMIREZ – Madrid, 1880 (1857-1923)
ANTONIO MOLINA – Málaga, 1890
FRANCISCO ORTEGA – Granada
ZORZANO – Logroño
MANUEL RAMIREZ – Madrid, 1885-1910 (1866-1916)
ANTONIO TORRES – Almeria y Sevilla, 1885 (1817-1892)
ENRIQUE GARCIA – Barcelona, 1890-1922 (1868-1922)
SANTOS HERNANDEZ – Madrid, 1890 (1873-1942)
DOMINGO ESTESO – Madrid, 1900 (1887-1934)
(possibly born 1882 in Cuenca 12 May)

Twentieth century
FRANCISCO SIMPLICIO – Barcelona, 1920-32 (1874-1932)
ENRIQUE SANFELIÚ – Barcelona, 1930 (1882-   )
JOSÉ RAMIREZ II – Madrid, 1915-55 (1885-1957)
MARCELO BARBERO – Madrid, 1925-55 (1904-1956)
JOSÉ RAMIREZ III – Madrid, actuales (1922)
ARCANGEL FERNANDEZ – Madrid, actuales (1922)
HERMANOS CONDÉ – Madrid, actuales
MIGUEL SIMPLICIO – Barcelona, actuales
IGNACIO FLETA – Barcelona, 1897-1977
MIGUEL RODRIGUEZ – Cordoba, actuales
AGUADO y HERNANDEZ – Madrid (1895-1975 Hernandez)

Also mentioned are makers outside Spain:
HERMAN HAUSER, Jnr. – Germany
ANTONIO VIUDEZ – Buenos Aires
ROBERT BOUCHET – France
GALENOTTI – Italy
VELAQUEZ – Puerto Rico
MANUEL RODRIGUEZ – United States (now in Madrid, Spain)
BOLIN – Switzerland, Korea and Japan

List of Guitars in the Ramirez Collection
1. JOSÉ RAMIREZ I — 1913. (flamenco) peg head, sides and back, flame maple
2. ANTONIO TORRES — 1862. Cypress (flamenco) renovated by Manuel Ramirez 1902. 3-piece back, cypress

3. VICENTE ARIAS — Ciudad Real 1874. Palosanto back and sides, peg head
4. MANUEL RAMIREZ — Flamenco, cypress
5. MANUEL RAMIREZ — Flamenco, 3-piece cypress back. 1872. Arlaban 10
6. ALTIMIRA de BARCELONA — (Paris). Birdseye maple
7. FRANCISCO GONZALEZ — 18-2. Palosanto 1-piece back. Madrid, Carrera de San Jeronimo 15. Won medal in 1867, Paris
8. JOSÉ SERRANO — Seville 1871. Pegs. Mahogany sides and 7-piece back of mahogany and cypress
9. JOSÉ RAMIREZ II — 1972. Cypress. Pegs
10. MANUEL — Cava Baja 24. June 1889. Cypress, Pegs
11. JUAN PAGES — Cadiz 1787. 12-string, 3-piece. Rosewood B
12. DIUNISIO GUERRA — 12-string, 3-piece cypress back. 'I have been made in Cadiz in 1784 San Jose'
13. MANUEL MUÑOA MIHIZO — Madrid 1804. 12-string
14. FRANCICO SIMPLICIO — No 328, 1931. 'I am the pupil of Enrique Garcia', Chicago Exposition 1893. 1st prize
15. ANTONIO DE TORRES — Seville 1854. Palosanto. Calle de Ballestella 11
16. JUAN MORENO — 1830. Madrid. Peg head. Flame maple top, sides and matched back
17. FRANCESCO ORTEGA — Granada. Cypress
18. MANUEL RAMIREZ — Luthier of the National Conservatoire, 1911 Arlaban No 10
19. VIUDA de MANUEL RAMIREZ — Cypress. Arlaban No 11 workshop for Violins and Guitars; initialled SH (Santos Hernandez)
20. SANTOS HERNANDEZ — Aduanna 27, Madrid 1930. Flamenco. Pegs. Cypress. 3-piece
21. JOSÉ RAMIREZ III — No 7. 1946
22. JOSÉ RAMIREZ IV (aged 20) — Cypress No 1. 1972, signed
23. JOSÉ RAMIREZ III — Brazilian Rosewood 1960. Original guitar played by Segovia from 1960-63. String height at 6th string 4-5 mm
24. JOSÉ RAMIREZ III — In Ebony

Chapter Twenty-five

THE CRAFT IN SPAIN

Paulino Bernabé
Of all the luthiers who have worked for Ramirez, Paulino Bernabé is, in my opinion, the greatest perfectionist and a superb craftsman.

Paulino Bernabé is an expansive, tall, loose-limbed, friendly, cigar-smoking, brandy-drinking individual, who finds life, people, and guitars a source of wonder, inspiration and creativity.

He is a Madridlenian, born on 2 July 1932, the son of a stonemason, who became his own master in December 1969, with a shop at 8 Cuchilleros opposite the famous Botin's Restaurant and within view of the Arcos de Cuchilleros, with its steps descending from the adjoining Plaza Mayor, the centre point of old Madrid.

The small bright workroom behind the shop is a picture of tidiness, and there is never a speck of surplus dust or a tool out of place. While he works he usually has the stereogram softly emitting guitar music. He hardly ever constructs two guitars *exactly* alike and he is still experimenting in order to produce the world's best guitar.

One flamenco model, which is not for sale, is made in the style of the nineteenth century with alternating strips of rosewood and cypress. To my ear the tone was everything a concert-flamenco guitarist could ever desire.

He also works with camphor wood, Palo Santo, Palo Rosa and pearwood and does not think that a sprayed lacquer finish is detrimental to the tone. In fact, he ran a test on four guitars, two with hand applied varnish and two with sprayed lacquer, and found no difference in their development of sound. He says it depends on how you apply the lacquer and remove it.

He prefers to work in Brazilian rosewood rather than Indian rosewood because the Brazilian rosewood looks more beautiful, is possibly more stable, and perhaps produces more treble tone which mellows with time.

Even so, stock of old matured wood keeps running out and always requires replacement.

He is meticulous with every single strut or bracing and bounces each piece in order to ascertain its resonance.

His main workshop is on the garden floor of his newly built house, where he keeps his store of wood, and where backs and tops and necks hang maturing. A veritable treasure-house for a connoisseur.

Paulino now has an assistant who is fascinating to watch when he is at work perfecting a fingerboard on an otherwise completed guitar. Not a spot is missed, every fret receives undivided attention; the slightest imperfection in the finish is deftly touched up. Nothing escapes his twinkling eye which also takes in the surrounding action.

Paulino, who works on most of the body contruction at his home workshop, showed me two tops which he had prepared in which the grain ran diagonally; one from right to left and the other in the opposite way; one top had just three struts fitted diagonally opposite to the grain.

He hopes by means of these experiments to discover ways of improving the sound of these instruments, which he builds only to specific orders.

Every guitarist has his own idea of what constitutes the ideal guitar but all must admire the superb beauty of Paulino's craftsmanship and the perfect balance of his instruments. His enthusiasm for building a better guitar is always on the boil.

This enthusiasm is also reflected by the phrase 'No problems' when encountering any special difficulty, and this is only matched by his other favourite phrase 'Fantastico!'

Fortunately he has a bright wife, Angelita, who helps on the business and secretarial side, giving her husband freedom to pursue his creative flair with 'No problem'. To which I say, 'Fantastico!'

A Paulino Bernabé guitar, like a Rolls Royce, is in short supply and almost as expensive.

Hernandez y Aguado

Manuel Diaz Hernandez, known as Manuel Hernandez, born 1895 in Vamojado, Jaen, died 22.2.75 in Madrid.

Victoriano Aguado, born 1897 Madrid. At the time of writing in a home for the aged.

When I first began to visit Madrid in the early 1950s, the best known luthiers were Marcelo Barbero, Conde Hermanos, the Ramirez shop rather than his guitars, and the shop of Santos Hernandez's widow.

Although Hernandez y Aguado had been making guitars in their workshop at the Ribera de Cortadores since 1941, it took me years to find this courtyard, tucked away through an alley at the top of the street known as the Rastro, the location of Madrid's fleamarket and antique centre for old guns and other 'finds'.

In England their fame began after John Williams had been using one of their guitars, and in whose hands it produced a clear gentle sweet sound.

Eventually, with the assistance of a Madrilenian from whom I discovered this hidden courtyard I met this wonderful old team of highly skilled craftsmen from whom I ordered an instrument for which I had to wait almost a year. I paid my deposit and the short chubby one (Aguado) – who did all the polishing and was also responsible for the secretarial work – wrote out the receipt on one of their cards. Both were very gentle and polite and gave me the run of the workshop, so that I could photograph everything I wanted. It was evident that the craftsmanship that went into the guitars was the most highly skilled and immaculate.

They worked carefully and unhurriedly, producing about one guitar a month – no wonder there was always a long waiting time – and their whole output from 1941 to 1975 is said to be only upwards of 400 guitars. One feature of their guitars was the varnishing of the interior and another (although unseen) was a drawing of each of their faces on either end of the flat strut fitted under the bridge placement on the inside of the 'tapa' (top or sounding board).

The other distinguishing mark was the incisive carving down the headstock on contrast to all the other Spanish guitars which are always simply polished. Guitars, like beautiful ladies, have their following of admirers, and although beauty is in the eye of the beholder, people have different tastes, but one whose admiration for the Hernandez y Aguado guitars was always constant was a guitarist by the name of Regino Sainz de la Maza.

Sainz de la Maza was, in his time, one of Spain's leading concert performers, and was also greatly acclaimed in South America where he gave recitals. He became Professor of Guitar at Madrid Conservatoire where he remained for many years turning out players like José Tomas, José Luis Rodriguez, José Luis Gonzalez and other prominent guitarists.

How was this team of Hernandez y Aguado created? Well, it happened this way.

Hernandez had worked in a piano factory constructing the piano bodies (a position reached after much study of acoustics and other necessary crafts) and Aguado had come in as a polisher. When the factory was closed, the two, who had become friends, took the workshop at Rubero de Cortadores and set up as piano repairers. Hernandez, who rather fancied playing the guitar, made one for himself. It was seen by de la Maza who thought it was quite nice and encouraged them to make another. Eventually they dropped piano repairing and devoted their time exclusively to guitars. De la Maza has a number of them, which he highly prizes and would not think of playing on any other make.

When I next visited the workshop, in about 1968, things had slightly changed. Hernandez y Aguado guitars were in greater demand and were, in fact, one of the most sought after by the Japanese. Nevertheless, I was surprised to find a young Japanese working at a bench. I asked him his name and he said it was Toshihiko Nakade. His father was the first real modern guitar maker in Japan, and I had been buying guitars from him although I had not yet met him. It transpired that Toshihiko had been sent to Madrid by his father to finish his guitar-making studies, and had no doubt paid a good premium for the privilege. Toshihiko's apprenticeship was well rewarded because, by the end of 1969 when I returned to Japan and met his father, the son was already on his own, making very good instruments costing more than his father's.

A few years before the death of Hernandez in 1975, I had a letter from his son-in-law, Jesus Belezar, informing me that Aguado who had had trouble with his legs, had now left the workshop to become a resident in a home for the aged, and that he was now working with his father-in-law. Now, of course, he is carrying on on his own account. And that is the way a unique and talented partnership has ended. Alas, the gentle, old-world, leisurely traditions will never be repeated but remain just a treasured memory.

Marcelino Lopez Nieto

Another maker of the Aguado y Hernandez school is Marcelino Lopez Nieto, a man of many artistic talents – painting, drawing and the history of classics. He works on his own, apart from receiving some help from one or two of his sons, who number five. His guitars have a clear delicate tone, and he has made one specially for Segovia. This model, which was first made for me in 1972, is considered by some as one of the greatest he ever made. Marcelino Lopez lives and works in a very pleasant house quite a way from the centre of Madrid, and now devotes most of his time making old instruments such as lutes and vihuelas and studying their history.

Ansalme Solar Gonzalez was brought to my notice in the late 1950s by a guitar aficionado, who told me about the excellent toned instruments Solar Gonzalez was constructing from very old mahogany. The wood came from old doors which Solar Gonzalez had bought at a demolition sale, and while the wood lasted the guitars were excellent. Their sound was light and crisp, they were easy to play, and they were reasonably priced. But like all good things, the wood did not last for ever. Solar Gonzalez' workshop developed and he began to construct guitars of rosewood and cypress as well as African mahogany, which were good, but no longer exceptional, nor reasonably priced.

Fernando and Cesar Vera are two clever craftsmen, born in the late 1930s, who set up a new workshop in Madrid during 1963. This was well organised and turned out some very good classical guitars which both sounded very good and were very well finished.

They were so good at their work that Jose Ramirez engaged them to make a special student model to which he put a special label with the Ramirez name but which sold at a lower price than the No 1A concert guitar.

Fernando, always experimenting with new materials, decided to use a plastic fingerboard on his guitars instead of ebony, hoping that it would eliminate the danger of neck warp. Unfortunately, the pull of the wood is stronger than the immobility of the man-made fibres, and when, after developing buzzes, we attempted to shoot the fingerboard in order to refret the guitar, two things happened. The blade of the plane repeatedly snapped on the hard surface and, after it was refretted, I found that the natural perspiration or oils of the fingers, could not be absorbed but remained on the surface of the plastic, which was no help to the movement of the left hand. Needless to say, the practice was discontinued. Today, the Vera brothers specialise in making the finest lutes to come out of Spain.

There are a number of other makers in Madrid, of whom Juan Alvarez and his brother Francisco are very good, but have not aspired to the heights of those previously mentioned. They, too, have a shop in Madrid near the Cortez (Parliament building) and make instruments for the House of Arcangel Fernandez.

Mention must also be made of **Luis Arostegui** of Madrid who makes a very reasonable priced concert guitar of rosewood, which produces a very bright and healthy sound, but has, so far, not succeeded in equalling the quality of the most famous Madrid luthiers, but he is still in his thirties and may well succeed in that respect.

Andres Martin is a much older man, who was once in vogue, but is no longer in demand by the younger generation, although his guitars are very well made and sound quite good.

Ignacio Fleta e Hijos, Barcelona (b. Huesca 1897 d. 1979 Barcelona) Ignacio Fleta, was born in Huesca province of Teruel in 1897. He made his first violin at the age of 22, but it was not until 1951 when he first heard Segovia play, that he took up guitar-making seriously. A case of one great master inspiring another.

His keenness was unlimited as proved by his hours of work, sometimes as long as 12 and 14 hours a day. Even in 1966-67 at the age of 70, he put in 8 to 10 hours a day.

He both lived and worked at Angeles 4, Barcelona, where the entrance hall of his flat is the 'showroom', one front room used for the stock of wood, and the main front room where Ignacio and his two sons Francesco and Gabriel (both married and with families of their own) worked under his firm but kindly instruction.

It would also seem that in 1966 Ignacio considered that his sons had finished their apprenticeship and so changed the name of the label from 'Ignacio Fleta' to 'Ignacio Fleta E Hijos'.

When I first visited him in 1958 there was a waiting list of six months before one could obtain a Fleta guitar. Fifteen years later, the waiting time became a staggering 14 years. The reason is not far to seek – a world demand unmatched by the supply of about 32 per annum.

The magazine *Blanco y Negro* for December 1962 published the following figures of Señor Fleta's complete output until then: 82 violins, 39 violincellos, 5 violas, and 270 guitars as well as some other instruments. Most luthiers do not like being questioned about their output, but when I tentatively put the question to Señor Fleta on one of my visits to receive a new guitar in 1966, he faced me, with a glint of fun in his eye, and replied 'Just look at the number inside the guitar you have in your hand and you will see how many guitars I have made'. The number was 382 (dated 1965) which, divided by 15 years of guitar-making and experimenting, reaches barely 26 annually. My next guitar dated 1970 numbers 536 making an output of about 31 per annum.

Throughout the 25 years Fleta guitars have maintained their outward appearance, but there have been constant improvements to the sound due to slight adjustments in the strutting, measurements, selection or thickness of wood. Varnish was, of course, a very important factor and it took him four or five years to discover what he considered the ideal formula. The ingredients for the varnish consist of linseed oil, various types of gum (gum mastic, gum benjamin or benzoin), saldarac (a type of resin), fragrant aromatic resin of a Javanese tree and gum lacon (a red brittle resinous substance). Saffron and sandalwood are used for colouring but the exact formula of every maker's varnish is a treasured secret.

Señor Fleta used the same tender care from the selecting of the wood for every guitar, to its finish. He used palo de santa de jicaranda (a type of rosewood) for the back and sides, a cedar or spruce top, and pine struts which are perfectly fitted and cut to required thicknesses. The final filing of the frets is made by a file the width of the fingerboard, and while the file is in operation the body of the guitar is protected by a shaped 'bib' placed on the table and tucked into the sound hole.

Ignacio Fleta broke with the Spanish traditional way of fitting the sides into the neck stock, followed by glueing on the top then fitting the back. He finished the whole of the sound box (body) first *before* fitting the neck – probably due to his training as a violin maker.

The wood always went through a humidifying process and was then treated with infra-red and ultra-violet rays before it was cut to the shape of the instrument, then shaved down to carefully calibrated thicknesses. Then came the varnishing process which could not be hurried.

According to Señor Fleta, a violin can retain and improve its sound or sonority for about 300 years but a guitar which is a much more delicate instrument, retains its tonal qualities for a much shorter period – probably 100 years.

Unfortunately, this gentle genius underwent a number of operations and towards the end of his life could not work as much as he desired on his beloved guitars. He left much of the work to his trusted sons, who have continued to make the Fleta guitar since his death in 1979.

The measurements are as follows:

Overall length	$39\frac{3}{4}''$
Body size: length	$19\frac{1}{2}'' \times 11\frac{1}{2}'' \times 9\frac{1}{2}'' \times 14\frac{3}{8}''$
Body depths	shoulder $3\frac{3}{4}''$, waist $3\frac{13}{16}''$, bottom $3\frac{7}{8}''$
Fingerboard width	nut $2\frac{1}{16}''$, 12th fret $2\frac{7}{16}''$
Height of strings 12th fret	$\frac{3}{16}''$ (at 6th string)

Bridge	$7\frac{1}{4}''\times 1\frac{1}{4}''$
Height of saddle	$\frac{7}{16}''$, treble side $\frac{1}{2}''$, bass side
Diameter of sound hole	$3\frac{7}{16}''$, width of mosaic $\frac{15}{16}''$

Players who have recorded LP albums using a Fleta guitar:
Ernesto Bitetti (1943 Argentine)
Alberto Ponce (1935)
Gonzalez Mohino (1930 Madrid)
Oscar Caseres (1969 Montevideo)
Jorge Morel (Escobar BA)
John Williams

The Guitarreros of Granada

There are six guitar constructors in Granada whose instruments have become known, or will become known in guitaristic circles. The most famous one, Manuel de la Chica, who has already been mentioned, was born in the first decade of this century.

It is with regret that I cannot honestly say that the promise he showed around 1950 has materialised and I think that if he had been closer to the centre of the craft, say in Madrid, he would have been able to eliminate the weaknesses which developed in the bass tone of his guitars. The basses lacked crispness because of lightweight body construction.

In Granada, the glamour of the region, its history and its beautiful architecture, may well affect an introspective artisan with their magic, thereby increasing his imagination rather than his skill. The glamour must to a certain extent also affect his customers who imagine that his guitars are better than they really are.

The senior guitar-maker and teacher is 70 year old Eduardo Ferrér who has taught a number of the younger makers including his own son, Jose, Luis Arostegui and the two bright hopes of the future, Antonio Marin Montero and Manuel Bellido (b. 1939), both in their 30s, and the much older Isidro Garrido (b. 1922).

Eduardo Ferrér has the distinction of having spent three periods between 1966/68 in Japan teaching guitar making to the Japanese under contract to Yamaha, then returning to Granada to continue running his own shop.

Isidro Garrido is really a maker of flamenco guitars, and works on his own, having begun at the age of 15. He is not well-known because he has never courted big business, always making guitars for personal customers, who are usually professional players. He has never deviated from using pine tops which is in keeping with his traditional way of working in his shop, tucked away in a corner of old Granada, where he is to be seen chatting to his cronies.

Antonio Marin Montero and **Manuel Lopez Bellido** used to be partners, and although they have now gone their own constructive ways, their workshops are next door to one another, openly adjoining. Nevertheless, their instruments are quite different from each other.

It must be said that the general opinion, including my own,, is that Marin a former pupil of Manuel, has the superior talent and his guitars take their place among the world's best, and are continually improving.

Bellido works on the prinicple of diagonal strutting rather like the piano soundboard and hopes to develop the tone in this manner. He, too, began making guitars at the age of 16 and, working on his own makes no more than about 30 instruments a year. He still has a great regard for his old teacher, Eduardo Ferrér.

Manuel Bellido has a younger brother, Jose whom he taught and who makes more flamenco than classical guitars. He is married to Eduardo Ferrér's daughter.

Rafael Morales (in his 50s) has carried a certain mystique about him because of his own original ideas, particularly in relation to his flamenco guitars. He often used flame maple for the backs of his flamenco guitars (rather then the traditional cypress) and although they were not bad generally, they did not produce *all* the qualities required of a first class flamenco guitar, being rather thicker in sound. Since his chest and lungs were affected by the wood shavings and dust, he does not construct himself, but employs guitar-makers to work for him. Although his present flamenco guitars are made of cypress back and sides, they lack the guts of the more formidable sound of the great Andalucian maker of Cordoba.

Before coming to Manuel Reyes of Cordoba I must mention the latest recruit among the best artisans of Granada. He is a young man Antonio Raya Pardo who makes excellent concert and flamenco guitars which ring freely and play easily.

Manuel Reyes – Cordoba

Manuel Reyes is undoubtedly one of the most sought after flamenco guitar makers in the world and today the demand is so great that no more orders are being taken, as he has sufficient orders for at least five years.

His workshop could hardly be in a more romantic-looking square than Plaza del Porto, No 2, where he owns a corner house, inhabited by his pretty wife, children and himself.

Manuel Reyes was quite a good flamenco player before becoming a professional luthier, but had to give up professional playing when he had an accident, which resulted in his right arm being repaired with a fixed joint to the elbow, so that he is unable to straighten it. Although he still plays, this slight disability in no way detracts from his guitar building talents, and today a No. 1 first class Reyes is indeed a prize worth having. He is now making classical guitars.

Mention must be made of **Miguel Rodriguez** who also lives in Cordoba and is a renowned maker of flamenco guitars, and a product of the Ramirez Dynasty. He, in turn, was the teacher of Manuel Reyes of whom he must be very proud.

Carmelo of Ronda

Ronda is about 50 kilometres north of Marbella on the Costa del Sol and is built across a volcanic divide or crater which is spanned by a bridge. After a dangerous mountain climb, during a morning covered in low mist, I discovered Carmelo by asking his neighbours to find him. When I finally located him, all he could show me was tops, ribs or backs, not having one complete guitar in stock. I ordered a number of flamenco guitars from him, which were quite good, but they did not like the English climate, and suffered from various splits on the table and back. I have not seen any of his guitars since that time (1965).

Jeronimo Peña Fernandez (b. 1 April 1933 Jaen)

I first met Jeronimo Peña in 1973 after hearing about him from my friend, George Bowden of Palma, Majorca, a Canadian Hispanophile, forestry student, guitar maker and owner of a guitar store.

Without wasting time, I took the journey to Marmalejo, a tiny little town in the province of Jaen, which is only to be found on the most detailed maps of the region.

Married with two children, he had a light, well-fitted workshop in his backyard, and being originally a carver, makes his own frames and anything else required in the making of guitars.

His father was an agricultural worker who apprenticed his son in 1942 to a carpenter at the age of 9. There he served his apprenticeship until 1947. Jeronimo was not just an ordinary carpenter, but an excellent woodcarver who, in common with many Andalucians, played the guitar. So, in 1950, he began to make his first guitar, and completed it in four months, which gave him the incentive to continue, making guitars and violins during his military service. Having got the 'bug', he continued making guitars after his return to civilian life, and finished one instrument in six months.

One year there was a Festival in Jaen which featured 'Pepé' Marchena the flamenco guitarist, and Peña was bold enough to show him one of his guitars. Marchena liked it so much that he took it with him and showed it to a guitar collector friend of his, Don Indalesio by name, who was head of a Mathematics Faculty. The professor was very impressed and encouraged Peña by presenting him with a beautifully sounding guitar which he advised Peña to copy, and arranged for him to go to Barcelona in order to study with Carlos Ramos (who originally came from Malaga). The professor also calibrated the measurements of the fretting in a more accurate way.

In 1967 he was advised to become a full-time guitarrero and became, in my opinion, one of the most outstanding of all guitar makers and when, during my 1973 visit, he showed me a flamenco guitar he had just completed, I was amazed at its tone and volume. Not only its tone and volume, but its meticulous workmanship, carved ebony inset in the neck, the carved end of the fingerboard and the carved decorative head and bridge. Peña is rather proud of the special guitar he made for the famous bullfighter 'El Cordobes'. He has certain definite rules which he applies to the making of his guitars. The wood is at least 25 years old and some cypress comes from houses, and from furniture 200 years old. Almost all the tops are made from old wood. Peña studies the wood for five years and from the end of each August the contraction of the wood is measured every month, while hot air is also used to help to season the wood.

Peña constructs his instruments only in June, July and August, when it is the driest part of the year in the region of Marmalejo, the home of Jeronimo Peña Fernandez, who loves his craft so much that he spent two years carving the headboard and lower end of his matrimonial bed.

There are of course, a number of good craftsmen other than those I have mentioned, who construct their guitars in different parts of Spain, among them Gerundino Fernandez who makes flamenco guitars in Almeria, Santiago Barber, Jose Ortiz, Manuel Romero and Pantoja in Seville (el Centro del Mundo), and Antonio Duran in Granada and probably a number of others whose work may be good, but they have not come into my orbit so I will leave them to plough their own furrows.

Alhambra Guitars

The Alhambra guitar factory has existed since 1963. It is situated in Muro del Alcoy between Alicante and Valencia 12,000 ft. above sea level where evidence still exists of Roman building and occupation.

Alhambra guitars were initiated by two cabinet makers, Ricardo Lorens and Jose Maria Vilaplana who, in 1955, formed a limited company with help and money from a larger holding company, for which two brothers Jaime and Camilo Julio, acted as Managing Director and Marketing Manager.

During the 60s we did receive some guitars from them, but in spite of their low prices, then starting at £12 for a full size guitar, I did not care for their tone or finish, and discontinued stocking them.

However, by 1976 the standard of Alhambra guitars had risen considerably, and after a visit to Muro, and making my modifications clear, they agreed to supply the guitars for the Musicentre labelled 'Specially made for the Ivor Mairants Musicentre'.

Since that time the Alhambra guitars have become a staple diet in the lives of the British guitar fraternity, and no wonder. Their tone is loud and clear, they all have solid cedar or spruce tables, and except for the cheaper models, the sides and backs are also of solid timber, rosewood, mahogany or walnut.

They have a staff of more than 60 and produce upward of 30,000 guitars every year, and expect to raise this figure to 50,000. Although the workers are highly trained, only about three of them are capable of making a complete guitar. In spite of the very expensive sophisticated machinery that has been installed, it takes five hours to cut all the parts and fifty-nine hours to assemble each guitar.

Alhambra takes a lot of advice from the many good players who test the instruments (Jose Luis Gonzalez lives in the district), and also from Madrid's leading luthiers José Ramirez, Felix Manzanero, Paulino Bernabé and Arcangel Fernandez who not only sell Alhambra guitars in their shops, but offer good advice which is used to improve the guitars.

The more expensive guitars are, of course, entirely hand made and polished and I can safely venture the opinion that the Alhambra factory is the most up-to-date guitar-making plant in the whole of Spain (but it is not to be compared with the top luthiers workshops such as Ramirez).

The scale length of Alhambra guitars is 656 mm. The 656 mm. is divided by the constant figure of 17.817 and the result is again divided by 17.817 until the 19 frets are measured:

Distance between the frets:	NUT 656 mm. from Bridge	
36.8187 mm.	619.1813 mm.	
34.7522	584.4291	
32.8017	551.6274	
30.9607	520.6667	
29.2230	491.4437	
27.5828	463.8609	
26.0347	437.8262	
24.5735	413.2527	
23.1942	390.0585	
21.8924	368.1661	
20.6637	347.5024	
19.5039	327.9985	12th fret
18.4093	309.5907	
17.3761	272.2146	
16.4008	275.8138	
15.4803	266.3335	
14.6115	245.1220	
13.7914	231.1306	
13.0173	218.9133	
12.2867	206.6866	

Jose Maria Vilaplana

If the reader will refer to the beginning of this description of the Alhambra operation, the name of Jose Maria Vilaplana will have been noted. This Jose Maria is his son who has been in Muro del Alcoy since 1947 and has been working at Alhambra since 1961 when he was fourteen.

He was apprenticed to his father for fifteen years before he began making his own guitars. About three years ago a special workshop was set aside for him in the Alhambra factory and he put all his talents to making his own concert guitars. I had two of them, Nos 7 and 8, and they were magnificent, the materials being the finest Brazilian rosewood and the tops of superb spruce.

It was fascinating to watch the care and dedication he puts into the making and fitting of every piece of wood.

His guitars met with an immediate response from those who tried them at the Musicentre and were soon snapped up. The latest batch are even better and in my opinion compare favourably with the best in the world.

When, after meeting Jose Maria, I asked to see his father, he told me that he was at the seaside building a boat for himself, and he asked if my wife and I would like to see a model boat that his father had recently constructed. Off we went to his house near the factory, and in the drawing room, displayed in a large glass case made in perfect proportions of 1 to 100, stood the Spanish Man-o-War which led the Spanish Armada against Sir Francis Drake and which was sunk in the Channel. Every fitting, row lock and gun was in perfect proportion. Each mast and rigging was an exact replica of that famous flagship.

And that is the kind of master carpenter who still has a 15% interest in Alhambra guitars.

Chapter Twenty-six

A WORLD OF CLASSICAL GUITARS

Mexico

Considering the fact that Mexico was invaded by the Spaniards four and a half centuries ago, and that many of them settled there, it is not surprising that the guitar should have become one of the most popular instruments in use there today.

Although, in the 1970s rock music and electric guitars took hold, it was in addition to the traditional Ranchero groups, harp and guitar trios, and Mariachi bands, and by no means replaced them. In fact, as far as I have experienced, there is more outward evidence of nylon-string guitar playing in Mexico than in Spain.

Unlike the Spanish made classical or flamenco guitars (which are more or less the same size) and the half size requinto with a 60/61 mm. scale length instead of the full scale length of 65/66 mm., the Mexican guitars come in all sizes, tunings and numbers of strings. The smallest type I saw is known as a Harana, a five-string 55/56 mm. scale length instrument with the top string tuned to D, and the third string F♯ tuned one octave higher than normal.

The next largest is also a five-string guitar-shaped instrument, but with a swell back and rather high bridge, known as a viola. The viola has normal guitar tuning with an octave 'g' but with a shorter fingerboard.

The Ranchero group often has a tubby looking cutaway six-string guitar as well as a normal sized classical one, and in addition the Jumbo sized four-five-or six-string bass guitar which reminds me of a bear, looks like a double-deep 'cello and is known as a Guitarron. This outsized fat cat rests with its back on the player's belly and produces short plunky notes.

All the guitar groups took part in a fabulous performance I saw given by the Ballet Folklorico de Mexico which provided dancing, singing and playing too thrilling to describe.

To my ear the tone and balance of the guitars sounded perfect, but upon close examination of the instruments I was rather disappointed, and to my surprise found them poorly finished.

When I played some of the instruments they produced a dry thin tone that lacked sustaining power. Those I saw for public sale were even worse and high priced compared to guitars from the rest of the world. The fact that these guitars sounded just right when performed in their native context led me to the conclusion that it was a case of 'horses for courses' and I had to admit that as far as the Mexican guitarists are concerned, it is a case of 'T'ain't what you do, it's the way that you do it!' and that's what it's all about.

Japan
There are still some people who find it hard to accept the fact that the Japanese are capable of constructing or playing the guitar. Automobiles, cameras, Hi-Fi, transistors, TV, yes. But guitars? No.

What causes this disbelief? Well, seemingly, Japanese guitars reared their six-strings in about the middle of the 1930s and exploded on the world in the sixties, but in order to discover the how and why, a little more delving is necessary.

I had the advantage of two tours of Japan; one with Mantovani's Orchestra in 1963, and the other on a buying expedition in 1969. Both visits gave me an on the spot, first-hand experience, but for the history I am indebted to Akinobe Matsuda, the guitarist, and to Shiro Arai, a leading guitar manufacturer and exporter. Shiro Arai, himself a good guitarist, owns the brand name Aria and claims to be the first to distribute mass-produced guitars in Japan. He had also studied the early history of the guitar in Japan and passed on to me the results of his researches, for which I thank him. I therefore feel that I am able to present an historic picture of the phenomenal rise in the popularity of the instrument among the Japanese and so dispel the doubts that cause unacceptance of a fact of life.

It is generally believed that during 1549 the first Christian missionaries landed in Japan, and brought with them the musical instruments then popular in Europe namely the clavichord, the lute, the harp and the rebec. It is also considered that, because of the attraction of these instruments, and the devoted work of Jesuit priest, Francis Xavier, a number of converts were made among the Japanese. There is also evidence that the lute was played at Mass, and that in the second half of the sixteenth century there were very good lutenists among the Japanese converts.

So much so that in 1582 four Japanese students were sent to Rome to study, and they returned eight years later fully-fledged performers of the above instruments, and it is recorded by the Society of Jesus that they gave a performance for tycoon Hideyoshi, who was very much fascinated by the music.

One can only conjecture about the possible progress of Western music in Japan had it continued uninterrupted but in 1616 Tokugawa Shogunite promulgated the Christian Prohibition Law and put an end to European musical instrumental influences for nearly three centuries.

It was not until an American admiral named Perry arrived at the port of Uraga (near Yokohama) in 1845 to seek trade agreements with the Japanese that the guitar made its first appearance. A picture now in the library of Yokohama, taken at a reception held on board the admiral's ship, clearly shows two guitar players performing, but this occasion had little influence. It was only after Taijin Hiraoko (Japan's developer of railroads) had stayed in the United States for five years studying Railroad Technology and returned to Japan carrying a guitar, that his countrymen really saw the instrument. However, Hiraoka was not a real guitarist but just strummed to accompany his own vocalising. Therefore, he, too, had little influence.

The introduction of the guitar to Japan can be accredited to Kenpachi Hiruma who, having graduated from the Music Research Bureau (later the Tokyo Art College), travelled to America and various European countries including Italy, where he studied both the guitar and the mandolin, and upon his return in 1896 began his life's work of teaching the guitar.

The first mandolin ensemble known in Japan was formed in 1900 at the Gakusyu-In School, and the following year the Tokyo Art College formed its own ensemble in which Mr. Hiruma played the guitar.

Later, in the year 1911, a well-known Italian guitarist named Adolfo Sarucolli settled in Japan and did a great deal to popularise the guitar, teaching both guitar and vocal music.

The methods of the Italian masters, Carcassi, Carulli and Giuliani, had by this time found their way to Japan, and, as the Mandolin Orchestras increased in popularity, so did the number of guitarists included in the ensembles increase, and the number of solo guitar performances. The three most notable players in the early 1900s were Baron Morishige Takei (1890-1949), Yoshi Ohkahara (1904-1925) and Jiro Nakano (1906-   ), although their guitars were steel-strung.

Baron Takei, who had been to Europe, was most enthusiastic about the fretted instruments, and in 1915 founded the Orchestra Symphonica Takei. He also published a monthly magazine known as

Mandolin and Guitar. Furthermore, he brought from England, Phillip J. Bone's *Collection of Guitar Music,* and his book on the *Guitar and Mandolin* all of which contributed to the increase of guitar knowledge.

Japanese who remember Segovia's first visit in 1929, say that this was the epoch-making event that touched off the beginning of the second Golden Age of the Guitar in Japan.

It was the influence of Segovia and the music of Sor, Aguado, Fortea and Tarrega, which lead the Japanese guitarists towards a more authentic method of playing, and in the early 30s Japanese players were playing music by Tarrega, Torroba and J. S. Bach in concerts and a number of Japanese Guitar Associations were established independently of the mandolin ensemble.

In 1927 a bi-monthly magazine was published by Dr. Isao Takahashi and Chuzaemon Sawaguchi, while Seiichi Konishi (a bosom friend of Baron Takei) translated *Guitarra in Delgrave Music Lexicon* by Emilio Pujol into Japanese.

Shun Ogura translated *La Guitarra y su Historia* and in Nagoya Jiro Nakano published the *Guitar Study Magazine.* Mention must also be made of Masao Koga (1905-   ) who composed many Japanese popular songs (Kayo-Kyoku) using the guitar as the accompanying instrument. He wrote so many hits that a range of instruments known as 'Koga-Melody' guitars were at one time sold everywhere.

The question of who began making classical guitars in Japan can safely be answered. It was the violin makers and, in fact, some of the early instruments look like a cross between a guitar and 'cello.

As far as is known, the first man to construct a classical guitar was Kinpachi Miyamoto, a famous violin maker and Sakazo Nakade (b. about 1905-   ) was a pupil of his. Sakazo Nakade's guitars are known for their sweet, firm, penetrating tone and his two sons have followed in his footsteps.

I have already mentioned that in 1957 the Japanese contestant at the Moscow 'International Festival of Youth' won a gold medal, proving that there were devotees of the classical guitar in Japan. Then, when Segovia returned to Japan for his second concert tour in 1959, many guitarists were presented to him and showed their prowess. After he had heard them all, he explained that it was necessary for one good young student of the guitar to go to Europe for further study, and from those who had played for him he chose Akinobu Matsuda.

Matsuda did, in fact, go to Sienna, then to Santiago di Compostela and received tuition from Segovia. He entered the guitar competition in Santiago de Compostela in 1961 and was credited third place to Jose Tomas from Alicante who gained first prize, and Jose Luis Gonzalez from Madrid, who came second.

Segovia transferred him to John Williams for tuition, and it was during this period in London that I became acquainted with Akinobu Matsuda.

Matsuda was born in Himeji in 1933 and became interested in the guitar when he was about 14 and tried playing his sister's guitar aided by her old practice books. Noting his interest, she obtained a letter of introduction from a famous Tokyo teacher named Obara, recommending the boy to a monk who lived near Himeji. This monk was well versed in the works of Sor, Aguado, Coste, Llobet and de Visée, and explained the value of this music and its study to young Matsuda, illustrating his lessons with the help of some Segovia records.

So far early history and living experiences match up very well in the story of the growth of the guitar in Japan, even to the point of Segovia mentioning that in 1959 he thought there were about a half million guitarists in Japan, even if the majority preferred to play folk songs like *Wine and Tears*, a big Koga 'hit' which greatly influenced the Japanese people.

By the time I went on the three week Japanese tour with Mantovani in 1963 to take part in the Osaka Musical Festival, the guitar players and its makers had come a long way. I personally witnessed a grand concert in the huge Mainichi Hall in Osaka, given in honour of the sixtieth birthday of a leading guitar and mandolin teacher.

I saw the results of what could hardly have been more than 15 years growth in the progress of the guitar in Japan. There must have been 2,000 supporters and players in the audience and on the stage. The large dressing rooms were full of groups sitting on the floor, rehearsing, practising or conferring, and there were performances of solos, duets, trios, quartets and, of course, the mandolin and guitar orchestras providing continuity with the early part of the century. When one compares the lack of similar support in Great Britain for such a venture in 1963, one should no longer be surprised that Japan is also a land of the rising guitar as well as the rising sun, for by this time Segovia's estimate of a half a million guitars had doubled.

The number of guitar makers had also doubled. Arai & Co. Inc. had become established, with headquarters in Nagoya, as manufacturers, importers, exporters and wholesalers with their Aria guitars. Sadao Yairi was making an excellent range of guitars, which we imported and sold from £20 upwards (in 1978 the lowest priced Yairi retailed for over £100).

Ryoji Matsuoka guitars were also of excellent quality; Yamaha specialised more in the steel-strung variety, although also producing a nylon-strung range. Suzuki were one of the earliest manufacturers, having begun by making violins, etc, but their guitars were rather drier in tone than the Yairi and Matsuoka.

In Nagoya I was shown products of a number of manufacturers who, instead of using the traditional mahogany, maple, walnut or rosewood for the backs and sides, supplemented with local woods for their cheaper guitars. They were zebra, shina, luan and other strange names, as well as maple and rosewood. The tops were spruce, but when Jose Ramirez changed his tops to Canadian red cedar, many of the Japanese makers followed his lead and used cedar, solid or laminated. They not only followed Ramirez with his selection of tops, but plagiarised his headstock.

Segovia, of course, was playing a Ramirez guitar, so what was better than to copy the distinctive elegant Ramirez head. Imitation might be termed the sincerest form of flattery, but a head that was once immediately recognisable has now become commonplace.

The copying, of course, can be extended to every famous make of American acoustic and electric guitar, i.e. the Les Paul copy, Martin copy, Gibson copy, Fender copy, Rickenbacker copy – need we go on?

In 1963 I first met Masaru Kono who has since changed the spelling of his name to Kohno.

He then produced a whole range of excellent classical guitars from No 2 to No 10, and when my order was delivered in London in the autumn, Julian Bream happened to come into the shop and asked if I had any new 'machines'. I showed him the Kohnos and it did not take him long to select one of the lower priced models (about £80), take it away, and use it in concerts. He tells me he still has it and uses it.

The people who may still be wondering what caused the Japanese to become guitar makers may well wonder how Masaru Kohno learnt his craft. Well, during 1959 he went to Madrid and presented himself at No 12 Jesus y Maria, the workshop of Arcangel Fernandez, and, through a friend who spoke Spanish, asked if he could watch Arcangel at work, Arcangel, being a most friendly and straightforward person, did not object, and so the visits began. Masaru Kohno would often take Arcangel out to lunch or dinner, and

A WORLD OF CLASSICAL GUITARS

generally treated him with great friendship which Arcangel reciprocated. Between interpreters and drawings, Arcangel's work was carefully noted by Kohno, and after visits almost every day for about six months, Masaru had seen enough for his purpose and left Madrid to establish his own workshop in Tokyo. I relate this story without comment as it was told by Arcangel.

Masaru Kohno entered one of his guitars at the Liège Concourse National de Guitares in 1967, and won the first prize for guitar making out of 31 entrants. The chairman of the adjudicators was my late lamented friend, Ignacio Fleta (who died in 1977) and he told me that when he examined Kohno's guitar (which was, of course, unlabelled at the time) he thought it was very much like his own.

The next time I visited Japan was in October 1969 when USA and the UK were clamouring for Japanese guitars, but could not get the quantities they required.

I was sitting in the sumptuous office of Mr. Shiro Arai when the telephone rang. It was a call from New York begging Mr. Arai to keep up deliveries. In spite of Mr. Arai explaining that there was a six months backlog, the caller would not take 'No' for an answer.

One of the most interesting visits was to the small factory of Takamine guitars, situated halfway up a mountain near a spa called Nakatzugawa where we met the President of the company, Mr. Hirade. It seemed to have ideal working conditions and 60° humidity – good for guitars. The workforce numbered 75, all of whom played guitar, and they produced 2,000 guitars per month, half for the home market and half for export.

Considering that each guitar required 150 operations to complete, the going was not at all bad.

I must mention our host's hospitality. We were made so welcome that a special lunch was laid on for my wife, self and our Japanese agent at the newly-built restaurant in the spa. In the large private old style Japanese room we were served with a nine course meal that might have been suitable for an eighteenth century Samurai gourmet but hardly for Westerners or even our man from Tokyo, served in the traditional Japanese manner at a large low table by two kimono clad serving girls. The delicate china dishes contained mysteries never before seen by Western eyes. I made a gallant attempt at eating some of the courses, even to the sautéed unborn bees, but even our man from Tokyo had to replace the lid on the china bowl, after he had viewed the roasted whole bat hanging on the sides by its claws.

Since 1969 however, many American dollars have poured into the Japanese guitar industry and agreements reached, giving certain distribution rights to American companies. For example, the US manufacturers of Ovation guitars, Kaman Inc., have taken over the Takamine distribution in the US; C. F. Martin have their Japanese Sigma brand; Norlin who, as Gibson Guitars, bought the Epiphone name in 1956, transferred their manufacturer to Japan; Guild have their lower-priced Madiera guitar from Japan; Fender have lower priced acoustic Fender models.

The Japanese manufacturers themselves also supply rival distributors with different name brands. One of the most famous, namely, Masaru Kohno, reserves his own name for his Nos 5000, 3000, 2000 and 1500. What used to be the Kohno No 10 and my lower numbers bear the label 'Saiko' with the words 'Supervised by Masaru Kohno'.

Ryoji Matsuoka, a manufacturer of very fine sounding guitars, also makes a brand known as Takumi; both Ibanez and Tama guitars are made by the same manufacturer and my own Sakura and Mitsuma brands of guitars are made by small manufacturers who are keen on improvements and, as I mentioned earlier, Aria guitars are manufactured under the auspices of Shiro Arai.

New classical guitarists abound and increase in number; one of the most notable is Norihito Watanabe who has won a number of competitions and has a terrifyingly fast technique.

Having read this section, it will now be more evident that one should no longer be surprised at the ability of the Japanese to make and play guitar.

The Guitar in West Germany
From my own experience of classical guitars there seems little doubt that Herman Hauser (1882-1952) was the best luthier in twentieth century Germany, if not the best in the world, and when he died, his son Herman Jnr. continued.

When I met him in 1957, he did not look too well, but was working very hard at trying to follow in his father's footsteps which was, of course, very difficult. In fact, I had some troubles with neck warp on one or two of his guitars. Today, however, he ranks among the best, and my present Hauser, made in 1974, is a guitar of great beauty in every way and tonally, it is loud and clear.

Dieter Hense whom I first met in Leipzig and now lives near Wiesbaden, is a man who has retained his integrity in the 20-odd years I have known him. He has been making exceptional concert guitars ever since he was able to come over to the West from Markneukirchen in East Germany. He uses either spruce or cedar depending on the tone preferred by the customer.

Dieter Hopf, son of Willi Hopf, who has a very large manufacturing company in Wehen, has studied violin and guitar construction and has produced many fine guitars of all standards, using some of the most superb Brazilian rosewood I have ever seen. I would say that, commercially, he is the most forward looking guitar enthusiast in Germany, whose guitars have lately improved tremendously. He also employs other luthiers, chief of whom is Koruskenyi,[1] a Hungarian by birth, who has recently been making very good guitars.

There are guitar makers, too numerous to mention, whose workmanship is good, but whose tonal results are very mediocre and not worth mentioning, but among the production makers, Horst Teller stands out as the one who steadily produces a good range of guitars which improve every year. His father was one of the real old craftsmen, working in the village of Bubenreuth in Bavaria, and I first met Oscar Teller in 1953 when I went there to ask him to make a folk guitar similar to the Martin 0021, then played by Josh White. He did, in fact, make an excellent copy in rosewood, which was marketed by Boosey & Hawkes as the 'Josh White Guitar', a rarity today.

In one Frankfuter Messe, the International Musical Fair, I counted 52 guitar makers from East and West Germany exhibiting their instruments.

The Guitar in East Germany

In March 1961 I extended my German visit to Frankfurt to include the Leipziger Messe which follows the Frankfurter Messe and includes a show of all musical instruments made in East Germany, including guitars.

Getting there wasn't all that straightforward. First we (Willie Wilson, the buyer for Boosey-Hawkes and I) flew to West Berlin, then took a crowded train from East Berlin to Leipzig. When we arrived after a few hours there was a mixture of sleet and snow falling down from the heavens, and when we got out onto the platform we discovered that such a thing as a porter did not exist. So there was nothing for it but to descend the many stairs down to street level, getting soaked through and carrying our own luggage. Somehow or other we found transport to our digs with Herr Muller-Becker at Foeke Str. No 2 and were glad to sink into armchairs. We were lucky –

[1] Who has since passed away.

the Rolls-Royce representative (who were displaying their engines) had digs too, but possibly less comfortable than ours and the Armstrong Whitworth digs had not been prearranged. Having spent an enjoyable afternoon in West Berlin where we revisited Kempinsky's very modernised cafe-restaurant, I did not think much of the Leipzig welcome.

Soon we made our way to Peterstrasse, where the musical wares were exhibited at the Petershof. We walked along in the eerie silence of the snow-covered street, devoid of motor traffic, and eventually reached the hotel, the bright lights, and the many booths displaying masses of guitars. Being conscientious, or maybe just hating to miss something good, I visited them all. The funny thing I noticed while looking around was that I was being followed, at a respectable distance, by the buyer from one English wholesaler, who in turn was being followed by another. After I had examined the guitars at one stand, my friend from the rival British firm would ask my opinion and whether I had ordered any guitars. Had I made a positive comment they would have been in there like a shot with a counter offer. So I had to be non-commital, which wasn't difficult. Out of 72 guitar makers or manufacturers I found two good ones.

One was a young man named Dieter Hense (27) who showed great promise as a classical guitar maker and the other a firm named Otto Windisch, makers of Otwin guitars, excellent steel-strung instruments.

Dieter Hense did, in fact, make some wonderful steel strung folk guitars similar to the Martin 0021 size, which sold at the unbelievable price of just over £20 under the Josh White name, but very few were made because of the restrictions on raw materials.

Ten years later he was permitted to go to West Germany (as I have mentioned in the previous section) where he has become one of the best luthiers of today. The reason he was unable to make progress in East Germany was his refusal to join the Communist Party.

Mr. Otto Windisch received a large order for his small cello-style Otwin guitar which quickly became very popular in England, selling for about 16 guineas. In my conversation with Mr. Windisch I discovered that he used to work for Gibson guitars in Kalamazoo. Need I say more?

My journey was both fruitful and extremely interesting, especially one nightclub incident. Willy Wilson and I were invited to the magnificent Leipziger nightclub known as 'House Antifa' where we enjoyed the food, drink and music. There were two bands. One, the most magnificent Hungarian Zigeuner Orchestra I have ever heard, led by brilliant violinist Toki Horvath, and Kurt Henkels and his Rundfunksorchester. We were having a marvellous time, when one of the big shots sitting at our table discovered that I was a guitarist. 'Please let us have a performance' he begged. I hedged, but was put on the spot by the big shot who happened to be the chief of Dominions Export in Berlin, and acted with gangster-like insistence, probably because his girlfriend was sitting next to him.

Well, I could not very well let the side down, so I crossed the dance floor and asked the guitarist for his instrument. I named an old standard tune and began with an introduction. As soon as my left hand pressed onto the fingerboard I knew I was in for a period of concentrated hard labour. The string action was about a half an inch high but there was nothing I could do about it. Suffering agonies, I plodded on. It was like being crucified, but not as bad as being electrocuted (of which I had had experience).

My performance won me a good friend in Toki Horvath, who, many years later came to London for a TV Spectacular, and entirely depended on me as his guide. After the Hungarian uprising he had fled to the West and settled in Munich.

I nearly forgot to mention my discovery of the Gittre 'Sichola', a three-necked monstrosity with a chord contraption, enabling the holder to play chords without effort immediately, subtitled the 'Everyman Guitar'. It was of course a 'No Man's Guitar' and has sunk without trace.

Holland

I must not omit to mention a maker of guitars, Baroque guitars and lutes in Holland by the name of Niek Van Der Waal who makes an extraordinarily clear sounding guitar which deserves a place among the aristocrats.

One of his instruments is played to great advantage by the American virtuoso Michael Lorimer who also produces sounds from the Baroque guitar of which the Baroque Era would have been justly proud.

France and Italy

France has its Robert Bouchet who was the favourite of Presti and Lagoya and Julian Bream until his best Bouchet was stolen from his car, alas, never to be replaced. Today it is a rare privilege to possess a Bouchet.

At present, Daniel Friedrich, a maker who won second prize to Kohno in the Brussels Exposition, is playing a prominent part on the classical guitar scene, and his instruments are much in demand.

The maker who received the third prize for his guitar at this competition was an Italian named Orlando Raponi who is patronised by Alirio Diaz. He makes a long scale guitar with a very strong tone and, like all leading luthiers, has a long waiting list. Now we come to Great Britain.

The Classical Guitar in Great Britain
Of all the places in the world where the guitar may be heard, London, at times, must rank as the Mecca.

In the season, there are many recitals of classical music in the Wigmore Hall, the Purcell Room, the Queen Elizabeth Hall and even the 3,000 seater Royal Festival Hall for the occasional Segovia, Bream, Williams or Yepes concert.

The Royal Academy, and the Royal College, and all the musical establishments, teach guitar as a first subject, and there are numerous virtuosi among the young students and players. The serious guitarists from all over the world come to study in London and not only in London. The main provincial cities have branches of the established Conservatories and their own Colleges of Music; provincial students come to London to seek fame and fortune.

The Inner London Educational Authority (ILEA) begin guitar tuition for children from the age of six, and we have a small-sized guitar known in Spanish as a Requinto, specially made to accommodate youngsters.

In the recent Bach Festival in London, concerts of flamenco music with singers and dancers were given in the South Bank concert halls.

Jazz is also catered for with Joe Pass, George Benson, Barney Kessel, Jim Hall and Georges Barnes at Ronnie Scott's Club. It does not need an expert to realise how much the folk and country styles have caught on and the many radio stations which pump out incessant pop and rock. Blues is no longer the prerogative of New Orleans or the Mississippi. Everyone who picks up a guitar plays a blues lick and London still swings in one way or another.

We even have famous luthiers in England whose instruments are sought after in other parts of the world.

Not since the first half of the last century has guitar making in England been such a popular craft. It far eclipses the eighteenth/nineteenth centuries.

Then, Luis Panormo and his family were the premier guitar craftsmen catering to the guitar-minded public. Luis Panormo (1784-1862) even had the ear of Fernando Sor when the latter came to play in London.

From 1819 to 1829 his address was 26 High Street, Bloomsbury, from 1830 to 1849, 46 High Street, Bloomsbury, and from 1850 to 1854, 31 High Street, Bloomsbury. Now it is known as High Street, St. Giles, and runs from Centre Point to St. Giles Church, where the lovely church spire is dwarfed by the 39 storey Centre Point.

The musical trade has never moved away from the district, sometimes known as the 'square mile', from Charing Cross Road round the corner to Shaftesbury Avenue, where most of the West End musical instrument shops are to be found, and Denmark Street, where some music publishers are still hanging on in face of redevelopment.

As I have previously mentioned, Jack Abbott and I almost went into the business of guitar manufacture but in the last stages my accountant threw a spanner in the works. No doubt he was right, but I foresaw the great need for good instruments and tried twice more without actually taking the plunge. I also tried to interest the Board of Trade in establishing a British Guitar Industry but without success. Nevertheless, there were pioneers who were not deterred. The first one of these was Harald Petersen (b. Denmark 1910).

Harald Petersen arrived in England round about 1949 and came to see me when I lived in Cricklewood. He announced himself and I asked him to come into the house, carrying with him a wooden crate. He unpacked the protective stuff and took out a classical guitar – well, it wasn't really much of a guitar, but the bare requirements, and, although it had some sound, I then did not have the time or the spirit to finance or interest myself in what I expected to be a long haul.

Harald Petersen struggled on, and by the early 1950s had come a long way, at any rate with the production of a good looking, well sounding guitar. He settled in Lancashire (now Cumbria) and worked steadily, although taking some time before he cured the weakness at the bass side of the bridge where the table had a habit of sinking. Sometime before he died in 1969 his guitars had greatly improved and the fault had been totally cured. It was then that I became a regular customer of his and continue to buy the Petersen guitars from his two sons Tom (b. 1939) and Peter (b. 1941) of whom he would have been justly proud, both as people and as craftsmen.

Not too long ago a Japanese guitar export-import agent came to see me and bought a Petersen Model 'C' which he displayed back home, and about a month later the Petersen brothers received an order which took them a year to complete to the exclusion of all other orders, some reward for the uphill struggle of the Petersen family.

Guitar students of Hector Quine (who was the first person to be appointed as a guitar professor to the Royal Schools of Music in about 1965) may like to know that he was, among other occupations a guitar maker, and for some time Julian Bream played a guitar made by him. But the first English maker to receive international acclaim since Luis Panormo was David J. Rubio.

David J. Rubio

Before he became a luthier his name was David Spink, and I have my doubts if that name would have brought the same glamour to his guitars as the one he 'adopted'. After all, David is fair, and Rubio in Spanish means 'fair' so fair it is.

If Harald Petersen had a struggle so did David Spink but in an entirely different way. He was a medical student in his final year who fell for the romanticism of the flamenco guitar. He not only became an aficionado but took it seriously enough to take lessons from Pepe Martinez and play professionally at the basement coffee bar known as 'The Flask' in Flask Walk, Hampstead. To say the least it was disappointing to his family and to the establishment.

He finally broke away from his studies and home by going abroad and on tour with a Spanish flamenco company, with a Ramirez guitar from me, which he could ill afford. But while in Madrid he became interested in the way guitars were built and took some mental notes. The company went on to the USA where he met and married Ness, an American girl, who helped him to set up house, home and shop all together in the small shop he rented in Carmine Street, in the area of Greenwich Village, New York. I paid him a surprise visit in October 1965, and he was really surprised to see my wife and me out of the blue as it were. He was delighted to see someone from home and showed me a flamenco guitar he had made which I thought was more classical than flamenco, and voiced the opinion that he ought to make classical guitars, including one for me.

He was also busy making a vihuela and showed great ingenuity by making all his own jigs, while Ness designed and fitted the mosaics. His living space was to be found behind the shop.

We now jump two years, and find him on the top floor of a warehouse in Bond Street, Manhattan, where he had built himself a self-contained home and a workshop, and built up a good stock of timber. What is more, Julian Bream had tried his guitars and ordered one. More than that, he had invited him to come to Semley, Dorset, where he could live and make guitars. After weighing up the pros and cons, David decided to take his wood and return to the Old Country, where he became established as luthier extraordinary and, of course, luthier to Julian Bream.

The nature of the human species being what it is, David wanted to stretch out and gain full independence, and after almost insurmountable difficulties and obstacles, bought a seventeenth century thatched house in Duns Tew near Oxford which had, at one time, been the local post office.

He more or less rebuilt the house with the result that it became an ideal workshop and a lovely home.

His success is well-known and Duns Tew has become a Mecca for players petitioning to buy one of his instruments.

Now the guitars are nearly all made by his erstwhile assistant and pupil Paul Fischer who works independently in the Rubio workshop producing guitars but signed 'Paul Fischer'. In addition another young disciple E. B. Jones makes his own guitars, thus carrying on a tradition similar to that of the Madrid makers for this century where the pupils and assistants of Manuel or Jose Ramirez became great luthiers in their own right. The Rubio story is, in my opinion, producing a noteworthy hoist in the 'wheel of fortune'.

George Love is a luthier who has made some excellent guitars for quite a few of the younger concert artistes and, in fact, has a full order book.

John Mack also makes some respectable concert guitars.

Jones (not to be confused with E. B. Jones) has been known for his Jones guitars and has come a long way from the time he made his first rather clumsy efforts. Today, they are very refined and can match the rest.

John Ainsworth of Chorley
John Ainsworth is a BSc in Zoology with an interest in Biology and Forestry and therefore well attuned to the properties and nature of the wood required to make a good sounding guitar.

His love of the instrument and natural ability to create in wood soon had him 'hooked' on constructing guitars of aesthetic and sonorous beauty.

This has become the time-consuming passion to which he has devoted the past few years and after playing two of his instruments I was struck by their penetrating clarity of sound and physical beauty, and was, therefore, very pleased to introduce the John Ainsworth Concert guitars to the discerning player as we entered the new decade of 1980.

R. E. Spain

Despite his name, Ray Spain was born in Cumberland and came to London to teach engineering at a Secondary Modern School where he became senior master. Naturally, you have guessed that he became an amateur guitarist, and began to make guitars for himself.

When he thought he had succeeded in producing a good sounding instrument, he asked me to examine it, and its free full tone impressed me. Only a maker with some talent for the subject could have been able to put a box together which produced that quality of tone. But this was just a beginning. We spent much time in seeking improvements and gradually the sound and appearance of each new guitar proved the value of these tests and scrutinies. He has added two more models to his range, one a real Flamenco sounding flamenco guitar and a flat top steel-strung.

Mr. Spain, as my chief repairer of classical guitars, has had opportunities of dissecting all kinds of makes right from eighteenth and nineteenth century guitars which he has restored to perfection. I am quite sure that when he had finished with them, they looked and sounded better than when they were made. Fabricatori of Naples, Lacotte of Paris, Luis Panormo of London, Stauffer of Vienna, Gaetano Vinaccia of Naples are all guitars which he has restored to playing order. He did a job on No. 32 of Antonio de Torres (1856) which had a reflector inside the soundhole. When it was finished its sound and appearance were a joy to hear and behold. Julian Bream was so impressed that he sent Jose Romanillos to examine it and take measurements.

Ray Spain has restored more than one Jose Ramirez which has either split apart from being out in the sun at Aden or come apart from extreme damp and humidity. Due to his training as a technical engineer, the intonation of his guitars is very accurate, and the fretting smooth and without buzzes.

His output is around 12 guitars per year so naturally there is a greater demand than supply, and in the last two years he has made two models, one with exceptional materials and, perhaps, a little more love and attention devoted to it. Each new guitar is compared with the previous one in the hope that some improvement has been effected.

They have found their way to many parts of the world from Cincinnati to Tasmania and those players that have one hardly ever part with it.

Ray Spain is still in his early forties, and full of enthusiasm for his chosen craft, so much so that he has gone one step further by making flamenco guitars which can vie with the best in Spain.

Martin Fleeson is an art teacher who succumbed to the lure of making guitars, so this makes two of my 'guitarreros' who are also teachers. His guitars are light and clean in weight, appearance, and sound, and his mahogany model is quite remarkable for its price, although not as rich sounding as his best rosewood one. Once again, I have been happy to support and encourage another one of our 'staid' Englishmen in this romantic occupation.

Don Tatum is not a schoolmaster but a full-time guitar maker who produces instruments with a tight clear tone, more baroque in sound than the warm Spanish character. Perhaps one may describe the contrast as clarity versus density. Don Tatum has quite a following already, which is well deserved, and those players who have one of his guitars are very pleased with them.

There are an increasing number of young guitar makers who have been smitten by the fascination of creating an instrument.

Finally, a word must be added about the good work of the London College of Furniture, which is producing both repairers and guitar makers, whose work I have examined. Two of the students have worked as repairers at the Musicentre for a period before leaving to establish themselves in England and in the United States.

Jose Romanillos

Last but, as they say, by no means least, is the later star in the firmament of guitar building, Jose Romanillos. Jose Romanillos one day presented himself at the door of Julian Bream's house in Semley, Dorset and asked the maestro to examine a guitar he had completed, and Julian, who is always ready to give a hearing to something new and, perhaps, worthwhile, considered that this young émigré from Spain had possibilities, so he arranged for this poor woodworker to come to Semley, make his home there and begin seriously as luthier.

Julian's aim has always been to find a guitar with the tone of a Hauser Snr. and a Bouchet rather than a Ramirez. Perhaps even a similar tone to a Torres but more of it. Anyway, a keen worker of

Romanillos' calibre aided by Julian's deep insight into guitar sound, must produce something worthwhile and success was not far away.

It did not take long, with the backing of Julian, for Romanillos guitars to be in great demand. Of course, not everyone is a winner as any luthier will understand, but he has risen to international fame faster than almost any other present day constructor.

Today, with new young players eager to come to the fore as solo artistes, everybody connected with the classical guitar field either learns from or makes some contribution to the general stream of interested parties or experiment in playing, making or writing.

It is just as exciting in every sphere of guitar playing whether it is pop, rock, folk, blues, flamenco, acoustic or electric, 6-string, 8-string, 10-string or 12-string.

One would hardly have envisaged John Williams playing a solid electric guitar, but then, who in their wildest imagination would have expected the guitar to become a household musical instrument, second only in number of players to the piano and perhaps rising to become the world's most popular?

CODA

In the 1920s the new instrument of the era was the 'cello 'f' hole steel-strung guitar, whereas prior to that there were only flat top steel-strung guitars of the Martin type and the gut-strung Spanish Classical or Flamenco guitars. The function of the flat top steel-strung guitar was to play Country and Western music, and the 'cello body guitar to play rhythm and some solo passages in a dance band or to accompany a vocal group.

In the early 1950s there were few signs of the enormous extension in the popularity of the guitar, a phenomenon which no one forecast. Yet today, the guitar seems to be an accepted addition to every household and can if so desired be adapted to sound like other instruments due to the advance of electronics in the sound-effects industry.

Today we have classical and flamenco nylon-strung guitars, flat top steel-strung guitars of various shapes and sizes, a few 'cello body 'f' hole guitars, 'cello guitars with electronic pick-ups, and solid wood electric guitars. These solid guitars come in various shapes and sizes; square, oblong, V-shaped, snake shaped, diamond shaped, and with curly horns like a bison, but they are fundamentally variations on the Les Paul and the Stratocaster solids.

All types of electric guitars are used for Rock and Roll, Heavy Rock, Rhythm and Blues, Country Blues, Bluegrass, Country and Western and Pop music. There are many players who play electric guitar and almost as many who favour acoustic flat tops, but sales of records undoubtedly prove that the bulk of the music is played on electric guitars.

The Cinderella of the electric guitar field is the jazz side and of *all* record sales only five per cent is reputed to be of jazz, i.e. extemporised rhythmic dance music. In spite of these small sales, there are some wonderful jazz guitarists developing all the time, and more and more rock-playing youngsters are taking an interest in jazz. All in all, the interest in the steel-strung guitar is growing all the time.

There is just as steady a growth for the classical guitar which seems to me to be of a more lasting and deeper interest. The amount of classical music now being consumed by students is enormous and the revival of the guitar and lute music of the 16th and 17th centuries is remarkable. More music of the 18th/19th century guitar composers is being discovered and recorded by the leading players, which popularises it among the aficionados. There is hardly a limit to the ages of beginners. Six year olds are given the opportunity of having a guitar. This encourages the parents to join in and help the children. Some over 60s are just beginning to learn.

Serious composers have now written, and are continuing to write for the classical guitar, and now and again a composition becomes very popular. The slow movement of the Rodrigo 'Concierto de Aranjuez' has probably done more for the mass popularity of the guitar than any other guitar composition, except perhaps for Stanley Myers' Cavatina. This leads record companies to include the nylon-strung guitar in many record releases and so it snowballs to further popularity.

Even Flamenco music has more adherents and one can detect the small steady increase in its popularity by the number of well attended concerts, new recordings and new transcriptions. People in many professions use the guitar for relaxation and therapy from the daily toil − doctors, lawyers, scientists, teachers and journalists; so do many manual workers from labourers to skilled craftsmen. The people of the Third World of Black Africa are very rythmic and musical, and many of them use the guitar for native and Western music.

In the midst of the conflicts we are asked to supply guitars to Black African organisations to help their morale, and whole families in Ghana and Nigeria study musical instruments of which at least one is a guitar. If therefore, amid the present crisis the guitar has become such a universally performed instrument, I can only forecast that when conflicts are settled and work and leisure assume a reasonable proportion of the human existence, more time will be taken up with music, and what is simpler than to be enchanted with the gentle sound of the versatile guitar?

If my forecast sounds too romantic and unreal, perhaps my recent experiences may provide good reasons for optimism where the guitar is concerned.

Every two years or so, my wife and I visit the National Association of Musical Merchandisers (NAMM) Exposition in the United States, and in 1975 it was held in Chicago.

We made our way first to Miami, then to New Orleans, and while in Miami we were invited to lunch by Mr. Charles Hansen, one of America's most dynamic music publishing personalities − he bubbles with ideas. 'Why don't you write a guitar solo for the US Bicentenary Year of 1976, and since you are going to New Orleans let's have some of its flavour.'

In New Orleans the air was so impregnated with music from Jackson Square to Bourbon Street that it was not difficult to be inspired, and a few days later I posted off a new finger-style guitar solo entitled, *Spirit of New Orleans*. When I met Mr. Hansen again in Chicago the following week, he informed me that the cover was being designed and, sure enough, a week later in New York, I saw the proofs.

I was then commissioned to write *Arranging for the Guitar* and other original guitar works including a Sonata, Meditation, Moto Perpetuo, a Bundle of Blues, Master Theory (A Composer's Guide to the Guitar) in three books, *Perfect Pick Technique and Basic Jazz Improvisation*. In fact, at a time when I thought my writing days were over, I had embarked on a completely new phase in another country.

I used to think that when one reached 70 it would be a time for reflection, but here I am concerned with new adventures in writing for this instrument, whose possibilities keep expanding. EMI have also commissioned me to write a number of folios of arrangements entitled 'Popular Solos for Classical Guitar'. The first two of which have already been published.

Now it seems that destiny has provided me with a suitable finale to my story. It so happens that 1979 marked the 75th anniversary of the establishment of the Gibson Guitar Co. and to commemorate the occasion Norlin (makers of Gibson guitars) created a *Gibson Hall of Fame*, and each year guitarists found worthy of the honour, will be inducted. For this selection a Board of Directors has been appointed of which I am the European representative.

My first candidate? Who else but Eddie Lang, who, with his Gibson guitar transmitted the message to me fifty fretting years ago.

George Van Eps – Chicago July 1980.

PERFECT CADENCE

I finally met George Van Eps in Chicago at the end of June 1980. It happened in a most unexpected way.

I had slipped into Rick's Jazz Club at the Holiday Inn, Lakeshore Drive, where Barney Kessel and Herb Ellis were performing and had chatted with Barney before the show.

Near the end of the performance, Barney, after playing a solo item, announced that George Van Eps was in the audience (apparently he had just noticed him). While Barney was describing the high esteem with which all guitarists held this legendary guitarist, I wondered who it could be, but when George Van Eps' name was announced it was obvious to me that only *he* qualified for such a eulogy. When Herb Ellis returned to the stage for the last duet, he, too, made an announcement to the effect that he was using the string damper that George had invented many years ago and that had he known George was in the audience, he would not have been so relaxed and might even have made a slip-up or two.

When the performance was over, Barney asked me to come and meet George and all I can say about the meeting is that George seemed to be as delighted as I was.

George was there in company with Bill Bay (Mel Bay's son), Maurice Summerfield and his assistant Tom Charlton, and soon Maurice insisted on all of us being photographed together.

Not having seen George before, I was expecting to see an older looking man, but to my surprise I encountered a sprightly, trim, wisecracking individual in the prime of life and vigour.

These were momentous moments for me and did much more than 'make my day'. I arranged to meet George the following morning at the Mel Bay Booth (in the 1980 NAMM show) where he was in attendance, helping to launch Volume 1 of his *Harmonic Mechanisms for the Guitar*. This book, said George, was the work of a lifetime and looking through it I would say it would take a lifetime to study thoroughly. It was, in fact the very work that George had described to me on the telephone, back in 1969.

The Mel Bay stand was inundated with visitors seeking a handshake or an autograph from the great man, but during a lull I presented him with my book *Perfect Pick Technique* which includes my dedicatory piece to George Van Eps entitled *Moto Perpetuo*. When he saw the piece he said he was thrilled to see this dedication for the second time – the first time in manuscript and now in print, and showed it to all and sundry, insisting that I autograph it for him. In doing so, I could not help but admire the generous nature of a man who had the ability to make those he met feel elated.

At this moment Mel Bay entered the booth and seeing George with my book, said to me 'Why don't you write a book for me?' 'What about?' I asked. 'About everything you know' came the snappy reply.

After a day's consideration, the upshot was a book to be called *The Complete Guitar Experience* from basics to professional playing.

In the circumstances I feel that any further comments on the subject would be an anti-climax.

A meeting of guitar personalities, Chicago, June 1980 (left to right) Maurice Summerfield, Bill Bay, Herb Ellis, Barney Kessel, Ivor Mairants and George Van Eps.

APPENDIX

GUITAR WORKS by IVOR MAIRANTS

Compositions for Classical Guitar

Publisher	
EMI	6 Solos for Classic Guitar
EMI	6 Bagatelles
Chappells/Hansen	A Bundle of Blues
EMI	6 Progressive Pieces for Solo Guitar
EMI	6 Easy Pieces
EMI	6 Lute Pieces
Breitkopf & Hartel	6 Part Suite
Brons/Hansen	Sonata (to a Sonic Age)
Chappells/Hansen	Meditation
Chappells/Hansen	The Spirit of New Orleans
EMI	Travel Suite
EMI	3 Rhythmic Dances

Arrangements for Classical Guitar

EMI	Sonata in D, M. Albeniz
EMI	La Catedral (The Cathedral), Barrios
EMI	3 Studies, Barrios
EMI	Aire de Zamba, Choro du Saudade and Danza Paraguaia, Barrios
EMI	Air on the G String, Bach
EMI	Fur Elise, Beethoven
Breitkopf & Hartel	The Carman's Whistle, Byrd, arr. for 3 guitars
Chappells/Hansen	Fiddler on the Roof
Brons/Hansen	Godspell (advanced classical guitar)
Chappells/Hansen	Religious Themes for Classical Guitar
Chappells/Hansen	Selections from *Mr Wonderful*
Chappells/Hansen	Music of the Modern Masters
Southern	Los Cuatros Muleros
UMP	Cancion y Danza (Mompou)
Belwin Mills	Ay-Ay-Ay
Walsh	Romance d'Amor

EMI	Popular Solos for Classical Guitar Books 1 and 2

Works for Flamenco Guitar

Music Sales	Flamenco Guitar method
Spark	Accompanying LP (The Art of Flamenco Guitar)
Belwin Mills	Flamenco Album Nos. 1, 2 and 3 each
Music Sales	Seguiriya Andaluza
Music Sales	Gates of Bethlehem

Tutors for Classical Guitar

EMI	Fingerstyle Guitar in Theory & Practice. Tutor. Book 1
EMI	Fingerstyle Guitar in Theory & Practice. Tutor. Book 2
Boosey & Hawkes	Simplicity Tutor
Chappells/Hansen	Part 1 Anatomy of the Guitar
Chappells/Hansen	Part 2 Visual Aids
Chappells/Hansen	Part 3 Guide to Guitar Writing from the Renaissance to the Present Day

Solos for Plectrum Guitar

Publisher	
FD&H/EMI	Little Bo Bleep
Bosworth	Mustard & Cress
EMI	Once in a While
Bosworth	Overhead Drive
Bosworth	Pepper & Salt
EMI	Personal Call to Barney Kessel
Bosworth	Russian Salad
Bosworth	Sea Food Squabble
Bosworth	Spring Prelude
Belwin Mills	Walking with Wes
Belwin Mills	Greensleeves
Belwin Mills	Ay-Ay-Ay
Peter Maurice	La Majestica
Peter Maurice	In Charlie's Footsteps

Tutors for Plectrum Guitar

EMI	Complete Guitar Tutor in Theory & Practice
Foyles	Play the Guitar
Music Sales	Graduated Course; Books 1, 2, 3 and 4
Chappells/Hansen	Perfect Pick Technique
Belwin Mills	Visual Aids to Chord Arpeggios
Chappells/Hansen	Arranging for the Guitar (Finger Style. Popular Music)
EMI	Book of Daily Exercises
EMI	Modern Chord Encyclopaedia
Belwin Mills	12-string Guitar Tutor
Music Sales	Folk Music Accompaniment for the Guitar
Belwin Mills	Bass Guitar Tutor

LIST OF ILLUSTRATIONS

Front Solomon, Sarah, Thema and Ivor Mairants 12
1. The Valencians, 1926 25
2. The Florentine Band, 1927 25
3. Fred Anderson's Cabaret Band, 1928 26
4. Percival Mackey's Band, 1928 26
5. Emile Grimshaw Banjo Quartet 27
6. Clifford Essex 27
7. Eddie Lang with Mound City Blowers 27
8. Vega Banjo Catalogue, 1928 28
9. Marius B. Winter Orchestra 29
10. Louis Levy Orchestra 1937 – 'Lord Babs' film 29
11. Roy Fox Orchestra 30
12. Roy Fox Band 1932 – about to embark for Brussells 30
13. Advert for 'Spring Fever' a guitar solo 31
14. Advert for postal guitar lessons 1938 32
15. Mario Maccafferri, Chappie D'Amato and Jack Hylton 50
16. Ivor Mairants with his C.I. Martin guitar, 1932 51
17. 10,000 dancers on the floor at the Wintergarden Ballroom 52
18. Ambrose 52
19. Ivor Mairants with Premier Vox electric guitar 1936 52
20. Geraldo's Orchestra embarking for Germany, 1946 53
21. Geraldo Orchestra, Samson and Hercules Ballroom, Coventry, 1947 53
22. Ivor Mairants and Albert Harris, Decca Studios, Upper Thames Street, London, 1935 54
23. Ivor Mairants with Vega acoustic/electric guitar, 1945 54
24. This time a Zenith guitar with Eric Robinson at BBC Television Studios .. 54
25. On set for Ealing Studios, 'Saraband for Dead Lovers' 91
26. Scene from 'The Battle of the River Plate' the singer, April Olrich 92
27. Jean Simmons – the Film Actress of the Year, 1949 92
28. With Winifred Atwell at the London Palladium 93
29. Adelaide Hall presenting *Melody Maker* poll awards, 1951 93
30. *Melody Maker* Award, 1950-1 93
31. Red Square, Moscow, 1957 94
32. Alexandra Ivanov, Kromskoy 94
33. Lily Mairants with Russian 'bobby' 94
34. Original staff of Central School of Dance Music 95
35. With the late A. P. Sharpe 1950, Editor of B.M.G. for many years 95
36. Ivor Mairants Guitar Group 96
37. Ivor Mairants Trio, BBC Spotlight Programme 96
38. Ivor Mairants Musicentre, 56 Rathbone Place, WC1 97
39. With Mantovani, Decca Studios, West Hampstead, 1968 98
40. Guitar section of 'Manuel and His Music of the Mountains' 98
41. A copying machine at the Framus factory, West Germany 99
42. George Benson, Ivor Mairants, Attila Zoller 99
43. Cartoon by 'Sallon' 100
44. Gibson L5 Guitar as used by Eddie Lang 142

'MY FIFTY FRETTING YEARS'

45. Jimmy D'Asquisto 121
46. Carmen Mastren 161
47. Charlie Christian 162
48. Eddie Lang 163
49. Teddy Bunn 163
50. Django Reinhardt with Harry Volpe 163
51. Chappie D'Amato, Mario Maccaferri, Ivor Mairants 164
52. Promoting Maccaferri guitars, 1933 164
53. Ivor Mairants Guitar Quartet 165
54. With Barry Galbraith, Elstree Film Studios, 1954 165
55. Roy Plummer with a 'Roger' Guitar 165
56. With Kenny Burrell, 1965 166
57. With Herb Ellis, 1955 166
58. With Josh White, 1955 167
59. With Les Paul and Bert Weedon, 1952 167
60. With Joe Pass, 1975 168
61. Jamming with George Barnes, Frank Clarke (bass) 168
62. Barney Kessel giving an instore guitar clinic at the Musicentre 169
63. With Perry Botkin, 1959 169
64. Three rare D'Angelicos from Pete Townshend's collection 170
65. Laurindo Almeida displaying his cutaway classic guitar 170
66. Gibson's Nashville guitar factory 171
67. The famous Harmony Stella 12 string guitar 171
68. A 'Gibson' welcome 171
69. Reception to launch Maurice Summerfield's book 'The Jazz Guitar' ... 172
70. Mario Maccaferri tells I.M. the secret of his success 172
71. Siegfried Behrend 262
72. Andres Segovia 263
73. Julian Bream at the Musicentre, 1958 263
74. With Narcisco Yepes and his wife, 1960 264
75. Jose Luis Rodriguez, 1970 264
76. Alirio Diaz 264
77. Panel of pictures, Ramirez's old shop 265
78. Paco Pena, Sabicas and Ivor Mairants 266
79. Antonio's Flamenco Company 267
80. With Pepe Martinez, recording 'The Lyrical Guitar', for Phillips Records 267
81. Serranito's London Debut 268
82. Carlos Montoya 268
83. Mario Escudero 268
84. With Pedro de Lunar, Rosa Duran and Perico el del Lunar 269
85. Mariano Cubas Martin and his collection of guitars 269
86. Ignacio Fleta, 1966 270
87. Ignacio Fleta, bending a guitar side, 1966 270
88. Paulino Bernabe, 1971 270
89. Faustino Conde with Nino Ricardo 271
90. Marcelo Barbero 271
91. Arcangel Fernandes and Marcelo Barbero Hijo 271
92. Manuel Contreras 272

93. Jose Ramirez III 272
 94. Felix Manzanero 272
 95. Edgar Monch 272
 96. Hernandez y Aguado 273
 97. Luis Maravilla and his son, 1963 273
 98.-101. Ray Spain at work 274
102. Rose Augustine and Lily Mairants 275
103. The D'Addario family 275
104. Trying out new Barcus Berry pickup 276
105. The Fleta family 276
106. David Rubio 277
107. Ramon Montoya with Pepe Martinez 278
108. George Van Eps 384
109. Guitar Personalities, Chicago, June 1980 386